THE SHADOW MINDS JOURNAL

KIA CARRINGTON-RUSSELL

To those who fear the dark and what may hide in it-
Write about it, talk about it and accept that it's real. Fight your internal
demons head on and don't let them rule your life. Only you can shine the
light in your own nightmares. So shine bright like you were always
meant to. I believe in you.

ISBN 978-0-6484981-5-5

CHAPTER ONE- VIVIAN

I stood on the edge of the balcony of our lake house aware of the demonic swirls beneath the water. I anticipated that these demons might have ventured towards the harbor considering the holiday season, but rather cocky considering how close to our estate.

I watched over the children that played and laughed as they jumped off piers and into the water on either side of the mansion. I looked up at the sunny day wondering how many more thousands of days I would see the same thing, trapped in this residency and city. I was confined to my post within the city of Shabeah and revered as a celebrity of the underworld. That title was not where I saw myself a year ago.

Tahmeed and Destiny's laughter echoed behind me, cutting my loose thoughts short. They were reading over the tabloids that recently came out scrutinizing that they were romantically involved. It wasn't true but they definitely acted on it teasing the media. They were more famous now than what they were in their human life. Destiny had been an upcoming actress of age twenty-six only having landed a few gigs. Tahmeed had been a professional tennis player, titled champion two years in a row before she was 'reborn'. And they were my roommates so to speak, much more adapted to the way of life, riches and fame than I could ever desire to be.

We all handled the same dark contract and one that could not be reversed but only in the most indescribable and tortuous death would we be freed–well if you could even call it that. We were contracted to the Underworld, more specifically, a demon lord called Haymen Davolch, who had carried his notorious reputation, power and riches for thousands of years. He was revered in the media as the lord of demons, some even called him a god in his own right, the God of Demons. Some titled him as the King of Kings and the titles continued endlessly depending on what dimension and world you lived on. No one defied Haymen and if you were so lucky as to be socially introduced to him, you also had a name in the underworld and media, where reputation and power was all that mattered. But to be contracted and bound by blood to him was to be his slave as he saw fit. Some called it an honor. I personally thought he was a giant dick but I would be fed my own tongue before I had the chance to say it so loudly. Many died an excruciating death for simply looking at him wrong. I personally at times was the one to execute them.

In a world where angels and demons were renowned and even celebrated; we were the hounds who would convict the stray demons and send them back to where they would never resurface. It's not a gig I chose for myself, at first, I had spited my role and task, the other two having already adapted.

But alas apparently, I was chosen. It wasn't the day that I feared, in fact killing demons was something I did exceptionally well. It was when night came and it was time to sleep that truly jeopardized our safety and life. There were once five of us in this district. Now down to only four in recent months. There were demons more powerful and became very real in our dreams. An internal war that came to life against demons that could possess us if we weren't effectively able to fight off the intrusion. We were vulnerable and weak and what they sought out most was to possess our body to use as host. Not all entities had a form and not all could be contained by a living body for a long duration before rotting themselves. It left these demons vulnerable and their power leaked, they were once again forced to the shadows until they acquired a new host.

There were things that could not be explained. Things I didn't want to relive or see. But as per our contract and protocol, we had to journalize these dreams and attacks so we could seek them out in the physical realm, to ultimately kill those who challenged Haymen's territory and power. We were both the bait and the soldiers. Not all came out alive and numerous generations had been wiped out. There were numerous warriors who had the same respective role in other cities similar to ours but we were publicized and considered as the 'elite'. We were the guardians of Haymen and the door to the Underworld, or so what the media was told and all that they knew.

A treaty was created between the world of humans, demons, and angels, for a balanced living space after the last Great War between demons and angels. Naturally, there were rebels from all races and species who did not agree with such madness of structure. That was originally the reasoning as to why Haymen's guardians were created, it was more of a poetic title than anything considering he could wipe out an entire civilization with the brush of his hand if he wanted to. I had been told stories of Haymen doing exactly that in a different world when he reacted poorly to a business negotiation. To say the least, it didn't end well for the other party.

The term 'guardian' was more so structured for ease of the transition into the human world. Tell them it was a 'lethal force' to kill demons who rebelled and continued to feast off humans, they would've screamed–tell them it's a guarding force of beautiful women and somehow it's understated and less threatened... go figure. Since the humans had seen us take down many demons, intercept catastrophic incidences and public tortures, we were now idolized. Humans loved to idolize what they both feared and did not understand. The same for the angels, who we had mutual agreement but begrudged. It was inevitable. Light and darkness couldn't too often stay on the edges to make grey, but hey, sometimes we were allured to one another while off duty. I mean power seeks power, and no one can match that of an angel lover. That passionate hate, war and rivalry really does create something rough in the bedroom, or so I've been told.

The treaty had now been in place for little more than four hundred years and now in the time of 2,986 we were watched and our duty revered to take the 'monsters' away. Little did the humans know of the true intent and purpose of the Guardians. The monsters they saw and were attacked by were not the ones that would devour them whole and take their earth. We fought them simply for the riches in return, well simply we were told to do so, so Haymen could gain further his power. We fought for the land of the living, but it was in the world that was dark, sleeping, and corrupt that would truly break all. I understood that now. Not being human any longer and walking through the darkness every night... the humans had no idea of what terrors truly sought for their blood.

I searched absentmindedly into the water disregarding those thoughts. I was here now, this was my new life. I stared into the surface of the water still tracking the beat of the demons under the dark water. They haven't yet made their move, they were simply circling-waiting. Maybe not so dumb.

My hair when I had been reborn from my human life after a tragic death-which was nothing short of demonic-had dulled into a light crimson instead of its once strawberry blonde. My skin seemed paler and more unearthly. It cascaded around my shoulders in its bountiful curls which had been revered as beautiful in tabloids. To stir the tabloids, I threatened to cut it off and was placed into confinement for two days by Haymen as punishment for actively attempting to defile his property. He pestered me more than anything during those two days making it seem hellish. He knew I actively avoided him even though I worked for him and surprisingly he hadn't yet called me out on it or punished me for it. The Guardians were owned by their master. Our vanity and appearance a further tool for him to exploit in the press and for personal gain. Our tattoos appeared after our blood oath, mine being physically forced upon me-not that I could recall much from the day of my death. All of our tattoos were different. Mine charmed like vines from both shoulders and between my breasts were droplets to the core of my belly button. The exotic and beautiful markings met with the medal piercing of my belly bar. At night it would glow a dull blue. It was a tattoo that only other members of the underworld and angels could see, it marked us as property of the world beneath. I had never been there, only making it so far as the door.

I pushed back my hair and tucked it behind my ear, scraping past the four piercings of my right ear.

"Vivian," Tahmeed yelled out to me. "Would you like help?" I continued to watch the swirls and felt the rattle of their movement beneath. I followed the sharp movement in the dark water when a woman's scream grabbed my attention. A silken thin line of a tentacle wrapped around her little girl's ankle and pulled her beneath the water with rapid speed.

"I've got this," I said, despite knowing that the invitation was in humor. We didn't help one another when it came to our duties and killings. The shimmer of my blue tattoos glowed brighter as I dove into the water, the black coolness over my skin rather refreshing. The sharp pain of skin stretched over my ribs and split as small gills tore open on both side of my ribs. My ears elongated and further gills broke out under my arms and legs so I could fluidly breathe beneath the water. *A bit excessive,* had been my first thought the first time I attacked a water demon and my form changed to adapt to my environment. But my water demon was the third to my seven to join me and my contract. This was the true power of a Guardian. Contracted to seven demons who resided within us. We could shift into and use their abilities at any time. All for the sake of being contracted to and to do Haymen's bidding. Every Guardian was different. My nails and canines elongated and my hands and feet changed to webbed.

I shot through the water hearing the little girl gargle screams as she was being dragged with unrelenting force to the bottom. My sensitive hearing could hear the pressure begin to crush her voice. Below was one of the baby demons which had twelve black silk tentacles and an open mouth of nothing but razor fangs. Others started wrapping their tentacles around her to fight for their food. With a sharp jolt of my legs I cut through the water and sliced through all four tentacles before they tore the girl's body apart.

They were in the dark hiding, and their screams were deafening. I grabbed the girl and propelled for the surface. When there were baby madrins there was always a mother close by leading them. As soon as I broke to the surface of the water, I placed the little girl in her mother's arms on the deck. The sun was so bright in comparison to the darkness below. The mother looked at me wide eyed fearful of my form and slitted eyes. She took her daughter who was still not breathing but resuscitation would bring her back. I placed my finger on my throat to project my voice along the coastline of the lake.

"Get away from the edge of the harbor." I didn't care much for the humans but I would get a decent pay out for this one and the less carnage the better. "I repeat–" That one thick tentacle wrapped around my waist and dragged me beneath the water. I twisted my hand beneath the strangling tentacle to cut through with my nails. The baby madrins divided in size, fearful of their angered mother. I looked down on her eyeless form as her razor-sharp teeth were one which had devoured ships.

Two things ran through my mind in that moment. One; I had never actually fought a madrin before. Being programmed as I was, there was an ancestral knowledge of the demons I fought because of the demons I was contracted to. Two; That was one ugly ass demon. I split her tentacle with my razor-sharp nails releasing her grip on my waist. The scream that came from her was so echoing and impactful that I was blown to break through the surface of the water. I flipped through the air looking down on her location. I'd never had the chance to see how long my sharp spaded nails would go. I aimed my hand to the location of her membrane. One way to find out. With excruciating pain my nails elongated rapidly and shot straight through the water and hit home. Still holding on to my wrist for support I hung in the air looking like some pole vault champion with my fingernails as the beam. Although excruciating, I had to admit this must have looked epically cool and disgusting at the same time. I could feel her squirm beneath my thick nails as her body slipped and sagged around them. The baby madrins left black ink in their escape as they darted back into the thicker parts of the water and towards the ocean.

I relinquished my hold on the demon and retracted my nails slightly wincing as they retracted into the tips of my fingers. Black blood swept up over my nails and hands as I flipped and hit the deck in a crouch.

I was naked and bony, and in a form not entirely my own. I looked over my shoulder at the closeness of the camera that went 'click'.

And that is how in the city ruled by demons, renowned as Shabeah–you made the front headline. And so looking over my shoulder with black blood running down my naked form, I smiled and licked at the blood which was not my own. Another demon down, another penny rolling in to my bank account, and this one want to be big!

Chapter Two- Vivian

Slap. The newspaper was sprawled on the coffee table in front of me by that afternoon. I was sitting cross legged on the couch in front of the big screen in our open living room. I continued reading my sweet romance novel with little interest in the newspaper article.

Tahmeed looked at me with arms crossed impatiently after she had slapped the paper down with a smile. "Not even six hours and you're already on the front, I'm sure Haymen will be impressed. It should be a descent payout with the size of demon and catastrophe it could've been."

I picked up the newspaper and evaluated the graphic yet sexy photo of my spiny back. Being able to actually see the demon that I had become was beautifully haunting. I looked bad ass. I was crouched in front of the water, my slit eyes alluringly crazed. I looked like a water siren and I had the feeling that if I were truly that species of demon, humans would not survive in the water around me, men in particular.

"A decent angle, to the cameraman I give credit," I unleashed a ruthless smile.

A small beep began in my ear and I didn't even have to look at the screen to know who was calling. I was going to ignore it until I saw Tahmeed look between the beep in my ear and me expectantly. Of course she could hear a private call. To defy Haymen was asking for torture if not a death penalty. I smiled brilliantly at her feigning my ignorance to her too watchful eyes. Tahmeed had noticed my reluctance of being contracted to Haymen shortly after my recruitment. I learned early on to have the control and restraint as to keep that secret. Although they were also the Guardians of this city, they were as much friend as they were foe.

I brushed my finger over the small metallic chip on top of my ear to take the call. If I had brushed it the other way it would've initiated a small screen in front of my eyes to type away or treat as any modernized phone. Instead I simply chose to take the audio instead of visual. The shorter the call the better.

"A full-grown mother madrin, and my–don't you look beautiful sprawled on the front cover," his low voice purred through the ear piece. Most women's toes would've curled at the way he spoke to me. Haymen was by far an extremely attractive man, but it was what dwelled beneath the surface that was nothing but ugly and destructive. His true nature that my demonic self was drawn too but hated at the same time.

"How much?" I said asking for my reward.

"You never play with me my beautiful Vi, it makes me so sad," he said sounding as if he were sobbing.

"We don't get paid to play," I simply said walking out of the lounge room and back on to the balcony where Tahmeed couldn't overhear. I looked out at the setting sun which glistened over the black water. It would be such solitude to live in there, the depths of its cool water and isolation. There was a yearning for me to dive into it and never return but I wondered if that were me or the demons blood inside of me. Especially the one which I had just called upon hours before. I looked to my right where I had been earlier. It had now been closed off where the humans cleaned up and hovered a large suspended crane to pick up the remains of the madrin. I smiled looking at the size of the cage. Looks like they will be calling back up because it was a lot bigger than that. Oh yea, it was so much bigger. Haymen's voice brought me back to reality and our battering.

"It's in every demon's nature to play," he said and I knew he was smiling. "I will show you the real meaning of it one day when I have you in my chambers."

I pressed my back against the railing with my hands resting on either side of me. "You make it sound like a dungeon and there is nothing you can offer me that I can't get elsewhere on my own. Thanks, but no thank you. Just pay me my money."

"I could pay you nothing if I wanted. I find your customer service lacking," he said in a tone that reiterated his ownership of me. It was distant to his usual playful one. I had heard him use it on others before and it was usually a done deal that nothing would work in their favor there afterward. I gritted my teeth. I had been saving up for something phenomenally expensive and this payment might be just enough to purchase the item.

"You are not my customer," I tried to say sweetly instead of gritting my teeth. I went to say something smart ass but he cut me off.

"Watch your tongue my darling Vi, your allure won't work if you don't have one," he said. Another Bing on my phone. I held down my metallic ear piece for three seconds which crafted a visual blue screen in front of me. I looked down at the screen pleased with the amount that had just been directly deposited into my bank account. It was more than generous as all my pays had been.

"Thank you Haymen," I said. "Pleasure as always."

"Vi, go with the blue dress tonight," he said on the other end of the phone. "It does always bring out that hair of yours I love so much." He hung up on me and I looked down on the screen which had recorded our communication. One minute and twelve seconds. And let that be the last of him for another two weeks, please. There was something about Haymen despite my displeasure of feeling like a slave for him that made me uncomfortable. For some reason I liked to challenge the man who thought he could rule and own everything and in his own right he probably could but I wasn't allowing him to fully own me, when he'd already taken everything else. At least that's the defiance I had to learn to reel in if I wanted to live.

"Come on girl!" Destiny said bursting out from the lounge room with a bottle of champagne. "The night is young, let's go out on the prowl tonight in celebration." I touched my ear to close the screen and telecommunication not at all surprised that Haymen knew the girls had been planning a night on the town. I *was* feeling a little frisky after such a great kill and I knew that it wasn't in celebration of my kill, we did this all the time. It was simply because Destiny loved going out almost every night and so to speak we were immortal until something bigger came along and killed us.

Destiny, Tahmeed, and I, stepped out of the long stretch limo two blocks from the entrance of the club. We preferred walking the two blocks and having it as a preventative in case people began to swarm our limo at the entrance which was utterly irritating. Within our treaty we weren't allowed to hurt humans. Well, publicly anyway. If you didn't get caught it didn't count as far as Haymen was concerned.

Shabeah was glorified for its gothic architect, consisting of older buildings and lack of advancement in technology in comparison to other cities. Some parts of it still maintained cobbled streets and churches which long passed their time of being holy. Haymen had a preference and that was to hold back the technology for as long as possible preferring the more remnants of his 'old' days, which no one was actually certain as to how far back that tracked. I had seen photos, media and movies of cities that were far beyond our 'primal' city and yet that was what glorified and beautified Shabeah, enriched with its history and dark alleyways that were easy for murder by a certain few demons. Humans claimed that the area which the poor lived was haunted. It might be, sure, countless murders would've been conducted there but why worry about that when you have actual demons to look out for?!

"Alexa said she can't come tonight," Destiny began as we approached the club.

"I have a feeling that she is still with Doc, do you think she is having issues with her sleeping?" Tahmeed asked as her throat widened to empty the remains of her bottle of Champaign... that she had opened only moments before. She threw it into the back of the limo and smiled as she wiped away a few drops from her mouth. I figured out quickly that my tolerance to alcohol was much greater than when I was human. That was apparent for the others as well. Tahmeed was the most formidable in that department.

"Maybe she had a major hunt that's taken a few days," I said as we began walking to the entrance. I had the same suspicions as the others. But it was nothing that we would advise of one another even if we were having issues with the demons that sought after us when we slept.

"Who knows," Tahmeed said shrugging her shoulders. "Maybe she's hunting. That or she's the one being hunted. She's been odd lately. Maybe she is near compromised."

There was a silence. I had no interest in talking about this anymore. It wasn't something we usually spoke about. It wasn't the demons we hunted during the day that killed us usually. Although of course it happened. Eventually, it was those demons who waited in the dark of our sleep that would possess our body and take it for themselves. That was the implied ending for all of us, unless we found them first which had been a failure for generations before us.

"Enough of this talk! We didn't get dressed up to talk about depressing shit! We're all on our own here, her fate is only hers. Let's drink instead. It's her battle not ours," Destiny said bubbly as she readjusted her hair while we approached the glassy entrance.

Destiny wore a short purple dress that didn't leave much to the imagination, it curved her bountiful chest and curvaceous hips splendidly. She wore knee length black boots and so many bangles you could hear her like Demon Claus coming a mile away. Her blonde, bountiful curls had been straightened into a high pony tail and her usual blue eyes were ivory tonight with black and greens of make-up smeared onto her face in a hauntingly beautiful allure with black lips.

Tahmeed was a little more modest in the sense that she went out in one of her demon forms which was fully naked but covered in an ivory plated skin. Her usual tanned skin completely vanished and her usual brown eyes were completely swallowed in black with no pupils to show. She had a very specific species of demon she liked to take to bed. From what I heard, they were rough and her skin was an armor that could take that kind of... pounding. She was the shortest of us three but made it up in the height of her heels which were an excessive six inches. She walked in them flawlessly. The fashion of the rich and famous was elaborate in comparison to what I was used to wearing in my human life. I had certainly seen quirky wardrobes since my 'career' change and being involved with the media and the humans and demons who marvels in such pleasurable things.

I defiantly wore a simple leather black dress in comparison to the recommended blue one. I knew the exact dress Haymen was suggesting because he had sent it to me a month ago in a neatly wrapped box with a red bow that was the same size. It had sat under my bed ever since.

The music was suffocated by the glass domed entrance. The line-up of humans trying to get in stretched past the corner but to our credibility I hadn't waited in line once since I'd been turned.

"Vi!" One of them called out. It was a young male whose hair stuck to the side in one of the latest styles with feathers poking through, "You were amazing today! I love you, so much!" he said as if to reach out and touch me.

Destiny pulled me tighter into her and looked to the group of men. It wasn't just one but a whole bunch of them who looked at me starstruck. "No touching tonight, boys, she's mine," she winked and continued pushing me to the entrance. She had stopped me from giving them a piece of my own mind. Humans were disgusting in their excitement of having to touch and make contact. Looking was never just enough. I didn't mind being admired from afar but don't gasp at me close and try to touch me. No one was ever to touch me unless invited. I wondered if that was my own true feelings or the energy of one of my demons. But humans touching me was something I detested.

Tahmeed finished another bottle right before the entrance before throwing it a fair distance away into a side street bin, and triumphantly getting it in. Was that illegal, yes. Did anyone care if Tahmeed did it, no. Onlookers looked at her with awe, if you were daring to come to this club as a lower demon or human you wanted to make sure that you were entirely obsessed and crazy to even dare come in here because there were usually deaths and little traces to how and who.

The bouncer saw us and pressed his hand against the glass. It reacted with his touch, a plain human bouncer, to claim it being 'fair' for all species. The glass opened through the side where we could walk straight in. The dome glowed red for a second, it was scanning to make sure we didn't hold any weapons. The process began two years ago when ownership changed. It was a way to stop the weapon and human trafficking that used to happen in here when the mafia was involved. After running it for so many years it was investigated that the humans were being sold and fed to demons. This was once the bloodiest and reputable dangerous club to go to and now the most high classed where everyone wanted to be. Mostly because the demons thrived in a place where so much human blood had already been shed. That, and it wasn't in the center of the city or the red light district. It was a complete world of its own. The bouncer checked above his head where a small green dot flickered. He smiled and looked back at us.

"Enjoy your night at Ravish, ladies," he said letting us through. Despite its ugly dome like entrance as soon as the two wooden doors were opened by the fellow security guards, the music poured out and the lavish red walls were revealed. Small lights on the ceiling led the way through the dark hallway, music of scratchy and heavy pounding alike encased us. I turned to Tahmeed who was downing another bottle of Champaign. I raised an eyebrow at her as if to say, 'where did you even hide that?' She winked and polished it off as we walked into the next set of open doors.

Demons from all over the city, of all species danced through the club and naturally more than half had taken on a human form. Demons found it almost entertaining to do so, for those who could. For some reason humans thought they were more civilized or 'safe' in this form. It was a decoy often to allure humans in for their own intent. Tahmeed swept the room with her eyes and found exactly what she was looking for. Coming in at seven foot, a little small for his kind, and shoulders that I am surprised fit through the frame of the door, she beelined the red looking beast. His blue teeth flashed at her. Either he was a regular patron of Tahmeed's or no words had to be spoken between them as to what they both expected that night. Within seconds, Tahmeed was lost to the crowd of ravers.

"Well shit, that was fast," Destiny said. "She could've at least had one drink with us and played hard to get," she smiled while linking her elbow with mine. "Just you and me." Destiny was touchier than I liked. She seemed to be the only Guardian who acted in such a ditsy way but the others including myself allowed it. It was harmless for the time being.

Caged dancers hung above our heads, their sequenced and glittered bodies not leaving much to the imagination, especially when I looked up into those glassed cages that levitated in the air.

"Breakfast," I said under my breath.

"What?" Destiny asked absentmindedly as she looked for two available seats. As soon as we approached the bar, two women were asked to leave. The women in silken silver hair and an unnatural glow like the moon were not happy to be ushered along.

"My two favorite girls," the barman who was used to Destiny's flirting, said. He gave no further attention to the two he just requested to leave. She smiled as she took a seat at the long modular glass bar. Within it tiny fish circled. I watched the all black obsidian man next to me coax the human male he had with him to try one of the fish. Good luck to him. There were small holes drilled into the top of the bar where patrons could take one at a time. The demon traced the movement of one of the small fish and caught it efficiently with two fingers; he scraped it out. The fish floundered to be in the water again but his grip was firm, much like the hold he had over the human who looked no older than twenty.

The bartender in front of him lined up a trail of salt which could be snorted after the fish was eaten.

"I don't know, I haven't done any demon drugs or anything like that," the human said nervously. I watched curiously as to whether the human was dumb enough to try. That fish would outlast him and possibly his internal organs, if his demon weren't kind enough to put measures in place first. If he had, well the fish was definitely an aphrodisiac, where in most cases you would dance and have sex for days without realizing or remembering what happened. Snorting the salt afterwards, made the fish react, almost instantly as it scorched its skin and it flamed up within.

The demon that reminded me of obsidian looked at me. His skin was leathery black and his eyes were yellow slits in his head that seemed too small for his body. He had one elongated nail on his pinkie which I realized he was tapping on the bar. I had never fought an Obsidian before but I heard they could make your greatest nightmares seem like reality. If an ally however–they could, if they wanted, make your greatest fantasies seem real. I very much doubted anyone saw that side of them. They fed off the horror and pain of others and I very well might be watching as he coaxed his next victim.

"Pretty," is what he purred at me with a voice that was far more heightened than his blinding darkness. The longer I watched the more I felt like I was being swept into the depths of his allure. It was almost transfixing.

A drink was pushed into my hand, snapping me out of my daze and leaving me to my own affairs.

"Don't stare too long," Brady the bartender said to me. He was cute, with red hair and few freckles across his face. Very much averagely human. "And before you ask, no he's not going to murder that boy, he comes into town now and then, picks up his fun, and sticks to his own business. If that kid is stupid enough to mingle with him in the first place then I'm sure he knows what he's getting himself into."

"Come on Vi, don't go all work on me now. Tonight is our night, and you need to get laid, seriously, what has it been two weeks?" The reality of it made me swallow, hard. That was the odd thing about becoming a Guardian. I had a phenomenal allure to appease my appetite, to kill, and have sex. Unrelentingly so, and as soon as one of us somehow managed to get to the two-week mark we were hell to live with and it affected our work. Of course, I had to keep in the back of my mind that those who I slept with died within three days.

"Yea but I've got to deal with those bodies lining up behind me. Someone's surely going to come a knocking and question why," I said getting a laugh out of Brady. I threw back my drink and requested another one. I was hoping the drink would knock back the edge of requiring a regular sexual partner. Well, that's the technical term. I just wanted to fuck the shit out of someone. There was so much anger and frustration in me just from my appetite not being met. If time allowed it and a there was a suitable partner, I would relinquish my job momentarily and just fuck for a week straight, hoping it would drill this constant frustration out. I felt like a dog on heat as my eyes acutely scanned every male in this room and my eyes even trailed over a few women out of wondrous curiosity.

"Oh please that's just a rumor, and besides, you can't help it. Who knows maybe it's a backlash of one of your demon's blood. But let me tell you just as much, you can't live going without," she said sipping on her cocktail as she actively scanned the room. "No offense but you've been a bitch to live with for the last week. You need to sort that shit out."

I smiled and picked up the skewer with my small olive to my new drink. "I'd hate to see your mean side," I said with a smile and ate the olive. She charmed one back and slid off the chair. She grabbed my hand to lead me onto the dance floor.

"Let's go make a spectacle and dance. We can't let Tahmeed have all the alluring attention." I looked over the numerous dancers trying to find her and instead Destiny pointed across the room, where against the wall Tahmeed was showing her impatience of having to wait for a demon, she all but beelined before walking through the door.

"Time. Twelve minutes," I said to Destiny who looked over at Tahmeed with a smile. We had only been here for twelve minutes and Tahmeed was already trying to drag him away. She was a woman that did not mess around. The music pounded around us but she made sure to speak loud enough for me to hear.

"Darling, we live in the world and are a mixture of demons, this isn't a fairy-tale. We are and act exactly like our demonic counter parts. If there's a thirst then no one is to deny any demon theirs for the taking and the need for it to be quenched," she said taking a sip of her pink drink. She watched others out of the corner of her eye, on the hunt for something new. The reality was, she was right. And I knew the consequences if I didn't squash this building frustration now.

Chapter Three- Vivian

A handful of free drinks from men and demons alike with terrible pick-up lines, I found myself finally feeling the buzz of the alcohol. The music vibrated and pulsed on the dancefloor as I danced with Destiny who was flicking her golden locks back and forth. Tahmeed had left about an hour ago and we already had two demons thrown out from the club who had offered us drinks which were laced with interesting drugs and concoctions. I could smell it as soon as they offered it to us. I didn't react well. Before I ended their lives, the bouncers thought it best that they drag them away.

I threw my hair back and then something glorious on my left caught my attention. The dark skinned muscular angel charmed a smile that was all but to die for. He was talking to his friends which was a surprising mixture of demons, humans and only one other angel. As he laughed and spoke to them, his eyes were definitely on me as he took another sip.

"Wow that is some eye candy and he's coming over here now," Destiny said with a promiscuous smile. I wasn't a woman to play coy and so I watched him as he approached. I wasn't going to pretend to not be interested. I wasn't one to play such games.

"I didn't actually think the angels and demons sex thing was true," I said to Destiny. "Wouldn't both find the other revolting?" I said, keeping the beautiful specimen in the corner of my eye.

"That's not our battle or war; we're just the middlemen," Destiny mused before making herself very busy with the neighboring dancer. That's when all tonnage of the handsome muscled man walked up to me. His wings were tight on his back to make sure no one touched them, because of all their 'angelicness', if anyone were to touch their wings without permission, it was a death sentence and one that was not pardoned. Another thing about these oh-so-holy specimens that was yet another contradiction to their 'good' persona.

"Vi, I assume, from all the media I've been hearing these past few hours, your hair makes you unmistakable," he purred into my ear, instantly disregarding my personal space. If it were unwarranted I could've just as easily pushed him away. His white wings expanded past his shoulders and melted down into an orange, the feathers explicably clean and looked rather silky. The very reason why they fetched such a high price on the black market, commonly used for fashion, spells and channeling. But to successfully catch one was a feat in itself, but to do so without consequence was a near miracle.

"And yet, I don't know your name. And to not put a name to such a pretty face would be so cruel." And it was a very pretty face. Strong jawline, luscious pink lips and soft orange eyes. And that natural touch of something magical and all things good. It just made him divinely fuckable.

"I heard you're bad for my kind and even yours," the angel said yelling over the music, instead of giving me his name. He swept in closer once again so his rock-hard body was against mine as we danced. He placed his hands on my hips possessively and I knew the deal was sealed. We both knew what we wanted and why. I could tell from the look in his eye, of all masculine hotness and desire. The attraction of something we shouldn't have drew him in even more, as it did I. "I've been told that you have a reputation of being called the Widow because all those you sleep with die from unnatural causes within three days."

"Scared to tangle with something dark?" I asked.

"Well I'm here dancing with you, aren't I?" He replied with an arrogant smile.

"I've never fucked an angel before," I said with wild curiosity.

"I bet you haven't with those manners. I've always wondered what it would be like to fuck a demon. A beautiful one at that."

I snaked in front of him and wrapped my hand around his balls. "I am *not* a demon." I said arching an eyebrow and watching him squirm. He stood into the grab further, standing over me with his chest close to my face. He smelled of fresh air and sea, of flight and freedom. He grabbed my ass tightly cocking his eyebrow.

"No you're not, but you are contracted to the underworld. A demon slayer at best. But tonight, I can make you feel like you're so much more."

"Why don't you put your money where your mouth is," I said loosening my grip and stroking it up him making sure to feel out his impressive size while I did so. And I knew from what I felt he was ready for this just as much as I was. Sleeping with demons now seemed no fun in comparison. I loved the thought of fucking something considered so 'pure'. It was true, all those I had slept with to date were now dead. I still didn't have a reason as to why, bad luck I supposed for them. There was a line-up of corpses behind me and I wondered if an angel would be different.

It would cause more damage for any demon including me to not quench my sexual thirst and often we would go feral if our needs weren't met. Fuck or kill. It's why you rarely saw any devoted relationships amongst demons. As soon as something shiny grabbed their eye and they wanted it, they would make sure they got it.

"Luke," he whispered into my ear and drew part of my hair back. "My name is Luke." He pressed his lips to mine, his hotness compressing against my coldness. He coiled his hands in my hair, our breathing heavy as his tongue fought for dominancy over mine. I growled into him and bit the bottom of his lip as he drew back. I looked down and could see his cock pressing against his jeans. My own stomach and urges pulsed with that hungry need. It was now sexual aggression and I had to pounce.

"We're done here," I said and began leading him through the crowed to the exit.

As soon as I opened the door to the lake house he flew me across the room with shattering force and pinned me against the wall. I allowed the forceful strength momentarily as his kiss trailed down my neck and onto my collarbone. I ripped his shirt apart and tiny buttons bounced across the room. I ravished his muscular chest and abs with my eyes. His shirt hung on either side of his wings. How they put shirts on I wasn't yet sure, but I wasn't in the mood to ask now. He kissed my neck harder, leaving a bruising mark. I pushed him back with force making him stumble and fall onto the couch. He seemed surprised by the force, but hardly interested as I straddled him. There was nothing sweet and innocent about this–nothing angelic. This was pure hot and adrenalin pumping sex. I undid the zip to his jeans and splayed my panties to the side–just kidding I wasn't wearing any–and as his fingers lapped under my dress, his eyes sparkled as he realized.

I took the size of him in one painfully bliss swallow. He pounded me from beneath the bruising sure to arise in the morning from the sheer strength of him. I bounced hot and heavy, the nails of one of my demons coming out and clawing his back. The tendon in his neck strained by what I knew to be added pleasure. I licked the sweat on his neck raking my teeth which drew blood. Oh, how some part of me wanted to bite him. He went still and I arched an eyebrow at him.

"Oh honey, I'm not poisoning you or anything," I purred. "If you're not willing to play in the big leagues then you shouldn't have made the suggestion."

"Oh, I can keep up," he growled, no longer creeped out but taking it as a challenge. He flipped me onto my fours and pushed the dress further up my waist. He grabbed my hair and pulled my head back hard. My neck bent back so much that I thought any more force and I would find myself in a very deathly and compromising position and then he glided into me. I was wet and slick and ready for his size. Claw marks tore down the side of the lounge as I moaned in pleasure. I couldn't help if I shifted at times, especially during sex. My tattoos glowed bright blue and before I knew it I had changed into one of my poisonous advisories and succubus form.

He paused again not sure. My skin was softer, like a creamy silken snake's, but the claws, tail and fangs that often dripped with poison were all but soft and enduring.

"You can heal right, not overly affected by poison?" I asked and looked over my shoulder back at Luke, who I knew was definitely someone within the angel military from the branding on his chest. A small circular tattoo. It wasn't large and told no story. The ones who had been there for hundreds if not thousands of years had stories in their tattoos. He was a new soldier, maybe a few hundred years old, but it meant he went through training and by military standard he should be able to withstand my poison. The perks I had previously found out with this particular demon was when I was aroused, that poison would mix with endorphins and his rock hardness would last for hours, as if I thought that it wouldn't. "It won't hurt you, it will bring you…. Pleasure," I coaxed.

I rubbed my silken ass against his cock and he all but rolled his eyes at the feathery touch. I knew it would be hard to resist as I splayed so beautifully in front of him, even for an angel who might have righteous discipline. I flicked my tail back and forth as if devilishly. I trailed its tip slightly over his chest, it wasn't much poison but it left a slight green scratch on him. He broke out in an instant sweat and I could see that for a sheer second he panicked until his rigid body relaxed and he grabbed his cock.

"Holy shit," he said. "It's painfully hard." I looked over my shoulder and rolled over to him.

"My poison can give you the most pleasurable night you've ever had and it will be gone from your system in the morning." I stroked one silken finger along his cock and he shuddered–a drop of precum forming. I smiled and licked only once. He grunted as he blew his load over my shoulder and onto my back.

Once his rigidness stopped, I took a slight bite on his inner thigh, my poison naturally secreting. Again, I knew he feared it but his dick shot right up. I smiled and knelt in front of him and wrapped my hand around his cock. He shuddered but his eyes were all but lustful.

"You will build a tolerance to it," I promised. "And then you can please me," I said running my hand down my stomach, enjoying the feel of my own silken flesh. I was humming to be touched and couldn't help the small moan that left my lips.

He reacted and drew his own fingers below, thrusting into me. I closed my eyes, in pure bliss as he leaned me back and pumped into me. With only a few strokes for himself, he came again on my chest. I lavished in the feel of it moaning and looked up at him with the haze of my now red eyes.

He leaned over me and kissed me tightening his grip on my jaw. His fingers continued to pump me. This time he dragged his own lip against my fang. His dick thickened in size again.

"It's so painfully hard," he said grabbing himself again and pumping a few times in wonder. The sight was glorifying as his wings naturally spread out behind him and glowed a light orange. And I knew from research, it was an indication of an explicit and intense emotion. He rolled his eyes in the pleasure of his own feel. I stroked my silky hand against him again and he shuddered. His wide wings fluttering gently.

I wrapped my legs around him and pulled him into me etching for him to dip his cock in me again.

"Give me a night I will remember," I purred. "Your tolerance will build and I can have you buried in me all night." His cock was hot against the moistness of my silken flesh. "Fuck me in the clouds," I purred imaging the sheer force of gravity.

"Aww baby got no wings?" he teased. "I won't fuck you in the sky. That's exclusive for our own kind."

I raised my eyebrow. First, I'd heard of that. He chuckled and slammed hard into me, taking me by pleasurable surprise.

"But I do give consent. As long as whatever this is, is out of my system by morning, let's fuck baby," he smiled and leaned into me for a kiss as he thrust one more time.

"I thought you'd never ask," I said with a smile and came undone in front of him. As long as he had given me consent, I could give in to the nature of this demon. And oh, how I wanted to ravish him. I flickered my tail back and forth before angling it and piercing it hard into his ass. He arched as I did, his size seeming to only enlarge into my now swollen lips. I shredded my claws into his back as his eyes rolled into the back of his head from the pleasure and sensitive touch he was experiencing.

He might've been an angel, but that's got nothing on the pleasure of a demon woman all but liquefied with erotic poison.

Chapter Four- Vivian

*T*he problem with sleeping was it left me vulnerable to the creatures that would prey on me at night. In this place, a very distant and dark reality, I could not fight, scream, or control the environment. All I could do was run. The world and experience were completely controlled by the entity which was imposed on me. All I could do was my best at escaping its clutches and not fall for the numerous ways that they would come to me. Was I terrified? Extremely, because every time was the matter of life and death. Was I strong enough?

Sometimes I dreamt normally, like any other human. Little did anyone know that before I was turned into a Guardian I already had run-ins with these creatures of the night. Those attacks started when I was a teenager and entirely human. No one knew, not even Haymen, and I would keep that information hidden. The attacks increased when I reached adulthood but I was able to better identify it, prepare myself for the lethargic effect it would play on my body. It increased and it got worse. But I was able to handle it somehow until Haymen turned me and forced the contract upon me. Death would have been my better option. Now being a Guardian, I was the very host that those entities savagely struck and now I had to find a new way to handle it and disperse their interest in me.

Just like now, I was dreaming, rather standard and easy sleeping. But then there was a shift, like my dream had connected into a different channel on an old tv antenna. The dream went slightly distorted, or should I say, it felt like I went distorted. Sometimes instead of a new attack, I would relive memories of the old ones.

I was already running along the dark road which surrounded me with dim houses, the light posts flickered off as I ran past each of them. The man or creature behind me was laughing as he chased me with a slight limp that did nothing to affect his speed. I was no longer the sixteen-year-old girl who had first lived this but tears still welled in my eyes as I panicked. I could not fight them. I knew I couldn't. I could not change into my demon forms and I knew that to linger, to try and oppose the entity of whomever it was, would only allow it to get closer to me.

I ran faster; my lungs heaving and shards spreading up from the chill in the air. My breath began to lock from exhaustion as I felt him getting closer and the odd niggle on my back, a brush with coldness that I feared was him catching up and his fingers reaching for me. I could not let him touch me! He would possess and take hold of my body. He would kill me from the inside and I feared not to face death but the uncertainty of what kind of afterlife or darkness it would spiral me into. These creatures were unholy and the touch of demonic spirit that not even I wanted to confront in the light of day.

I noticed an old warehouse which splayed lights on and ran for it. I knew I shouldn't have. But it seemed like every other option around me had disappeared. He was leading me into there.

The bright lights of the warehouse which catered for a retail store speckled my sight for a second. I panted for only a moment before dashing between the shelving, forklifts, and jumping over crates. I looked behind me but couldn't see him. My shoulder smashed into the corner of one of the crates throwing me off balance. I caught myself and instinctually clutched for my shoulder heaving. The hair on my arms rose as I circled around in the small shelving I was at. My breath was heavy and I willed it to stop. Please. He will hear me. A tear slid down my face. This was my sixteen-year-old self reliving the moment. Ready to wake and cry to my mother about a force against me that I could not explain. I knew what was to come but I still tried to change the fate of it. It didn't make it any less terrifying.

I turned to run into the other direction when a splash of cold water hit me. It felt like shards over my already too cold body and I screamed from the pain. The chuckle from the chucky doll ran up my leg and across my shoulder with an open wire. I didn't have time to react but only to scream. As soon as the wire touched my entire body I convulsed and hit the floor with the current of electricity that my body could never handle...

My body was convulsing as I woke despite the sleep paralysis I woke up with every time I had one of 'those' dreams. Tears slid down my eyes as I felt like I was that sixteen-year-old girl once again. I knew what would happen. It was the same as last time. Eventually, the convulsing stopped and I could move. Slowly but surely, I sat up to sit in my King-sized bed, the silky light blanket dropping to the floor with my movement. I wiped away the drool from my mouth and wrapped my arms around my legs. I sat in the dark unable to identify anything in my room. Luke had left hours before and I made certain of that. I never slept with another in the room. It was a vulnerability and a risk I wasn't willing to take. No one else could know about the night terrors that haunted us.

I sighed heavily trying to balance my breathing. So much has changed since I first had that dream at sixteen. Now twenty-four, I no longer had my mother to cry to. She died when I was seventeen. She didn't understand, didn't want to. Saying that it was just a nightmare. But at least I had that companionship and someone to talk to instead of others who would say I was going crazy. In a twisted way I wondered if it was the reason why I was handpicked by Haymen to become a Guardian. Not that he ever said anything from that day and I couldn't remember how I was turned. I just remember that it was against my will. I never dared ask the others if they had the same experiences in their human life too.

I touched the large silken marble on my bedside table that summoned Doc. I had to report this to the Shadow Mind Journals. The only thing I would keep to secrecy was that I was reliving the nightmare, I had to tell Doc that it was all anew. The Shadow Mind Journals was the recording and deciphering of those who reached out to us in our dreams. It was in hope that we could identify the entity and it could be tracked so then we could hunt them during the day. There were many secrets of the Guardians but no outsiders knew that this was our true purpose. To find those who Haymen considered his greatest threat, or so I presumed. I couldn't imagine anyone going to all this trouble to find one species of demon unless threatened by it in some way.

I walked up the hallway from my bedroom and placed my hand on the marble panel of the door. It instantly slid open. The white room was bright in comparison to the darkness of the hall I had just walked through. It was the sector within our home that Doctor Tellith would appear at as soon as we summoned her. She was a witch that worked for Haymen and kept track of our stability and the physical toll that the dreams were taking on us. Not out of concern but as to whether we were close to being compromised. We were simply property in Haymen's eyes and that thought was extended to those who worked for him. The attacks drained us physically more than any of us would admit and that was because while we were running and fighting for survival the entities were sucking the life out of us, hoping to drain us completely so they could take our bodies upon the next attack. It was still questionable as to whether the soul was sucked out and eaten or if the person remained and screamed beside their laughing possessor. It wasn't something I was ready to find out.

"Those leaves fall into your hair, Doc?" I asked her as I looked at the colored feathers threaded through her black tangible hair. She arched an eyebrow not raising those wooden brown eyes from her task at hand. The room was surrounded by few white benches and she ushered me to sit back into the white leather chair.

"Were your poor manners a result of being dropped as an infant?" She asked as she pressed the needle into the vein of my arm. I smiled at her and her own were filled with the same lack of delight. My dark mahogany, almost black blood threaded through the tube, reminding me that I was far from human.

"I don't know why we have to do blood tests each time," I said in agitation. Despite my warrior like attitude, from human life to now, I still did not like needles.

"I told you last time. I will take a sample out each time to see if there's any variance and besides, I need more from you than the others. We still haven't identified the heritage of four of the demons who you're contracted with," she said.

"I didn't contract them," I said laying my head back and looking up to the bright light. "They came to me and for whatever reason that might've been they just have no appetite to appear in front of me yet."

"But unlike the others you seem to be hazy on those who accepted and contracted with?" She said now taking the needle out. It was true. After the initial contract with Haymen, I was faced with demons who encouraged my growth and would aid me in my task as a Guardian. They were demons who had already died in their lifetime and were willing to resurface when I needed their strength. And yet unlike the others, I completely blacked out and awoke in this very house with tattoo markings that stretched out further than most.

"Oh, come on. It's kind of like a surprise every time I turn, what's in the box?!" I joked with her. She shook her head and as usual did not find it funny.

"You're lucky so far that in most situations you have the descendant of a demon who can challenge the ones you are hunting. But I fear without this data one day you might be caught off guard and you might be seriously injured." She labelled the clear bag which held my thick substance of blood and scribbled down in her diary a language which I couldn't identify. Witch scribblings. The black ink shortly went invisible and I imagined only eligible for her eyes.

"I don't fear fighting in the real world, Doc," I said with much purpose. "It's the demons when I sleep that will end me." She looked up from her notepad with a grim expression and that was fact. That's how more than seventy percent of our kind had died to date. And Tellith had been around for many years opposed to what her naturally youthful skin looked like.

"It's necessary so we can find them. These entities are what truly challenge the treaty. On top of that, they are an immediate threat to Haymen and his empire. That is why you are contracted." I knew not to argue with her or tell her how I truly felt about that statement. It wasn't disclosed to us why they were such a threat to Haymen, but what I couldn't voice to people was that contract to him wasn't signed willingly by myself. All those that worked for Haymen would never speak ill of him. To do so would be death.

She brushed away my hair and I presented the back of my neck all too used to the process now. "I heard you had a pretty little angel at your hip last night," she mused as if trying to distract me. How things circulated quickly around here. Then again, the entire house was monitored.

"And most of the morning," I added. "Four hours to be exact until I kicked him out because I heard Destiny coming back. To say the least I think she is burning the couch."

She smiled with little humor and raised the small metallic chip which had four sharp prongs on it. She pressed my head down and injected it into the back of my neck.

"Shadow Mind Journal activated," the room sounded in a woman's robotic like tone. I closed my eyes not wanting to relive the experience of my dream. But that would be to feign ignorance and weakness. I looked up to the ceiling again where now the room had dimmed and my nightmare was displayed on a projector. Tellith was the first inspector as she watched and studied it, as she always had done. As she did, she monitored the small screen beside her which read information about my body's reaction during that time. I watched on as I ran through streets, the experience threatening to make me want to coil up again. But to do so would be to show weakness. Especially in front of a witch employed to Haymen.

And so, we watched on until the last moment of my convulsing and then the image distorted and sharply cut out.

"This one seemed different. You didn't look back or try to confront the attacker. You lacked in trying to identify them or the location," Tellith said scribbling in her book with ink that would soon disappear. "Your brain waves are also overlapping like a few of your previous collections. I will ask you again, Vi, is this a memory, have you dreamt this before?"

"Not that I know of," I said and held her gaze. Tellith had her suspicions of that I was certain. She eyed me and ripped the reader out without warning. I rubbed my hand against the back of my neck, trying to remove the itch that remained. She pressed a small cloth there to wipe away the blood that would've already begun to clot and heal. "I'm sorry, I figured it was too dark to see him, which is why I was looking for better lighting in the warehouse." I lied.

Her face was expressionless as she continued writing. Doc was the first to examine it. I wasn't sure what happened to the journals afterwards and if there was another program or team on it afterwards. I suspected there was more to the story of the Shadow Mind Journals and our purpose but I learned long ago to not press for answers. There were always consequences. Especially when that demon I had in mind was Haymen.

"If you recall anything else or would like to enter new data please let me know. Until then, you are dismissed Vi," she said widening her hand out towards the door.

"Hey Doc, we haven't seen Alexa for a while," I said thinking of the fourth in our team. The fifth was killed weeks ago and a new member would be deployed to us in coming weeks.

"She is with me for the time being," Tellith said. "It shouldn't be too long before she comes back." Doreen, the prior Guardian that we hadn't seen for weeks had spent one of her final weeks with Tellith. She didn't disclose much to us but told us she had a close call. Tellith made her physically stable and healthy but we knew Doreen hadn't been the same since. One week later she went missing. No body to remain, only the knowledge that she had been possessed and a message painted in her own blood on the walls in a language far older than any of my ancestral demons could read. Only Haymen who immediately ported in seemed to know what it read. He simply told us to clean it off the walls and repaint over it for the next Guardian who came.

Knowing that our discussion was over I nodded goodbye and left the room. I took a moment to catch my breath on the other side of the door. I rolled my shoulders and cracked my neck. I embraced the demon blood within me, taking a deep breath and feeling comforted by the power that radiated within me and of the knowledge those demons brought me. This was now the real world and day. I could protect myself and kill as I pleased.

"Vi! You're parcel arrived!" Destiny yelled out. "I threw it on your bed. Also, I charged the new couch to your account. You shredded the fuck out of it and I don't even want to go into further detail as to why the dry cleaners couldn't even attempt it."

I smiled. Two months ago, Destiny had to pay for the entire refurbishment of the kitchen. At least I was a little restrained.

"Light dim," I said activating the lighting in my room. It was lavish in size, almost a studio in its own feat assuring that none of us Guardian's felt crowded. My king-sized bed was beautifully wooden and rounded against the grey of the walls. To its right was a wall water feature which hid the entrance to the walk-in wardrobe. On the right was my private bathroom. The shower was in the center of the room, the water never able to get past the groves in the ground which trickled delicately out into the side of the room and into the lake. A mirror took up the side of an entire wall with the wooden basin running along. In the corner, the toilet seemed almost unfitting for the architect. On the ceiling was images of angels fighting demons, images that spoke of a story long before my time. Across from my bed was a wooden table and laptop. I specifically ordered this in for myself, removing the television. I hadn't much time for it even as a human.

I had removed the kitchenette that was once in there and instead lined it with wooden shelves of romance novels I loved to devour. Trailing the shelves led me to the end of the room, where a Jacuzzi was positioned right before the glass sliding doors which would lead out onto a private balcony that overlooked the lake. I was on the third level of the mansion and the view inched me to look into the city which was not far from our home. Our location was pinnacle and reputable.

As Destiny promised, the parcel was on my bed in a box which required my fingerprint to open. This jewel cost me majority of my savings. I pressed my thumb to the pin pad and watched it as it registered and clicked open. The inside of the case was golden silk. I pushed it away and my eyes fell on the necklace in admiration. It was a chunky necklace with large blue gems. But it was what the Trinity necklace could do that cost me a small fortune on the black market. I hooked it around my neck without hesitation. I held them away from neck and sighed preparing myself. I let the weight of it drop through my fingers onto my skin and focused on its activation.

Within seconds I was in a barren and quiet place. All but the mutated crows which squawked around me. The ground was rocky and cracked and the sky held a dull grey. I was positioned beside a dead tree with roots that twisted in the ground. I pressed my fingers to my face, noticing that I wore a mask which covered my identity. I looked down on my pale skin, noticing the long navy dress that enveloped me. The tattoos which marked my contract with Haymen and my demons weren't to be seen. It was the first time I had seen my bare skin preceding my Guardian years.

Peace, serenity, loneliness. I sat on the rocky edges in pure bliss. I couldn't feel the presence of my demons and relished in the first breath I felt that I had taken in a year. The Trinity necklace, depending on which jewel you owned, transported you to an abandoned world. It was the rare gems within the necklace that transported you there. I didn't know what world or place this was but as the seller promised me it was very secluded. This was my private dwelling. A world without demons, angels, or human civilization. A place to simply be in comparison to the world that catered to noise, gore, and unsightly fashion. I closed my eyes and despite the dusty and stormy smell of the wind, I inhaled it–in peace.

CHAPTER FIVE- VIVIAN

I only allowed myself the luxury of an hour in the silence. The crows that surround me assuring that they were no foe.

I allowed my mind to transcend back to the reality of day by taking the necklace off. The shudder automatic as I was sucked flawlessly back into my room.

"Trinity necklace." The male voice made my insides squirm as I had been caught red handed. I looked over my shoulder to where Haymen sat. The dull lighting only made his pale skin shimmer with an off-orange hue. His piercing blue eyes are breath taking as always. They were sharp and consuming, as if you could see the very worlds he tore down before him to get what he wanted. His black hair was well groomed as it always was. The black suit he wore indicating he might have been attending human meetings prior.

I was still wearing my short polka dot silken pajamas and high cut shirt that my nipples clearly peeked from and my chiseled stomach on display. His glance did not go unnoticed.

"How long have you been here?" I said with a steady voice. If it were anyone else that had snuck into my room uninvited the consequence would have not been a simple conversation. I haven't had to confront him physically for weeks now. The pure power that radiated from him was overpowering and near suffocated the words from my mouth. A thin layer of raw power and darkness always surrounded him, unable to be contained. His presence was always overwhelming and my voice wanted to lock but I took a stand, like I always did. I eventually got my grip and bearings around him. It was just the initial shock of his presence every time. Menacing. Powerful. And a specimen who created an in-depth reaction from my own. It made me only hate him more.

"As soon as you went off the grid," he simply said, his expression still not changing. "So, this is what you've been saving all your money for?"

"I didn't know that there would be consequences if I bought such an item. I could think of worse things," I said walking past him to hide it from his reach in a vain attempt to distract him from the item. I swaggered my hips in a way that I knew would distract most from the necklace and straight to my ass. I headed towards my walk-in wardrobe but he grabbed my wrist and the burn of his touch ignited my tattoos and they lit brightly. He smiled at the sight. Just a reiteration that he owned me.

"I didn't say I was displeased. I simply wanted to check on my kitten," his rough voice charmed with an arrogant smile that was hard to resist.

"I am not your kitten," I said through gritted teeth because my body said otherwise. He stood up, his height towers over mine with my head at his chest level. Those harsh blue eyes always intimate as he searched for something within me, of what I wasn't yet sure but not curious to find out.

"Not yet, but you will be one day," he said stroking the back of his finger over my cheek. I wanted to push him away, because my arousal was apparent, and I hated that even more. He chuckled to himself as if knowing and leaned in to whisper into my ear. "You forgot to protest," he charmed. He vanished within a second, a black mist remaining like a black poof of magician dust. I took a step forward not realizing that I had been leaning into him.

"Grrrrrr!" I grabbed a pillow and threw it across the room agitated. Now not only was I hot, flustered, and my needs not met, I had been completely caught off guard. If I had hackles they would have risen and I had to check in the mirror that I didn't physically have any at the time in case one of my demons has come through. I was so angry! I hated him and yet my body reacted to his so freely like every other woman and man I knew. Why did he tease me in such a way! Next time I would be prepared for his charm and like I usually did, I would resist it. What worried me more is that he now knew I owned a

Trinity necklace and I doubted he was here to check up on me and make sure I was okay. Haymen simply didn't like his property to go amiss. Especially of its own choosing.

*

Word was that the local orphanage was experiencing some bizarre phenomenon and children were going missing. I knew that it could be almost any species of demon that would be daring enough to prey on the weak and innocent. I drove through the city at illegal speeds on my chic black motorcycle zipping between cars amongst the many sky scrapers of the city. The wind whipped back my crimson hair in lashes of waves. A lot of people on the streets in crazy hats and crazy colored tones yelled out my name waving as I drove through the streets. My hair and bike were unmistakable. The fashion of the humans had gone extreme as soon as demons and angels came out of hiding. Those who had money went under cosmetic procedures and fashions to try and even look more 'paranormal'. Even the city, Shabeah itself had gone under major reconstruction the moment Haymen decided to make this his 'human' residence and where most of his business was executed. Most of that reconstruction was to nicely preserve the old cobble streets and buildings on the outer streets of the city. Internally, it had already been crafted to the demands of human evolution. Other high demons and angels alike usually held rein over a city of their own. Some chosen from preference, others by rank of wealth, power, and even being the victor of some cold blood wars. It was certain that those city keepers had far superior rein over the money invested in the city and control over it than the human mayors themselves. Some completely cut out the human counterpart. Much to my surprise, Haymen had kept generations of the Mayor's involvement. Perhaps that was simply because he rather deals with business in the Underworld than the human one.

I zipped through cars even driving onto the footpath at times and dodging people so that I didn't have to slow down. A few intersecting cars were displeased by the way of their horn. People continued to point at me in awe as I zipped past and were excited by the clocked speed I was reaching. I wanted this to be a visit that the public knew exactly where I had been. It only made the humans trust Haymen's lead more so to see his Guardians out on the prowl for justice. It simply looked better for the treaty that we looked like we cared. I planned on interviewing those in charge of the orphanage. Usually when dealing with demons, I left that to the discretion of the night, because usually it wasn't a simple conversation.

Demons who decided to go against the treaty were often the ones in power in their human careers and took that as a stable position to start feeding off of their humans. It was an act I saw all too frequently and now went straight to the top of the food chain to see if it were the same thing. This was a public investigation but I would do the remaining of it at night when most of the demons dwelled and revealed themselves.

I pulled to the curb, the back end of my bike lifting slightly as I lowered it in a quick halt. I looked up at the sad looking brick building. The signage on the left read 'Shabeah Orphanage'. Black gates surrounded the building and green grass was lavish around. It was clean and well-structured from the outside but I could feel the animosity from where I stood. It was the remains of something powerful and demonic. The demon might not be here now but there is definitely residue of something being here. I could sense it. The building was in a back street of the city. Plenty of unsafe alleyways surrounding in a part of the city that I wouldn't deem safe to have children dwelling.

I wondered if this was Haymen's or the mayor's decision but then again, I couldn't imagine Haymen putting much thought into what happened to the children. In other words, the mayor simply didn't want this on display like most things on this side of the city. This was also where the homeless, poor, and sick lived. I rolled my eyes at the structure of the city. In comparison, my human life was much like this opposed to what and who I was now. I had very little in materialistic objects and a small apartment which I rented for an excessive price. But that was my life and I was happy with it.

I pushed away the thoughts of my previous life disturbed by the distaste. My demons didn't much like the human comparison either. I stretched my leg over the bike and walked through the black gates which automatically opened for me. I saw people on the streets who might've been so desperate as to steal my bike, if they didn't know who I was. My reputation alone would keep their mitts off of my property or the penalty would certainly be a painful death. My demons were almost daring someone to try, taking pleasure in dealing with the consequences.

I walked up the stairs onto the second level and an older lady walked out of the two open wooden doors offering her hand in greeting. I looked at it and ignored it. I wasn't one much for human contact.

"We didn't know if the Mayor would pass through the message. Thank you so much for coming Miss Vivian. My name is Dorothy," the older lady with wrinkled skin and white hair pulled back in a ponytail, said. I tried not to scoff at her Miss Vivian. No one knew my last name and it was never to be made public. I wasn't famous in my human life like the others so it was the only thing I could truly burn from that time. I didn't detect Dorothy to be anything other than human and there was absolute desperation in her eyes. "Please come this way. I will lead you to Mr. Greenhouse, he is in charge of the Shabeah Orphanage."

She walked me through the brick building which gave me the sensation of being in a slaughter house more than it did an orphanage. That disturbed me greatly. It meant that death was in the air for these children and they were being hunted. The lights were on and bright but I could imagine them flickering back and forth. An odd sensation that made me question if perhaps exactly something like that had happened. I heard little girls crying one side of the walls and others that played. All of the doors were opened, letting me see them as I walked pass. Some still had innocence in their eyes and enjoyed to play, some even unaware of who I might've been. But others stared at me. Some even through me and I knew that they had seen or been touched by something any child would be traumatized by. Their looks were blank as if they were already being manipulated into being a demon's puppet.

I rounded the corner following Dorothy. The shuffle of the rubber of her shoes squeaked against the floor. On the left-hand side were two rubbery doors which led into a kitchen. In there, adults and children were preparing meals. I took the moment to assess it properly with that keen eye of mine that took in everything within seconds. For some reason I could almost see the walls bleeding. I wanted to halt and assess the room further but couldn't feel the presence of any demon. My eye caught that of a girl, maybe not yet twelve with braided brown hair. She stood beside the bench where she had been rolling dough and looked at me with a concrete stare that I couldn't quite read.

Our gaze was broken as I was greeted again with brick wall and rounded the left corner of the hallway. On this side of the building there were square glass windows where the curtains were drawn back and peeled open. It overlooked the green grass and an attached building to the side.

"What is that building?" I asked. She looked down and gave a grim smile.

"That's the pool. We like to teach the children to swim since Shabeah is surrounded by water. We closed it down three weeks ago after the first incident," she said shamefully.

"Which was?" I pressed. I was only given the minor details. It wasn't the mayor who had passed the message but a direct request from Haymen this morning.

Dorothy went to speak and then looked to the children who hid behind the corner staring at me with curious wonder. As soon as I looked towards them they hid again. She nodded her head to the side to say we would speak behind closed doors.

At the end of the hallway was an office with open doors. I didn't have to read the signage to know whose office it was because it looked like it was set up as a principal's office. A man in his forties looked up from the scribblings he was writing and smiled. He was seated behind a large wooden table with bad posture. The computer screen in front of him turned off as he was copying text from a book to his own note form. Behind him was blinding light from the windows very similar to the ones in the hall. The side of the office had numerous volumes of books and I couldn't help but notice that a lot of them were notably credited to demons and their species. Before the wheezily man in front of me could introduce himself, I spoke.

"Demon books and descriptions seem to be an odd place in an orphanage. One would even consider it encourages contact with one," I said arching an eyebrow. Although I knew the leather seat in front of the desk was positioned to be inviting I studied the room more carefully. Dorothy stood to the side quiet. No introductions needed to be made.

"It was a personal interest of mine since I was kid," Mr. Greenhouse said. "But I've never encouraged it. This collection has increased since I've tried to find what demon has been taking our children." A demon Mr. Greenhouse was not. But there was something about him that was dark and menacing. Something even cruel and I felt the presence of the exact demon of mine which wanted to come forth. Without warning, my tattoos glowed bright blue and I allowed her to come through, merging flawlessly with her. Bells rattled as my cat demon appeared. Perfectly black with green eyes that glowed in the dark. Her black coat delicately laced my skin to cover the nakedness. My claws were retracted in a non-threatening manner and the bell laced around my tail jingled as it twitched back and forth tentatively. "Hmmm," I purred almost in ecstasy from the change and the sense of freedom. Mr. Greenhouse shot from his chair in shock.

"No need to worry Mr. Greenhouse," I purred as I sassily walked over to the bookshelf brushing over the titles in curious wonder. "I'm here to help remember," I purred raising an eyebrow. My tail flicked attentively to his every move. He wasn't the demon here. I couldn't sense a demon anywhere within the compound but darkness still swept throughout the entire building. And for some reason this room pricked my instincts most. "Did you know that a cat's sixth sense is keener than any other animal's? Or maybe I am just biased to that thought," I all but laughed. Dorothy was pale in the corner. "Sometimes much like the gypsy's, a cat's eye can see things even us humans cannot."

"But you're not human," Mr. Greenhouse stammered.

"No, I am not." I was certain that my eyes glowed with that statement. He had a strong reaction to my demon form. Perhaps for all his study and research on demons he had never seen one himself. He finally collected himself and sat back down in his brown leather chair where I noticed very tiny scratch marks on. They were tiny, only the surface on the leather slightly disrupted but with my keen sight I noticed it. They looked to be the size of a small child's nails. My gut told me I knew the reasoning but I had to confirm. I was certain that was why my cat demon came forth. There was no demon present now, and perhaps I would see something as soon as I made contact with the core of this place, but there was another darkness lurking here that I could easily remove.

"Do what you must. I want these demons gone and to leave my children alone," Mr. Greenhouse said with concern that met his eyes. But not entirely to convince me. I charmed a smile that I knew rattled him. Whatever hopes Dorothy had put into me had vanished and she was now terrified. It seemed humans forgot we weren't angels but those who could summon and took pleasure in our demons. And yes, we often looked terrifying.

I touched my hand to one of the books and allowed my sixth sense to open. I narrowed my vision to the core and roots of all that would lay open to me. I saw children playing. Children being bullied. Some even finding homes and the overwhelming sensation of finally being saved from this place. I scanned back through and everything became hazy as I swept through the main hall. My vision narrowed back and forth and I felt lethargic as I dug deeper. There was resistance so I had to push a little more and find the keyhole to open the images of the past. And then I heard the screams. Children being chased and tortured in the night. The darkness that enveloped me only enough to show its touch but protected to not let me see more. I knew this feeling and was certain that these were the same entities and presence I felt when I had my Shadow dreams. I could only brush past the memories not able to see anything clearly. They blocked me from encountering anything more, being careful to hide their tracks.

I could usually see and hear the footprints of demons, most aren't able to hide from my cat's eye. Like a vacuum I was sent back to the room I was in now. The entity's not allowing me to see any further in the halls. I kept my cat eye open as I was now in a memory of the same room I stood in. And there was the evil that lay bare and probably drew darkness to this place.

"Please Mr. Greenhouse," a little girl said backed into a corner by the human who held an evil within him that could not be seen by other adults, but the children who were his victims.

"Shhh, shhh," he said leaning his weight over the little girl. "It's just a little game and a secret between you and me. You can't tell anyone okay. It'll be fun. You be the robber and I will be the police officer." The graphic images I had to watch afterward only validated my previous instincts and it was why my cat demon–although I usually used her for investigation–so quickly wanted to come to surface. I knew that the hair on my back rose and I was probably hissing at the image. Although a demon, my cat demon was most adept to children. Surprisingly she was the most maternal of all my demons and did try to protect their innocence.

I allowed myself to be sucked into another part of the property, the pool I had inquired about earlier. It was a large room with a lapping pool, few chairs around and ornamental plants. The shutters to the windows were closed dark in the night. No light came through but with my cat vision I didn't need it. My eyes glowed green as I walked over to the eight-year-old girl whose mouth and eyes were open in horror. The paleness of her skin told me that she had been dead for hours. And yet she still floated on the top of the pool. I looked around but nothing remained. The damage had already been done and the murderer vanished. I was sucked into the back of the grassy establishment where a boy hung from a tree. My cat all but curled and snarled at the gruesome kill. I knew as I brushed past the remains of his mind that it wasn't voluntary. Something had pushed him to do this. I was drawn to the local dumping ground where amongst the rubbish which had been splashed on top, another little boy had buried himself, with added help from the boy that had hung himself afterwards. I knew that no one has yet found his body.

I stepped out of my cat eye now and into the present moment. "The little girl was killed and found in the pool three weeks ago. That was the first incident," I said to Dorothy.

She tried to speak but nothing came out. She then cleared her throat amazed that I knew and said, "Yes."

"There was a boy who hung himself on the back tree," I added. She nodded as tears swept down her face. My hackles rose again as I knew this boy was also a victim of Mr. Greenhouse's disgusting actions towards a child. "And you're missing another boy?" I said. Her eyes lit up and she let out a sob.

"Timothy," she said with hope.

"Is dead. Buried at the local dumping ground." Tears swept down her face as she began to wallow. She genuinely cared for these children.

"And the demon?" Mr. Greenhouse said infuriated. "What type is it?" I sneered at him. *Type?* It's almost as if he wanted to validate his knowledge in some sick manner.

"Dorothy I would like you to send me a file to my personal email on the other experiences and your findings," I said bending over Mr. Greenhouse's desk and writing down with pen and paper my email to her. I could tell he was confused as to why I hadn't asked him.

"I need to investigate this further," I said to both of them. "What I strongly suggest is that you evacuate your children from this property by tomorrow."

"We have nowhere else to go," Mr. Greenhouse said almost defiantly. "We needed you to come to get rid of the demon."

My eyes glowered at him and my claws sheathed out. He jumped back still in his chair. "Mr. Greenhouse," I purred with smug expression. "I plan on doing exactly that. Just know that I kill all evils that I see befit for the Underworld. My cat eye sees everything and even if my prey might run, I will find them at dark." He paled understanding my threat, his eyes large and shocked as he realized I had seen everything.

"If you can kill the demon by tonight then do we truly need to evacuate?" Dorothy asked.

"Yes," I said to her less bitter and changed back into my normal form. My leather dressing fitting my body tightly.

"The treaty," Mr. Greenhouse began to stammer. "You can't hurt anyone but demons," he said almost in desperation. His rounded face wobbled from fear. I could sense that Dorothy was confused behind me as I began to walk out of the room.

"Have a good afternoon Mr. Greenhouse. My cat will definitely find a mouse tonight," I said pissed that I couldn't kill him right now.

Chapter Six- Vivian

I was laying on my stomach on the roofing opposed to Mr. Greenhouse's apartment block watching him as he frantically packed his things. His paranoia got the better of him as he frantically looked out the window and closed the curtain. It was a rundown building fit for the scum that lived in there. And I could smell that there were plenty of menacing people inside but I wasn't here for them tonight. Evil had a presence and darkness around it. Particularly because of my job I was sensitive to it. Humans pathetically and easily gave into it. Not for the purpose of even wanting to become a demon themselves but because humans enjoyed to test what they could do behind closed doors when others weren't watching.

The overcast moon made it easy for me to hide in the shadows. I smiled flicking my tail back and forth listening to the jingle that followed. I didn't necessarily need a demon to kill him but I called forth my cat demon because her primitive nature took delight in this justice. I purred with satisfaction as I was ready to taunt, play, and pounce, on my prey. So many ways I could kill him. I could easily kill him within his room. I could have already been done by now. But I wanted to wait until my mouse came out of his hole, squirming as to whether he would make his escape. The main exit was in the alleyway that I watched over. Hmmm yes, I think I would delight in that. He had no right to be killed in the comfort of his home. He knew he wasn't safe. Just as those children felt. He deserved to be killed right beside the dumpster of trash just like what he was.

I began rubbing over my claws, polishing them as I waited oh so patiently. It was a dark alleyway and the street wasn't far from his reach. But he would never make it. Not that he knew that yet. I didn't have to wait too long until he came through the door, looking out skeptically before exiting with one small suitcase. As soon as he closed the door behind him, with sweat beading down his face I flicked my tail once. That one singular jingle made him erect in a posture his back might've known long ago. He began to run and I smiled as I leapt off the top of the building and landed in front of him softly without a sound. I was crouched over, my ass in the air as I flicked that one tantalizing jingle.

He screamed, rather girly actually, as he desperately ran back towards the door. I was careful to make sure that no one heard and there was no shuffle of curtains. No one would witness this extermination. I wanted him to feel that he was alone. Like how all those children felt.

"When you decide to become a monster, Mr. Greenhouse," I purred. "Make sure you're the biggest one out there." He twisted to look behind him and I slashed at his face. He screamed a gurgling scream as an eyeball flew across the filth of the pavement.

"The treaty!" He screamed thinking that it held power against me.

"You know," I purred again approaching him as he tried to get off the ground again and run further into the alleyway which was a dead end. "I was human once. And even if I still were. I dare say I might've done the same to you after knowing what you had done to those children."

He scurried as if actually to climb the wall. He saw a piece of wood and collected it. My hackles rose and I suddenly realized that I wasn't alone. Someone was close by and heading in this direction with exceptional speed. The joys of a cat's sixth sense. I growled in anger not being able to play with my prey.

I hurdled for him, dodging the one pathetic swing he attempted and plunged my claws down to cut off his manhood. He screamed, horrifically. I punctured my claws into his neck, not wanting to taste him with my own fangs. I wasn't leaving his bleeding out to chance. Sensing that my follower was close, I scaled up the walls quickly and ran across the rooftops. I couldn't see them because of the overcast clouds but I knew they were flying in the sky. I lunged over masses of space from rooftop to rooftop trying to lose them with the skill of speed. When I realized it was pointless and they surprisingly kept up with my speed, I landed on the ground and reverted back to my usual self. No evidence of the demon with claws that just killed a human. I had now put enough distance between myself and the murder.

I ran amongst containers on the pier. There were a few lights remaining after the late workers had finished hours before, which is exactly why I led my pursuer in this direction. I skidded onto the pier and circled in my spot ready for my attacker. Let's welcome this demon and I'll decide how to kill them from there. I was close to the water in case I needed to call forth my water demon. I was on the wooden side of the structure opposed to the cemented cargos in front of me. I estimated that my opponent would land right there. My crimson hair wavered in the wind as I watched the clouds pillow away. Great white wings stretched out at lightning speed and when my opponent hit the cement, it shook the very wood I stood on. Cracks and holes were crated around his fists and knee. I widened my eyes at the sheer beauty and size of the white wings that glittered with golds and light reds tipping the wings. Black pictures and swirls of tattoo reined on every inch of the angel's body. Unlike the one I saw last night, this one was older and had plenty of war stories to tell because they were ingrained on his skin.

His blonde hair didn't move in the wind that pushed my own as he stood up. Emerald green eyes met mine and they were pissed! What was an angel doing searching for me?

"You can run can't you cat?" He seethed. It seemed this man hated me. I smiled. So, he had seen me in my cat form. If he saw me do anything else then I might have to kill him. No witnesses to killing humans.

"I'd rather nap," I charmed back. "Why is such a big old burley angel looking for little old me?" I asked surveying his chiseled stomach and arms. He had a strong jawline which I so wanted to pet. He wore black loosely fitted pants and I realized that maybe, those were his, "Pajamas?" I asked. "I get a visit from a beautiful mystified angel in the night in his pajamas. Haven't I hit the jackpot tonight!"

His hatred for me only thickened and death wandered into his eyes. I don't know what I did to piss this angel off but whatever it was amplified his hatred for me even more.

"By order of my council. You, Vivian who is contracted to Haymen are coming back with me to face the courts for killing an angel." He tried to restrain himself from coming at me straight away. I snorted thinking back to the guy I had just killed. Surely, he hadn't meant him. Because he was far from an angel.

"Just call me Vi," I taunted. "As much as I am enjoying being in your dazzling presence. You have the wrong girl, officer," I said innocently.

"Do you know a Luke?" his words were barely audible but it carried on the wind to me. I left nothing to show on my face. I had slept with Luke last night. I didn't say anything or ask any more questions. This guy was kidding. Which meant that Luke was dead. Yet again another victim who slept with me and died within three days.

"I know many Luke's, but no I haven't killed any recently," I said.

"I'm done," the angel said in a rough voice before lunging at me. Within that second my tattoos glowed blue and I shifted into my water demon and dove for the water. My skin stretched over my ribs and split to create gills. My ears elongated as I hit and went deep within the water. Gills formed under my arms and legs as I continued to go into the depths of the water. The moment he dove into the water, it ricocheted the depths of the sea. I could feel other demons and creatures scurry away and run for life. Instead, I smiled. Oooh, I do like these games.

I wondered for how long he could hold his breath and how far down could he go? After all, angels were meant to fly not swim. The laws of the treaty meant nothing right now. He attacked me first. It was game on and now I had the right to defend myself.

Suddenly the water around me was sucked away and replaced by a bubble of air. I didn't like that and projected the coils of my bony spine to project into shards. I did the same with my hand aiming it into the direction I could sense him and shot. My claws painfully projected forward and I nicked him. Of what part of his body I wasn't sure. My spine clawed up the bubble of wind that constricted me and my breath. Finally, my spiny back slit the air bubble open and water gushed back in so I could take a breath.

He was trying to catch me like a damned fish. I swung my body to the side and decided I would do this the best way I knew how. Head on. Within seconds, the force of our impact met one another as he tucked his wings behind his back and propelled through the water. He wasn't as fast as me in the water and if I wanted, I could have escaped. But I would never let anyone who attacked me, live.

I let a high-pitched siren go. Instead of clutching his ears like most did, he grabbed at my throat despite his bleeding ears. I pushed his hand away upper cutting my claws into his stomach. He blocked it and kicked me in the stomach pushing me away. I grabbed hold of his calf, piercing my claws into it. And that was the bait I realized as soon as his wings spread wide and pushed strong against the water. We broke through the surface and I let go of my grip. I was meters in the air. I had no demon that could fly and I was in the middle of the sea. Before he could grab me, I painfully allowed the spikes attached to my spine to painfully form around me like a shell. It looked like a purple coral from the inside and I knew the colors of pearl were outside. I allowed enough space to project my hand out and unleashed my long claws trying to pierce him.

He dodged it. I almost hit the water when another brush of wind gathered me high and a brush of disastrous smelling substance hit me in powder form. I screamed in pain. It felt like my insides were burning away. The powder forced my demon to retract. Whatever that powder was, it coiled my demon in a painful manner. My body couldn't move as the glower of my tattoos faded and my back hit the water. Hard. Despite my body near being unmanageable to move I still swam but it was nothing in comparison to the sheer force of when he imploded into the water and scooped me in his arms.

I kicked and punched at him but my normal form was nothing in comparison to his sheer might. I had never met a match like this. The only person whose strength I couldn't oppose on such a scale was Haymen's. My hands were tied behind me and I made a last effort to wriggle out. I kicked him in the nuts which gained me the reaction I expected. When his grip loosened, I kicked off him and propelled for the water again.

I internally clapped for myself. Well done Vi. You're plunging into water when your hands are tied behind your back. Well thought out, Sport.

Before I hit the water, he scooped me again. His face was pissed and as I went to wiggle away again his lips met mine in a wave of fury. That poisoning kiss instantly put my body to sleep.

CHAPTER SEVEN- GABE

I crouched on the terrace of a small townhouse in a small suburb of Shabeah. I knew it would be a few hours until Haymen's Guardian, Vivian, awoke since I put her to sleep. I was anticipating Haymen's attention at any moment and was surprised he hadn't yet discovered me in his city. Especially when I had swooped down on one of his flashy demon summoners.

Vivian was her name and I knew with a face like that she would've enticed Luke very easily. I was so pissed at him for giving into it. I was surprised by her guts to fight against me and even more so that she actually landed a few marks. I looked down at my calf that she sliced open and the puncture wounds to my stomach. Only dry blood remained, not even a mark to remain. It didn't heal as efficiently as they usually did. Which meant this little Guardian was contracted to some high-class demons. The tattoo across her chest stretched wider than ones I have encountered before. I was curious as to why this Guardian in particular had the strength to even oppose me momentarily.

I wanted to kill her to make a statement to Haymen. A head for a head. But there was a greater purpose of confining her and taking her to the high courts. I wanted Haymen to be held accountable and slowly destroy this empire which he so proudly built. I knew he was up to something. Always have been and always would. This pet Guardian of his was my excuse to unravel that. Then I would dispose of her. I would never forgive someone who killed one of my own. This was personal as much as it was political. I loosened my tightened fist reminding myself to rein in that temper. Luke was my own. I had to make sure to play this correctly. If I lost my temper now, his sacrifice would all be for nothing.

I expect to see Haymen soon. He didn't like it when his property was taken and I imagine he'd be pissed over this pretty doll of his. It had been a few hundred years since I last saw him and I looked forward to having something of his in my own possession. If she didn't repulse me so much I might've even teased him with her in my clutches. But one thing was certain, I did plan to kill her in front of him. I needed the council's approval and to serve her justice for the crime she committed. Either Haymen would step out of line from the treaty or I would take an eye for an eye with a public execution. None of it would bring Luke back but I couldn't stand by and do nothing.

I watched the man in the small townhouse. I found classified information about Vivian's former life including her previous housing. I needed more information on her so I knew who and what I was dealing with. No secrets that could discourage the high court's opinion on her justice to be served. Haymen was selective about his Guardians and most already had some status about them. But I had found very little and an average background on her. I was woken up when Lukes body was reported dead. Lacking a cool head, I ported straight to the outskirts of Shabeah and swooped in sniffing her out. I hadn't even thought to dress appropriately.

The male living in the townhouse was Vivian's boyfriend five years prior to her rebirth. He still lived in the same complex that they had shared. She was a dog walker and worked part time at a café. Very ordinary and nothing that Haymen would usually go for in all his years. When the lights went out, I swooped in silently to the hinge of one of the open windows that was slightly ajar. Very unguarded for someone who lived in a central city that was run by demons. Especially with a former lover who was now demonic herself.

I opened it and held my wings in tight so my sensitive wings wouldn't scrape the window. It was pointless, I still barely fit. A golden Labrador ran at me. Before it could bark I eased it telepathically. I could speak with animals, sooth them as a second natured gift. It was a minimal power of mine but one that comforted me at times. It was different in this era from the war horses I had spoken to years ago to now neighborhood hounds. It grimaced low and came over to sniff at me. I held out my hand where it licked and wagged its tail.

"It's okay," I said to him quietly. As soon as I patted him I realized that he had smelled Vivian on me and that he was crying for the owner that he had lost long ago. The pooch openly showcased memories to me of her.

"Hey boy," her voice was sweet and so human. Her crimson hair was pulled up in a ponytail. I could feel that she was fragile. So simply human and happy.

I pulled back to the now and looked at the dog which missed his owner so much. Animals were much like children, so innocent in the sense that they would so openly display their feelings and emotions to one that they trusted. Some were more guarded than others but not this one. He had no reason to be. This dog remembered her to be a good person. I lifted up the tag of his collar and scoffed at the name.

"Lassie!" She yelled out at him in the vision I could see to be the kitchen in the room next to the one I was standing in. She was serving a dish for him.

"Hey you," the boyfriend pushed away Lassie in playful measure to hug her from behind. Her skin seemed to flush and glow in comparison to its cold demeanor now. "Why don't I get my meals dished up with such glee?"

"Because the dog has my full heart," she mused and kissed him.

I was pulled out of the vision. She was telling the truth. This dog had meant everything to her. I didn't have the heart to tell the dog that she was now a demonic evil bitch. It was best that he thought his owner were dead.

I looked around the dark room which had boxes in it. Very little furniture remained, he was obviously moving. I didn't bother going into the room where he slept and only inspected the rest of the house. The dog followed me around with curiosity and hope that I would return him to his true owner. An open bin caught my attention which held photos that had been thrown out.

I collected the photo from the top. It was a photo of them happily hugging with Lassie in the front. I realized that she was with child. I don't even think she knew that she was pregnant. Women had a natural glow to them when they had conceived. For an angel of my age it was easy to see from a mile away. I took the most recent photo of them and placed it inside of my pocket.

Lassie came to me again and brushed himself against me. This time the memory was the demon summoner who watched him from afar through the window. Vivian's crimson hair covered most of her face as she hunched over in the same spot that I stood before. Memories flooded to me of many nights when she would sit in the same spot. There was no emotion in her face only a distant stare as she watched on. Lassie would bark at her but she always made sure not to be seen by her lover.

"You seem to have verbal-vomit like your master," I said to Lassie who looked up at me with his tongue hanging out in a smile. "Dear friend, I would like to take something from you. I need it to return to your master," I said. I pulled out a small knife and Lassie only pulled back his ears. He wasn't scared of me but weary of what part I guided the blade towards. I cut away apart of his lock. I would never hurt an innocent creature but the demon summoner didn't know that and I was curious as to whether it would bring a reaction out of her. And if it did I could use it to my advantage. Because emotion was what made people unstable and I had every intention to make her and Haymen to unhinge.

Chapter Eight- Vivian

Another shadow dream memory from when I was eighteen and moved in with my boyfriend. A year had passed since my mother had died and our relationship was only new. He stuck by my side despite the hard beginning and then we decided to move in together. I had hated our first apartment. I told him that there was something about it that unsettled me. One room in particular that I couldn't stand the feel of and made sure the door was closed at all times. It was a small house, befitting for the two of us who wanted to start afresh together. My two cats were unsettled in that house as well feeling the same unnerving presence linger. I thought that maybe it was the house, until I realized that the entity was following me. I had always seen these dreams and knew their touch that could hurt me within my sleep.

The memory was clear and it was as if I was reliving it all over again. It was a small combined living room and kitchen, very small in size. The old wooden floors had holes in some parts where you could see the ground beneath. When turning to the left, I was greeted by the three doors of my rooms in the house. The left was our room. The small one in front of me was used as storage and the third on the right was always closed. I went into my room to collect my handbag before I left for work. When I came out I stared at the flooring of where blood began to pool from that room which remained always closed.

The dream went fuzzy and lucid like it always did when I was no longer alone in my sleep. My dream was being controlled and leading me to some devastating end. The blood spread quickly towards my feet. I ran into the living room with tears, terrified of whose blood that might've been on the other side. I ran for the back door through the kitchen and laundry room but something grabbed me and pulled me to the left and into the bathroom.

I was grabbed from behind and a hand wrapped around my throat and angled my face up. I looked through the mirror to the stranger who

held me from behind. I was greeted with the blackness of a figure, who
had no definition, no eyes nor lips or anything that I could fixate on.
Tears blurred my vision as it forced me to stare back at it in the mirror.

"How do you kill something that isn't real?" The male voice purred
into my ear with laughter. And he was right. It was the question I had
been asking myself since I was fifteen and began receiving 'visits' from
these entities. His laughter swelled my ears as I closed my eyes and so
badly prayed to wake up. Wake up. Wake up.

My eyes burst open and I rolled over to touch the small icon on my
side table. I would have to record this in the Shadow Mind Journals.
Instead, I was greeted with cold stone. I properly opened my eyes and
jumped up in one clean movement to search my surroundings.

There was nothing but brick walls enclosing me in darkness.
Only the light blue of my tattoos brightened the room. I tried to call
forth my cat demon for better sight but she was asleep. All my demons
were. I put my hand to my stomach getting flickers of memory and
then growled.

"Angel boy?!" I yelled, aggravated now. What on earth was that
powder shit he blew on me that forced my demons to recoil and that
sleeping kiss?! How had I been beat? Just because I couldn't call forth
my demons didn't mean I was left for weak. My strength wasn't
anything to be taken lightly either. I searched the walls surrounding
me even the one above which was too high for me too reach. I tapped
along trying to find a weakness anywhere in the foundation. No
variance. Giving up on intellect I went back to my most primitive
nature. Force.

I took in a deep breath and punched into the brick of the wall.
My hand crushed under the impact and I instantly retracted it.
"Mother fucker!" I started cursing as I shook it back and forth realizing
that only created more of a throb. I held it close to my mouth grunting
into it as if the noise would bring it back to life. "What the fuck?" I said
looking down on my hand that was now clearly broken. What
happened to my strength? If it weren't for the deep maroon almost

black blood coming out in blotches I would've thought I were human again in this sedated state.

I looked around having nothing to wrap it in. Great. I sat back against the wall. I was in some kind of angel prison for a crime I didn't even commit. Well unless this was all over Mr. Greenhouse. Then I most definitely killed him. I charmed a smile remembering his face as I emasculated him. Worth it.

I heard noises around me but couldn't identify which side they came from. There was no clear opening to this prison. A light shot down from above and I filthily looked up at the angel boy who looked down on me. Great I was in a pit about twenty meters in the ground and had no way of scaling the walls with a broken hand. Fantastic. I wanted to personally congratulate myself on the idea of using brute force.

I could hear others speaking to him but couldn't see them. He dismissed them and jumped into the hole. His drop was silent but his landing rocked the ground I sat on. Purposefully, I considered. A display of power. Boring.

"Rather showy wouldn't you say?" I said wavering my good hand and clutching the other close to me in hopes that he wouldn't see it. I wasn't entirely sure what my healing rate would be like in this current state and I didn't want him to know that I was weakened. Alas, it was the first thing he saw and he cocked a dirty smile.

"Broken hand?" he asked, his emerald eyes finding amusement mixed with his resentment for me. Sweet justice, he might have well said.

"More like broken heart from being so poorly treated. Most would offer to buy me a drink before they locked me in their dungeon," I said charming a cocky smile.

"I want to kill you," he said. "But I can't until you admit to everything that you've done."

"Yea, here's the thing," I said as I stood up dusting the few strands of straw on me. The floor had a few strands of hay lying about. Rather primitive. "I didn't kill your angel lover. I'm sorry I didn't realize you were an item. I suppose that makes this the awkward mistress talk," I said wavering a hand between him and me.

He wrapped his hand around my throat and raised me off my feet. "Do you think this is funny?" He cussed at me, a few flecks of his spit hitting my face. Disgusting.

"Momentarily, I did," I said as I wiped away the spit. My words came out strangled but I kept my composure. This wasn't my first time dealing with such conflict. "If you wanted to kill me, you would have by now," I said through one gush of breath. "But you haven't which means you can't. Funny thing that treaty," I said through a cracked smile that I knew drew blood. I didn't close my eyes as I waited for the backhand that would come. Instead he dropped me back onto the ground. I landed on my broken hand cursing under my breath.

"I preferred you in your pajamas," I spat, enjoying how riled he was becoming. It was too easy.

"Why did Haymen choose you?" he asked me directly. I side glanced him with a coy smile. So, he was trying to get some information on me. Perhaps Haymen and him knew each other. Suddenly, I realized this might not be about me at all. "You were nothing special before. Yet you seemed to have signed some pretty serious contracts with the sizing of your tattoos. Who are you?"

I looked down at my short-sleeved leather shirt which revealed parts of my tattoo. I looked up at him with a suave smile. "Angel Boy, did you take a peek while I was sleeping? First you disempower me, then you steal my first kiss, and now, you're doing ennoble things to me as I sleep?" I said abashed.

He pulled a photo out of his jacket and threw it at me. I only had a brief glance and looked back at him. Aiden. It was a photo of me and Aiden. And Lassie my Labrador which I adored so much. Suddenly all humor had vanished. Which wasn't good. For him.

"Where did you get this?" I growled trying to sound reasonable. It came out feral. I looked up at him. The size of his wingspan, even when tucked behind him, they stretched close to the walls.

He smirked at me, actually smirked. All reasoning was gone. I lunged for him. He sidestepped and pinned my good hand behind me.

He pressed me against the wall. I could feel the heat radiating from him onto my back because it was so contrast to the coldness of my own. My broken hand was crushed against the brick at my stomach. I breathed out frustration, flicking my hair out of my eyes. Although pinned tightly I raised my feet against the wall and pushed back with all my might. It made him take a few steps back and I swung at him with my broken hand. He had already caught me and now pushed me into the ground my mouth tasting the straw.

"Such a humble life you once lived," he said on top of me. His breath flushed hot against my ear, which despite my anger for him only made me aroused. I cursed the primal hormones of what I was now. There was no thing as modesty or self-control. But I was so pissed at him.

"Why don't you eat your own fucking humble pie instead of trying to steal mine," I said to him. Not even Haymen had dared speak to me about my previous life. That was one thing that would not be toyed as a game.

"Maybe you should've better protected it." A piece of golden hair was placed to my eye level and I knew by keen smell whose it was. My body went rigid. Lassie.

"Here's the thing, Lovely," he purred into my ear again. "Today when I take you to the high court you are going to admit to killing Luke. That way I will have the right to publicly execute you, which I will take great pleasure in. If not... The choice is yours," he said and got off me.

"Do you really think I'm going to trade in my future for a dog?" I said to him with my back still facing him.

"Oh, I'm counting on it," he said. "Human emotion is a funny thing and I wonder if even a mighty demon warrior like you might still be sentimental for it." The wind swept around me from the strong beat of his wings. The ceiling closed behind him and left me once again in the darkness. I was stuck within the cell staring at a picture which was taken a lifetime ago... literally. Suddenly I realized the weakness in angels all too clearly, or perhaps Mr. Angel Boy in particular. They were sentimental. I was born and trained not to be.

CHAPTER NINE- HAYMEN

I sat on my leather seat assessing the chest board in front of me with Destiny's head bobbling on my cock. I pushed her further into it, lacing my hands around the curls of her blonde hair enjoying her soft tongue which was so delicately moist on me.

A knock at the door. I growled in frustration and pushed Destiny's head down further to indicate for her not to stop.

"It better be good," I growled wavering my hands to unlatch the privacy key I had put on my door. It was pitch black, how I preferred to be left. One of my scavengers walked in. Ugly bird like demons with black tattered wings from age. Their long beaks struggled to speak even their own demon language. The glow of its beady red eyes was all that I could see and I made sure I didn't focus on its ugly form. That was sure to turn me off.

"Master," it said, its tongue slithering through the size of its beak. "Your Guardian, Vivian has been contained by an Angel."

"I see," is all I said. "Do you know whose squad imposed on her?" I wondered which squad it was that had the balls to run in on my turf, let alone my property. Every high angel had their own military team. Which one was it that took sudden interest in my beautiful crimson haired girl? Knowing my sweet Vi, she certainly wouldn't have gone willingly. How many angels did she kill in the cross fire of that.

"Not squad sir. Only one. We believe it was Gabe Christain. Intel suggests that they fought at the Pier on 99." His rascally voice sounded.

My cock straightened further into Destiny's throat making her choke. I soothed back her hair and pressed her again to continue.

"Leave," is all I said to him. With that he dismissed himself. Gabe Christain was the last angel I thought would involve himself with such a small matter. The results were even better than anticipated if he came personally. The players on the field began to move and whether they realized it or not, they would all start revolving around my dear Vi. It had been many years since I saw my old friend Gabe. I smiled allowing the bliss of Destiny's lips to sweep over me again. If he caught her he had no intention of killing her. Yet. This should make the game more interesting.

CHAPTER TEN- VIVIAN

"I know this might surprise you but I actually have a job that I should be doing. You know, just like saving kittens out of trees and stuff," I said antagonizing Angel Boy. He dragged me by the metal chain that was wrapped around my wrists. They didn't go on willingly either. Just like my legs that suddenly wouldn't walk behind him, and I dragged my body lethargically slumping. I smiled at the memory of his frustration. He blindfolded me for extra measure. My right hand was still healing but I kept that out of my mind. Instead, I made it my personal task to see how effectively I could irritate my captor.

I had the feeling that we were still within Shabeah. This shabby city had a demonic vibe to it constantly. If I were in a city that was governed by an angel, I imagined I would of smell cups of lemongrass tea and flowers. . . assuming that's what the fancy fuckers did with their time.

His lack of response irritated me. Despite my floundering steps and walking into walls on purpose he now gave me no attention. I didn't like that. I walked at his pace pointedly for a minute. He continued to ignore me only to try and walk ahead. We must've been power walking a moment later as he tried to outrun me. I listened to his steps aligning my own with his. Suddenly, I stepped my foot in front of him trying to trip him. He stopped before falling for the bait. I laughed at the growl that came through, deep and aggravated. Well there, now we have a little bit of attention.

"It's such a shame I can sense others around us. Because of the treaty you probably can't hurt me unprovoked until this council says so, right?" I nudged my shoulder into his and I knew that he was fuming. My laugh echoed through the room which was intentional. The sound of my own voice bouncing of the walls indicated that we were in a large open room. Most probably a large hall room. He collected his pace walking in front of me again. "Should've killed me when you had the chance," I murmured so only he could hear.

Suddenly the room felt as if it sunk in. The moaning and rattle of the room, indication of the power that was to follow. I knew this darkness all too well and could almost smell the coal like flames of Haymen. I heard the click of fingers and suddenly I was beside Haymen, my chains removed and blindfold gone. A thin layer of darkness wrapped around me from Haymen's quick teleportation.

We were in a large marble hall. The ceilings high and trimmed in gold. There were white statues surrounding ornamentally but other than that, empty. Well, besides the twenty odd angel soldiers armed and surrounding Gabe as he stood there. His lack of motivation to retrieve me made me realize he had been waiting for Haymen. I was just the bait. I hadn't been in this room before but wondered if someone had transported it here momentarily for the council. I couldn't imagine Haymen to own something so... godly. No, he preferred darkness over the flashy marbled walls.

The two stared at one another silently. I kept my gaze from Haymen unsure of how he would react to my capture. I had failed and possibly shamed him and I had seen his reaction to others before me when such a thing occurred. Instead I winked at one of the onlookers, making him shuffle uncomfortably. I charmed a smile.

"Vi," Haymen said pulling my attention to him. I looked into those killer blue eyes that missed nothing. His rough voice that echoed my name raised the hairs on my arms. The angel spoke out to Haymen but his attention was only on me. Not even I could understand what he was saying as I was sucked into Haymen's power. He reached out and collected my broken hand. My heart raced at the possible outcomes— further twist it until it was unrepairable, amputate it, execute me here and now. His head which bowed to no one suddenly dipped and the cold touch of his lips pressed against my hand. My entire hand jarred awkwardly and healed. I flexed it back and forth, assured it was properly fixed. I gave nothing away but I was surprised by his... generosity.

65

Weapons began to unsheathe within the room and I suddenly looked around and realized that twenty angel guards who were heavily armored with gold plating had their weapons pointed at Haymen and me. His gaze held onto mine a moment longer, lingering with what one might have thought to be assurance that I was alright.

He was totally indifferent to the weapons that were pointed at him. Not one of them would come close to touching him. "You seemed to have taken my prized possession, my dear old friend, Gabe." Haymen said as he finally turned to the angel who was my captor. So, Gabe was his name. Haymen's eyes were ice cold and death danced within them. The emerald green of Gabe's was as sharp and cutting. These two had history. "And you even polluted her with your old tricks so she couldn't summon her demons. How despicable." Haymen brushed the back of his finger down my cheek and stroked down to my collar bone. It was the feeling of cold ice running down my neck. "She's my favorite, did you know?" And that question was a lethal threat.

Gabe didn't flinch. The others surrounding him weren't as certain. Even I didn't want to stand amidst the tension between the two. The sensation of their two forces of power by look alone was enough to cut the air out of my breath.

"She is to appear in front of the high court for murdering an angel. No matter the claim on your property, a treaty is a treaty unless you want to create war," Gabe said stepping forward, almost hoping that was what Haymen would do. Haymen only stretched a sickening smile and began playing with the tips of my hair in distraction.

"You know I do like a good war," Haymen purred absentmindedly. He seemed infatuated with me even as he spoke to Gabe. He was looking at me as if I were his prized possession. I met his eyes once for a chance glimpse. My gaze dropped from his intensity. What was he doing?! I looked to Gabe instead who was furious by the contact. I wanted to say, 'You and me both sister,' but even I didn't dare try when Haymen was next to speak.

"As much as I want to entertain you, Gabe," Haymen said dropping his hand from my hair and seriously looking at him. "I've come to represent my darling Vi in this trial you've orchestrated yourself. So as of now, you no longer speak or even directly look at her."

"Perhaps I've taken a shining to your new trophy wife," Gabe antagonized. I tightened my jaw to not spill the filthy words from my mouth. The large white doors to our left opened. Both with serious expression Haymen and Gabe looked up the twenty steps that led to the inviting room.

"Shall we?" Haymen adjusted his black suit and waved his hand towards the steps. Gabe straightened himself and walked ahead. I was surprised Haymen was even entertaining this. I really am going on some ridiculous trial.

I began to walk after him but Haymen caught my wrist and grabbed my jaw. He angled my head to look up at him. The sheer force and power that swirled from him was both intoxicating and terrifying. "You belong to me," he purred. His lips were close to mine as we shared breath. My body couldn't help but react to his. It was savoring the coldness that pillowed off of him. He smiled and brushed his lips along my cheekbone and to my ear. My entire body straightened and my nipples ached to be touched. "I want you to find Alice Kendrid within Aztec and find out what you can about their Master." I blinked once. My keen mind cut to the truth of this matter. Haymen was already using this incident to his advantage. He already planned to have me convicted and sent to Aztec prison.

"I don't have time for that. I have a lead on my case at the orphanage. I think-"

"Then I will have Tahmeed watch over it until you return," he sharply cut me off. His whisper in my ear was an order. I wasn't to argue. Ever. His shallow breath was already against my neck and I found myself arching into him as he spoke. "I'll give you two days." His lips brushed up against my neck and along my jaw again as he pulled away. My hand had been pressed against his chest and I was on my tip toes breathing into him. I lacked all common sense until his cold smile broke the tension.

I questioned as to how much of this might have been premeditated by Haymen or if it was simply chance that he jumped with opportunity. I was being convicted of murdering Luke, an angel, and a crime that I didn't commit. I wanted to plea my case if not for my own pride but knew that was now out of the question. I didn't let any emotion flicker on my face. We were his tool and had to act like it. At least I knew that he wasn't so easily going to dispose of me and had no intention of allowing my public execution.

Two days my ass, what if I was in there for longer? When would I have time to report about the orphanage that was showing traces of the very entities we were hunting? I had just started my case and one thing I hated was leaving a hunt without conclusion or death.

He stepped around me and began to ascend the stairs with hands in pockets. Dick. He can hunt himself if he plans on sending me to prison. I bitterly began my walk up the stairs looking up as if to see the noose that would soon be the object of my hanging.

*

I wasn't surprised that majority of the jury were angels, 'the warriors of justice' I sarcastically sung in my head. Amongst the angels, there were few demons and humans who watched on with a skeptical eye. The angels looked at me with disgust and the humans seemed to be raising their nose further than was needed. It was entertaining to watch how humans acted in front of a room full of angels. The demons looked on with smug expression. I had no doubt they would've had the same face even if a fellow demon was killed. They just loved cases like this. They were secretly laughing at the fool who got caught killing someone that they shouldn't have.

I looked towards the podium in front where three angels sat in white... so cliché. Behind them was a golden scale that I imagined to represent justice. The podium oversaw everyone in the entire room. So many political and unequal rights came to mind. Why was it only angels? How was that fair in the grand scheme of things? I pondered whether I should begin spelling my rights and inequality just to annoy them. But I knew more than anyone how unfair this world was. How were the results ever going to be fair for a demon when the high court was only angels? I was going to be convicted of murder anyway so I might as well piss off as many people as I can on the way.

A camera to my left sparked a flash. The lanky man behind it smiled at me. Great, this will be the scandal of the year. How beautifully organized this was and arranged so quickly. They even had time to involve the media which was hardly ever involved in internal matters. This was purposefully organized because Gabe wanted me to sink and drown. Hard.

This would only end one in two ways. One, I would be killed like most demons who reached this panel. Or two, which was the way that this would go because Haymen wanted it, was that I would be imprisoned. It wasn't unheard of but very rare and usually offered to those who the panel was scared to kill because of the backlash that might occur. That or they were being protected for special reasons. I heard of one case that they were the last of their species and so the 262 accounts of murder were pardoned and he was locked away instead of being killed. That was the written press version but those who had real connections knew that the backlash would be too great if he were killed. Some demons and angels had power, real power in the human world. And so to keep the treaty safe, that was accounted for. The words of war rattled many different worlds and it was one that wasn't desired here.

The male angel who sat in the middle was old in all accounts. His dark grey eyebrows twisted up in comparison to his long thin beard that hung down. The beautiful blonde to his left had her sharp eyebrows raised and soundlessly scoffed at me when I looked at her. She already wanted me dead. The older lady wore a scowl from age but her expression was unreadable. Perhaps she would hear out the case unbiased. I chuckled to myself. Yea, right.

Gabe shot me a sharp stare. I only smiled at him before he looked back towards the podium with a clenched jaw. He stood to my right in front of the jury. There were no chairs or podiums for us, we stood out in the open being looked down upon the angels in front of us. I yawned as if bored, hoping to gain a reaction out of Angel Boy. He could blow his own case if he lost it in this court. Still yawning from the boredom, I turned around to the cameraman to smile over my shoulder provocatively. Snap! The photo was taken. The jury began whispering amongst themselves throughout the echoing hall. 'How disrespectful', 'She has no remorse', yada yada. Haymen's smile stretched wide at my attitude. He pressed his hand on my lower back as if to look at the judges and cleared his throat.

I looked over at Gabe whose eyes screamed 'Death Penalty'. "I suppose you couldn't run and fetch me a latte? I think I might be here a while," I said with a cocky smile. His eyes remained on the front but the vein in his neck bulged. It was rather disappointing that he didn't bite.

"Miss Vivian Lair," the older male said grabbing my attention. I hated when my last name was used. I buried that with my past the day I died. Those who knew my last name had done extensive research because I tried my hardest to destroy all connections to my previous life.

"Present. With no choice in the matter," I said. I would've raised my wrists in chains if Haymen hadn't already removed them. The blonde woman scoffed at me.

"Just call me Vi," I added looking directly at the younger angel hoping to irk her further. The two older angel's expressions didn't change and they had no comments to make. The blonde one followed suit but I knew she was biting her tongue. So, I smirked at her with satisfaction wondering how long I could wind her up before she broke. Her stare only narrowed further on me.

"You are here today within our Court, specified only to be the judgement panel of Angels under the impression and violation of the treaty. You are alleged for the murder of Luke Tailor, a soldier under Gabe Christain's legion, how do you plea?" That I didn't know. Gabe's jaw was clenched and his fists curled to show white knuckles. So, Luke was under his lead huh? That's why it was so personal for him. That kind of dedication appeared as a shock considering I was disposable to my own boss. Or maybe they just liked to make a fancy protest and look righteous.

"Not guilty," I said. "Let me assure you that when I was last with Luke, he was very much alive and happy," I said with a suggestive smile. Gabe's knuckles turned white as he focused on the screen that began to descend the wall. A projector from the corner of the room blasted through the room with evidence and footage of Luke and I at the club. We were getting acquainted as he whispered sweet things into my ear and I smiled. Haymen's hand on my lower back seemed to heat and press further into me. I hesitated to steal a glance at him. He was not at all impressed by the video. I was his property to an extent but not when it came to dealing with our sexual frustration. I was doing what all Guardians did. I tried to step out of his hold but his hand firmed on the back of my hip. A low growl that wasn't human came from him in warning. I focused on the screen until the surveillance was done trying not to think much on the imposing hand at my hip from the boss who was ready to have me convicted for his own gain. The film ended as I led Luke out of the club.

"He was found dead the next day," the old man said.

"Well he was very much alive with me that night and left around three in the morning," I said. "He certainly exhausted me after all of the late-night movies we watched together," I toyed deliberately. Whispers circulated around the room. I could feel the rage flowing from Gabe even if his facial expressions said otherwise. I wanted to poke him just to see if he would snap. He dared threaten Lassie yesterday but, in this court, if I could make him lose it, he would only shame himself. And that was exactly what I wanted him to do. I wouldn't allow anyone who threatened me go unpunished. "And before he left there were certainly no complaints," I added speaking directly to Gabe. It was loud enough so everyone would have heard. His dark green eyes found mine and I made sure not to look away. The intensity in that gaze hitched my breath but I refused to back down. I wondered how old he actually was, looking at him now, I could see death dancing in his eyes. A very forceful darkness from a white winged angel. That certainly grabbed my attention. I just had to wind him up a little bit more and maybe I would see that venomous side of him that would jeopardize his case.

"Vivian," the older woman on the right said. "You do realize that these are serious allegations." I smiled through my eyes at Gabe before turning my attention to her.

"Correct. I am answering them honestly. Just because I was last with him and slept with him– repetitively and for hours on end," I added hoping to wind Gabe up more. "That doesn't mean I murdered him. I didn't have the slightest energy to lift a coffee cup let alone murder once he was done with me," I said pointedly towards Gabe. Before Gabe lashed out with a remark, the pretty blonde on the panel stepped in.

"You were the last one seen with him. You baited him and then murdered him. Like all of your kind do!" I was surprised she wasn't spitting venom. Jackpot. Gabe might have not yet cracked but this little angel did. The room was silent as she thought about her words. The two elders looked at her with distaste. Looks like I got under this one's skin.

She blushed in embarrassment and I clicked my tongue.

"Ah, racist," I said in a tone that I knew would grate against her anger further. "Because I'm a Guardian? Because I can call upon Demons? You know your kind created this treaty and yet you don't seem so faithful to it," I said.

"Enough," the old male said irritated with the bickering. He threw an effective look at the younger angel. She sat back into her chair keeping her pretty mouth shut. Haymen so far had been quiet. I only questioned as to when he would step in and start manipulating this into the direction he wanted it to go.

The older angel began skimming through files that also projected on the screen.

"You've been within the employment of Mr. Davolch now for a little over twelve months it states here. One of his regional Guardian's in the city of Shabeah." She stopped on a page and looked to Haymen with a scornful expression. "Haymen," she said now not so formal. "It is within our treaty that you announce the demons which your Guardians are contracted to. This one only has four entered." I let my face show nothing. I only knew of three. Only three demons had come through so far and I still waited for the rest to awaken.

"Siren, a form of water demon; Succubus, both poison and sexual." I noticed the look that Gabe gave me and I arched a suggestive eyebrow. He looked away as soon as our gaze met. "Cat demon, rather rare considering how little they produce offspring. Foreseer and sixth sense." She stopped on the final one and looked up at Haymen. She then read it again. Her eyes then dropped to me. "Reported as of yesterday, Hellhound."

The room went silent and so did I. That was new.

"Hellhounds have been extinct since the last war," the old man began as he pulled the files from her to check it himself. There, on the screen in clear writing and image was a description of the Hellhound. "Explain yourself Haymen." Formality was being lost the further this case went on which indicated they were all familiar with one another.

Haymen dropped his hand from my waist and stepped forward. And now he would begin his show. "My Darling Vi is rather special. Most of my Guardians are aware of the demons that they are contracted to as soon as they wake. Vi it would appear isn't aware until they come forth to her. My finest witch has been taking blood samples weekly to experiment and decipher her blood. And as of yesterday, she was able to identify only one other, being the Hellhound. Now obviously I can't control what contracts are made and what demons come forth. Perhaps not so extinct after all," he charmed them a smile. I knew very little about the Hellhounds but what I did know was that they were the shadows under Haymen's control in the last war. They were ruthless and bloodthirsty and only he could control them. They were brought in from another world and so during the war they were the sole target to destroy for numerous angel units. The Hellhounds were the first crack to Haymen's empire to fall. That was the war that eventuated into this treaty.

Whispers began to spread and I noticed that Gabe stared at my chest as if trying to burn through my shirt and see my tattoos for what they were.

"A Guardian can harvest up to seven demons, there are three not accounted for," the older lady said.

Haymen shrugged his shoulders. "Gretel," he said using her name. "I cannot produce information I do not have. I don't know what she harvests either. Not until they awaken within her. I can't help the paranormal that occurs. That is why my Darling Vi is so special to me." I realized that was the second time he said 'Darling Vi' and it was reoccurring because it was a threat.

"Then perhaps we can easily manage this case by allowing me to slip into her mind," the younger angel insisted. "I will confirm if she is innocent and actively help the record as to all seven of her demons."

"I'm sorry Buttercup but I'm not going to allow that," he said readjusting the hem of his suit jacket as if uninterested in speaking with her particularly. "All of my Guardians have personal information that I cannot have compromised. And if you have done this to any of my own previously then it's a direct insult to myself." His eyes met hers with the rage of a storm. "If that were the case I would have to deal with it accordingly."

The older angel who was called Gretel intervened. I quietly enjoyed watching the younger one get nervous at Haymen's threat. I wondered if the reason why he entertained this entire hearing was to be in a position where he could ask *them* questions. "Haymen, you do realize that with this case and accusation it might be the only way that you can prove her innocence. This is no small matter or charge. Unless you can prove otherwise, there is consequence to her actions and that will result in a public execution. The killing of our kind is not tolerated."

"Let's round this up quickly then, shall we?" Haymen said clapping his hands together. "I know that Vi didn't murder that angel because she was with me after he had left."

"That's a lie!" Gabe spoke up.

"Is it? I don't like speaking ill of your dead friend but she was quite unsatisfied after he left," Haymen taunted. I charmed a smile. Although that was a lie, Haymen was doing the same as me. He was riling Gabe.

74

With all restraint Gabe stood there like stone. "What your Guardian felt afterwards is irrelevant," he hissed. "The fact is that she was the last one seen with him and there is no tracking, surveillance, or even contact made from him after he was coaxed to her bed. I have a strict mandatory call in every few hours from those who have been pardoned outside my city. Prior to entering Ravish Club was the last time my team had heard from him."

"Well you sound smothering to work for," I said and looked over to Haymen who smiled. Menacing pride filled his eyes.

"Opposed to your puppeteer of a boyfriend," Gabe hissed.

"Enough," the older angel said silencing the room. Images of Luke's body splashed across the screen. His wings had been ripped from his body, the bone broken into shards and were found in dumpsters. His body which was located elsewhere was swollen from an unnatural form of drowning. Crisp green poison had oozed from his face from when it had been slashed by three long talons. Bone was shattered and bled out from the muscle of his wings being torn off.

"All the elements involved in his death was that of what your demons have the ability to do," Gabe gritted out and looked at me. "You seemed to have really enjoyed your night with him." For once, I didn't say anything. I wasn't sentimental and I didn't care for his feelings. But sometimes I knew when to remain silent. I had been set up. Not that my demons could have killed him this exact way but it did make it very easy to pin me for his murder after we spent his last moments alive together. Haymen's hand found his way around my hip again.

"I will have my Guardians find your killer out of good faith considering that it was within my city that your soldier was killed. Until then, and to assure you, that no one else is hurt during the time that we have a rampant demon who is targeting angels, I want a lockdown and agreement that no angels are permitted in my city until the matter is fully resolved," Haymen said to the three on the podium.

"Bullshit. You think that you are going to gain from this?" Gabe sneered. "There is no way you are taking her back under your protection and requesting for your city to go off the grid. That's not how this works."

"I'm just trying to protect your soldiers who clearly can't defend themselves against this rampant demon. Perhaps while I focus on my city you should focus on the training your own." The tension in the room thickened and I could feel the power of the two pushing against one another with me in the middle. I was near choking on the hatred that I could taste was brewing for years.

"Don't think that you will slip out of this one, Haymen. All evidence leads to your little pet here," Gabe said not even looking at me. His stance had changed, his full height and broad shoulders stretching to show all lean muscle. He was ready to fight. Haymen's fingers began to dig into my hip, whether he realized it or not. Both of them were restraining themselves in the face of the court.

Haymen disregarded Gabe and looked to the angels. "Of course, I understand you will need a certain leverage until I can produce the truthful killer. I permit for my Guardian in question to be detained but once I prove her innocence she will be released."

"You're just buying time!" Gabe harshly shouted throughout the room. The camera flashed and Gabe shot a fierce look at the cameraman. He looked away and reined in his anger. He should've just killed me when he had the chance instead of going through all this justice and political bullshit. Despite his irritability, I thought he was smarter than that. He had to have a separate motive just like Haymen. I could feel that I was just the pawn to whatever game these two were playing and for the time being there wasn't much I could do about it.

"You do understand the magnitude of your suggestion Haymen? She isn't just going to any detainment center, she will be going to Aztec," Gretel said. "She will not be released unless you can find evidence of the real killer. If nothing is found within a week she will be publicly executed and the media will be informed," she said pointedly to the cameraman. Which meant currently this case was not to be made public.

"I object," Gabe said stepping forward. "He is going to manipulate the truth to suit him when we already have the evidence we need now. If she is pardoned for this act, I will personally watch over her until a mistake is made and justice is sought through."

"You seem to have taken a liking to my Guardian, Gabe," Haymen growled and it shook the room. Everyone waited until the aftermath stopped. Those on the podium weren't as concerned over the power display. Wind began to howl through the room and I could almost see the flash of a storm in Gabe's usual green eyes.

"I am not letting you get away with another bullshit stunt," he said. "You made a mistake the moment you allowed such a hideous creature to kill one of my own." Somehow, I had almost become irrelevant in all of this argument despite standing in between them.

"I ask you, the jury," Haymen said in a manipulative tone. "Do you believe my Vi is guilty of such an act with such little evidence except for *this* angel who points his marshmallow fingers?"

Gabe's wings and chest expanded and the leash to his fury had snapped. All that kept him back was the hitting of the hammer on the front podium by the old man. He rolled over the information and looked to his other two angels. I had the sense they were talking telepathically. Blondie sat back unimpressed by the outcome. The older man proceeded. One thing I now noticed was their wings were tucked it in and almost hiding. I couldn't see any of their colorings or tattoos that might've marked them as warriors like Gabe. If I weren't about to be convicted of murder I might've been curious as to how their hierarchy and roles worked.

"Due to current information we have at hand and the seriousness of the prosecution we will allow both parties to do private investigations. Haymen, as agreed if you can curate us enough evidence of the rightful murderer then she is free to leave Aztec, if still alive," he added. "Haymen, you are not pardoned to have exclusive rights to your city in this matter. We deny your request. If enough evidence is found to support that Vivian Lair is not the murderer, Gabe Christain has the right to have one of his officers or he can personally follow your Guardian's actions for thirty days after being released from Aztec."

"That last sentiment is ridiculous and I do not adhere," Haymen snarled.

"The other option is, Mr. Davolch," Gretel announced. "Is that we finalize this matter now and with no further evidence she will be locked away in Aztec for the rest of her lifespan. We respect you Mr. Davolch, but this crime is too serious to overlook."

"And what is your reasoning behind this decision?"

Blondie spoke up. "Justice and reassurance. Despite Shabeah being known to be a city for demons, on behalf of the treaty we must know that things aren't being overlooked. The death of an Angel has drawn our attention to the possibility of an imbalance and perhaps too much demon influence. What better way to assure the commitment on your part to the treaty than to have one of your personal Guardian's followed, who by registration is your leading law enforcement. We wouldn't want to worry or follow you for such reasons, Mr. Davolch. And that of course is out of respect, which is why we will follow your law enforcement instead."

"You can start following one of them now if you will," Haymen seethed. "I don't know why you care to specifically hinder my Guardian here who already has been effected by such accusations." I was surprised that he was actually entertaining them. If he wanted he could burn down this entire room with the click of his fingers. And yet he listened, something I saw Haymen do very little of.

"Justice, Mr. Davolch. If she makes it out of Aztec and you are able to prove her innocence then we need to guarantee she is not covering up evidence or intel. This is a serious matter and I am sure you can understand that we would treat a suspect similar if it were one of your own kind that was attacked." Wrong. He would've killed them by now. I looked over at Gabe in question. Why didn't he kill me? What was he after to draw out this painful political shit show?

There were so many things I wanted to say and to be able to speak for myself. Possibly even sky kick blondie here in the face but the moment Haymen spoke up I knew my word was irrelevant. He was silent for a moment, thinking and manipulating the outcome to his benefit as always. His grip loosened on my hip and he finally let go. I felt almost relieved as the tension he emitted dropped off me.

"Then I should make her quarters more accommodating for you, Mr. Christain," Haymen said with an underlying suggestion. Before Gabe could respond, the hammer was brought down and my sentence was final. I grimaced at Haymen. He laced his icy fingers around my hand and kissed the back of it. "Two days," is all he said and then blackness swirled in the spot he once stood. Poof. Just like that my almighty savior and boss vanished, sentencing me to the most brutal prison. Two days my ass. I would go insane in that time and there wasn't a thing I could do to go against Haymen's word.

I was jarred by Gabe who grabbed my arm and began to drag me out.

"Listen here Angel Boy," I said trying to grab my arm out of his strong bruising grip. "I might be going along with this whole thing but that still doesn't give you the right to touch me as you please." He pretended not to hear me as we walked towards the now open doors.

His brooding expression only focused outdoors. I smiled and placed my foot out in front of his. This time he tripped. He caught on to one of the chairs as he brought me down with him. I was ready to hit the ground face first. It would've been worth it. He regained his composure with me still in his grasp.

Click. The photographer had taken the cheeky photo. I laughed hysterically as he grabbed the man's camera and crushed it in one hand. Well I guess none of this would be sprawling on headlines after all. Within seconds, he chained my hands and feet together. I didn't even see where they came from. Maybe this little angel had a few teleportation tricks up his sleeve. Tape went over my mouth within seconds as he threw me over his shoulder and walked out. I could've fought him until the very end but I knew I had to adhere to Haymen's words. Didn't stop me from laughing at the pissed off angel who dragged me out of the courts.

CHESS PIECE

As light and dark remove themselves from the podium and
enter the chess board-
They realize not everything can be overseen and planned.
When you are at eye level with your enemy, you begin to have a
sense of your surroundings.
The initial strategy will not be the winning one.
The winner will be the one who can best adapt to his
surroundings;
To the new players of the game;
The understanding that in war, there is no such thing as rules;
And the stamina to last until the end and hold the King's throat
to blade.
Let the game begin and the victor be righteous.

CHAPTER ELEVEN- VIVIAN

Aztec. Fan-fucking-tastic. I had the glorious honor to be confined with the cheerful Gabe in a small carriage attached to demon horses who trailed a path deep below water in an ocean I haven't even heard of. I felt motion sickness from the speed alone. I was blindfolded prior to boarding and it wasn't taken off until we submerged far below where I had no way to flee. The chains around my ankles have been removed but the ones on my wrists remained.

I squinted out into the darkness and depths focusing on the small bulbs of light at the forefront of the horses. Their hair wavered in the water unnaturally. That was the only part of them that could be described as still living. The rest was rotting flesh and bone. The one that I was focusing on had a small fish suctioned to its rib. Without speaking to my demons, I had no idea what kind of demon horse it was but I knew it was focused on only one thing; and that was transporting me to Aztec. Six of them circled the carriage propelling us further into the water with an unnatural pressure that didn't crush us.

I sighed irritated and closed my eyes trying to push away the nausea. A part of me wanted to encourage it just so I could vomit on Gabe who sat across from me. My only reassurance that he wouldn't attack me now that we were alone was the fact that he wouldn't have gone through all this trouble in the first place. He sat across from me staring at me intensely the entire time.

"I might vomit on you," I said putting a hand to my stomach and pretending to gag. He didn't flinch. I smiled back at him until looking back into the darkness of the sea. It was oddly silent. Not because Gabe didn't speak back but because my demons were still dormant. It was the first time since being contracted that I couldn't feel them pumping through my veins. I felt oddly free but weak at the same time. I had become so used to their company that the silence of my own thoughts was overbearing.

Under the circumstances of how I got here and the inability to do anything about it, I was definitely brooding. Every part of my nature told me to escape. But, it was Haymen's direct order. My life was for his purpose and disposal. Even if I ended up in Aztec for the rest of my days. There was nothing I could do about it until I somehow freed myself from the chains that connected us. And somehow, I would find my freedom even if that came in death. The other Guardians might've been content with their fame and living conditions but I wasn't. There was a restlessness in me that I could never fully explain even to myself and one day I would pursue that. I was in no position to disobey him now and might not be for hundreds of years depending how long I survived this job.

With the absence of my demons, unnecessary thoughts came to mind. My old life. My death which was shortly followed by intense training and education of my new one. I quickly buried my questions and curiosity as to whether the old me remained. She was gone. Eaten by the demons that now consumed me. Shortly after being reborn I would watch my old home in silence, expecting to feel some spark of emotion. But to my own disappointment there was nothing. Even when I looked at the man I loved deeply for five years, there was no connection nor appeal to walk towards him. Vivian Lair was dead.

I learned quickly after that not to engage with my old life in any way. Everything I did was closely watched. I was nothing but a dog on Haymen's leash and so I learned to bark at his request. I trained to become the Guardian he wanted and emerged myself into the world that was befitting for my killer instincts. And now was no different to that. It's not that I lacked in pride, I was simply born and programmed to be Haymen's hound.

"I've always wanted to fuck in a carriage led by demon horses under the sea," I said aloud to interrupt my own thoughts. The revolving questions in my head would only make me sloppy. I could feel the anger radiate off him as he continued to stare at me intensely. I enjoyed getting under his skin. I smiled and looked into the darkness of the sea. Well at least I knew he was listening. "Come on, I might be imprisoned for a while. Why not help a poor girl like me?"

His strong jaw tightened and that wild storm was livid in his eyes dulling his usual emerald green.

"Maybe it's sexual frustration?" I continued. "Are you being serviced often?"

Finally, he bit back. "I suppose that would be your self-worth wouldn't it? How will Haymen move on when I finally kill you?" He gritted out. Speaking seemed to actually release part of his frustration. Every ounce of his hatred spited on every word. I wondered who he hated more, me or Haymen?

"Why are you thinking of Haymen when I am asking you to focus on me?" I said brushing my hand absentmindedly over my breast. The motion did not go unnoticed and that pissed him off even more.

"If Haymen asked you to noose yourself as well, would you?"

I leaned in towards him with a smile. He didn't move as I rested my cuffed hands close to his knees. "Of course. I am to serve. But Haymen's not here right now."

I loved irking him and I couldn't deny that if given the chance I would take him to bed. He was a warrior that radiated power, clean cut muscle and strength. Despite his asshole personality I could imagine the intensity of having him as a lover. I could appreciate a fine specimen even when I had to put work first.

"Not every prisoner survives Aztec the first night," he said spitefully changing the topic. "You might want to be careful with that mouth of yours. Especially when you can't call upon your demons."

I shrugged. "Everyone's at the same disadvantage. I actually considered my communication skills my greatest asset."

"This is a prison of real demons. Not fakes. Your human like body is at a disadvantage to those with fangs and claws."

"My second greatest strength is optimism," I said crossing over my legs and leaning back into my seat.

"Some of these prisoners were captured by the Guardians themselves. I'm sure they have unsettled business," he said now leaning towards me with his hands between his knees.

"I have yet to meet someone in this job who likes me," I said disregarding him. I would never let it show, but I knew too well that I was at a disadvantage. I could only rely on my combat skill to defend myself. I wasn't planning on dying in this depressing prison but I wasn't eager for the challenge to survive either. On top of that, it was going to be boring.

"Always some smart ass comment to make. I wonder how scared you actually are right now?" His tone has changed. It wasn't as vicious as before but curious almost. I held his gaze trying to read his expression that gave nothing away. Was he trying to see if my kind felt? If we ran on emotion?

"Oh, she finally has nothing to say?" He said arching an eyebrow.

"I was just wondering if all angels were hypocrites. You're convicting the wrong person and hoping for their death within the first night. Doesn't seem very angelic of you," I said now getting pissed off.

"Shedding some tears doesn't seem very demonic of you. Or are you just not used to getting your own way?"

I looked at him dead in the eye and gave him the cattiest smile I could muster, I leaned in making him uncomfortable with my proximity. "I was being nice, I actually like you," I lied. "Let's just be done with this and let me go. I do have a job to attend to, you know?" And that was the truth. I thought about the children in the orphanage. I didn't like handing my cases over to another Guardian. That was my hunt and I didn't like to hand it over so willingly. Despite being unassigned from the case my mind still pondered over the possible leads. After my run in with Mr. Greenhouse, I didn't have the luxury to investigate it any further.

"I don't think being on the front cover of a magazine naked is classified as work," he said leaning in so we were nose to nose. Power play and dominance show, that's all this was. I certainly wasn't going to back down from him of all people.

"From your pretty, moisturized hands I'd assume you don't know much about killing demons. Maybe when you come up the ranks I can give you lessons." His smile was nothing but feral and I was surprised he hasn't yet reached for my throat. The look he gave me told me he wanted to wrangle it.

"Oh, I know too well how to kill a demon," he threatened.

"Oh, really? I figured that you would have been up in cloud nine, on level heaven at tea parties, with your beautiful little pinkie poised with that stick up your ass that seems irreversible."

His hand reached for my throat but his hold was soft and controlled. I wasn't scared by the obvious threat. I was certain that if he took the liberty of personally bringing me to this prison he wasn't going to lose his self-control to kill me now. He stroked the pulse at my neck. The warmth of his finger opposed to my natural coldness made me shudder. My body was reacting to his. If it weren't for the circumstances I might've fallen for the open display of power to silence me. His strength that could kill me within a second but had the control not to, turned me on. He was trying to silence and intimidate me. It was a shame I have used the same methods on others. I had gone quiet for too long and realized that was his intention. I offered him a charming smile and spoke back to him huskily.

"If this is how you kill demons, with their hands bound I'm not at all surprised you came out the victor."

"Demons are an abomination," he cussed and his grip tightened. He was seeing how far he could push. At what point I might become scared and unravel in front of him? He could cut off my hand and I would make a point not to even hiss at him.

"Need I remind you that I'm not a demon," I growled back breathing into his ear. He still didn't move from this little game we were playing and I wondered how far *I* could push until he would fling me across the carriage. I began to slide my hand up his leg.

"No, but you can shift into them. That's basically the same thing." He let go of my throat and pushed me back into my chair before my hand glided too high. He tsked in disgust and looked outside the window. It would seem that perhaps I won that little game. I didn't have the same righteous pride as him. I would do every dirty trick in the book to win even if I had to sleep with him. Gabe however was the opposite of that.

"Anyone can turn into a monster," I said. Members of his own had become dark angels. Good turned evil all the time. "Don't think you are better than me because you have some glitter wings strapped to your back, Angel Boy. It wasn't my choice to become what I am today. I am nothing but a creation made by my master. But you," I said pointing my finger at him. "You were born an asshole."

The tension and silence only grew and we looked out on either side of the carriage. I had no choice but to wait until we arrived at Aztec.

*

An odd current surrounded the castle that was isolated in the middle of the sea. I could barely see the outlines of its full shape until we were closer. The current was howling as we got closer and I questioned what sort of magic was crafted to conceal it from the world. The carriage began to rattle as the demon horses got closer to the current running alongside it. Suddenly they barraged into it. My head hit the top of the carriage from the impact. Gabe didn't move, his wings were firmed on either side of the carriage so he wasn't thrown like I had been. Much to my surprise the demon horses were able to pull us through the vortex. It was only seconds until they dipped towards the entrance of the castle leaving the vortex behind us. Once we cleared it there was no more water. It was like being in a confined bubble of air protected by the rapidly moving magic on the outside. Aztec was an eroding castle concealed in the depths of the sea by magic that I imagined very few could break. If it did, the entire bubble would implode and drown those who lived in Aztec. I wondered what witch was mighty enough to craft such an imprisonment in the first place.

Despite the water not reaching the castle, algae and seaweed still grew in a phantom breeze on the rocky castle. We glided in the air towards the cobble entrance. There were numerous high towers fabricated at both the front, back, and the wings of the castle. To my right was a large pitted area that was caged. There were few tables and chairs which had been affected by the algae as well. Very little lighting gave much away as candles were isolated and flickered in the phantom breeze. We were surrounded by darkness. The time of day would never be known here.

The demon horses dropped lower and ran to a halt on the cobbled landing in front of the entrance. The opening of the castle looked like an open mouth as the edges eroded in what looked like tiny pinned teeth.

Gabe opened the carriage door and looked at me pointedly. He would either let me walk of my own accord or drag me out. I don't think he cared much for which style I would be handed over. I stepped out and my chains clinked together in dramatic effect. He tugged on the small chain that was attached to my wrists as he walked past to follow. I looked over to the towers that were clouded in darkness. From one of them I could see beady red eyes peering at me from the small window. I was already being spied on. I was not going to enjoy my stay here. I dragged my feet slowly taking in as much of my surroundings and exit points.

Solidified soldiers and gargoyles were cemented into the exterior of the castle. Their eyes followed our every step towards the entry. One of the gargoyles shoulder began to drip from the rocky wall as it lowered its top half to snarl at me in warning.

"Man, I am way too pretty to be in a place like this," I said under my breath. Gabe ignored me as he tugged on my chains to hurry my pace. It was definitely to my disadvantage that I couldn't call upon my demons in a place like this. The powder that Gabe had blown into my face the day we fought still had me crippled and I imagined that would only continue as I was in here.

From the darkness and mouth of the castle, a long scaly creature twice my height walked out. A black robe enveloped his disgustingly thin figure and he produced a candle. I was grateful the robe concealed everything but his scabby lips. Without saying anything he turned and indicated for us to follow. Gabe looked at me and I shook my head.

"That is one ugly ass-" He tugged on my chains and dragged me behind him. I walked further into the mouth of the castle. Looking behind me, one of the gargoyles watched on. Chanting murmurs from below echoed through the numerous hallways within the castle. I didn't understand the language but instinct pricked at me to run the other way.

A curdling scream echoed from one of the hallways and the clanking of metal hit the ground. All three of us stopped and looked in that direction. After a deafening silence, Gabe and I both looked towards the scaly demon. He turned and continued walking. Gabe was watching me carefully and so I made sure not to make eye contact. I clenched my jaw in agitation. I didn't know fear but I knew when I was in a place I shouldn't be. Without my demons this might very well be the place that I would die in. Every pump of my blood told me to run the other way. Instead, Gabe tugged on the chain for me to keep walking.

There was something confined within Aztec that held a raw power that I'd never felt before. By the way Gabe was walking, he felt it too. The hairs on my body rose and I didn't care if Gabe gave me shit for it–I grabbed onto the chains closest to his hand so I wasn't too far away from the one creature in here that might have a fighting chance. That and I would throw him at the beast that might dare attack me.

I paused for a moment to look down at my feet. There was nothing but I felt slithering snakes around my ankles. I caught Gabe's gaze who had just been looking at his own feet as well. If looks could kill he would be dead. I was so pissed that he brought me to such a creeper of a place. We ascended spiral stairs that grew darker the longer we walked. The uneven cobble steps would've had most tripping. Gabe's broad shoulders and wings were almost dragging on the sides by how confined the staircase was. The chanting murmurs followed behind us as if chanting the demons within to sleep.

Something snaked around my legs and constricted. This time I actually fell. Gabe caught me by my elbow and pulled me to the next step. I looked behind squinting in to the dark trying to find the creature that had snagged me. Whatever it was that tripped me, felt like the very demon my instincts warned me about.

A flicker of another tentacle that couldn't be seen struck at my cheek. The smell of blood instantly wafted the room. I hissed at the strike I couldn't defend myself against. Gabe stopped and pressed the back of his knuckle along my cheek as if to confirm. I pulled away from him snarling but he tugged me forward by the chains. When Gabe looked back at the hooded demon for answers he was already gone still ascending the stairs.

Gabe turned and followed him. I couldn't so much as see the demon but I felt it. Small tentacles surrounded and followed me. Whatever it was, it had taken an interest in me.

"Great. I'm going to be eaten before I get up the bloody stairs," I hissed under my breath. That and the number of stairs I was climbing had my legs in jello mode. I had no choice but to slow down as I fought against the constricting tentacles and uneven stepping. Gabe continued to tug on my chains half dragging me up. I hissed again as the demon took another small lick at my arms. This time the demon who was leading us paid attention. He began chanting with the others and very slowly I could feel the demon cower away. Was all that chanting really just to trap one singular demon?

I wasn't sure which I preferred. The constant chanting that sounded like a child's meditative lullaby or an invisible demon who wanted to eat me?

The robed demon led us to the first floor and fell silent. He stood in front of a door and stretched out his scaled arm. I was hesitant behind Gabe. I didn't like being crammed into small spaces, especially when it wasn't my choice. Gabe tugged my chains, encouraging to inspect it myself. When I walked towards the low door he grabbed my chin to inspect the wound on my cheek further. I pulled my chin away from him. He was the one leading me to this death sentence and I had no interest to entertain his curiosity. If he wanted to know what demon dwelled in Aztec then he could bloody well stay here himself.

Inside the tiny room was nothing. All except a tiny slit suggesting it might be a window. A completely bare room. I nodded my head in humor. "This is to my liking," I said looking at Gabe and being sarcastically enthusiastic. "Exactly what I requested. Wonderful. Fucking great."

"I'm happy for you," Gabe added with a bitter smile.

"Yea for sure. Just kill me now and get it done with," I said. He tugged on the chains overpowering me and flinging me into his arms. He caught me and unlocked my chains. Gabe collected them and pushed me back into the room. For the first time, I actually hoped that Haymen did care for me only a little and kept to his word. I looked to Gabe as he closed the door and rose my finger to him in salute.

CHAPTER TWELVE- GABE

In all my years, that was the first time I had personally taken a prisoner to Aztec. I wouldn't leave any room for Haymen to try and break her out or meddle in her conviction. Now that I have delivered Vivian personally, I could focus on my own precautions of Haymen being able to break her back out. I had the rights to detain her but after the case was judged I needed to make sure that it stayed that way and not enabling Haymen to find a loophole like he always did. I needed to find more evidence that would cement her execution.

Aztec was as bad as the whispered stories I heard. Very little information was released about Aztec and not everyone knew about it at all. Its whereabouts was only given to a certain few who overlooked the treaty and the only way to get there was by way of the demon horses. Only with the seal of the court to imprison and the escort's blood would they appear for the summoner. Old magic. Only with their aid and cartage would anyone survive the crushing water pressure or the witch's magic that surrounded it.

When it was first built, I was against the blueprints. I couldn't trust a demonic realm to contain our most dangerous prisoners. But I was overruled and outnumbered by the majority. They wanted it far away from our own daily living. Aztec was Haymen's idea and suggestion. It was monitored by the Angels to make sure equal control was harbored over the project. Thus, the Gargoyles and soldiers that are in place. They were created specifically to keep a watchful eye on behalf of the Angels who wouldn't dare step in there themselves.

I was on guard the entire time walking through Aztec. Not because of the prisoners who watched us but the demonic creature that followed us up the stairs. It didn't dare touch me after its first inspection. It had slithered around my legs and my light was quick to push it back. Vivian however seemed to be to its liking. I quickly assessed her cheek before I left. It was only blood. No poison or saliva.

I hadn't felt the raw power of a demon like that for centuries and questioned where the familiar entity came from. I decided not to concern myself with the matter any further. If it was contained in Aztec now it would forever be concealed there within. The constant chanting of the keepers would keep the demon dormant.

Despite her tough exterior and attitude, I knew that Vivian was shitting herself and so she should. She would get what was coming to her after what she had done to Luke. I was done with remaining silent as Haymen shadowed over the treaty and continued to play puppeteer. Numerous spies had been found in my cities over years and although I could never prove it because they commited suicide when captured, I was certain that Haymen was behind it. He was up to something. His compliance over recent years and quietness put me on edge. After years of opposing him in the last war I knew that his silence was only a tactical pause. I would display to the world the true colors of Haymen who over the years seemed to be on his 'best behavior'. The public execution of one of his own Guardians would be the start of his bleeding rein. Luke's death was what made me shift my hand earlier than expected. Now I would not retreat. I had to out Haymen before he acted first. His very existence needed to be eradicated and as the Angel of War, I had no issue in being his prosecutor.

I remained in the shadows of Shabeah. Even if Haymen found me, I had the right to continue my own investigations as he did. The sentence has already been made. I just had to make sure that it wasn't rescinded. All the evidence showed that Vivian was the killer. What unsettled me was Haymen's willingness to put her in Aztec. He had other motives like always and I had to make sure he couldn't see them through.

I was fully aware of those who tracked my movement. They might've considered themselves stealth but I was wary as they shadowed me from the rooftops. Haymen didn't like unwelcomed guests in his city. If I was attacked now it would bring too much suspicion so instead he had someone watch over me. That didn't deter me from being guarded as I walked through the late of night. I could feel the demons that scampered throughout the city like vermin. I covered my wings with a large black trench jacket in hopes that it would conceal the bright white of my wings. It would only draw unnecessary attention and as much as I loved to kill demons who might've dared attack me; I too had to act appropriately until the final verdict and lead up to Vivian's death.

I looked down at the flashing GPS on my watch screen. One of the spies I had working within the police force in Shabeah sent me this record and murder only this morning. Anything considered relevant or out of the ordinary in Shabeah was reported to me directly. I rounded the corner of an apartment building and into an alleyway. This was the location under inspection.

The body of Mr. Greenhouse had already been removed from the scene. The end of the alleyway had been blocked off by a glazed police screen where only officials could enter. This way none of the public or media could tamper with remaining evidence or take photos.

Alongside the location and time of death, he had sent me photos. The man had been brutally savaged. Claw marks to his face where his eye was removed. His genitals had been ripped from his body and a slash to his throat which bled him out in minutes. I looked up into the night sky confirming that I was familiar with this area. This was the first location where I tracked Vivian's presence.

This case has already been removed and deleted from the system. Obviously Haymen was quick to remove any remaining evidence of his Guardian who was a human killer. I was grateful I received these prior to that because it matched exactly where she had been the very night and moment I began my hunt. If I hadn't been tracking her that night I could only imagine how long this murder would've stretched out and that she was clever enough to dispose of his body herself. Despite her attitude I could see the quick wit within her and I was pleased to know that I ruined her plans that night.

Finding evidence that she was a human killer would add to my case. To my left and above two stories was an apartment window that had glazed police screening. Evidently that was the victim's house. I looked around the ceilings of the surrounding apartments and found a sloped roof which I would personally perch on if I was spying on someone. She more than likely had been waiting for him there. I recalled the photos that had been sent to me not daring to open them now. With my little tag along who was perched three apartments away I could risk compromising my spy and the police files he had sent me.

It was a shame for Haymen really that a human had found him first and stupidly called the police enforcement before his own. That was the only way I could've possibly been tipped off. Not that he would know that. It was by coincidence that she was in this location when I first swooped down on her and I could claim that I noticed the disturbance and came to investigate personally later.

The images that I quickly flicked through before stepping into the open had been graphic and I tried envisioning them behind the screen. Vivian's cat demon would have been a perfect fit for this kind of murder. And that was exactly her first form that I caught glimpses of before she turned to her human one. She probably thought she got away but I had noticed those glowing tattoos of hers shift her form in the night.

A small meow caught my attention. I turned and knelt down to offer my hand to the alleyway cat that was drawn to my presence. To my onlooker it wouldn't look suspicious. Only few knew of my side gift and it was one I was certain even Haymen didn't know about.

"Hey there kitty," I soothed. She walked over faster and rubbed the back of her head against my hand and then leg. "What do you have to show me?"

As soon as I asked the question she opened up to me. She had been here that very night. Vivian's shortcoming was that she might've been wary that no humans saw but her cat demon drew the attention of this stray alleyway cat. The cat had a very strong impression of Vivian and was in favor of the slaughter. I didn't lead on my own impression of Vivian. I wanted this cat to trust me and show me everything.

The cat had been hiding in the dumpster watching on as Mr. Greenhouse scurried out of the building. He was frightened by the slam of the doors behind him. By how weary and frightful he was it seemed like he was already expecting Vivian's visit. The alleyway cat hissed at him as he walked into her direction. Everything fell silent around one frivolous jingle of a bell. They both looked up high from exactly where I had anticipated Vivian might've been watching from. Two green eyes crept out of the darkness, even the outline of her black fur blurred with her surroundings.

Mr. Greenhouse panicked and ran for the road as she majestically fell. Even I had to admit that although demonic, her cat demon form was beautiful and bewitching. She landed softly on all fours and I could tell she was excited to play. Her figure was silken with black fur and that one singular bell rang again as her tail swished. She had one golden hoop in her right ear that reminded me of their kind that were often known as the gypsies to the underworld.

The alleyway cat felt relieved that she has finally come to kill this man. I looked down on the kitty surprised by its disgust in the victim. She swept me into another memory a few years ago. She had been walking alongside the edge of the opposing apartment building and watched on as Mr. Greenhouse was doing illicit things to a child no more than eight. My jaw clenched as I watched on and realized what the cat was showing me. The next morning, he walked out of his apartment block with a bag that was small enough to fit the body of that child. He threw it into the back of his car parked on the side street. He skeptically looked around before closing the door. It was early morning and no one was around. Jingle. That one singular jingle swept me back into the original memory of Vivian murdering Mr. Greenhouse.

"When you decide to become a monster, Mr. Greenhouse," she purred. "Make sure you're the biggest one out there." He twisted to look behind him trying to escape, she slashed at his face. A gurgling scream erupted from him as his eyeball flew across the pavement.

"The treaty!" He screamed at her frantically. I couldn't help but wonder myself for that moment if this is what the humans thought the treaty would protect.

"You know," she purred again approaching him as he ran further into the alleyway and into the dead end. "I was human once. And even if I still were, dare I say I might've done the same to you after knowing what you have done to those children."

I pulled away from the alleyway cat thanking her. I knew what happened after that. "Thank you, friend," I said to that cat as it meowed and continued to rub against my calf. I looked back to the location that Vivian had once been waiting for her mouse. That one singular jingle echoed in my mind. It was reported that Vivian made a public visit to the orphanage Mr. Greenhouse overlooked that very same day.

I sneered at the thought of how many other children in the orphanage might've been affected by his evil doing. I hated that woman and killing humans was against the treaty. But, a part of me was aware that she had fought for those children when no one else did. I wanted to use this evidence against her. Killing humans was not tolerated. But the man should've been convicted one way or another a long time ago and when it came to the harm of children, I don't know if even my own kind could've gone through the proper channels.

"This area is restricted to Shabeah police force," a woman's voice crept into the alleyway and the click of her heels followed. Finally, my little tag along decided to reveal herself. The tattoos weren't as big as Vivian's and by comparison she wasn't as beautiful either. She was still a beauty as all the Guardians were to encase the evil within them.

"I was wondering when you would introduce yourself, Destiny," I said patting the cat one last time and standing. "I figured the only way to lure you out would be to stand by somewhere I shouldn't be for too long."

She charmed a smile, similar to the attitude that Vivian held. But this one was different. I could see the absolute despise and hatred in her eyes. It was very similar to the hatred Haymen held for me even when he smiled. Vivian might have been his favorite but this one certainly seemed to know about our past. Interesting. Maybe he was sleeping with all of them.

"If you're not going to do anything, then I will take my leave," I said walking towards her. I deliberately put my hands in my pockets.

This little pipsqueak had no chance against me in combat and I hoped my comfortable stance egged her to try something.

"Go back to where you came from, Angel," she seethed as I passed her. I continued walking, ignoring her small threat. Maybe this one wasn't as dumb as Vivian and kept to only verbal threats. There was much to be said about Shabeah and even more that had to be destroyed. The city of demons was a breeding ground for evil like Mr. Greenhouse.

A call came through my ear piece and I swiped the top of it to answer. A simple voice message from Gretel. I was to visit her immediately. I selected the files from Mr. Greenhouse's death and transmitted them to her device. I teleported my jacket to my own closet freeing my wings so I could take flight. Most angels required a small implantation that would fabricate clothes around their wings. It could host up to hundreds of different shirts and jackets and remove them just as quickly. Only few had the gift to teleport, which I personally found more convenient.

I didn't want Destiny to witness my teleportation first hand. The removal of the jacket could've been considered as the implant program. I imagined Haymen had pre-warned her of my gifts but unless she had witnessed or fought against someone who also had the skill, then she would always be caught off guard. So instead while in Shabeah, I chose to fly. I spread my wings wide and darted for the sky. I wouldn't teleport to Gretel until I left the city.

My little tracker tried to keep up as she jumped from rooftop to rooftop but the distance became too great. I never expected her to keep up. I waited until I was far from the ogling eyes of Haymen and his city before I teleported into Gretel's office.

She sat in the corner of the room on her white leather couch. A cup of tea was placed on the coffee table in front of her. The moon was positioned perfectly in front of her open windows where she would often leap and fly from. She was no longer in her formal attire from the judgement this morning but instead wore high waisted white pants and a fitted silk shirt. Considering her age that surpassed over one thousand years she looked no older then forty in human years. It was the scowl that made her look older and wiser. I took a seat across from her ignoring the rest of her office that was surrounded in old archives and the large wooden desk in the center.

When I sat, she raised an eyebrow at the files I had sent her. A small screen was projected in front of her where she slid through the images.

"The Guardian, Vivian, killed this human male just before I caught her last night," I said.

"This came across my desk two hours ago from Haymen," she said taking her glasses off and flicking a file to my own communication device. I opened it instantly. "Alongside this." She handed me a newspaper article which read: "Demon saves our children! Pedophile slaughtered!" One thing that ceased to amaze me was the accuracy and ability of the reporters who were able to gain information so fast and spin a story. That, and Haymen would've had influence over this publication.

"The treaty states that neither angel nor demon are allowed to kill humans."

"You know that I can't do anything with this," she said cutting me off. "Yes. This Guardian girl went against the treaty. But then to explain to the public who have idolized her for such actions that we are sentencing her to death will destroy their faith with our judgement. Sometimes justice isn't always black and white. You know that, Gabe."

"I didn't realize our law was so wavering," I said harshly. She gave me an even stare and took a sip of her tea.

"You are a warrior, Gabe. You fight the wars when they come about and it is my job to deal with the politics, especially oversights with the treaty. I am telling you that this cannot be raised. Not now while we have one of Haymen's sealed away in Aztec. Are you really that eager to start another war, Gabe?" She hushed.

"She killed Luke. An Angel—our blood! When did we become so weak?!" I said shocked at what I was hearing.

"And I am no happier about it than you but we must treat this trial fairly. We sentenced her, that is what you wanted."

"I wanted her dead!" I savagely said. There was a long pause in the room as she gave me time to recompose myself. She took another sip of tea and placed it on the coffee table.

"Perhaps I am doing you a favor... It must be a burden to be the Angel of War. I wonder how close at times you are to the edge of becoming a fallen angel. Seeking blood is not always the healthiest for our kind, perhaps you should step away from this one since it has affected you personally," she lightly lectured.

"You might be scared of Haymen but I'm not. He is planning something. I'm not the only one who caught wind of his spies or movement through my city. You know that something is brewing just as much as I do."

Gretel didn't say anything. She only nodded her head slightly and looked out into the open night so I continued.

"You gave me permission to continue my investigation throughout Shabeah which I am grateful for. But if I don't have your support past that then I will act of my own accord."

"Why the girl? Why are you so fixated on her?" She snapped as if not listening to me but finally voicing what has been on her mind. "You are the Angel of War. If you really wanted to, you could've killed her and possibly have gotten away with it. Instead you chose to keep her alive and bring her to our court. I've seen you take down armies at a time so why did you hesitate on this one Guardian if you so badly want her dead?"

I paused. I didn't expect that question. I almost wanted to laugh at her. The entire point of the treaty was so there were rules and guidelines to protect all races equally and deter further war. And yet like all the higher angels who only involved themselves in politics, when it got heated, they simply wanted someone else to do the dirty work. Gretel's eyes that saw too much read my silence. She was all too knowing with that critical eye of hers but she said nothing. Out of all three on the panel, Gretel had been the only one to have fought in previous wars. It was with age and retirement that she focused her sharp mind elsewhere. This was a question from warrior to warrior. She wouldn't have dared ask anyone else that question but me. Her trust was deep and I spat on my original anger towards her for asking what I might've opened.

"She's different," I said after a long pause. "I was in two minds as to whether to bring her to the courts the official way, that way I could stand where I am now against Haymen; or I could kill her right then and have my immediate revenge. When we fought, she was actually able to land a few marks. It's been a while since someone has been so lucky. It's certainly not the strength of an ordinary Guardian." I contemplated that for a moment. A lot of movement was subtly happening around certain cities, including my own. There were certain demons that were testing boundaries and creating minor havoc. But it was a build up to something larger. I knew when war was coming and somehow it led me here to this Guardian.

"You think the girl is hiding something?" She asked skeptically. I frowned, still unsure of exactly what I thought and why I even kept her alive. I had convinced myself that the avenue I had taken was the correct one. But there was a part of me that had numerous questions about her particularly that I was too scared to open. Instinct kept driving my attention to her. That fought against all logical thought I had to execute her. That's why I decided only to focus on the logical reasoning.

"I think Haymen is hiding something. The Guardian was only an excuse to get closer to his empire. But this Vivian has only been working for him for a year. She wasn't a human of fame or fortune. She is the opposite of all generations he's rebirthed. Even the few that harbor in my own city were well known before being turned. She's the only one that was off the grid to start with. Just a normal human." All of this I said out loud as I considered it myself.

Gretel stood up and walked around to her desk in thought. I twisted in my chair to watch her. "I trust your judgment. You know Haymen will do anything to get her back."

"I know," I simply said. "Even if he does I'll be chained to her side for those thirty days. If not, then I will have the right to publicly execute her. Either way I will find my way to unravel what Haymen is doing. It makes it easier now that I know how important this Guardian, Vivian, is to him."

"You know I have to judge unbiased if he does bring proof of her innocence," she said rounding the large wooden desk to stand in front of the open windows. The breeze silently drafted her hair.

"You do your job Gretel," I said standing up. "And I'll do mine." I teleported from her office and back to the outskirts of Shabeah. The muscles in my wings stretched out as I glided effortlessly towards the city. War was coming, of that much I was certain; and when it does, I would make sure that my kind was not unprepared.

Chapter Thirteen- Haymen

I looked down on the filthy demon that has been dragged in and interrupted my meal. He looked like a male human but I could see the slither of magic that circled him to hide his true identity. Destiny twisted his arm behind and forced him to drop to his knees in front of me. I sat at the end of my long wooden table lazily with numerous plates before me. I snapped my fingers and a few of the candles that floated in the air instantly lit, illuminating parts of the darkness I enjoyed to dwell in.

Destiny raised her eyes over Alexa who sat at the other end of the table. Her jealousy didn't go unnoticed. She always went feral when other women were so close. I considered it to be a primitive part to one of her demons and was not something I tolerated. I flicked my finger and a trickle of the darkness that always seeped from me slashed her cheek in reprimand. She only looked to the demon in front of her then as it oozed with black blood.

Her fellow guardians hadn't seen Alexa for little over a week now. They probably already thought that she was dead. Dark circles ringed her eyes and the sharpness of her gaunt face shadowed the bright skin she once had. She once was a beauty. Her black curly hair was tattered and thinned in patches. Her state disgusted me. This had only happened in a matter of weeks.

I took a sip from my goblet eyeing Destiny as she prompted her prisoner to speak. My stare reminder her I didn't like my time being wasted. She growled and broke his arm behind him. His howling scream encircled the room.

"I didn't do it!" He finally wept. Tears began to hit the floor. Not from the pain of a broken arm, no, to most demons that was child's play. He was shitting himself about what *I* would do to him.

"Didn't do what?" Destiny growled before twisting his bones further.

"I didn't kill the angel. I'm not that stupid!" He cried. Destiny had healing marks on her body where they would've fought when he detained him. Dry blood remained on her sleeveless shirt and her hair golden blonde was teased by chunks of dirt.

I growled at the magic that continued to swirl around him. It clung to him in protection. A witch's spell that many wouldn't have noticed but was offensive to my eyes. No witch or her magic was more powerful than me. I knew the moment he had crept into my city hoping to have gone unnoticed. Instead of killing him for his imprudence I waited until a time just like now.

Even with a high witch's spell to change his form I sensed it as soon as soon as he entered. I had created Shabeah for that exact purpose. Any demons or angels to come into my city were never unnoticed. His breed of demon was one I had been wary of for a while since his Queen went silent when I demanded her to bring me soldiers.

I stretched out my hand watching my darkness that always encompassed me to strike at him. I knew it would hurt him to so forcefully rip the magic off his body. I looked forward to his screams. I could feel every edge of my darkness worm under his skin like needles. It pulled apart the cloak of magic like skin being torn from muscle.

He screamed in agony as my talons hooked deep into his skin and pulled out the witch's transformation spell. He dropped to the ground as Destiny let him go. He would be too weak to stand let alone try and run now. Blood seeped onto the floor as it oozed from his nose and mouth. It wouldn't kill him but it certainly could be considered as close.

Destiny couldn't remove the magic but she had a keen eye and nose for investigation. Especially when it was something I wanted in a matter of time. She had caught the exact demon I was searching for.

"My best Guardian has been taken to Aztec because of you," I growled. I disregarded Destiny's hurt expression. She meant nothing to me. She was only my property and it was sickening to see her expression which should've always been stone.

His back was spiny and the small spikes in his back had snapped from previous fights. More than likely from territorial fights within his own kind. He hissed at me, his snake like tongue spitting out as he continued to weep. His form was like a human water snake. One that was highly venomous. Most Demon Snakes found themselves imprisoned in my own personal Underworld.

They were uncontrollable at most times which is why I had current issues with his Queen.

Despite being notorious for their solidarity and personal space, they did answer and follow their royal heritage.

"Was it your Queen that asked you for the blood of an angel?" I asked. "You were witnessed walking from the dead body. Poison, drowning, even his wings being torn from his body. Did your Queen ask you to do that?"

"No!" he sobbed into the ground crying and hissing. He disgusted me. His kind were strong and would at least dare to fight me. Then again, that is why I had Destiny hunt him instead. Scorch marks fringed his scales from the conflict. "How could I possibly take on an Angel, my Lord? I wouldn't stand a chance," he begged. All lies. An Angel would always have the upper hand in strength and because of their training and tolerance to poison. But if taken off guard, it could be believable.

I looked at Destiny annoyed. I didn't have time to talk to this disgusting creature. She grabbed his neck and jarred his scaly face to look at me. His green slit eyes tried to focus on me as tears of blood dripped out. Maybe I did almost kill him.

"You," I said pointing to him. "Will admit to everything that you have done. You were the one that killed the Angel. And you will pay for your crime," I said. He begged and sobbed at me. I threw my silken napkin at him in disgust hoping that it would magically clean up his disgusting display of weakness. I looked at Destiny. "Make sure it happens."

"Yes, my Lord," is all she said as she grabbed him by the tail and dragged him out. She eyed Alexa warily. The jealous expression was unanswered by Alexa who now hardly spoke.

I would make sure that enough evidence and his confession would free Vi and that's all I cared about. I knew who had killed Luke but they would never take the fall for it. I had to start the game and Vi was right in the center of it all.

"I need you to manufacture some fake evidence of his whereabouts with a surveillance video. Liaise with Destiny to make sure the evidence matches the statement," I said cutting through a piece of bleeding meat and eating it. Alexa's form of technology demon had brought me years of luck. She could manipulate or create any evidence I needed her to. It had benefited me for many years until looking at the disgrace she was now. She only nodded in response.

Tellith had tried her hardest to rehabilitate as much as she could even through old magic of her tribe. This shell was all that was left. Once she achieved what I needed from her I would dispose of her. She has been compromised.

"Did you interrogate the human police force?" I asked taking another bite of meat. Tellith said that her rehabilitation might depend on conversation with me, her master. I didn't care for such things, I would just create a new Guardian. All of them were disposable. All but one.

She nodded. She looked down and typed a few things into her watch. A file shortly beeped on my own. I opened it and the blue screen widened in front of me. I didn't like this technological era but very few demons could communicate like the old days. They were all so weak now.

I briefly read over the profile of the man who had been spying within my human law force. I was certain he was Gabe's. I had been suspicious on small intel that would leak out. Alexa could back track even confidential and deleted files. Her demon was an asset to me.

"Don't kill him yet," I said taking another swig of my wine. "We might find use for him." I closed the file and watched on as she nodded. I tapped my finger on the wooden table. I wanted her silent presence gone. I ate with very few and she hasn't eaten anything from her plate. My enemies had been close to capturing her. This was how all my Guardians acted the moment they were compromised. Some were consumed instantly. Others like Alexa fought until the very end, until they had no strength left and were taken.

"What did they say to you?" I asked. Despite her communication with them, even her Shadow Mind journals couldn't isolate or pinpoint to their whereabouts. I was done with searching for them. I have been out in the open for so long now, practically inviting them to fight me head on. Leaving their kind to gain strength would be problematic for my rein. I had to kill them while they were weak. The years since the last war had passed quickly, I wondered how much strength they had already gained.

"This is a request Alexa. I am asking you a question," I said in my tone that owned her.

Alexa opened her mouth. She then remoistened her dry lips to speak. After moments of attempting her voice was shaky and barely audible. "They haven't forgotten what you have done," she said. The voice hadn't even sounded like her own. "They are coming for you, Haymen."

I raged at the threat and threw my goblet across the room. They were taunting me still with these games!

CHAPTER FOURTEEN- VIVIAN

I watched on as Gabe walked outside the castle and disappeared by carriage into the water vortex. I spited him dearly. He left me in this dreary hell hole where I could only see portions of the outside through the slit window.

The door dragged against the cemented floor as it was opened. I turned with my arms wrapped around my chest calculating my odds of escape. I decided it was too soon. I had to watch more, see how the rounds and functions worked. Then again, Haymen had specifically thrown me in here for one thing. To speak to some person called Alice. He was as vague as always. I didn't even know who Alice was. Despite Haymen being in charge of the Underworld which was a prison in itself, I had somehow ended up in this tropical death sentence.

Two gargoyles walked in, their cemented frame was very much alive and like Gabe, they had to contract their wings to squeeze through the door. A pair of black cotton pants and a shirt were thrown at me.

I scoffed at them as I looked down at the prison attire. Despite my own clothing being dirty and ratty I would defy them until the very end. I refused to wear some prison garment. For all my tough talk, the powder Gabe had blown into my face significantly made me weaker.

I tried to rebel, if only to see how far and long it would take to push the patience of a cemented gargoyle who was possessed by some living angelic force. I learned the hard way that they didn't have patience or a sense of humor. Within thirty seconds of me staring at them they had unsheathed their weapons and were not messing around. I realized either I dressed myself or they would do it for me. Being stripped bare and clothed by a Gargoyle wasn't on my 'to do' list.

I resisted the first time they tried to touch me and frisk me. A small fight broke out and I discovered after being manhandled by two gargoyles and being pinned to the chest of one, that the option of head butting the other wasn't to my liking. White stars blurred my vision and blood began to drip down from my eyebrow. They frisked to make sure I had no weapons and closed the door behind them.

I felt around the floor and walls to find any weakness or form of escape. There was neither. The only thing I had was the small window where I could see another tower on the wing of the castle.

After Gabe and the gargoyles left, the demon's curiosity only increased as the hours went by and I sat silently in the darkness of my room underneath the window. I felt its presence hovering at the edge of my door. It sporadically struck out to have a taste of my blood. As it did now.

The scratch of its invisible talon raked down my cheek ever so gently, as if just for a lick. I sat there with knees to my chest and hands propped over them. My blood began to slowly trickle down my cheek. There were numerous cuts on my hands and feet, tearing up my black cotton attire. It was as if it were an animal simply coming and checking on its most recent toy–a little nibble here and there as it pleased.

I couldn't identify what demon it was but it was excited by my arrival–that much I could tell. If those who chanted endlessly at the core of the castle stopped, I doubted that anyone within Aztec would survive if the demon truly awoke. Whatever they chanted, sedated it almost completely to sleep. I wondered if it was some kind of guard to make sure no prisoners escaped or a demon that was also being suppressed and buried deep in this prison.

I pulled back my hair and untangled it from the blood it had been stuck to. Besides chanting and screaming there was an eerie silence and I knew that if Haymen didn't keep to his word I would probably go mad within a week. I stayed still not wanting to disrupt any of the darkness that swept through. It pillowed through my room. It was the promise of twisted torment and death. Something that even the most fearless of demons might be scared by. The hairs on my body were constantly raised and I was on high alert for every shift in the cold wind waiting for what might happen next.

There was a clink and I looked to the door. *Well, how's that for timing*, I chastised myself jumping up and readying myself for the fight to come. I edged to the door with my back against the wall, ready to attack whomever would walk in. It eerily creaked open. Darkness wafted in. I waited with my fists clenched... but nothing came. After a minute of still waiting for someone to walk in I peered outside and realized that no one was standing there. I looked down both hallways and noticed that in the distance all other prisoner doors had also been opened. I pressed my eyebrows together and heard an outbreak from outside.

I looked downstairs to the caged area I previously walked past and noticed that numerous demons who looked *very* appropriate to be within Aztec were gathering. I surveyed them and watched as some sat down at one of the tables eating something that I knew even from this distance shouldn't be edible. Gargoyles and the cemented soldiers surrounded the cage. And then I saw it, the small woman who walked out with pale skin with the light glow of blue. Her tattoos glowed like all Guardians, exemplifying the contract with both Haymen and seven demons. Alice Kendrid, I realized. This had to be the person Haymen wanted me to speak with. Although obviously a Guardian, her movement wasn't the grace of one. It was stifled and awkward. Her long black curly hair was untamed and the paleness of her skin was not of natural color. Although her tattoos still glowed lightly and I could only see them because hers were situated on her arms, it seemed like they were crusted and ugly. Her skin had an underlying black taint where her veins instead of being transparent were grey and muggy.

Her head twisted almost like an owl, unnatural even for a Guardian as she looked up at me and those rotten yellow teeth smiled at me. Her black pupils were small and pinned as she raised an eyebrow at me and pointed to a table. An invitation. All the other demons within Aztec suddenly became irrelevant. Not that I would ever let my guard down to that extent. As Gabe mentioned, prisoners didn't have access to their demonic power but some of them were born with claws, blades, and poisons. I was definitely at a disadvantage.

I looked at the gargoyles and soldiers wondering if a fight broke out; what my options were of stealing a weapon if I took one of them down first. What would my escape route be? I couldn't let myself die in such a horrendous and disgusting place. A fight already broke out between two demons. One looked like an oversized bat with razors extending on its wings and a human figure. He opposed the woman who looked gigantic in size, the size of six men. The bat demon swept his razor wings over her and she grabbed onto his wings and pierced her thumbs through them to pin him. She bit into his neck with solid and crooked teeth, grinding down part of his bone. The bat sliced up the side of her stomach, a gash wide enough that I knew it was a serious injury but neither budged as they backed off one another and re-evaluated each another again. They have both been seriously injured. Everyone just watched on. And from the scarring of the two, I wondered if this was a regular thing.

Before Alice's face could twist to mine again, I headed for my door. I suppose there was only one way to find out if I would survive this or not. As soon as I stepped out of my room my door was slammed behind me and the floor beneath me fell. I dragged my nails along the small wall trying to catch myself before I fell completely, but luck wasn't on my side. I hit the ground and coughed into the dirt I had fallen into. My fingers were bleeding as I looked up and around into the darkness. The only tinge of light was in front of me and from the noise I could hear, that was where the others were.

It was built like a fighting arena. I stood up touching around me on the gravely wall. Yep, this was definitely the only way to walk. I brushed myself as I walked out. Only few candles prevented this from being a place of utter darkness. Although I couldn't call upon my demons, I was grateful to the contract I suddenly had. If I was still human, I would've been fumbling and tripping over in this crippling darkness. Well, to be precise, if I were human I wouldn't be in this mess in the first place. The difference between the human court and supernatural court was massive.

Usually I'd have some smartass dialogue I'd say to myself just to ease the tension. But in this situation, I was silent and on alert. There are numerous demons within Aztec who had exceptional hearing and I didn't need to draw more attention to the 'new girl'. I walked out and all eyes of the prisoners fell on me. I ignored them and only focused on Alice. I was aware of their every movement and the proximity of the closest demon which catcalled out to me as I walked out. My tattoos weren't visible. I wondered whether I should have them on display but decided against it. Although I looked human, they knew I was anything but to be in a prison like this. But if they find out that I was a Guardian who couldn't summon her demons within this prison they might attempt to overpower me.

Even the gargoyles and cemented soldiers snarled at me as I walked through the caged dome arena. There were only a few demons here, eight including myself. I darted my eyes around a few other towers and noticed that not all of them had been let out. I knew the act of killing an angel had consequences. But being detained in Aztec, I personally thought was overkill. Especially considering that the ogre looking woman probably slaughtered hundreds of children and that bat thing over there was probably the demon I had long ago heard about called Count Dracula who slaughtered villages at a time. Mind you as I look around, of course there are no angels, there aren't even any fallen angels. Double standards when it came to our white winged friends. If a demon hurt any other demon or humans, then we would be hunting your ass to either kill you or take you to the Underworld. But Angels had no such thing. You hardly ever heard bad things being said in the media about angels. In many ways they just sounded like pompous snobs.

I approached Alice, still aware of the others who rounded me with curiosity. I watched the small movements and displays of strength. In a group like this hierarchy got sorted out pretty quickly and I had to make sure that I was on the top of that list. If I wasn't crippled, out of all my demons, I would've called upon my Succubus. She would've laughed and swaggered in as if all these boys were hers to enjoy... even the woman for that matter. She had a very cunning way of getting to the top... would charisma be the word?

Alice didn't twist as I walked behind her and rounded the table. A show of confidence that I wouldn't attack her from behind. I sat directly across from her hunched figure on the cool metal seating. Her shoulders were inward and scars and scabs were open all over her flesh. I wondered if the wounds were from the dormant demon who had the same curiosity for my blood.

She began laughing and it wasn't a feminine laugh which I half expected from the small figured woman. It was a masculine and wavering laugh. When those dark pupils flicked up at me, she lunged for me. I smacked her hand away from my throat and shoved her back hard into her seat. The act itself was half-assed and she didn't retaliate again after that, she only laughed. Others watched on in interest. I wasn't sure what to call Alice anymore because it wasn't who I imagined the Guardian originally might've been.

"How does such a pretty Guardian find herself in here... or let me guess, Haymen found an opportunity to send you here?" When Alice looked up the blackness of her veins were more visible in her face and around her mouth. Her lips were flushed and blue. Everything about her was wrong and the feeling around her was an all too familiar presence. She *felt* like those who attacked me in my shadow dreams. This was real. This is what happened to those who were devoured and used as a host.

"What are you?" is all I asked. I was still focused on Alice but my attentiveness was all around me and on those who shifted from side to side edging closer. Another fight broke out amongst the previous two, captivating majority of the fellow prisoners' attention. I looked up at the cemented gargoyles that hung over the cage watching. They were fixed on growling but not intervening. They didn't care if anyone died down here. In fact, that is probably what they were hoping for.

Alice laughed in the voice that was not of her own. No, something was definitely possessing her. There was no longer an Alice Kendrid. "This is such a nice body, no? I've violated it more times than I can count, even when she was present for it. Lovely Alice. So supple," he said grabbing hold of his breasts and moaning in a manner that made me cringe. But I didn't because that was what he was after. To scare me and make me uncomfortable. Those tiny pupils landed on my body and rolled up with an intensity that made me want to rip out her throat. "I think I would have preferred yours. Would you like me to tell you what objects I'd use on you?"

"Here I thought you would be something interesting. But instead it turns out you're just a talkative pervert. How pathetic," I said as if to leave.

"Wait!" It rasped while reaching out for me. The problem was that he was far from a dirty pervert… he was more and I could only imagine the torture he did on Alice. Once I extracted the information I needed, I planned on killing this thing in hopes that Alice might find peace. I wasn't much for sentimentalism, especially to a woman I never met, but this was too close to home and was the only thing that terrified us Guardians. We would never admit it out loud. *I* would never admit it out loud. I arched an eyebrow at it and sat back down. It was obvious that it was excited by my presence. I didn't know how long Alice had been in Aztec. It must've been a while because she wasn't on the records for the past three generations of Guardians in any city. I had read the archives of Haymen's Guardians as soon as I realized no one spoke the truth and if any of them had found an escape from Haymen's clutches.

In here her body had not aged, it only rotted with the filthy thing that possessed her. Alice began to laugh again, and again the black veins beneath her transparent grey looking skin seemed to brighten. The tattoos were an insult as they still glowed a faint blue. Haymen didn't have to specify what he wanted me to ask, I already knew. This demon was the very kind we ran away from in our dreams. And our main task to hunt by day.

"Where's your master?" I asked. His laughing ceased and her neck crooked awkwardly as if trying to understand my question. But no, his eyes were on me, acutely aware of what I asked.

"I haven't spoken to him for some time. But things must be moving nicely if Haymen's sent you in here out of desperation," he cackled again.

"Haymen fears nothing. I think your presence is simply becoming an annoyance. One I would be happy to destroy for my Master," the words I spoke sounded that of a true loyal Guardian. He laughed in response.

"Haymen is filth," he said suddenly serious. Alice's yellow teeth were grinding against one another. "And he is not the true Demon Lord. *My* master is the only one befitting that position." I took note of that, and everything he was telling me. I had never met one of these demons during the day and I never understood their purpose, until perhaps now.

"He seems to be doing a shitty job at that if he's in hiding and can't approach the throne because he doesn't even have a body." It was a guess. I imagined that if his lackeys had no physical body then neither did he. Alice's shoulders rolled awkwardly trying to contain his anger. His lip cracked and began to bleed as his eyes pinned me for the insult towards his master.

"My master will come for you. They all will, every single one of you until Haymen can no longer hide behind his walls and pretty fighters. My master will take his throne, like he once had before, you seething bitch." Spit began to expel from his mouth and I knew his control was losing out. I noticed the other inmates that purposefully circled me. Alice had her head angled to the side peering at me.

"You will be my message to your beloved Master," he said seriously. "I will let your blood splatter on the walls of Aztec. You will only be another casualty in this prison but he will hear the message loud and clear. I might've been in here for over three hundred years but for my lifespan, that is hardly anything. He thought you could gather information for him but all that tells me is he still can't find us. I may be locked up by his accord but I will never betray my own." *Us.* I wondered how many of 'us' there was.

"In a place like this, neither of us can summon our demons. Hand to hand. I will kill you," I said confidently. It was a ruse because I noted the others who still circled me waiting for Alice's signal. They were following the demon within Alice.

"My dear, you will not make it out of here alive. I will rape your dead body and use that blood to write a message to your beloved master. None of your kind will defeat us. You will never be powerful enough or worthy enough for our new world!" She began seething and cackling like the crazy and possessed person she was. Or should I say what the demon was.

"My last question before dying, then." I said noticing the shuffling amongst those who were ready to attack me. I was stalling time as I looked around me, for anything. There weren't even utensils for the molded bread that was served as food. "What are you?" I looked at the closest gargoyles wondering if somehow, I would be able to reach for its weapons but the cage came between us still.

There was a slight nudge then lick from the invisible somber demon. I felt the small trickle of blood and wondered what its nudge was for. It was almost as if it had been making sure that I was the inmate it was looking for. Over time, despite its vicious licks, it felt familiar. It no longer licked at me but I could feel it wrapping around me slowly, as best it could under its silencing of the chanters. Would it... help me?

"Call us shadows, since that's what you like to call your little dream states when we slowly eat you from the inside and take possession of your body. Call us whatever you like. But to you... today... I am your death." There was a moment of silence before everyone pounced.

I flipped over the seat I was on and ran straight for the bat-like demon. I dodged his bladed wing that swooped for me grabbing ahold of the holes that the giant had pierced before. I used the holes to control his wing movement for a moment catching him off guard. I slashed across the face of one of the demons that tried to scalp me. It worked on the first one until the bat demon used his strength and flicked me into the air. I smacked the cage, latching my hands on the top of the dome before I dropped. The gargoyle above me sniffed and came to bring his hammer down to crush my fingers. Fuck. I looked down where they all waited and knew crushed fingers would probably make it harder to survive this. The bat demon and another one with wings swept up towards me. I anticipated their blades and jumped for the side of the cage. I barely caught hold of the metal, hanging from only my fingertips on one hand until I gripped and pulled myself up. The impact of the two flying demons collided with the gargoyle that brought down his hammer.

There was a ricocheting sound and bits of the metal began to glitter the arena. A space had been made at the top. The bat demon grabbed the gargoyle with his wings, widening the hole and ripped him into the pit. Suddenly, all the gargoyles and soldiers began to drop from the walls of the castle. Another two gargoyles swept in attacking the two that had just flown out of the arena.

I took my opportunity in seconds and climbed over as my feet hung and threw my body over and into the outside. A cemented soldier brought down his axe over me. I let go of my grip and slid down painfully on the metal. As soon as I hit the ground I rolled to the side to dodge another gargoyle. A thick nudge and lick pushed me towards the entrance. I followed the guidance of the demon that seemed to be hovering behind me. I ran for the entrance that Gabe and I had walked through. Another large lick up my back from the demon who nudged me in faster. Clashing of weapons, roars and screams erupted behind me. I looked ahead and ran being attentive to how close my pursuers might be.

Six of the bony hooded chanters crept out of the darkness and their chant has changed. An invisible hand wrapped around my throat, levitating me in the air. I choked as I tried to grab onto the hand that wasn't there. The pressure began crushing my throat. The demon that had been following me around suddenly was somber. I felt it push past me and an invisible tentacle of power wiped them out. Blood splattered against the wall as their bodies hit... hard. I allowed myself only seconds to catch my breath. I wasn't certain what I ran towards but my heart raced with adrenalin. Something I rarely felt anymore. It seemed like the invisible demon that helped me gained power as soon as six of those chanters focused their attention towards me instead of it. I frisked their crumpled bodies in search of weapons. Nothing.

Another lick on my back that was already dripping with blood nudged me towards a tunnel. The demon was leading me. It was as if in its own way it was communicating to me. The darkness and bloodlust that swept off it rolled around me as it grew impatient. Now that it gained more freedom I could feel its presence growing larger and stronger. Either I followed it or it would kill me. Because it had the ability to do so in seconds. That ruthless nature of it surrounded me. The fight outside was futile. There was no way that even if they did kill all the guards they could ever escape. There was no way underneath all of this water and our demonic powers still dormant.

This time, five more approached me and hooked me with another blow of magical chanting. As they focused their attention on me it loosened the reins on the demon that was following me. I was flung into the air by the hooded demons. This time before I could be choked, they were impaled by tendrils that couldn't be seen. But I could feel it. The holes in their chest swirled open. They screamed for only seconds until they were dead. The demon retracted its tendrils and they dropped to their knees. I prepared for my landing but was caught by something. The demon wrapped its tendril around my waist and aided me to the floor. I looked around me trying to find some evidence of its existence. Why was it helping me and what was it? The chanting was now quieter. Eleven had been killed and if it continued I was aiding this demon to be released. I wasn't certain if that would be worse or better for me in this situation.

"Little Guardian…" I heard Alice purr behind me and I knew that in this darkness I was no longer alone. I flicked my hair over my face and stood up from the crouch that I had been lowered in. I looked down two tunnels on either side. In one direction I would face Alice and possibly some of her fellow inmates. Or on the other end was an unknown demonic presence that held so much power that it constantly needed to be detained. The invisible demon didn't give me time to think as it nudged me towards the second tunnel. I ran in that direction. It might kill me straight away. But that was a risk I had to take. Hopefully the end of this tunnel would also lead to somewhere I could find anything that might be used as a weapon.

I ran panting heavily listening to the screams behind me of the hooded chanters. Others began killing them as well. Every step I took closer to the invisible demon, it seemed to awaken and unravel it more. It continued guiding me, making sure I didn't divert my path into the depths and darkness of the spiral stairs I now jumped down. I took lunges of four at a time. I could hear Alice taunting me not too far away. If it were just us two, I would be the victor. If there were more, I needed a weapon. The screams and evilness that swept around was like a pooling hot breath down my back. I hit flat ground and landed into the dungeon of a creature that I could not see. It was dark down here and as I jumped into its domain, the screams behind me had stopped.

I looked at the massacre before me. Limbs were outstretched and blood was splattered everywhere. The hooded chanters had lost their hold on the demon after so many of them were killed. Candles that might've been lit were broken on the floor. Utter darkness.

I could feel its breathing, hot and dense as I stepped closer. Slowly, I crept towards one of the candle holders. It wasn't much for a weapon but it was something in the shallow room that held nothing else. I knew Alice was only steps away. The demon wasn't positioned in one spot. It surrounded the room. It was the room. The very air I breathed was shared with it. I realized then that the presence of this demon that drew me in was more dangerous than anything I had faced before. I had only felt this shadowing power from Haymen. Screams erupted behind me from those who followed Alice down the stairs. Bits of limbs began to rein down the stairs as I stood there very still. Did it not know I was in its room? Was it protecting me? What did it want?

It licked me up the back again, egging me closer into the room, closer towards it. My feet dug into gravel as my back straightened and I knew... I could feel that it was towering above me and around me. A slice went down my chest and I realized it had scratched away part of my shirt to reveal the bottom half of my tattoos. The drops down to my stomach glowed bright blue. Almost blindingly blue. I raised my hands to my eyes trying to block the brightness. And then a red fastened through it, merging with the color of my blue. I looked at that one singular tattoo that glowed brightly on its own and felt the summoning it contained. Power that I had not yet felt or called upon with a demon that had not yet surfaced. As soon as that particular tattoo glowed red the demon around me frenzied and I had the overwhelming sense of familiarity. Of... *home*. It wasn't my home but the demon whose tattoo now glowed. This beast recognized that contract and demon. The room swelled with choking power and before I could step away from the ambush of power, it dove into me.

The beast clawed into me, my screams were snuffed by the overwhelming power I was being drowned in. It continued to merge itself within me and into my tiny form. The walls around us began to cave in as I dropped to my knees. The feeling of the creature was like a vortex within me. And then it vanished. I breathed in shakily not sure what happened. What the fuck just happened? I couldn't feel it inside of me. It didn't possess or hurt me. I patted myself over to make sure. A large rock from above dropped. The power had shattered the structure of the room and slowly it began to crumble as it still shook from the aftermath. And yet I had never felt so grounded or silent. Coming to my senses in time, I blocked the blade that Alice brought down on me.

I wasn't quick enough and the blade cut down my arm. She had been aiming for my chest.

"Wait until Master hears about this! It makes so much sense! You're contracted to her. When he-" Alice began squealing and blood pooled out from her mouth. I could sense a figure behind her doing the harm and before I could react that same power suppressed me. My knees gave way before my sight. Darkness.

Chapter Fifteen- Haymen

Within seconds I had finished off Alice and knocked my beautiful Vi out. She had actually done it. I knew the demon that was being kept there would react and remember the presence of its master. Vi didn't yet it know but she held the contract to a very special person, who still hasn't come forth. It only confirmed my suspicions.

There was only one way to come in and out of Aztec and that was by carriage. What most forgot was that I had created Aztec those hundreds of years ago. The angels thought they oversaw and ruled it with their own gargoyles and soldiers who could detect any intruder. I made sure that small loop holes were available to my teleportation and mine only.

I picked up my beautiful Vi and cradled her in my arms. Her shirt had been torn open from where the demon inspected the contract. I teleported her into her cell, neatly tucking her in the corner of the room resting her head on the hard floor. I pushed back part of her matted and blood soaked crimson hair. The demon had finally awoken after so many hundred years of slumber. I'm certain it wouldn't have gone unnoticed by the others and especially Gabe. It awoke as soon as she stepped into Aztec. That demon was purely devoted to protecting its master and I relied on that for her survival in here.

She was the one I have been waiting for. My Queen had finally reappeared and contracted with my sweet, sweet Vi. I brushed my fingers over the droplets of her tattoo. The moment I saw it, I knew and I have patiently waited for things to slowly unravel. Now, I would watch and wait until she would reappear and Vi understood who she truly was.

CHAPTER SIXTEEN- GABE

I went over the statement. Official and sealed from Gretel herself.

Haymen had officially found the demon who had killed Luke and went into a very detailed statement with the demon admitting to the murder. Despite all the evidence leading to its legitimacy, I thought otherwise. The snake demon Haymen claimed was his downfall because I had seen Luke take one of the exact same species within my own city. Luke was young but experienced. I had trained him myself on many accounts. It left a lot of doubt in Haymen's statement. That, and he conveniently gathered it so quickly. The demon was prepared to face the courts and plead guilty. Because he wasn't protected like Vivian, he would be publicly executed.

By the courts ruling and agreement Vivian was a free woman. Well, in certain terms. I wasn't convinced that she had no involvement and I intended to follow her for the next thirty days as agreed by Haymen and the court. I would find the truth behind Luke's death and it somehow centered around Vivian. I just knew it. I owed it to Luke's family and co-workers; the truth about his horrific death. When his body arrived with wings in a separate bag, his mother wailed. Young were difficult to conceive for angels and like many, one child was all they could birth through hundreds of years trying.

He had done so much for all of us and to be murdered within the Demon Lord's city was no coincidence. I forbade any of my own angels to come within Haymen's city until further notice and I urged other cities who were ruled by angels to do the same.

I had avoided confronting Haymen head on for many years. I could ask any of my soldiers to follow her in my stead but I couldn't trust the treaty. Against *the* Haymen, only I would stand for a fair fight. I asked my second in command to rule my city while I was gone. This involved us all and although I had many candidates to take my place in Shabeah, I wanted to see this through to the end. Something was happening here, I could just feel it. Luke was the tip of the iceberg. If Haymen was plotting to initiate another war we had to be ready and on the forefront. It was only Haymen who could start a global scale war.

I sat in the carriage on my way to Aztec. I read over the documents that had been sent to me just before I departed the docks. A mass fight broke out in the prisoner's communal arena. It was the first time that anyone had been able to break through the metal cage but with the amount of impact on either side from both prisoner and guard, a small part shattered and it crumbled from there.

Seven of the prisoners were now dead. No loss, really. Only one survived. Vivian. *Of course*, I thought. Even another Guardian that was detained in there had died. I remembered Alice's case well. She was a Guardian of Haymen's, loyal until she was possessed by a member of the Volv. It was the first time any of us had seen one come out of hiding after the last war and that was three hundred years ago. That was bad. It meant that the Volv who possessed her was no longer trapped in Alice's body. It's why we imprisoned her, so the vile demon wouldn't be set free. After three hundred years it could easily find its way back to its master.

Almost all of the chanters were dead. They were witches who had been chained and forced to live a life within Aztec to keep whatever unspeakable demon was sleeping. Even I couldn't find a track record of it, but I knew what I felt which meant that records were being hidden. Gretel was the only one I could trust and she was one of the few who kept an eye on the prison alongside Haymen who represented the demons solely.

I didn't find it a coincidence that Vivian had been detained in Aztec for less than forty-eight hours and a slaughter like this erupted.

Gretel had been so kind as to send me the sheet, security, and blueprints to Aztec. I pressed a red button on the flat metal sheet and footage of the breakout within the yard projected in front of me in 3D. I swiveled the images from side to side until I could get a perfect positioning on Vivian. All the Guardians and soldiers perfectly filmed and saved the surveillance. What they saw, we had records to as well.

Vivian had been talking to someone in there. I zoomed in on the ugly woman like creature until I noticed the tattoos on her arms which matched that of a Guardian. Alice. The way Vivian had walked out was very intentional and she engaged with Alice almost instantly. I zoomed in further on Alice and her identity came up into a separate side box. Alice Kendrid. Concealed by Haymen's Guardians Three hundred and two years ago. I frowned at the offenses. Serious, but mostly screamed rogue Guardian who was attacking her own kind. I remembered being briefed on this case. I tapped on the side of the metal sheeting. If it weren't for a Volv possessing her she would've been killed. It was because Haymen wanted to entrap that demon that he requested it to be sent to Aztec. Each generation of Guardians only lasted a maximum of thirty years. On the official records it was because their contract expired with their demons that devoured them whole. I wasn't entirely convinced. Although Haymen claimed to be transparent about his creations, the Guardians there were a lot I was suspicious of. Especially if the only Volv movement since their uprising in the last war was targeted at one of Haymen's Guardians.

I zoomed in on the image of Alice and noticed her pinhole pupils and the veins which protruded from her in a grotesque way. The video didn't have audio and the way her mouth moved I couldn't read her lips. Vivian flinched but didn't move. I hummed and reversed the recording watching it again. And then a third. A clean cut began to bleed from her calf. I zoomed in and went over those few seconds again. She had definitely been cut by something. Perhaps the demon I had felt before I left? It had taken an interest in her the moment we walked into Aztec. I zoomed out and watched in suspense as the others began to surround her. The records said that Vivian had made it out alive so I watched on as the seven surrounded her and then attacked.

I had to give her credit. Despite having no access to her demons she was a fluent and smart warrior in her own right. Her body moved of its own accord and in some of her movements I could see the cat demon within her even if not apparent. She had strength and brains which was a rarity; watching her fight was almost... enchanting. I stopped the video as soon as Vivian had broken out of the cage and was no longer visible on the surveillance. What happened to her after that? She was running towards the mouth of Aztec but was later found locked in her room passed out?

When I landed, thicker bars were being applied by the witches. They were chanting and reinforcing the magic that should've held out against even excessive force. A part of me suspected that communal arena was designed in hopes that the inmates would kill each other. Some demons were easier to capture than kill and majority of the species in here went within that category. The same hooded figure greeted me at the mouth of Aztec. Before I even reached him, he was already walking towards the stairs not waiting for me to follow. The chanting continued but wasn't as loud; more than likely because so many had been killed in the outbreak. The copper smell of blood and rubble now seemed engrained in the walls. I squinted down a tunnel where I was certain I could see blood splayed against the wall. My wings glowed bright enough to lead me up the stairs. Although guarded I still expected to feel the demon's presence like I had last time. I even lowered my guard almost welcoming it to have a taste like it did with Vivian. Nothing. It was as if it had vanished. That worried me. When we stood in front of the door to Vivian's cell, the hooded scaly chanter opened the door and left. Odd fellow. I creaked it open and looked down at her. She sat against the wall with her knees bent and hands casually covering her stomach.

I wondered then if Guardians actually feared death. I had killed and seen many demons panic for their life. I found only few that did not squirm nor did they beg. I imagine Vivian would be that kind. But the shadows beneath her eyes was the element that gave away she was both not a demon and not entirely unscathed. Despite that, it didn't prevent her smart mouth barking.

"What do you want? Don't you have a pretty blonde angel to gang bang or something?" she growled. Her grey eyes didn't leave mine. I bit back my own comment which could meet hers but wouldn't be a part of her childish and menacing games. I looked around and could feel the remains of Haymen's demonic energy. He was always overconfident in himself. Powerful yes, but he had forgotten that I have been around for hundreds of years.

"Has Haymen come to see you?" I asked, ignoring her childish behavior.

"Why would he? I'm just a criminal behind bars. My master would have no need for me." I scoffed at her choice word, 'Master'.

"No one is your Master and if you honestly believe that then you are more pathetic than I thought," I said coolly. I had seen her fight and knew that she was smart. Her eyes screamed of that with intelligence. But that cockiness was overbearing.

"I don't need to hear that from you, Angel Boy. Shouldn't you be head hunting whoever killed your boyfriend instead of pestering me? Unless you just want to fall into the same trap that he did with me," she said arching an eyebrow suggestively. "Now wouldn't that just be pathetic."

I clenched my jaw hard, refraining myself from giving her the treatment she deserved. She shifted and covered her stomach tighter. She was hiding a tattoo that further extended down. Her shirt had been shredded into two. I took note of that. Guardian's tattoos and contracts weren't usually that exaggerated in size. I could've pinned her to a wall and seen it for myself but I reminded myself that I had her for the next thirty days. I would find out the story of her tattoos sooner than later.

"You are free to go, Miss Lair. Of course as agreed you will be supervised by myself for the next thirty days. It would appear that your *Master*, was able to bring forth some befitting evidence."

She looked away from me bored and unmoving. "I said you are free," I repeated to her after the long silence which rolled over into minutes.

"I would rather spend the next thirty days in here than spend it with you tailing me," she spat. I smiled. Stubborn. I would make sure to drive her insane within the month. She had involvement in Luke's death. I was certain of it and I would make sure that she slipped up.

"I doubt that you would last another thirty days in here after the footage I've seen of you trying to play nice with everyone."

"Fighting for my life for the next thirty days still sounds more appealing than being stalked by you. Brood over some other mare, elsewhere," she said. And this time I laughed at her, seeing if a different reaction would appear. She slowly looked in my direction and mumbled. "What do you know, he laughs."

"More so at the fact that you think you have a choice. I'm done with this," I said and walked over to her. She jumped onto her legs and tied the tattered bits of her shirt making sure to conceal her tattoos. So that particular one irritated her.

"If you man-handle me I will find a way to squeeze your large dome head through that window," she said raising her fists ready to fight. It was pointless without her demons–she was no match for me– but credit to her for trying. She tried to smack my hands away from her but I grabbed one of her legs and pulled her towards me. I flipped her in the air and threw her over my shoulder. She punched me numerous times in spots that should have disabled a man from walking. I dodged each one flipping her this way and that. Much to my annoyance it was like a screaming child and I had dealt with numerous ones of those at home. I was careful to keep my wings stretched away from where she might be able to hit them. They were *very* sensitive. Much to my surprise she hasn't yet taken any cheap shots to try and harm those either.

"If you don't behave yourself I will put you to sleep." Her motions stopped and I could almost hear her thinking it over. She obviously didn't like being put to sleep when it wasn't on her terms. I wondered if she remembered the last time I had to press my lips to hers to put her to sleep. Obviously she did, because she stopped with her tantrums.

"Put me down. I'll walk myself," she mumbled. I placed her on her feet and she shoved me away. I gave her an insincere smile which pissed her off even more before she led the way down the stairs. If I could keep her on edge then she was more likely to make a mistake. That, and a part of me truly wanted to put this smart mouth in her place. I had thirty days to piss this demon summoner off and get closer to Haymen's real objectives. Since this was his favorite pet, I considered that the two would go hand in hand. She looked over at my still smiling face and scoffed.

"What, did someone get laid while he was gone? You seem awfully chipper with my release considering how hell-bent you were on having me locked up and dead," she seethed. We walked down the stairs in the dark.

"Obviously someone didn't while she was captive," I retorted. I had taken Gretel's advisement. I needed to catch this Guardian unguarded so I could figure out what really happened that night and what Haymen was up to. I knew that he was recruiting to build an army because I had a close watch on him since the day the last war ended.

She waited for me at the bottom of the steps. As I took my first step, she put her foot out in front of mine and before she could trip me, I pinned my hands on either side of her against the wall and blocked her escape with my body.

"You try that little trick again and it will be you rolling down the stairs," I growled. This was now the third time she tried tripping me and I wasn't going to concede to such childish games. A smile twisted on her lips and she pushed her hands through my hair with a smile that was all too cunning. Now knowing that she was contracted to a succubus demon, I wasn't at all surprised she knew how to create such an enticing smile. Her hands stroked my hair, each touch like a burning sensation. I didn't like it and her touch wasn't welcome but that's why she did it. It was a game. I slowly grabbed her wrists and put them to her side.

She laughed behind me as I continued walking in front of her. This next thirty days is going to be a handful watching her alone.

Chapter Seventeen- Vivian

"Kill me now," is all I said when I walked into the Guardians home.

We had to push through a few cameramen who were trying to get answers and news on the latest scoop. Already, questions and stories started spinning about the infamous Gabe Christain taking interest in my case and presences still within the Demon Lord's city. Scandalous. Romance. War. Oh, the conspiracies started rolling in. Yet none of them caught wind of the truth, that I had been sentenced and detained in Aztec.

Tahmeed and Destiny were tense as they sat at the breakfast bar with coffee. I walked over and grabbed one of the banana muffins from the plate that was supplied by our chef. He had already left at this time in the morning. They both scoped Gabe for what he was–a threat.

"Being tailed by such an adorable puppy doesn't seem all bad." Destiny said. The smile not reaching her eyes. It was a sweet and coaxing insult.

"I can see that manners are of no concern to Haymen's slaves." he shot back at her. Destiny blew air out of her nose infuriated and I wondered if a fight was about to erupt. I stepped to the side so I was no longer in her way. Like I was going to stop it.

"Don't think you can just waltz on in here. You aren't welcome," Tahmeed gritted through teeth and had turned into her silken blue demon which was notorious for taking a 'beating'. But against the force of an angel, that demon certainly had a chance. Destiny's tattoos glowed and she shifted into her smaller compacted siren. Although better designed for water, they were light and the siren scream would bleed out anyone's ears on land. She was swift and ready to fight.

Gabe took the threat seriously and extended his wings out.

"Now you can see why I love my girls. They are so lively," Haymen said teleporting into the room with a black swirl around him.

"I told the council that your input was unnecessary, we found your killer."

"And I told them it was," Gabe prompted back. I leaned against the bench and grabbed a second muffin watching the show unfold. Destiny stared at me with an intensity that could burn but I shrugged my shoulders and continued eating. Hey, I had two days now of having to deal with Angel Boy, maybe they might start to feel sorry for me. "I will host my own investigation to make sure that your intel is legitimate."

"As much as I want to entertain you, Gabe, I must protest. And I am surprised that under your own circumstances and the state of your own city, you want to spend so much time fawning over my Guardians. As beautiful as they are I will not release any of my harem," Haymen said walking over to me. I diverted my gaze but didn't stand upright. I was too exhausted for that. He leaned down and bit a large portion out of my hand. That caught my attention and Haymen smirked, all his dark features ominous as he straightened.

"My city is of no concern to you. It would appear your little bunny here has a record of those she sleeps with being killed within three days. What was it, the Widow they called you?" He asked me directly in a sneer.

Haymen stood in front of me, blocking Gabe's gaze. "Nothing of which has been proven and only gossip. Has your life become so boring since the war that you pick on little girls for entertainment? How depressing."

Gabe's wings flared only slightly. He had a different sort of movement from Luke. Gabe was more controlled, his wings didn't seem like an object attached to his back but were actually a part of him, fidgeting with every breath he took.

"You either humble my request or she goes back to Aztec. That was the agreement that you agreed to and permitted me leniency to stay within your city for thirty days." Haymen was quiet but the oppression of his power swept through the room. It was dark and even little black tendrils began to whip against the floor. He was pissed. Gabe wrapped his hands around the two handles on his back. The view when I peeked over was rather ravishing as his muscles flexed and chest bared to grab onto the two swords as if he might need to unsheathe them. Swords that he had never even bothered to use on me when we first fought. Rather insulting. What was more interesting was that he considered he had a chance against Haymen's power. I was curious to do more research on the last war, more specifically about Gabe and how far his history matched with Haymen's.

Although silent, Alexa walked through the room. Her skin had paled considerably since last time I had seen her which only emphasize the contrast of her thick black hair. "What did I miss?" I could tell that she had just come from the Shadow Minds room. I couldn't look away from the black circles under her eyes. Would I one day go through that, too? She looked like just a shell of the Guardian I knew her to be. Doc said that she was with her for the past week. We all knew why. Because something was getting to her in her sleep and she was slowly spiraling. "Doc wants you," she said, disregarding even Haymen in the room with all his pent up furry.

A tendril of his strength smashed her against the wall and he stormed up to her. We all diverted our gaze as he turned his back on Gabe and took his frustration out on her. He wrapped his hand around her throat digging in his now sharpened nails which appeared from nowhere.

"Do you deem it okay to come and interrupt when I am speaking," he seethed at her.

"No," she said diverting her gaze to the floor and making little noise against the trickles of blood on her neck. "I apologize, Haymen, for my behavior. It won't happen again."

He snarled at her and released his grip but not the power that still kept her to the wall. He backhanded her across the face, hard. Her eyes rolled in her head for a moment. She kept her eyes closed not willing to look him in the eyes.

Gabe stepped forward but I gave him an effective look of warning. I don't know why. Frankly I wanted to see his ass handed to him. But this was diplomacy and Haymen played to his own tune on everything he did. Especially being in a mood like this, we might all be caught in the crossfire. Alexa's lip began to bleed and swell from the slap. I wasn't sympathetic, we had all gone through similar treatment and it was just a reminder to stay in line. I did however want to step out of this tension and it was either going to go one of two ways. I would be bitch slapped as well or I would be allowed to leave the room. I took my third banana muffin, rather slowly, and then pushed off my casual pose against the breakfast bench. I began to walk for the hall and Haymen's eyes snapped on me, wild and dangerous.

"I need to report to Doc," I said simply. It had been two days now since my last dream and report. "When you have the time, I will report my other findings to you. Until then I would like to be permitted to work as usual?" I asked. Although having an angel tracking me wasn't ideal I wanted to return to the orphanage. After seeing Alice and a real living Shadow person that attacked us during our sleep, I was certain the same kind of activity was somehow involved with the orphanage. That and I wanted to find information on the demon that swelled my belly. I still couldn't feel it slither like it had once around me, but there was now a disturbing and larger presence within me. Like in the pit of my stomach I had a compressed amount of power I had no access too. I was certain the demon was sleeping within me and I had to find out what it would do to me over time and how to get rid of it.

Haymen's gaze pinned me for a moment longer and then Gabe, as he stepped forward as if to follow me. I counted down from three in my head. That's how long it usually took Haymen to react in a blood thirsty manner. Three. Two. One. Instead, he vanished. His black power misted to where he once was. Alexa dropped to the ground. She simply stood up and kept walking, not even bothering to brush off her clothes.

Gabe's jaw tightened, deplored by her wounds. "Don't get upset sweetheart," I started as I walked down the hallway. "We're just demon summoners, remember? Evil, disgusting creatures in your eyes... you couldn't possibly be seeing us as women, could you?" That snapped his attention away from his hero like behavior. I allowed him to walk the length of the hallway with me so I could see that one frustrated expression on his face.

The door opened for me to the Shadow Minds room. From the outside it looked like an honest enough 'medical check-up'. I took a step inside the room and watched him as he tried to step in. Doc was behind me unamused by my behavior. As soon as he tried to step inside to follow me the ward around the room pushed him back and bounced him against the wall expectantly. I laughed and hit my knee.

"The funny thing about having a witch for a Doc is that no one else is allowed to come into this room but her patients," I said still laughing and wiping away exaggerated tears. The truth was this was only heavily warded and guarded by her because no one else besides Haymen, Doc, and the Guardians were to know what was happening behind these walls. The recordings were only exclusive to us, well as far as I knew.

"Our agreement was-" he said stepping forward. Click–the door was shut. Once it did, I wiped the smug expression off my face. I used humor and laughter only to piss him off but his following me everywhere was definitely going to be a problem.

"You should be more careful. That isn't just any angel," Doc said as she began to set everything up. I wondered how she knew that I had data to record despite not yet having the chance to page her. "Before your time he was acknowledged as the War Angel. Some even thought of him as some kind of warrior god depending on how serious his followers were."

I rested on the white chair. A war angel huh? "I suppose Haymen and he weren't batting for the same team before the treaty." That much I could put together myself without doing research.

"Leaders on both sides. Those from the old days are curious of what the outcome would've been if the treaty hadn't been agreed upon first." She said taking my blood. I watched the black syrup like substance leach out of my veins.

"No one can match Haymen," I said absolute. She arched an eyebrow at me in a questioning manner. Could Gabe?

"Haymen is powerful. I also believe that he would've won. But that angel out there is one of the only forces I've seen that might be able to counter Haymen for days at a time. Like I said, he's no normal angel and rather infuriating that he was permitted to be within this city and keep an eye on someone so close such as you. You Guardians are Haymen's pride and joy. It's an insult."

Well, pride and joy got backhanded across the face three minutes ago. I watched the capsule of blood and her witch scribblings that I couldn't make sense of.

"You found one of my demons through the sampling?" I asked her. I haven't had time to discuss with her the Hellhound that she insisted was one of my contracted demons. She looked at me and it was only for a moment but I saw it there. Fear. The first I have ever seen on Doc. Hellhound's were revered for their ruthless nature and loyalty to Haymen. But they were known as extinct since the last war. Surely those results couldn't be correct. As if reading my mind, she said.

"The results don't lie. You will believe it too, when it first approaches you. What I might suggest is seeing if you can find a book or so and do your research before it comes forth. All I personally know is they had one certain weakness. Sunlight."

I considered that. My current demons had certain weaknesses. My water demon couldn't last long outside of water. My cat demon was sensitive towards gases and poisons. My succubus was quick to heal but my strength at my weakest.

"So, they can't walk in the day," I thought to myself keeping note. Luckily, I wouldn't be permanently stuck in any one of my demon's bodies and could change when it suited me.

"Not only during the day," Doc added. "But also, those who can manifest light against darkness." She said nudging her head into the direction of the door where I imagine Angel Boy was probably probing open with a pair of tongs.

"He can create sunlight? Well my goodness, the sun really does shine out of his ass," And I hoped that he heard it because I thought that was a really good one. Even though I already knew the walls were soundproof.

"You might want to be careful as to how much you antagonize him, Vi," was the sound advice she gave before the small device latched its four spikes into the back of my neck. I scowled at her from the lack of warning.

"Shadow Mind's activated," the system sounded. All humor had washed from my expression as I was left to watch the remains of my sleep. It had been another memory before I became a Guardian. That was two now in a row and I knew as Doc looked between the video surveillance and the pad in her arm that she was trying to decipher why it appeared as a memory. I didn't want a new one but if I continued conjuring my memories and the attacks I had from when I was younger it would only raise more questions. Ones that I wasn't willing to answer. A few minutes passed as my last dream was projected on the screen until the moment I had woken up.

"I'll ask you again Miss Vivian, is this or not a memory because your brain waves are-"

"It's not Doc," I said jumping off my seat and ripping the prongs out myself. "Now if you'll excuse me I've been locked in a prison for the past two days and feel filthy. I put my hand on the door and tried to open it but it was still closed. I looked back at Doc who hasn't yet lifted the ward to let me out. She looked at me for a long time and I effectively looked around the room for weapons that I could use if she wanted to go down this way. I still didn't have complete access to my demons but I could feel them slowly unfurl. That damn fairy dust shit that Angel Boy blew at me really knocked them out.

Taking the safer option, I could feel the protection of the room lift and the door clicked open.

"Have a good day, Miss Vivian." she said not turning her back to me. She eyed me as I walked out. Smart woman.

I raised my finger to Gabe as soon as I walked out. He was infuriated. "Don't. I need a shower and can't be bothered putting up with your rules and regulation spiel right now."

The brush of his warm thumb reached out to the four small holes in the back of my neck.

"What is this?" he asked. I slapped his hand away and covered it with my hair. I gave him a broody look which might've worked if it wasn't against the master of brooding. "I asked you a question." He said, following me into my room. I had to answer him with nothing. I stopped and arched an eyebrow at him.

"This is my room," I said pointedly. "Get out. Go hitchhike to a campervan or something."

"I told you I will be following you everywhere," he simply said. I cocked my head to the side hauntingly and expressing my hatred for the man in front of me; some might have even considered my expression demonic.

I smirked and began to push down my pants slowly and teasing. His eyes shot straight to the creamy skin tone of my legs. It was an initial reaction before he turned his head to the side and swallowed. Well look at that, he is a man after all. His face showed the expression of utter disgust but his initial expression glowed like most men when I appeared in front of them. His eyes had turned feral and with wonder. It was only a split second but it was there. My succubus had trained me well in the art of seduction and knowing when a man wanted me. She surfaced, my beautiful succubus no longer dormant and enjoying the smell of arousal in the room. He noticed my changed form but didn't comment.

"Do you really think that I've never seen a woman before?"

"I just assumed with that pole up your ass you were still a virgin," I huskily said. He shot me a look of irritation and looked my slim legs up and down. My tail flicked back and forth. I could tell he was disgusted by my demonic form but the enchanting part about the succubus was there. There was always an air about her that made her awfully seductive. She still had my figure which was lean and that of a warrior's. I walked over to him, not letting him take his eyes off me. I haven't even started taking off my shirt and I had no intention to, either. He asked too many questions and I didn't want him further questioning the extent and size of my tattoos. But it was all part of the fun. I would try to drive him mad.

"Do you think I'm not immune to your charm?" He asked towering over me with his arms crossed over his chest. I looked down with a smile able to see his bulge through his jeans that said otherwise.

"Your virgin brain might be but I think your body might have a very different reaction," I said, sweeping closer towards him. I'll give him credit. He didn't move from his positioning but neither did he press himself against me like most would have already done.

I smiled and put the succubus demon away. My crimson hair splayed around my shoulders and he continued to look at me with the same intensity.

"Shower," he gritted out. I smiled at him before turning and feeling his eyes burn into the back of me, watching as my toned ass walked away. Oh yes, I might have some fun with this. How long would it take for an Angel Boy, no, the revered War Angel to break either by lust or pure frustration? Well, I was aiming for a record.

CHAPTER EIGHTEEN- GABE

Menace. That's all she was. And I would haul her ass—all one hundred and fifty pounds of it—if I had to so she was reminded of who she was dealing with. I was frustrated that despite my self-control and hatred for demons, she did incite a physical reaction from me. She was beautiful. As deadly as her spitting venom and ability to kill. Most feared me but here I was being mocked. There was a reason why Haymen didn't want me so close and this little new generation Guardian was ignorant to the fact of who I was and what I could do to her.

The others had some sense about them which is why her roommates changed almost instantly into one of their demon forms. Their demon ancestry knew who I was so why didn't Vivian's react in the same defensive way? Why was she not scared of me? It has been a *very* long time since anyone had the audacity to speak to me like that, whether Haymen's pet or not. Others knew their place.

I looked towards the open doors of her balcony. I could sense an angel close by and knew it wasn't just any *one.* I heard Vivian singing some terrible girl power song in the shower and assessed how long I might have to confront our new guest. I would make sure that this conversation didn't last long. I jumped off the balcony silently. The strength and extension of my wings swooped me up into the sky of day. I would've preferred night and cloud coverage like most of my conversations. I kept soaring up until the air got thinner and I broke through the first layer of clouds. There, slowly padding her soft pink wings was Lyra. Instead of her fighter's gear she came to me in a silken gold dress that swept around her curves. Her blonde curls were unaffected by the wind. She sat on one of the clouds not that it could hold her weight if her wings weren't beating but it was for added effect that she had been waiting.

"What are you doing in Shabeah, I told you to stay and aid Torrin in my stead," I growled at her. I didn't want any of my angels in this city and I had directly ordered all of them not to come. Her disregard for my word was becoming far too frequent. I was also pissed by her cockiness to enter the city of demons without any military garment or obvious weapons.

"Would you believe me if I said I missed you?" she said looking at her nails and shrugging her shoulders. Which is exactly why I had never divulged in Lyra; for all her beauty and brains and ample offers she overstated her power.

"Go," I growled and it rumbled through sky. She looked up into the dark clouds that began to sweep over. I was angry and didn't handle control when my direct orders were being ignored. Panic slightly sunk in but not enough for her to leave empty handed.

"We don't understand your way of thinking. Please, Gabe. You are the king of your city-" I growled at her term 'King'. I hated the term it was disrespectful to who I was and what I stood for. King was the title of selfish human men. "Apologies, Gabe." She said dipping her head and started to concern herself with the dark clouds that began thundering above.

"Thirty days is all you have to handle. If not less. My investigation is underway and if you find yourself meddling on it again you will find that your wings won't be able to fly for a year." A crackle of thunder lit the sky and hit the ground in the forestry outside of Shabeah. I needed to release this anger and build-up of frustration. Her supple skin went paler and I knew she feared the coloring of my eyes which would have changed from a forest green to a winter storm blue. I have killed thousands of men with these eyes. She was only but one.

She came closer as if to comfort me, her voice ever so small.

"You don't need to concern yourself with this investigation, Let one of the others do it for you, let me be of assistance!" She said as if to reach out to me. Her admiration had gone too far and her desperation to touch me only thickened my revolt in that moment. Another bang hit the ground and this time it wasn't too far from her.

"Do you think I would jeopardize someone else in the city that is overlooked by Haymen himself after one of our own was just murdered?! Leave!" I ordered and this time for all the sass and overconfidence she swept in with, she fled with her tail between her legs. I inhaled, wishing I didn't have to be so cruel to my own kind. Not all of them had fought beside me in the last war, many of my fellow guards had been killed by Haymen's demons, only a few remained. They didn't understand what the edge of war looked like. It always only started with the death of one... and then the edges of villages and then empire against empire. This treaty and human world was the center point for all the other worlds and homes that had been destroyed in that war. That's why so many demons and angels now lived here. Demons had numerous worlds whereas us angels had only one, chose to live in only one. We were lucky to have protected our own during the last war. Never would I let it come to that again. Since then I dedicated my life and living quarters to the human world to watch those who might try to create another resistance or war.

When Lyra had completely vanished safely, I swooped back down trying to ease my fury. I lightly padded on the deck of Vivian's balcony and knew as soon as I touched ground that her usual dark energy that surrounded her wasn't in the room. The shower was still going and to double check I opened up the door. She was gone. I pushed the door back and, in a rage, swept through the doors and swooped up again. I headed back for the clouds so I could hide amongst them for coverage and sense out the demonic energy that surrounded her. I made sure to familiarize myself with her energy so I knew where she was when she decided to run. I thought surely she couldn't have gotten too far in the time I was gone... evidently I was mistaken.

CHAPTER NINETEEN- VIVIAN

The song 'She'll be coming around the Mountain here she comes!' Kept playing in my head as I darted through the city on my slick motorbike. This time I took the back streets and areas that had coverage and confusing trails. I had the feeling that the quickly brewing storm behind me had something to do with Gabe's temperament. Somehow even the overpowering drift of wind and smell of rain... felt like him. If I wasn't zipping through streets I would have considered wiping away the residue that sprinkled on me in disgust. But I wasn't a fool. As I had familiarized myself with angelic energy I imagined he had done the same, which meant that he would be tracking me right now. For some reason, humans had created the concept that angels could do no wrong and were forever happy and bright. Just because he was an angel didn't mean that his power and temperament didn't mix just like the storm that was now brewing. Angels could be consumed by darkness and evil and there were dark angels for this very reason.

If I were lucky, my tricks and zipping through the city might've mucked up a lot of my trail and scent. He could be searching for an hour and that's all I need for the business that I intended. He couldn't know about the Shadow people in our sleep. Or whatever they liked to call themselves. And I certainly couldn't let him follow me on this case where I might be tracking more like Alice. I pulled up sharply at the gutter in front of the orphanage. I took my helmet off and stormed towards the entrance wary of my time. Tahmeed had taken over my case during the few days I was gone with little success. Without her permission or knowledge, I took it back. This was my hunt.

My arrival was welcomed by Dorothy who waited for me atop the stairs of the orphanage. It has now been three days since I'd last been here and her being here meant that they didn't take my advice to leave. I paced up the stairs greeting her at the door.

"There was another attack two nights ago," she began as she walked me inside.

"The children?" I asked stepping into the ill and twisted residue in the air. Something had been here not that long ago.

"No, Mr. Greenhouse." she said, tears spilling over her cheeks. "But what he had done to the children," she sobbed. I had no time for her sentiment and walked through the main hallway which reeked of vile and evil. The hairs on my nape raised up high and I looked into each room skeptically, ignoring what Dorothy asked me, flustered and panicked by my rash behavior. Something was in here but I couldn't get an exact location on it because it surrounded me. It was watching me.

One child screamed as I opened the door, startled by my sudden entrance. I left it open allowing my keen hearing to overpower all of their breathing and now quiet noises. My tattoos glowed bright blue through my sleeveless leather shirt and I turned into my cat demon. Hackles instantly rose on my back as she hissed on the intrusion that was in this children's home. It was good timing to have entered while the demon was here. The chilling feeling was similar to speaking with Alice in the Aztec. Maybe it really were our nightmare shadows who has infested this children's home.

I rounded the corner after checking the numerous rooms trailing down the hallway. I didn't dare open my cat's eye and sixth sense in the presence of whatever evil it was that lurked. This was not a standard demon. I stopped at the kitchen doors where numerous children were once again cooking meals. The chill that shuddered through me pulled back my ears and the single ring of the bell on my tail rang. All the children went silent.

Some looked at me in fear and others in awe. I supposed it was not every day they saw a naked cat demon at the entrance of their kitchen. My clothes always vanished when I turned into a demon so their true form could be appreciated.

I searched the room unable to locate the exact positioning or concentration of the evil. The girl which I had noticed last time with brown plaited hair walked up to me. My eyes narrowed on her and I retracted my claws so she wouldn't be so scared.

"Have you come to save us?" she asked with tears in her eyes. The child was petrified. This small girl had seen something and survived it.

I pushed her out of the way as the teenage boy behind her jumped at us with a knife in hand. He swung at where she once stood and began swinging at the other children barbarically. I grabbed him and pulled him into the hall before he could hurt anyone.

"Close all the doors!" I shouted at Dorothy without watching her do so. I circled the teenage boy whose laughter echoed the hall. And there it was, the same projecting tone that Alice had. But this one was different as if it were a completely different soldier possessing the boy.

"Oh, how easy you are to bait," his voice said far older than the red haired, freckled face boy. "Children are always such an easy lure. And to think, Haymen claims that your kind doesn't feel."

"I'm going to beat the shit out of you until you release that boy," I hissed.

"But how do you kill something that doesn't truly exist?" He asked me, his head cocked to the side awkwardly. I had heard and lived that line once before with that exact same voice. This *thing* had once attacked *me* when I was younger.

His veins deepened in blue around his face and his eyes were black pins. My claws were out and bared. My ears pulled back as I felt the shadows of the room vanquish. The lights began to flicker and only a small brightness seeped in from the door in the distance. All the curtains shut tight and suddenly I realized I wasn't just dealing with one nonphysical demon that could possess but numerous. The walls felt as if they were breathing in and out around me trying to squeeze my very breath.

The freckled boy breathed out a husky laugh. "A Guardian's fear is always so sweet. And you have attentively grabbed our attention. We will enjoy eating your body from the inside."

I felt the mass of something coming towards me and I jumped from it. I couldn't see it but my cat's demon's senses were aware when something paranormal was close. I jumped again as a second dove for me. I rolled on the ground blocking the knife the boy tried to stab me with. It scraped past me as I jumped away, being caught off guard by the invisible force that tried to attach itself to me.

Despite being a teen boy, the child fought like a warrior, an ancient one. I jumped back and forth, agile like my cat demon. Screams began erupting from the kitchen and another two young girls ran out with sharp blades. I was cornered in the room.

The laugh that echoed out of the little girl with brown plaited hair erupted and it was familiar. It was the same laugh that had possessed Alice.

"So, you didn't die?" I growled.

"Human children are so easy to possess," he gleamed through the child's face. "Thank you for freeing me from Alice's body. I was trapped in there until her body died." I hadn't killed Alice but maybe the demon that hid within me had, like it had to all the inmates that tried to kill me.

My hackles had risen. Killing the young was against everything the cat demons lived for. They had purposely lured me here to the children, knowing that only my cat demon would be able to detect them. None of my other demons had sixth sense. I would be defenseless even if I changed.

"You took something very interesting from Aztec. I had been hopeful it would lure to Alice's body but it seemed to reject that ideal," the brown-haired girl chuckled. "So instead I watched it host inside of you. And my master would very much like that for his own body."

Even I didn't know what crammed itself into my body but if it held value for these demons, I wasn't going to hand it over. And for all that creature's power, if it truly was concealed within me, it certainly wasn't helping me kick ass today. Instinct to survive was drilling in for me to make my way to an exit–even jump out of the windows–if I had to but then the nature of my cat demon got the better of me. I had to save these children. I growled at the notion. Sentiments always got people killed. I wasn't a hero and would never be revered as one. But if

I could lure them far enough from the children then maybe they stood a chance.

The glass of the windows shattered and Gabe swept in. His landing shook the building. Fuck. Not even ten minutes. And how glorified he looked to watch my ass be handed to me in time. I jumped away from one of the phantoms that swept for my body only to have a second catch me off guard and throw me across the hall and into the door on the other end. The impact crushed my ribs and dislocated my shoulder. But that wasn't my issue. The impressive force felt like talons ripping apart my skin and trying to take my body. I pushed it back with my own demonic force, resisting it. My presence seemed to be weak against its force as those talons continued slashing into me. I gritted my teeth to prevent the screams that tried to claw out.

The door behind me crumbled under the force and I was thrown onto the balcony. I coughed at the impact but gave myself enough time to roll even under its force to prevent the young girl with plaits bringing her knife down on me.

Light swept through the hallway and I heard the screams of the children who have been possessed. Gabe stood in the hallway his, wings glowing so brightly that even my cat demon wanted to shrivel away. The force began to retract. It was a combination of Gabe and his light, a weakening of anything that was formidably dark. I rolled onto my side and noticed a hooded figure that chanted at the front gate with gold bangles around their delicate wrist. Witch. I struggled to get up considering my broken wrist and ribs. Whatever the chant was those who were possessed were struggling to stay in their hosted form. An exorcism spell perhaps?

I ventured toward the figure who stepped towards me, inviting me closer. Until I was overshadowed by that of a pissed angel. The witch before me scattered into hundreds of orange leaves, leaving its remains to the wind. No. I ran over, awkwardly trying to hold my broken body together. Left behind was a pentagon burn mark of the spell it had teleported in and out of. I knew better than to leave without evidence of the witch. I hooked the light green hair that was attached to the singed grass and put it in my pocket. Any material that was either theirs or a part of them could be used for a location spell. And I knew just the right witch to find them for me. I looked behind me noticing the steam that misted from the floorboards of the three children who had been possessed. All of them had pentagon markings from where the witch had exorcised them out as well.

I assessed the streets and the fog that lifted as soon as they were gone. What had happened? Things escalated from zero to a hundred in seconds. I tried to center myself and think clearly, past the pain of my body that began to try and knit itself back together. Gabe stood behind me and I ignored him not wanting to deal with his pouting mood.

"Three, two-" he said and with speed I couldn't anticipate, he popped my dislocated shoulder back into place. Black and white starred my eyes but I only grunted through the pain not giving him the satisfaction to hear me whimper. My broken ribs would take their time to heal but I made note to not let it show. My tattoos glowed bright and I turned into my succubus. She was the fastest at healing and I concentrated all my thoughts onto that one spot. It might take an hour or so but at least it was better than healing at human speed.

So many thoughts swept through me. For some reason these shadow people were after me specifically. The former Alice, whose name I didn't know had seen the beast from Aztec harbor in me. It mentioned that it was hoping it would choose to harbor in Alice's body, which meant that the demon was relevant to the Guardians. Even with the demon choosing to harbor in me I had no new contracts nor tattoos. I didn't even know if demons could do that after I was reborn into a Guardian. I thought the contract only held seven demons?

There was no one in this world that I trusted, especially to ask about this. If the demon that slumbered inside of me held value then others would come for me. I could never ask Haymen and if it was seen in a negative light I was as good as dead. I could however ask one person, who if I paid enough would always stay quiet. He called himself Black Crow and if I needed information I would find him in the Black Market. It was a gamble to ask even him who would never show me his face.

Even so, I still had to go to the black market to request a locator's spell on the witch with green hair. Why had she taken the children that were possessed and what spell was she chanting? Who was she?

"What is today?" I asked Gabe as I turned to face him finally. He looked at me with disbelief and pointed back at the orphanage. His gesture was implying for me to deal with the carnage that was left behind instead of focusing elsewhere. Dismissing him I swiped the medal implanted on my ear and my blue screen appeared in front of me. Tuesday. Those who could tell me when the next black markets were operative would be in the usual place today.

I began walking towards my bike but Gabe grabbed my arm. Tight. I hid the wince and cold shudder that ran through my body as he further hurt my ribs.

"You are going to tell me about everything that was just in there right now. That was old demonic energy. Predating the last war," he said his eyebrows knitting together in fury. "Why are you taking on something that big?"

"I thought they were just the standard possessing demons," I said trying to pull my arm away. I couldn't tell him anything but it did pique my interest to know that he had felt that kind of power before.

"Anyway, I've got time to kill now so why don't we grab a bite," I said pulling my arm free. But first I had to do the 'good guy' thing and talk to Dorothy. I had to handle this before it hit the press. Haymen would not be pleased about this getting out. Especially when it might be bigger than anything we had faced before.

Chapter Twenty- Gabe

Slowly, things were knitting together in front of me. I haven't felt that kind of ancient power in a long time and the notion that it was in Haymen's city now was bad. I had previous intel that the city crime and reports have increased and I always kept tabs on Haymen specifically because he was always up to no good. And for the few wins that I found him doing illegal subject matters that stood against the high court, there was no bulletproof evidence that led back to him every time. It didn't help that the Higher court, not just the Angel court that Vivian had stood trial on, had three high and powerful demons to show equality, and he was one of them. Forces like this were to be reported to the higher council by Haymen himself as it was his city, but I knew if questioned he would deny all knowledge of it. But watching Vivian in that moment when she was pinned against the wall by the phantom power, her stricken face with fear, not that she would admit, made me realize it was her first time against one, or being attacked by the Volv. Perhaps after Alice had been killed in Aztec the one that had possessed her was now luring and after Vivian. But there was more than one Volv there. The time of their hiding was now coming to a close.

I was almost immune to their attacks as most ancient angels were. Darkness could not find its way into those who were pure and had the power of light on their side for so long. Well such is the notion, but not all angels were pure and it was those that in the past war they fed off trying to gain access to their body. I had killed four angels from such possession. There was no way to call them back after a Volv had dug its claws in so deep. They were like a parasite and our young were just as vulnerable as the human children who had become their easy victims. Human bodies couldn't withhold the foreign entities for long.

The Volv had many names hosted over numerous records, but those books were burned in the historical war and so their kind was hardly whispered in fear it would draw attention to our homes. Such darkness was a threat to even those within the demon world. They were beyond other species of demons. They were creatures that held no physical form themselves and jumped from host to host. And they would become as strong as the ability of their host's body. Some called them Shadows, others referenced them to demon possessive species they could understand. But even with those demons they had shape and couldn't possess someone for the entirety of their life, it would leave their physical form weakened and vulnerable. Some called them entities, some humans in the day had even gone as far as 'bad' ghosts, or my favorite, the soul of witches that had once been burned. Even the witches denied it because that ancestral power and wisdom was passed on to the next generation.

In the last war the Volv had swept amongst camps, both angels and demons and even humans, and attacked those who slept at night possessing their bodies and smearing blood amongst their camp. They were an enemy that could not be countered and that's why their disappearance was celebrated. But much more happened prior to the end of the war and certain things made me question as to how relatable they might've been now. Their silence was instantly noted after the death of Haymen's Queen.

I knew that Vivian wouldn't tell me much. Why would she? No matter how much I tried to force it out of her and there were numerous ways I could try. But some were within the jurisdiction and others were not. By technicality I was considered a guest within this city and able to continue my own investigations. That didn't permit me to torture Vivian to extract information and by the obvious gestures at her trial, she was a favorite of Haymen's which was something I would have to be wary of. I could seduce her and make her comfortable to tell her secrets, but I was disgusted to think of even touching her in such a way. That and despite her irritable attitude and ability to jump into action without consideration of her surroundings or consequence, I could admit that she is a calculated creature who would out any form of manipulation on her... why? Because she was a grand manipulator herself. All of Haymen's Guardians were. Although their personalities differed and the demons they were contracted to changed, they were all trained for the same execution of stray demons but I considered them to have other purposes. Hopefully I would be able to discover what that purpose is while watching one of Haymen's favored ones so closely.

It was useless to ask Vivian more questions. She would never tell me and only play games. So instead I would follow her and obtain answers for myself from what I would see. The moment I was gone for only a few minutes she came directly here which meant that she was trying to keep this secret and she was already aware of the situation and perhaps the Volv's involvement here with the children.

I watched Vivian carefully as she walked back towards the older woman at the orphanage. I stared at her, pissed as all hell that these children were involved amidst such evil. I also didn't take kindly to not being answered, even if this wasn't my city and out of my control. It appeared that the little miss needed to educate herself on who she was actually dealing with and I would make these next few weeks for her an uncomfortable living hell.

She thought that I didn't notice the way she walked or the obvious wince of her fractured ribs. I took a breath trying not to spew my frustration at her pride. She took a heavy blow which even splintered apart the foundation of the door behind her. And then there was a witch involved who took the three children possessed, perhaps the witch was working with the Volv but that didn't make sense if she took them away when Vivian was clearly being overwhelmed. The pure light from my wings would've blinded the Volv as they had many times before in the war, a trick I picked up to pacify them but not all of my kind could do.

I ushered away my calculating thoughts and followed Vivian's lead of clean-up. I could've left it to her but it didn't sit well with me when children were involved. I scanned the rooms silently assuring the petrified children that everything was going to be okay. By the time I left, each room seemed less rattled and in awe to see a real living angel. It was somewhat rare to see in a city that was governed by demons.

By that time Vivian was done within only minutes, humans and demons alike came into the orphanage and began leading the children out. Clean-up. And I knew that it would've been the request of Haymen. Three children missing and an assault like this would be splayed in the newspaper and as I walked out behind Vivian the flash of a bright light and a photo was taken. Already the media were on it. I tucked my wings in tight making sure that no one would get too cocky and touch them.

Vivian sassily swayed her hips confidently in succubus form. Her pointed tail swaying back and forth. She smiled at the cameraman, only one as she walked up to him with a smile that would snap men in half to be looked at by her twice. She leaned in towards him and whispered something into his ear. He didn't even realize her fingers were curling around the camera. She stepped back and his glossed over effect came back to awareness. She hadn't done anything illegal but her succubus was a natural manipulator which was what made them so dangerous. Her presence alone was overpowering.

He complained hysterically when he tried to retrieve his camera but with the same smile she dropped it on the ground and speared her sharp tail through it. I noticed the slight wince she made. She went to place her hand on her ribs but instead flexed her hand. She warned him not to touch it in case she excreted poison on it. And then she continued walking, ignorant to me who walked past her. I looked down on the media clown as I walked past and his eyes lit up.

"Mr. Christain, you've seemed to take a liking to our Vivian, she is a beauty," he said. And there was animosity in his eyes as he held out his pen and paper ready to conduct the interview. Anything for a scoop.

"That she is," I simply said and knew that it would make headlines. So maybe I had to start playing this a little differently. Because that one caption would make it into the media and be spread with rumors and conspiracy. This was a way that I could unsheathe Haymen because I knew how he would react to such garbage, as would I. But it would unhinge him if his little pet was seemingly frolicking with an angel. Or me specifically. It might also take away from my sense of investigation. I would deny the media later, even if it stretched wider and into my own city which I was certain it would. But those who ruled under me knew my hatred for this city and everything in it, especially a Guardian who was property of Haymen.

So, let us play this game... Because I am certain Vivian is already playing it.

CHAPTER TWENTY-ONE - VIVIAN

It turns out broken ribs are extremely painful and I struggled to breath let alone properly ride my bike. If it wasn't for the hindrance of the impressive three meter wing span trailing me, I might've opted to have someone else take me. But pride is a funny thing and there was no way I was going to let my bothersome plus one know I was hurting. The call for the clean-up crew was short and sweet and already they would have most of the children relocated and refurbishing the orphanage as if nothing had happened for when the rest of the media swooped in. What I wasn't looking forward to was the conversation with Haymen if he thought all the extra activity as of late was bringing in too much attention.

I went to the outer edge of the city, to an old burger joint which made the best fries simply because they changed their oil daily. To the rest of the burger places out there, honestly, it's not that hard and on top of that their burgers were the size of my face. After a hard day's work, I had quite the appetite. My ribs have almost completely healed together as I pulled up on the curb to the dodgy looking burger joint and walked in. What I liked about these parts of the neighborhood was it wasn't glistening like the central city, there weren't many cameras and best of all there was silence.

I was certain the couple who owned and cooked at the shop knew that I was one of the Guardians, but they were discrete and served me all the same. They treated me as if I was a normal customer. Which at times was rather refreshing opposed to the elite meals and photos that would be taken of me. It became ridiculous that whenever we ate publicly it was considered a trend. Sometimes I just wanted a big old cheeseburger or chunk of meat that our chef refused to cook because he considered it too 'cheap' and 'not real food'. Seeing some of those posts on blogs have actually made me realize how much I could shove in my mouth at once. Even I was impressed. Not glamourous but still entitled to media coverage apparently.

The blue of my tattoos glowed bright and I shifted back into my normal form. The ribs were nicely knitted together and I didn't have to lift my shirt to know that bruising would still remain for a bit longer. That would heal overnight.

The burger joint was long overdue for a window clean and the door sometimes struggled to open as it caught on the bottom of the 'welcome' mat. I wanted to turn and see the face of Angel Boy who probably preferred his delicacies of rich snails and bleeding steak with a side of Crème Brûlée.

The old man smiled when I walked in and I looked at the board only briefly already having in mind of what I wanted to order. "Two chicken burgers with the lot and a large serving of fries with chicken salt. A large Fanta too, please. Oh, and two deep fried mars bars, please."

Gabe choked behind me and I gave him one effective look over my shoulder.

"It's not the meal size that shocks me but the use of manners. Like a child in a candy store," he retorted back.

I turned my back on him irritated. I had gotten giddily excited for my food, I always did. "And he will pay when he orders, make sure to charge double," I said pointing at Gabe and walking to the singular booth in the corner. The white and black squares of the dining floor reminded me of a very retro time. There were only a few chairs and tables and I made sure to sit at the one that had no window view and was tucked in the corner with only a one booth chair. I liked to remain out of sight here. It was like my own little moment of silence.

The wife of the shop owner walked over to me and placed three books downs for me to select from. "I liked these three, the other two were okay but I thought they might interest you. We have similar tastes so I would probably recommend this one," she said placing one on top of the others. I read over the blurb and gave her a smile. Oh yes, this is definitely one I would read.

I began reading it before my meal was brought out to me and scooted over my large Fanta, ignoring the masculine angel who looked far too big to be sitting in such a small room. He was careful not to brush his wings against anything.

"What is this, some kind of book club thing? And romance of all things, really? You're a demon-"

I tsked him to stop interrupting me and continued reading.

"Surely you aren't hoping to fall in love one day? Will I find an online dating profile?" he asked.

"I don't believe in love," I simply said as the woman came and placed my burgers and fries in front of me. With book in one hand and a burger in the other I began multi-tasking. Sir pretty boy hadn't ordered anything as I anticipated but he did pay for mine... shockingly. Such a do-gooder.

"You did once. I've seen the pictures to prove it," he said.

My gaze shot up to his. "That was before I died and was inhabited by demons. You'd be surprised how much that might change one's character and ideals." I said taking a massive bite out of my burger and breathing out from frustration. I purposefully made sure to eat loudly and with my mouth open. He said a few more things but I chose to ignore him. About halfway through my book and two burgers later I was still grazing on my chips when I came across the page I was after.

A day, time, and location were scribbled into the book of when the next black-markets would be held. One week from now. I held in my sigh. One week seemed so far away. Especially having to deal with an insufferable follower. I took a mental note. I would keep busy until then. Surely I would find something using other resources. I polished off my deep-fried chips, keeping my head down in the book as the next customer came in, hoping that they wouldn't recognize me. I enjoyed this quiet spot and although most that walked through here were those who were familiar with the black markets, there were a few who were just ordinary people walking off the street.

The man's audible gasp made me realize that was utter stupidity when a brilliant angel was sitting in the middle of the room staring at me. The man wouldn't be able to see me past the mass of his wings but I finished the paragraph I was on and put it down taking note of the page number. As if reading my thoughts, the woman collected my dirty dishes and told me to keep it because the ending to the story was rather good.

I walked passed and barged my shoulder into the gawker. I was getting up to a good part in my book too. I jumped onto my bike and allowed the thrill of zipping through the streets and challenging Gabe to keep up. He had given up on telling me to stop and just followed me in silence. I wondered who would exhaust first. Me or the angel who was hundreds of years old, if not more. I certainly knew I'd give it my best, old man.

*

After doing rounds in the city, I parked my bike in the garage to our lake house waiting for the electric gates to come down. With very little space remaining Gabe swept in low and came onto his haunches standing as the becoming dark room lit up with light from his wings. Damn, and here I thought he might either get locked out or the rolling door might crush him. I walked through the side door which led through the Japanese garden and pool and into the side of the kitchen. I noticed that he was scanning everything, exit points, entrance points, and surveillance cameras–and there were plenty. Haymen did like to keep a close eye on his property. I opened up the white French doors to the kitchen and was welcomed by Tahmeed's black blood pillowing out from her stomach and onto the white tiles.

"What the hell happened to you?" I asked. Destiny was pressing a towel against her, to help stop the bleeding. Tahmeed winced at the pain and pressure. The side of her stomach had been sliced open deep.

"Just seal it shut," she hissed at Destiny.

"You will still have internal bleeding. We should call Doc," Destiny said. I went over and compressed the towel to make room for Destiny. Internal bleeding was an issue but Tahmeed would heal in due time. It was the nasty smell of burning flesh and scar that would remain, that would be the bitch. Tahmeed didn't even have to explain why she didn't want Doc called. Because then she would have to admit her failure of a mission. We were weapons, if even for a moment of compromise, Haymen would be displeased. I looked over my shoulder at Alexa who had her hands crossed over her chest and watched from the door with a vacant look. I wasn't even ready to tackle that issue right now. I could feel Gabe's eyes glued to us from the door, taking everything in. I suppose it was odd that we actually helped one another from time to time, it wasn't a common thing for demons who we were made up of. But our generation seemed somewhat closer opposed to the others I had heard about. This was only something small and honestly, we had nothing to gain to see one another die sooner rather than later.

Destiny's blue tattoos lit up and not much about her physical appearance had changed except that every hair on her body had turned into flickering flames. Her fire demon was her most powerful and even I was weary of it. She had shown that at times she couldn't fully control that much power. She had set alight an entire building accidently. If she weren't snapped out of it sooner; if she had forgotten that she needed to rein in and control the flames, she could've burned down the whole city.

"Push it close together," she said. I looked down at the wide gash questioning how on earth I was supposed to do even that. With a quick second I threw away the towel and black blood began spilling over my hands. I pushed the skin as close as I could, Tahmeed was screaming from the pain as I tried to get the edges close. There was still a large gap and trying to make sure her guts didn't spill out the side was quite a serious matter. As soon as Destiny's finger touched the edge of her skin and began to meld the skin together, Tahmeed passed out from the pain. Before I moved my hands, Gabe came and collected her in his arms so she wouldn't fall to the ground.

Destiny merged the two pieces of flesh together melding it. It was gruesome and far from perfect. There was internal bleeding and with her little control, I knew Destiny had singed some bits internally. But Tahmeed was right, even with internal bleeding her body would mend itself. It was her weakened state while she slept that was the real issue now.

They would come for her in the shadow dreams. I hoped that she wouldn't be compromised.

"I glitched the cameras the moment she came in. Put her to rest," Alexa said from behind us. She had a tech demon which was rather savvy with all things modern and technical. Which reminded me to ask her for a favor later so I could research certain things that might be off the records. If anyone could dig deep it was Alexa but I had to be careful about how I worded what I was after.

Gabe collected her in his arms and asked which room was Tahmeed's. Destiny reverted to her normal self and shoved him. "Give me her. We don't need help from the likes of you," she spited. She was slickened with blood when she grabbed her from him and took Tahmeeds dead weight without issue. She turned back into her normal form so the flames wouldn't lick at Tahmeed. She walked her down the hallway. Blood glistened from the doorway all the way to where she stood. She must've only arrived when we had.

Not that I liked to clean but we had to dispose of the evidence before any one realized the cameras were playing funny business. I went straight to the cleaning cabinet, which I don't think any of us had used since being in here. We had a cleaner come in every day. But this would be reported. I grabbed paper toweling and sprays that smelled of lemon. I don't know why we all banded together to help her. We usually looked out only for ourselves. But then I wondered if I had been the only one that had made contact with the *others*. Were they just as scared as I was? I wasn't terrified of anything, it didn't run in our nature. But it was instinct to know when something was greater than ourselves, and that we were fighting against something larger which might've been there since the beginning of time.

"She went to clear some demons that are taking humans in the forestry on the edge of the city," Destiny said walking back in and staring deathly Gabe with hatred. Her blonde curls and arms were sticky with Tahmeed's blood.

"I'd say it didn't go well," is all I said as I scrubbed the flooring.

"No. They still need to be eradicated before they come into the city. They're still days out of Shabeah so we have time. We'll just have to wait to see who Haymen wants to reassign. He won't be pleased with her shortcomings.

A loud screaming gargle came from Tahmeed's room. Destiny and I looked at one another and continued scrubbing. That was a lot sooner than I thought.

"Is she okay?" Gabe asked as he mopped up a black pool on the floor. Destiny hissed at his question and involvement. Even Alexa came over and began making small circles with a cloth. We didn't talk about it. There had been an increase in attacks as of late, we were being attacked almost every night now. We never spoke to one another about it nor were we about to with a war angel in the room. Surprisingly he stayed quiet but I knew that he was absorbing and calculating all that he could.

A small beep dinged in my ear and I wiped away the hair that had fallen over my shoulders with the back of my hand. I swiped the top of my ear to initiate the implant. The blue screen opened in front of me and I read the brief of Haymen's new assignment. Great. So those demons who had just split Tahmeed's stomach open was now my problem to deal with tomorrow morning. *Thanks Homie.*

"Looks like I will be finishing the job off for Tahmeed tomorrow," I said and continued scrubbing. Destiny didn't say anything after that and we pretended like the large angel in the room wasn't looking over us intently with questions that would not be answered.

THE SILENCE

There is a silence in the world that will always fill with music
from another creature's story.
While you sit, someone else is standing.
While you eat, someone else is starving.
While you live peacefully in one day, someone else is dying an
intolerable death.
As I clean and scrub the blood from the floor of a life I wanted
no involvement with;
I wonder, do people think of me?
Do they care for my story that I cannot live without nor live
within?
Do the humans of today care about my demons that are eating
me from the inside?
Somewhere I became cold and I refused to listen to the music
anymore.
I became emotionless, if only to survive in this Underworld.
Can anyone else hear the music?

Chapter Twenty-Two- Vivian

"You're not sleeping in my room," I said standing at the door with my hands on my hips. "I will spike you with my succubus tail with enough poison to put you into an unmovable pain for days if you try to step past me."

He pushed past me, his size imposing. I wondered just how much it might piss him off if I were to actually touch his wings. Instead I did the next best thing to show how serious I was. I couldn't compromise my sleeping conditions with him around. My tattoos glowed blue and I changed into my succubus stabbing at him with my tail as quickly as he pinned me against the wall. I scratched down the side of his hard face as he stared into my eyes, as if a storm were brewing within them. The green was like a wild storm of hail as he hissed at the scratch mark. He barred his knee against my own, his weight pinning me. His other hand pressed against my tail so it could no longer sway. His wings twisted into me, pressing against my wrists and pinning my arms away.

Slowly, the mark on his face began to heal. I didn't let my eyes widen but I had never seen anyone recover from my poison within a matter of seconds. His breath mixed with mine as his heat wrapped around and began extinguishing my coldness. He held my chin and I could see the glint of disgust for the succubus demon that was in front of him, that he had to touch and restrain. I reverted to my usual self, suddenly very aroused by his heat and proximity.

When I changed, his eyes flashed and there was less… hatred. A demon's face he couldn't stomach but maybe the seduction of my human one he could. And what could I say… I might detest the guy but damn, he was a hot piece of meat. I rubbed into him, trying to buckle free and surprisingly enjoyed being overpowered for once which I would've enjoyed in my bed.

He stared at my lips and I knew in that moment; the proximity was too close for the both of us. We might be natural enemies but power was drawn to power and the excitement to overpower one another was instilled in very dominant blood. It could be a wonderful way for us both to pass time. I tried to push off the wall again but this time he pushed me back harder and his hand was around my throat. Threatening, but could also be pleasurable. I gave him a coy smile as he rubbed his thumb gently over my throat. He went to say something but my smile seemed to snap him out of whatever trance he was in. He didn't recoil fast enough until we weren't the only ones in my room.

"You seem to be making yourself too familiar with my property," Haymen said from behind. Gabe looked over his shoulder at Haymen and slowly pushed away from me. I reminded myself to take a breath as he turned to face Haymen who was cross-legged and sitting on my bed.

"She seems to have the tendency to attack me. Often," Gabe added.

"I permitted you to follow her. But not touch, play with, or fuck her," Haymen said and the darkness that swarmed around his suit felt as if it were pulling the room in. My focus could only be on him. Gabe instinctively understood the threat because his wings began to lightly glow as if keeping that darkness away and from touching him.

"I have no interest in fucking your toys," Gabe said. The two were a formidable presence in my room, it made me feel tiny in comparison as I rested against the wall, knowing at times it was best for me to close my smart mouth. The situation of being followed wasn't my ideal condition to be in either. "You and I need to talk privately."

"I came to talk to my beloved," Haymen said ushering me over with two fingers. I did as he said and sat beside him. I had to be on his side, especially opposed to Gabe who was a foreigner. We weren't to disobey Haymen ever, let alone in front of someone who Haymen found to be a threat. "Not you." He threaded his hand through the back of my hair and pushed his lips onto mine. I was startled at first. Not sure as to what was happening because the act was unexpected. But my body rolled in the power and seduction that he fed me. His tongue pushed hard against mine with expectation of submission but that was never my forte. His cold lips to mine broke away as he looked at Gabe pointedly. *His.* I was his property to do as he pleased. And the notion seemed to disgust Gabe which I wasn't at all surprised by. But I couldn't deny my arousal that Haymen quickly elicited from me. My nipples had gone hard and I wished for more. I tried to chastise that part of me and the liquid warmth between my thighs that drummed for more but I couldn't help it. Intensity of fighting and sex is what nourished us and already it had been almost a week since my last satisfying 'meal'.

"What I wish to speak to you about is a matter of urgency and if you deny me this part of the investigation then I will take it to the High Courts. There are forces within your city that you aren't being honest about," Gabe said. Two things. One. He was the Demon Lord, I don't know why someone expected honesty from him. Two. I was weary because I wondered if Gabe was stupid enough to approach Haymen about what I fought against today. If he began sniffing too close to home, Haymen would make sure to eradicate him. Not that I would mind, I mean how many times during this month are we going to get into mini brawls while he follows me around like some sniffer dog?

"I gave exemption for you to follow my Guardian, not for exclusive interviews with myself or you showing disregard for the privacy of my elite team," Haymen said. "Spew what you like at the old nayers but you can most certainly get the fuck out of my Vi's room while she's sleeping. There is a guest room on the left window of the house past the kitchen. Amuse yourself there. If you reject my kind offer I will retract all submission of you being entitled in my city. I would also appreciate if you refrain from causing nonsense reports." He snapped his fingers and a black puff of smoke dropped a newspaper from the air. It landed on the ground where we could all see a photo of Gabe and I leaving the orphanage together. Obviously, there was another cameraman close by. We weren't doing anything special or shocking. It was him walking behind me. We were positioned at where he would've been talking to the reporter. But naturally they cut him out of the picture. *War Angel and Guardian Vi, looking to adopt?!* Was the headline. I laughed at the heading. Well that was rather clever considering we were coming out of an orphanage but considering what actually just happened and without mentioning the three children missing was probably the scarier part of how media really spun some shit. Haymen gave me an effective look. Gabe pursed his lips trying not to share the same amusement.

"I will be down the hall if you need me," he said in the most seductive tone that stroked every vertebra in my body. I knew it was for show, to trump Haymen in whatever way he could. I didn't openly react to it but I imagined that tone had seduced many women into his bed. He gave me a smile with the flash of white teeth and stepped out of the room. I was surprised he went so easily and with the infuriation that played on Haymen, I gathered that Gabe felt like he won at something today.

"Thank you for favoring me my privacy," I said getting off the bed after Gabe had left. I wasn't going to mention the kiss but I certainly needed to distance myself from Haymen who caused such a reaction from me. Now that would be playing with fire.

"I want a full report about the attack on the orphanage by tonight," he said well mannered. The darkness seemed to liven up after Gabe's disappearance. I nodded to him. "Is there anything you need to report about this incident to me now?"

I looked at him wondering if he knew already about the entities that entered our shadow dreams. Perhaps he did and he chose to stay silent. I wondered if it was a test or measure of my loyalty. I would usually brush it off but if Gabe reacted in such a way I wondered if Haymen was aware of the presence within the city also. He was no fool and I wondered what he was up to when we were doing our duty within the city.

"There was an attack but I haven't yet identified the demon. I plan on eradicating it and will still investigate the matter alongside other jobs you give me. I will write a report tonight but will keep you updated once this incident has been resolved," I said matter of fact as I leaned against the wall that Gabe not so long had erotically held me by the throat.

"You usually have so much more bite, your submission makes me think that you are up to something and not disclosing information," Haymen said and the coolness of his blue eyes conveyed a lot of hurt if anyone were to lie to him. He uncrossed his legs, uncharacteristically and began to unbutton the edges of his black buttoned shirt. The contrast of the porcelain skin beneath began to poke through. It held my attention for a great length of time. I didn't know a male could unbutton their shirt so sexily.

"I don't think you like it much when one fights back," I said honestly wondering if I would get a backhand or get away with it like I usually did. He arched an eyebrow, the slight shuffle of his black hair grabbing my attention. Too much of him was grabbing my attention because I knew beneath that suit was the splendor of a demon lord who could have anything he wanted. All beautifully muscled over hundreds of years and perfected with a warrior's pose.

He stood up and walked over to me as he began to slowly undo his lower buttons, trailing to the top. I didn't let him see my reaction but I was both confused and interested on what might happen. A small part of me was crying out for sensibility to break through. My body often had a mind of its own in trying to suppress its sexual appetite. I was always… hungry. I regretted looking down because he cocked an all-knowing smile. He was playing with me. With his shirt now unbuttoned, he pushed me further into the wall. He cupped my liquid warmth between my thighs rubbing against the leather of my pants and watched for my reaction. His other hand reached for my hard nipples as he pinched them and a small hiss escaped my lips. He chuckled and pushed his tongue down on mine again, his motion through my leather pants, riling me and creating a small thrumming of lust that I needed.

The kiss was passionate and much to my surprise familiar and strange all at once. I purred into his mouth as he aroused the part of me that was all woman and despite logic screaming *don't do it*, I craved him now. My nails dug deep down his chest, sizing each ab that was perfectly carved. He pulled away and cocked a smile at me.

"I think I preferred you when you fought back," he said with that cocked smile that was nothing short of demonic, and yet somehow, made him look younger. With the puff of black smoke I was alone and the warmth between my thighs was drumming with expectation to be treated with a larger pounding. I stood there in shock, pissed and unsure as to why I had even led myself into that situation. And now I was left with an irritable drumming that could only be appeased by one thing.

I considered sneaking off to find someone to appease this tension for the night. I wondered how possible that was with Gabe trailing me. I needed a place to cool off and question what just came over me and why Haymen was suddenly so interested. Why had I given in so easily?! I hated Haymen! I loudly growled to rid some of the frustration. I wasn't a human high school girl swooning over a crush. Demons needed to be sexually appeased. That was it and he was truthfully, besides being the most powerful demon alive, visually appealing to the eye as well.

I immediately took a cold shower to try and wash away the feel of both Gabe and Haymen. What the fuck just happened? I shifted into my water demon who struggled for breath under the running water. The splashing water was enough to keep my body wet but not enough for me to entirely breathe. The gasping and self-infliction, eventually took my thoughts away from arousal and to desperation of breath. I changed back into my normal form now certain that my sexual appetite might hold out for another day.

I walked into my dressing room and entered the code on the safe. In it I took out my Trinity necklace and sat down on the comfy white pillowed seat. There were no windows in here where Gabe could spy on me if he pleased.

"Lock room," I said activating my alarm system so that no one could break in while my body was physically left in here defenseless while I teleported elsewhere. I placed the necklace on and within seconds was back to the dry and beautifully haunting landscape that I was taken to last time. I was wearing the same dress that flickered behind me and a mask which covered half my face. I was brought to the same dead looking tree and crows seemed to welcome me.

Although I wanted peace I was also curious to see whether anything besides comfortable silence existed on this dimension. I wasn't sure what dead world it was but I wondered what remained. There might even be a story behind it. I decided to explore. I skidded down the rock edge, barely cutting up my hands as I slid down with control. The dress caught on things but just as quickly released and flickered in its own direction as if it had a mind of its own.

When my feet echoed on the cracked ground it was as if it had woken the world I stood on. There was a slight shake but nothing appeared. It felt like something had simply woken after being in slumber for so long. It reminded me of the demon under Aztec which still slumbered in me.

I began walking across the vastness of what seemed like a never-ending desert. It wasn't just flat land. Reassessing the way it crept down and the skeletons of creatures I could only guess it was once a large lake, maybe even sea. I kept walking for what seemed like hours. Perhaps it was a dried-up sea because there was nothing in sight. There was no sunlight but it wasn't dark either. The sky seemed to illuminate a dreary clouded blue tinge. My breath was shallow as the world seemed like it didn't have much to give. So many bones scattered where I walked and I wondered what might've happened to them and what kind of demons they were. They varied in sizes and shapes.

Was this world annihilated in one clean sweep? I didn't research on any species in particular but there were many that hadn't survived, especially during the last war. Species of demons were wiped out and some homelands were even destroyed in the process. It wasn't uncommon and yet I was curious. I was never truly left alone here. There were always one or two crows that followed me as if to see how far I would walk. I decided walking in this direction was pointless. I was only surrounded by vastness of land.

If anything, the walk did me good, defusing any other frustrations I previously had. When I next had the chance, I would explore another part instead. Surely there was something else to see than this barren land. Not that I would be disappointed because I originally purchased the Trinity necklace so I could get away and get some silence. But I felt like this was now my world and place to retreat to and so I wanted to explore it. If there were hidden stories or powers to gain I wanted to know about them. I took the necklace off and was whirled into the modern day.

I arched my back inward hissing at the discomfort of my back that had slumped for so long in the chair. I stood up taking another big stretch and yawn before placing my Trinity necklace in my safe and locking it. I walked out of the wardrobe still naked from my shower. An orange cat that perched itself on the railing to my veranda caught my attention. Its green eyes watched on with interest as its tail swished. I walked closer to the door to see if it would run. Most animals did when they felt the presence of my demons. But this one didn't budge. I shifted into my cat demon wondering if it would scare it. It didn't. I smiled at its courage and walked out to pat it.

It looked a little feral, maybe an alleyway cat. It wasn't fazed by my fast movement as I began to scratch behind its ear. It felt rather surreal. I had never really been a cat person. Well until I could turn into one. "You're not scared of me at all, huh?" I continued scratching under its jaw which it loved. It had no collar perhaps not even an owner. Having enough of me it jumped off the railing and walked over to the next window, walking along the house. It wasn't a demon or a spy I would've felt it. It was just a curious alleyway cat.

I shifted back into my human form and walked over to my bed. I landed on my bed, face first. As soon as my head hit the pillow, I fell asleep.

CHAPTER TWENTY-THREE- VIVIAN

Going to sleep exhausted was a rookie mistake for a Guardian but at times was inevitable. Avoiding sleep would only make it worse. Fighting during the day and being exhausted left us exposed during our sleep, especially in shadow dreams. It was a very different experience in the Shadow dreams after having met them in person at the orphanage.

Aiden was with me. How nostalgic to see my ex-boyfriend after so long. We were evidently still together as he walked me through a parking lot holding my hand. I wasn't alarmed, in fact I felt at ease with him. Before I was changed I had loved him dearly, we had been together for just under five years until my... death. I have only seen him twice after that and that was enough to know that I have completely changed and love was not a real thing for someone like a Guardian. That and also, he hated everything that I have become. If more hateful words were in his vocabulary he would've bashed me without remorse. And all of that trust and loyalty of five years splintered away in that reality when I realized he thought this was a path I chose for myself. The fame and money might have been why some desired it, but it was never something I wanted for myself.

Guardians were handpicked by Haymen himself, why he chose me was still a mystery. I was a nobody in my former life. I was just a dog walker, saving money in hopes to move from Shabeah. Now ironically, I was chained to it.

I couldn't speak and his words came in and out as he pulled me across the parking lot which was slowly dimming from the sunset. He looked back and smiled at me dotingly like he always did. In his eyes here, I was normal. An old wound, which had healed very quickly. Mental instability or sentiment wasn't something we really held onto. I wish I felt more for him but I was programed to know that it was weakness and I would be exploited for it.

He continued leading me through the carpark and down the staircase to the underground train track. When we walked down the stairs two men grabbed my attention. I continued walking but turned to watch them leave. Every step I took after that felt as if I was slowly being drugged and my vision became hazy. I didn't understand how it had happened and if I had been drugged. I was becoming... exhausted and weak.

Aiden walked me into the toilet and suddenly he became an old girlfriend that I worked at the café with. She applied her lipstick as she spoke to me through the mirror. Her blonde hair was spilling over her sleeveless dress as she ranted about her ex-boyfriend. I couldn't concentrate as her words dipped in and out. My vision was rippling as I squinted at her trying to focus.

My legs became heavy and I began to panic. What was happening to me? I could hardly breathe. I stumbled over to the singular toilet booth. I just wanted to be alone so I could put my head between my knees and figure out what was happening to me.

I became paranoid as I could feel someone creeping up on me. Hunting me. My friend was only a distraction. I had to run away. My every sluggish step towards the toilet was haphazard and I stumbled about trying to reach it. To hide in there so nothing could get to me. I fell into it and instead of falling into a toilet booth I was inside an empty underground carpark. The flashing of lights flickered over me. I could hardly stand as my lethargic legs were about to give way. Wake up. There in the flickering shadows stood a figure. Wake up. Just watching me. Laughing at me but I couldn't audibly hear it. He was entertained as I tried to fight against him and his will that drained me. He was leeching the energy from me. Wake up. The shine of a knife in his hand glistened and he ran for me. He knew that I was trying to pull myself out before he could hurt me. My legs gave way and I dropped to the ground. He pulled back his elbow ready to plunge it into my heart as he ran closer. Wake up. He was almost here. He would kill me. This was real. Right before the blade reached my chest I focused on being awake in the real world. I had to free myself from this or he would kill me. Wake up. WAKE UP!

I dragged myself out of my sleep state but wasn't fully awake. I was laying in my bed in my room but I was in a state of... I don't know, in between. Awake and asleep at the same time, a state of mind where I might see things that I couldn't while being awake in the day. It felt like some middle platform like that. I couldn't move, my sleep paralysis was in full effect. I felt it before I could shuffle my eyes across. A black bony human like creature was hunched over my left arm. It had no mouth or eyes but still had the outline of those sunken features. It was cloaked in its black oily skin.

It screamed at me, a high pitch nasty roar, irritated that I had interrupted its meal. And I realized with fear, that its meal was my arm. Its claws were latched in as I felt it draining me and exhausting me of my arm's functions. Bile rose in my throat and I realized that fearing it or crying wouldn't get rid of it. Instinctually I felt like I had to fight against the presence and overpower it and so I roared back, like a lion would entitling itself to its own prey. No noise came out but the pushing and overpowering effect seemed to work as the thing withdrew and suddenly vanished and morphed into a red tentacle like thing. It looked almost like a spider as it slowly drifted towards my ceiling. My sleep paralysis only added to that stifling and fearful moment of not being able to jump out of my bed and run for the door. Sensing my spike in fear it swept a little closer. It was drawn to it. I tried to guard myself and focus. I needed to be confident. It glided back to the ceiling hovering a moment longer before finally vanishing.

Slowly I felt the full weight of my body, no longer being on the in-between plane where I could see the creature. Tears, actual tears streamed down my cheeks until I could move my body again. That has never happened to me before. Only spooky dreams that I could at times try to flog off as nightmares. But not this time, no this was real. That was something very present in my room and was feasting off me while I slept.

No alarms had sounded from a break in. Even that creature's presence wasn't detected.

When I could finally move, I rose to a sitting position and checked my arm. It didn't physically look different but it felt different. Like it had eaten and sapped all the energy in my left arm. It was sluggish to lift and use. I continued to look at the ceiling to see if I could see the attacker but it was gone. Whatever that thing was had vanished and with it a belly full of my arm. A lump formed in my throat as I wondered what else might've happened if I hadn't woken up and if I didn't realize something was wrong. Was this already the start of being compromised? Was this the start and end of how Guardians were eventually killed?

I brushed away the panic-stricken thoughts. They weren't going to help me; if anything they would just make me clumsy. I tapped on the implant on my ear to check the time. It was two in the morning. I had only been sleeping for a few hours. I knew Doc would come as soon as I called her but instead I felt like I had to shower and wash away the vileness I felt from its touch. I have been violated. And worst of all I didn't know how to stop it or prevent it from coming back.

Forty-five minutes later with freshly washed hair and painted toenails, I paged Doc. I wasn't at all surprised when I walked into the Shadow Mind's room that she was already there. I don't know how she appeared like some kind of magician but she always did.

"Sorry about the morning rise, Doc," I said sitting comfortably in the chair. The truth was I was glad to have someone near me, it helped me ease back into what should be the normal daily routine. I was a Guardian. Things such as fear and panic weren't ingrained in us. But there was that small part, I think instinct that fought for me, urging that something was wrong and I have become the prey of something even greater than me. It has me wondering why Haymen specifically wanted us to be the bait and hunt these demons. Maybe there was something that existed that even he feared or couldn't control. After my discussion with the Shadow person that possessed Alice, I was certain that its master might've challenged Haymen for the throne before.

"I was already here," she said flipping over a page that had already been scribbled with her witch writing.

"Alexa?" I asked about the fellow Guardian. I didn't see her walk past me in the hallway but I could smell her perfume lingering in the air. She nodded. I wondered if Tahmeed had been in today, despite the early time. That scream that came from her room meant only one thing–that she was being attacked in her sleep. Looked like it was a busy night for all of us. The attacks were more frequent now.

Everything was to be reported. That was why we were the bait and the hunters. The point of all of it was so we could record it in hopes it would get us closer to finding them. But I wondered if any Guardian at this point had actually been able to follow through with the hunt considering they all found themselves dead within years of taking the role.

"A rather early account for you. You've been reporting a lot more incidences as of late," she said. And that hung in the air. It wasn't a good thing. Progress of finding them... maybe, but not for my health or longevity. She did her usual blood sample and looked at me curiously when I didn't raise my left arm for her to take it. It was difficult for me to move it. It was heavy and felt like the life had been sucked out of it. I hoped that over time during the day it would come back. I wondered how much she would see on the Shadow Mind scan. Surely she wouldn't see what I did afterwards. But I wasn't entirely awake when I saw that red spider creature either.

She raised my arm herself and positioned it carefully on the ledge of the chair and began extracting blood. I wondered if she had yet sourced my last three demons. I still had to confirm if the hellhound was in fact contracted to me because I haven't had the chance to formally greet it, so to speak.

The blood was taken and then I had to relive the nightmare. I hoped she didn't ask too many questions because I sure as hell didn't know how to explain them. The four probes stabbed into the back of my neck. Being probed at three in the morning wasn't my idea of a fresh brew of coffee.

"Shadow Mind's activated," the system announced as the room dulled and my memory was projected onto the white wall in front of us. I wasn't at all surprised that Doc knew who Aiden was. "Do you think of or miss him?" She asked at the part where Aiden and I were casually walking through the carpark above the train station. It wasn't a remorseful question but an insurance to make sure that Haymen's property wasn't having human sentiments or being compromised.

"No." I said firmly and continued to watch the screen trying to get a clear sighting of the two men I walked past. It was after walking past them that the sense of being drugged had occurred and I was being entrapped. Maybe they were a part of it all. Or possibly they were just a figment of the dream I was forced to walk through.

I was desperate to see their faces and anything that might be a lead. I only had a few seconds to stare at them but they were both pale and well dressed for a colder day. They both wore cozy black coats and laughed at one another as they spoke. I couldn't hear what they were saying but by their complexion–rosy cheeks and blonde hair–I had the feeling that they weren't from my country. They had a very crisp English accent.

That's when my visual began to go hazy and even Doc leaned in intently. Bile rose in my throat while reliving it; to see my trauma on screen. I was relieved that she couldn't feel the panic and fear that drove me hard into that toilet and then into the underground carpark or she might've reported me compromised then and there. These emotions were making me unhinge. It wasn't the creature itself I was scared of but the inability to know how to prevent it. We couldn't show fear, we shouldn't know fear. Was I a failed Guardian for feeling this, if only for a moment?

The shadowy figure standing in the carpark was laughing. And then he was running at me with a knife; by the time he had gotten close to piercing his blade in my chest I couldn't make out his face because my vision was too blurred. Doc tsked in frustration. She didn't see my internal dialogue that forced me to wake up and get out of the dream state. The footage cut out. I was grateful she couldn't see the oily creature that I woke up to. What if they determined I have been compromised? Would they kill me? She burrowed her eyebrows together and looked at me. Then she began to scribble.

"Nothing else happened? It ends abruptly," she said.

"I think a bird flew into my window and woke me up," I lied. She considered it for a moment, but I knew she didn't believe me.

"Now Vi, you know you have to be honest with me in these reports," she began. She lowered her board so her gibberish witch writing was in front of me. I didn't let my facial features give way but suddenly that gibberish writing was starting to make sense to me. I found that some of those characters were piecing together right before my very eyes. It didn't read like English. No but it was a language that I understood and could somehow convert. *That was new.*

'Footage might have been compromised' was the setting tone for one sentence. Because I can compromise the footage of my own brain?! 'Mind stimulation was heightened. Perhaps panic. Physical pain might have been endured'.

"Are you listening?" she asked me clicking her fingers in front of me to wake me from my sudden daze. She looked at the board and then me.

"I am. Sorry it's just been a rough two days. I didn't mean to zone out on you," I said. "I understand and wish I could tell you more Doc, I really do."

She didn't seem to believe me but raised her hand to the door. She removed the four prongs from my neck. When I walked to the door she halted me.

"I mean it Vi, you can talk to me. It's your job to report *everything* to me," she said sternly.

"You don't have to remind me of my duty Doc, I was reborn for this one purpose, remember?" I said in a tone that vibrated the strength of my demons. We stared at one another. Psyching each other up and wondering who might win if we were to fight. And then I walked out. I wasn't in the mood to make enemies at three in the morning with the woman who directly reported everything to Haymen.

It didn't take me long to get changed into my loose pants and sports bra. That's one thing I did appreciate Shabeah for, a lot of it had been conserved even the fashion. There were still a lot of odd looks and fashions that made their way into Shabeah but it was an older preserved city. Other cities however were far more advanced and vivid. I have never left the city myself. My parents didn't travel and I didn't have the money for it either. Until now, and I wasn't permitted to leave.

I took to the gym which was a mixture of sandbags, target practices of all shapes and forms and various weapons of guns, spears, arrows, and throwing knives. Weights, extended poles, even spring vaults to help with flexibility and ability to use surrounding objects when confronted with an enemy. I took straight to the punching bag. Why dodge the classic when all I wanted to do was beat the shit out of something? I wound my knuckles with red tape which was rather a luxury since I never had the chance to say 'Excuse me, before we fight can I bind me knuckles?' in any fight but something made me feel more bad ass having them on while I trained.

An hour flew by and I was dripping sweat and bleeding knuckles. I had taken my frustration out on the bag. It was already in the past but a warning to be more cautious in the future. I couldn't allow myself to be compromised so soon. I refused to let myself be beaten by such an ugly demon.

I could feel Gabe's presence sneak up on me but I said nothing. I wouldn't let him disturb my vengeance on the boxing bag which kicked my ass the first few months of my training. I basically lived in this room for my first three months. A natural they called me, as if I had been fighting my entire life. All Guardians could tap into their demon's history and knowledge. That skillset was usually dragged over too. It's why all of our fighting styles differed. The months of training was to assure my body was fit enough to keep up. The first time I tried to do a back flip, I did exactly that and went splat straight onto my back. Oh yea, even a Guardian had to train.

"You look as though you could do with a sparring buddy," Gabe said from behind me, leaning against the French windows of the door. The training room was attached to the Japanese gardens around the back. It looked over the lake with wide windows surrounding us. I currently had the metal sheets over the windows, enjoying the lack of lighting that would seep through at sunrise. I punched harder.

"Are you offering to get your ass handed to you?" I asked taking another strike at the punching bag.

"Only if you can get me on my back," he said provokingly. I kicked the punching bag and looked over at him. He wore only his long pants, ones that he wasn't wearing yesterday. He wore no shirt, his perfectly formed biceps and chiseled stomach with pecks that were meant for shredding into. I looked away from the glory. Obviously, I didn't have much sleep because I was starting to become delirious with a sudden appetite for him.

I welcomed him with a bitter smile to the mat where we often sparred and practiced. Just muscle to muscle, no demonic or angelic powers involved.

"You can't use your wings," I said. "That's a rule." He smiled as he walked over.

"Already trying to get a handicap?"

"Unless I can use my demonic tail then its unequal footing," I countered.

"I was born with my wings, they are a part of my every movement," he sneered.

"Your mother must've been pretty loose to push out your proud wingspan," I said getting a little vulgar. He didn't find that funny. He smiled but all amusement was gone.

"You'd be surprised how many women struggle with my size even now. But let's not get distracted. Fine I'll bind my wings as much as I can," he said and they snapped shut flawlessly. A low breeze rustled through the room as he straightened them firmly behind him. And he was right, I was being distracted because what angel boy appeared to have forgotten to wear was some underwear to hold in his very apparent and dangling friend in his loosely fitted pants.

"Three tap outs and the winner's announced," I said raising my hands. He smiled at me and stretched his arms for a moment jokingly before loosely raising his too.

"I don't want to hurt you, you are a girl," he purred to irritate me.

"You've never seen me as a woman before so don't start now," I said and then I lunged.

CHAPTER TWENTY-FOUR- VIVIAN

My left arm was still dead weight but that didn't stop the rest of my body. I kicked at him to test the waters and to initiate the fight. I didn't expect to actually land a hit. My kick was countered by his hands and he pushed me back. We circled one another for a moment before he lunged at me. So, he wasn't the patient type I assumed him to be. His muscles flexed with stealth and skill of a man who has been a hunter and warrior his entire life.

He came down hard aiming to knee my stomach as a decoy. His real intent was to punch my chest and push me back. I circled around him to kick at the side of his ribs but he had already caught me and flung me around. I flipped in the air but despite his force, found control and landed on my feet. Already I was set to defend against his uppercut that promised to wind me if it connected. I dodged it and punched towards his face using as much strength as I could and used my clumsy left arm to block. He blocked my punch and with ease swiped away my left arm. He didn't even have to punch at me again because I fell into the force that my left arm had been thrown and rolled on the ground catching my balance.

I was crouching but not defenseless. He seemed to have noticed my left arm but before he spoke, I jumped at him again. I kicked knowing that he would grab my leg. As soon as he did I flicked my other one over it and tried to kick him off the side. The thing with having one arm and being half the weight mass of your opponent is that maneuver wasn't such a great idea. Especially when he locked his grip around both my legs locking me in place. I was suspended in the air on his two arms and he smiled.

"You know it will hurt," he purred.

"I bet that's what you say to all the girls," I smiled back. I knew it was going to hurt but it would hurt my pride more if he didn't go through with it. This was a one on one and fair fight.

He dropped me to the ground. I locked my feet around his shoulder to take away how much force he could bring down on me. As soon as my back hit the floor I lost my breath but flicked my legs back, taking his unbalanced weight over with me. His imbalance forced him to release me. Instead of pouncing on me straight away he let me catch my breath.

My left arm bowed a little as I tried to use it to push my weight up. Instead I balanced on my right arm.

"What could you have possibly done to your left arm in those six hours I wasn't guarding you?" he asked curiously having noticed my weak arm.

"Maybe I enjoyed myself a little too much last night and my wrists gave way to the feverish desires of my fingers," I said walking over to the collection of spears. I heard him tsk at my filthy comment. I was not a princess nor did I speak like one.

Before he could comment I aimed and shot the spear at him, only to clip his arm. It didn't make it that far. He moved and caught it, swinging around with the force of it. It twirled in his fingers for a moment as his eyes fastened on me not at all impressed.

"Cheap shot," he said. I grabbed another spear and walked back into the ring shrugging.

"I just wanted to see how senile your reflexes were. From what I've heard you're a very old man," I said noticing the flexing of his muscles as he spun the weapon over his fingers with ease. A sprinkling of sweat glistened his body.

"And yet your eyes seem to enjoy this senile old man's very healthy body. And mistake me if I'm wrong. I'm not the only immortal standing here."

That was true. Both angels and Guardians were immortal. But forty-four years was the longest any Guardian had survived. I wasn't about to tell him that but I'm sure it was noted by those who took interest in Haymen and tried to find a weakness to his guard.

Gabe tucked his right hand back and swung the spear with ease with his left. Interesting. I only just noticed now that he was left handed but he stepped forward with his right.

"Fair is fair," he said. "But are you good with only one hand with a spear?" He asked provokingly. I charmed a smile and jumped at him. The force and slap of the spears should've shattered if they weren't already pre-built to fair against a demon's strength. Minutes flew past as we countered one another again and again and those beautiful wooden pieces chipped away at one another. He got me once now, a slice on the cheekbone that provoked a cocky smile. That was two now that he had me on. I had to seriously pick up my game.

We smashed into one another, kicking and blocking with our knees as the spears went to our shoulders and face. With swift maneuvers and leaving myself open, I was over these games. I wrapped my foot around his ankle as I forced him to step back. He tripped as I pushed my weight down on him, knocking his spear away that would jeopardize piercing my shoulder.

I wrapped my knees around his waist as he keeled over and I sat on top of him. He was lying flat on his back. I heaved with breath as I inched my spearhead to his neck. His face gave nothing away. There were both the old echo of death many had seen; his forest green was the last thing they saw. But amongst that chaos was amusement. I looked down and noticed the sharp pointed spear that had caught in my shirt, slowly he glided it up, slicing it open with ease. Right above my heart.

I was still straddling his torso as my exhausted left arm was pressing against his chest. Hard and lean. The tattoos that scrolled over his torso spoke of the many wars he had already fought through. My eyes wanted to read those stories but I couldn't remove my gaze from his. We froze there for a moment heavily gathering our breaths that mingled with one another. His was hot and mine was cold. My chest rose up and down, the tip of the spear etching closer each time.

If we were serious we could end one another's lives right here and now. Neither of us would remain a victor. We would inevitably take one another out. And there was resistance to lower our weapon, because that threat became very real. Because despite the chemistry that burned through us, and I knew the look of passion when it was devouring me. It was the craze of madness and lust combined.

Sometimes a warrior even had the same expression when they slaughtered.

Destiny grunted behind us and we both slowly cocked our heads to look at her. Neither of us moved from our death holds and were both weary of the weapons. She tapped her wrist watch and waited. I looked down at Gabe again and slowly but still with my weapon pointed at him, rose to standing. He didn't raise his weapon to follow me but now that my weight has shifted and I was no longer pinning him he would have time to swipe my weapon out of my hand if he needed to. He didn't move and only waited as I stepped back and threw the spear to the side. I turned my back on him and walked towards Destiny. It wasn't me that she watched but Gabe. Her arms crossed and her hatred for him emanated from her eyes. If it weren't for the treaty and the point that Gabe could kill her easily, she would've tried to kill him many times over now.

"I didn't realize we monitored one another," I said as I came to stand by her. It was a threat and my eyes conveyed that as she looked at me evenly with the same intensity.

"Perhaps you are getting side-tracked from your task at hand and need reminding?" Her voice was flat and matched my own tone. I smiled, nothing but savage as I leaned in closer towards her. Our eyes never diverted.

"Since when did you become Haymen's lap dog?" It was a shot in the dark but I figured it was the only reason she was watching Gabe's and my interaction so closely. She would have no other reason to unless reporting directly to him. She didn't deny it.

"I like you Vi, but as soon as you're compromised I'll be the one ordered to put you out of commission." I stared at her for a long time, to counter that threat. If I had to, I would kill her first. My stare conveyed that threat.

"I think rogue would suit me, don't you?" I teased and walked away. I had no intention of going rogue. There was no way I could defy Haymen. Even if I ran away he would be able to find me anywhere in the world. But her absolution and following disturbed me. That was who we were and what we had to be for Haymen but I wondered if

Destiny held something more for him, perhaps even admiration. It wasn't hard to fall for Haymen to those who appreciated power and feared repercussions.

After a quick shower and preparing for my travels I threw my trusty backpack over my back. It held throwing knives, two guns and I strapped one sword to my back. And a lunch of course. They were all tightly strapped in for when I needed to collect the bag in a hurry. If Tahmeed didn't fare well against the demons in the outskirts of Shabeah, then I had to be as well prepared as possible. Tahmeed had the blessing of a demon who could teleport although limited to the amounts of times she could in one day. It lacked in stamina unlike Haymen who had no end to his power. Yesterday that very demon's gift was what saved her life and her ability to come back home.

I walked into the kitchen and was nodded in greeting by our chef. Gabe was sitting at the long white dining room at the end table. Destiny was staring at him with arms and legs crossed as he ate. The floundering chef came and scraped more bacon onto his plate and seemed rather flustered by his presence. Odd, he never so much as spoke to me. With accurate timing he looked at me and walked away. I stole two of the blueberry muffins which were freshly baked and cooling off the plate and his eyes chastised me. Maybe that was why he didn't like me. I smiled and walked out. Time to negotiate with some demons. Underworld or death. But after seeing Tahmeeds wounds, I doubted that there was much room for negotiation. I took a bite of the buttery blueberry muffin. Awesome. I wouldn't have to hold back today.

Chapter Twenty-Five- Vivian

Despite being scary to most, the mosquitoes seemed to have a requited taste for me today. Slap. I got one of the many bastards on the back of my neck. Swarms of them seemed to find me as I squatted among the trees looking at the tracks in the moist ground.

"I want to make a sexual banana joke," Gabe said from behind me. Haha very funny. Because eating bananas increase mosquito's attraction to you. How hilarious. I had been ignoring him all morning but couldn't help but look over my shoulder and give him an effective glare.

"For someone talking a mighty game against the mosquitos you seem to be wrapped up in those little pink cupid wings of yours pretty tight." I turned and stood up shuffling my backpack. I could sense the cocky smirk behind me. When I walked he did. I was getting irritated quickly by the constant surveillance. I wondered if I took a shit right now in the forestry if he'd offer to wipe?! "I'd rather you not get in my way and flutter about in the canopy or something. It's a bit much."

"I'm following you on the suspicion of murder. While you come out and prepare for what... another murder?" he said. I rolled my eyes at him. Like they cared much for the demons. Double standards really. Kill a demon who cares, and admittedly we often did like to kill one another, I mean we were demons. Kill an angel, oh no hands down and bring the shackles out because you are being put to trial!

"What was that?" he asked from behind me. Did I just say that out loud? He swept into the sky where I couldn't see him past the green of the treetops. I have to admit, I was envious of the prick–I wish I could fly. Hell, I'd probably fly a broomstick if it gave me the chance to drift through the sky. Bye-bye black slick bike I'd be all hot straw and sticks. Snap. I looked to the left and was confronted by a very huge and ugly looking bug demon.

It had no face that I could see and it glittered white that could be camouflaged in the snow. It was quite stark against the greens and browns of the forestry. Its giant pointed legs were edged with slick black blades. Well that would certainly explain the gash on Tahmeed. One clean cut and you would be beheaded, luckily it had nicked her stomach instead.

"Aren't you an ugly thing." I breathed measuring its weak points, which were looking pretty nil. Its height towered over me as it pressed two of its legs against a tree to look down on me. The implied weight forced its legs to slip through the thick trees like butter. A part of what I thought to be its head in the center looked at me and was quaking. I continued watching it but noticed the motion of another coming out from behind me. Silent. It's only noticeable approach was its white flesh.

I slowly reached into my bag for my gun. I wondered how quick their reflexes were. Another one came to my right and I realized the one in front of me seemed to be calling them. Its head in the center was still shaking. The forest went quiet and I watched their delicate steps. Each leg was a sharp point as they stationed themselves. Clever. They were surrounding me. I noticed the one in front of me was the largest and wondered if by chance it had something to do with hierarchy. Usually take out the biggest and you might have a chance of the others retreating. I couldn't hear or even sense Gabe anymore. Bastard left as soon as it got tough. How convenient. I placed my backpack to my feet and put my finger on the trigger of the gun.

"Let's see how this goes, shall we?" I aimed for the one in front of me and pulled the trigger aiming for what I thought to be its head. The demon reacted instantly and covered its face with one of the blades from its leg. I dodged the bullet that was backfired at me. As soon as I pulled that trigger all of them pounced with surprising speed. The blue of my tattoos glowed as I turned into my cat demon. I slid along the ground claws catching mud as I dodged the first sweep of their blades. I jumped back twice. Dodging with speed that I was certain only my cat demon could match. I jumped for the trees, gaining height to re-evaluate from the treetops. They were fast. Very fast. The tree I was balancing on was sliced in one clean cut. I jumped to the other tree and was greeted mid-air by one of the demons who had jumped to reach me. Fuck.

I flipped awkwardly in the air to divert my execution. Which didn't work in favor as my left arm lagged behind. It was only a nip but it was enough to extend down and instantly cover the fur of my arm with blood. As soon as I hit the ground on all fours I rolled and kept running. Right now all I could manage to do was run. I turned into my succubus form. It was risky but I had to get close to them. Somehow. I briefly looked at my left arm which glistened with blood oozing out. Better my left arm than its intentions of splitting me in half. I went for the smallest one on my right. They seemed to work in sync and the center, what I imagined to be their face continued to quake as if communicating with one another. I dodged the blades as best as I could, making sure that my tail wasn't caught in the cross fire.

Minutes passed as I dodged back and forth and clawed at them. When given the opportunity I sliced at their legs, on the side that wasn't bladed. They retracted in silence but I noticed that shortly after they weren't as quick on those legs. Good. My poison worked on them. I was yet to meet anyone who could handle the poison of my succubus. Gabe was the first exception. I focused on the little one mostly. Straining and obtaining small cuts as I dodged them back and forth.

Eventually the little one became slower and I took my opportunity and lunged. I wasn't at all surprised that its legs swooped up to keep me at a distance, but its legs were slow and I was able to jump higher, faster. I jumped and began to run along the top of its leg, dodging as the bigger demon tried to slice my head off to protect it. I ducked and jumped for the small bobble in its center. I jumped on its back and pierced my tail into its neck. My poison excreted and was a higher dosage from my tail. I pulled it out as soon as the larger demon tried to cut at me again. I rolled underneath the demon and stabbed my tail up and dragged it as I ran beneath it and out the tail end. I dove before it collapsed with me underneath. I continued running circles dodging the other two which seemed infuriated. Cardio was not my friend but it certainly was my savior at this point. I watched the third one as it slowly turned black and began to decay into the ground. Disgusting. I assumed that meant death.

I continued fighting the other two, slowly trying to exhaust them so I would be able to practice the same execution. Past the two of them I noticed that the corpse that was decaying began to crack open from the clay form it had taken. My eyes widened. Now that is disgusting. Smaller demons began to break out. Its corpse began to spawn. Fuck. What was worse than three giant blade cutting demons? Heaps of tiny ones. And here I had been complaining about the mosquitoes.

I felt Gabe's presence before I saw him. He swept in from the sky leaking a can of petrol on the ground. He took one giant sweep of his wings to stay out of reach of the demons reach and swept in fast, diving and lighting a match to light the petrol. Instantly they lit up and actual screams came from the offspring instead of the adult's usual silence. My succubus frenzied at the flames and I almost choked at how quickly she retracted and left me in human form. My succubus's greatest weakness was fire. I dodged the blade that came down on me but again my left arm was lethargic and couldn't keep up. This time it was a deep cut to the shoulder. I hissed, refusing to look at the damage. I changed back into my cat demon form and the bell on my tail jingled in agitation. I jumped again dodging the blade. I was slower now. I was wounded heavily but I still had a job to do.

I could feel something vile rise in the pit of my stomach. It was a darkness and savageness none of my other demons seemed to have. This was raw, powerful, heated aggression. As quickly as it swept up and offered its aid, I understood the demon I was contracted with. The blue of my tattoos glowed and part of it burnt announcing the contract with that demon being activated. We were now in alliance and my hell hound came forth. It was painful. Yet seductively enticing all at once. The power that flowed through me was dark and hot like fire. My body changed form, I thought that bones were breaking and knitting together within seconds.

Once I changed form I was eye level with Gabe. His expression didn't give anything away as he continued fighting against the larger of the demons. He turned his back to me. I was the size of a horse but more muscled and wide. The black paws were the size of a human's head with sharp un-manicured claws. I growled and snarled at the demon in front of me whose quaking seemed to quicken. I snapped at it and lunged. I was a lot faster than I would've expected from a demon this size. I was even faster than my cat demon. When I saw glimpses of my ragged fur I was black all over and if I hadn't had the experience of my cat demon I would've considered my large tail and balance rather difficult.

The demon was still slow as my succubus's slashes began to seep green from my poison. We could very well leave them and they would be dead within hours from the poison alone. I crisscrossed and out sped the demon as it planted its blades close to me trying to bring its weight down on me. After tiring it out, it became sluggish and I took my opportunity. I lunged for it and hung off its throat. My mouth clamped down on it and pulled. I ripped off its neck and the bobble thing that acted as its head and jumped back, avoiding the reflexes of its blades. I spat out the vile taste and threw its head to the side watching it drop in front of me. With satisfaction, I had killed it.

My hackles rose as a stir in the wind sent chills through the forest. I had felt this kind of demonic energy before and that was from a witch that practiced dark magic. Witches were neither demonic nor angelic but it depended on how the user chose to practice their magic that defined them. Call it good or bad or whatever you wanted, they gathered their power and materials from the elements that surrounded them. And because of that the forest went dire and cold. Something wicked came this way.

Gabe dropped to his knees and I could hear him gasp. I couldn't hear the chanting but I didn't need to, I had a sense of where the witch was and for whatever reason they were focusing on Gabe. The last demon took the interference and opportunity. Gabe was on his knees with some kind of paralysis as the demon sliced down on him. With speed that couldn't be matched by any other demon I had met, I jumped for Gabe and knocked him out of the way. The clean cut went through my lagging and dead weight arm. Clean cut. I howled as I felt the pain of my arm being severed while I rolled onto the ground.

I lunged for the creature, ignoring my pain and ripping out the bottom of its throat. I dropped onto the ground fighting to balance with one missing leg. Sometimes if severely injured my demons would leave the suffering and pain. But I found my hellhound rather loyal and tolerant of it. Before the demon could crush me with its weight, I balanced on my three legs, trying to focus most of my weight on my hind legs and jumped out of the way.

I looked back at Gabe who was wide-eyed and still suffering with paralysis. I think we were both shocked that I took such a fatal wound for him. I didn't even have time nor did I want to process that myself. Gathering all my strength, stamina, and balance, I sniffed out the coldest part of the forest and ran, looking for the witch.

I knew I didn't have much time before I bleed out, and that witch could be assured that I would take them out before I died myself. The smells of the forest began to engulf me as if trying to lull me to sleep within their trunks. To become one with the nature, to die and decay. Black blood oozed out of my shoulder. I only had minutes if that. It didn't take me long to find the witch who was in a black coat. As soon as she saw me she began chanting. A miraculous thing I realized and none of my other demons had such a resistance; was that her magic didn't work on me.

Beautiful. She was ravishing with red lips. I lunged for her and clamped my jaw around her face, shredding at the beauty and power that would be my ending. Her scream gargled into the back of my throat as I clamped down harder and crushed her skull. Splat. I could taste her death in my mouth.

I threw her around a few times assuring she was dead before I flicked her to the side and her corpse slumped against a tree. I hobbled starting to feel dizzy and knew that my time was near. I smelled the salt of water and began limping towards it. My hellhound was a determined and loyal creature and made sure to mix its own lively determination with me. I broke out of the forestry on a cliff edge to look over the sea. The blue of my tattoos glistened and my cat demon came forth. Oddly I found it comforting to die in this form. Much like a cat hiding to die solidary. I limped to the edge of the cliff to look out to the water and slumped into the ground. I wouldn't be getting back up from this one.

I was a fool for underestimating my left arm. I was even more of a fool for taking that blade for Gabe. I had no reason to. None. And yet I did. My body curled as I began feeling cold and the tiny swish of my tail rung only a few bells. I arched my head further to the water wanting to pull myself over and fall into the sea. At least I would be free. Finally.

My right paw twisted slightly in the moist dirt but no strength came from it. No flickers of memory, regret, or sentiment came. My duty was done. I had failed and I was to die. My eyelids slowly closed and instead of the crashing waves in the distance I heard that one defiant jingle of my tail. Death wasn't all that bad. I knew there would be other ways to leave this world. In this notion I was content.

Chapter Twenty-Six - Haymen

I watched over the proposed army that the demon king from Upid offered me. He was an ugly thing and far from human looking. So were his warriors. I looked over them from the edge of my city within the Underworld. The true city of Shabeah. The land was vacant of grass and gritted with a hot rock. They fought against one another in display for my attention. What I liked about these particular warriors was that they enjoyed killing even their own kind. Blue blood splayed everywhere from the brown demons that were solidified like rock and a horn in the center.

Most of them had installed blades down their arms as back up weapons, completely developing themselves as a weapon the moment they were born. What I took special interest in was their women and the electricity that they emit and could release at their fingertips. I let them pray on those who were imprisoned here. Those who went to the human world and defied my orders. The ones I had my Guardians drag back here. This was their consequence. I loved watching them try to fight and scream as one of the women jumped on him and pierced her delicate fingers into his eye sockets. His entire body trembled as he bled out of his face and nails while convulsing.

"Does my army please you?" Crad asked me from behind. I continued watching his army before I spoke to him. Crad was to die within the next few months. I had already planned it. Before then, I would take control of his army.

"Much," I said. I wanted to kill him myself, his imprudence and manner of thought, thinking that we were on par offended me greatly. He stood by my side, ever daring to stand as my equal. I patted over my suit jacket sleeve bidding patience. I could kill him now. Very easily and could even kill his entire army right now if they turned on me in his defense but I had other plans to execute instead.

His piercing black eyes watched over his army arrogantly and the sharp features of his rocky face was a ploy for what they could really do. And I was wondering how daring he was, how much he thought we could be allies and trusted me.

"Will you not show me the truth to your army," I said. It was a request. To deny me was requesting to be killed. I was wondering how cheeky Crad thought he could be. He seemed hesitant. Like most when I asked for their secrets on a platter. But it wasn't my first time having seen his demons operate. Especially considering this handful of warriors were the remains of his army because I had killed the rest. Those fifty years ago he had learned that I didn't appreciate being denied. I then took his wife for myself that night after I killed his army that would protect them both to remind him that everything was and would be owned by me. He killed his wife shortly after unable to look at her since I enjoyed my time with her. And it was consensual, like any demon, everyone was drawn to power.

Crad hesitantly whistled. As soon as he did, mists of dust blew through the hollowed canal. His warriors went invisible. There was a silence in the room until the remainder of the prisoners I had in there choked with slit throats and dropped to the ground. I pressed a smile. The perfect assassins. The reason why I kept a watch on Crad's army was because they were inclined toward virgins of all sorts. Now that would raise a lot of questions with the treaty when they let loose.

When Crad decided on his residence it was shortly after that Gabe claimed the city closest for him to rule. Crad stayed there but his army wasn't to step out of place, so often they ventured elsewhere to defuse their frustration. One day when I ruled over the humans and discarded of this treaty I would let them walk freely. Because by then they would be my silent army.

"They now belong to me," I said to Crad.

"They still rule under me but they will—" Crad's leg twisted and he dropped to his knee in a sharp burst of pain. I also forced his neck to twist up to look at me. I didn't even have to touch him to make him my puppet. His army remained silent and I could feel the presence of them surround us. What would they do, I wondered. Turn on me or turn on him? Here was their so called King whimpering because of a few broken bones. Bowing in front of me. Would they defend him? Did they think that their invisibility worked on me? One tried. He stepped forward only once and with little effort he became visible to me. I uncloaked him and looked at him with a stare that would kill. Literally. I wrapped my darkness around his tiny soft heart and squashed it into oblivion. I silenced his screams as I let my darkness creep into him and have its way with him, denying him of a proper death and tearing him apart from the inside. No one stepped forward after that.

"My lord?" one of my servants stepped forward having come from the closest tower. I had her there to report to me when the mission I had orchestrated was complete. I let go of my hold on Crad and walked away. Nothing else had to be said. His invisible army still surrounded me but no one so much as moved as I walked through them and towards my fawn eyed demon. She didn't say anything, only leading me to the remains of one lone survivor.

"I had sent out twenty," I said coolly. To the best I knew how. The silent demon in front of me dipped his head.

"And a witch if I recalled. Tell me, what remains of Gabe?" My dark tentacles already reached for him. I could smell fear and understood failure in any man's eyes.

"Your highness," he said dropping to his knees. "We had him captured and easy for the taking but your Guardian intervened. She jumped in his stead and was injured."

My nose flared and a million thoughts dashed through my mind in rage.

"When she fled we attacked him but not in time. Your Guardian had savaged the witch and his containment was broken. We-"

My darkness sliced his throat as he gargled to speak. I watched him drown in his own blood, infuriated as he gargled to try and justify his failure. The beautiful servant beside me did nothing and said nothing. I teleported out to find Vivian.

Chapter Twenty-Seven- Gabe

As soon as the witch had been killed I was released and with good timing. It took me only seconds to kill the nineteen who ambushed me and I hoped that they hadn't yet reached Vivian. One was able to escape. Instead of following him I burst through the canopies of the trees and searched for Vivian. My heart raced as I searched for her, maybe I wouldn't make it in time.

Witchcraft was a force that if caught unguarded I was weak to. Like this very instance. For whatever reason, Vivian had jumped in front and protected me. I tried not to think too much into it. I didn't want to seek an answer as to why a Guardian and host to so many demons would want to protect me, a war angel. For all her fowl mouth, bad actions and suspicions of murdering one of my friends and best soldiers–she has just saved my life.

I found her on the edge of a cliff. She was in her cat demon form and the claw marks that were etched around her paw told me she was probably trying to drag herself over and into the sea. Blood marred her as she was now unconscious and I could sense her life so close to extinguishing. I ripped my shirt off, placing it into my hands and pressed it against her hemorrhaging shoulder. Maybe a little too late but I just needed her to hold on long enough until I found somewhere safe. There was a hollowed tree close by that I saw earlier, possibly once lived in but vacant now. I clutched her unconscious body in my arms and flew there with the strong beats of my wings determined to not let her succumb to death. Although in her cat demon form she seemed surprisingly vulnerable and what I least expected was her cat demon opening up to me in the manner that all animals did.

She showed me images of certain hunts and killings they went on–passing time that went further into Vivian's memories. I blocked the images so I could concentrate on finding the hollowed-out tree. For whatever reason, her cat demon clung on with her instead of retracting from the contract. Very impressive considering she was fatally wounded. All other Guardians I had known died in their human form. With her cat demon opening up to me, I had the impression that it was almost loyalty, a suggestion that all the demons she was contracted to would stay with her until the very end. And that was the reason, I thought she hadn't yet died on that cliff's edge. They were desperately trying to keep her alive.

I found the tree and swooped in low. I entered the large hollowed tree that looked interiorly like a wooden cave. I put her down and removed the bandage to look down on her shoulder again. I had three choices. One. Let her die. And that seemed to be the easiest choice. It wasn't my obligation to keep her alive and stood against almost everything I believed in. Two. Very little people knew but I could teleport her to my own medical team but then it would violate the agreement between Haymen and me. She wasn't permitted to leave Shabeah. Even then it would raise too many questions and rumors from my own following and members for something I couldn't entirely explain. Or my third. Was costly to both her and me and almost a repulsive thought if I considered it seriously. I flexed my knuckles back and forth in consideration. I did owe her my life. And I had only ever owed a few that some of those that I did, weren't around anymore for me to repay it.

I inhaled and decided to act before reason set in. I knelt beside her and scoped her head in my arms. Despite being a demon cat, it still somewhat resembled her. Her unconscious face was somewhat serene until the movement made her wince. What I did need was her detached arm and so I thought of it, remembering it lying there on the ground and honed in on it. I teleported it into my hand. The cold limb was already lifeless. It had turned back to her human arm but would still do the trick.

I took a breath and prepared myself for the exhaustion that would come. I haven't done this ritual for a while. When I closed in on Vivian I was surprised to see that none of her demons fought against me. In fact they welcomed me to give her life. She had to unfold and bare open before me. She had to let me in. And my vulnerability was just as exposed in front of her. I haven't performed the ritual of what the commoners called Angel Kiss for some time. I burrowed my eyebrows as thoughts of the consequence rolled in. What would my people say? What would the high court say about this conflict of interest? It could be kept as a secret but for how long? This was a ritual made for our own kind and only performed by those who had lived the hundreds of years required to be able to perform it without inflicting death upon themselves.

I leaned down and kissed Vivian on the forehead. A life for a life was fair. Even if it was easier that I let her die. As I held her in my arms and closed my eyes I could sense that my wings began to glow a light pink. I couldn't help but smile at the smartass comment she would say if she saw the color. It lit the entire room as I concentrated on her, in place that some might call the afterlife. I had to find that little tether of her, of her life and bring her back. She was already slowly drifting in that darkness as I searched. Although her demon cat kept her alive on the physical plain, Vivian was slowly drifting and I wondered if I was taking her chance to escape. What if this life wasn't one she had chosen for herself? I tore away from the remnants of her own thoughts as questions rose in me that were of her own. It was a personal ritual to perform because from now on, not that she would enjoy to know and I had no intentions of telling her, we would be bound forever.

My life force would bring her back from that edge of death. She would always in one way or another be bound to me. That was the ritual of the Angel Kiss. And it was usually used on loved ones. It was a sacred and old gift, to use it on someone filled with demons was taboo. I pushed away my own sensitive thoughts and grabbed onto her, not letting her walk alone any further. This had been the second time I walked along death with someone. The second time I had performed the ritual. It had been many years since then but it still didn't prepare me for the serene and dark experience of walking along the edge with someone as they contemplated as to whether they should roll over and dive into the unknown for eternity. I held her hand as she was unaware of me. My light to her darkness. Most would have flashes of memory, of sentiment, laughter, those who they loved. Vivian was...

empty. There was nothing that surrounded her other than darkness. She didn't know the differences between rolling over into the unknown of death and the living. And I wondered if that was because, in a sense, she had already died once.

And then it hit me. As much as I think it rattled and woke her. We were walking together side by side, but I don't think she noticed me. I sensed her demon cat with us and what it dragged up was one of Vivian's most sacred and reserved memories. The one that defined her and even she had hidden from herself. The cat with its open eye opened the door and allowed us in. This was Vivian's trial and the matter which made her choose life or death. And so without realizing it, she stepped me into the memory as she revisited it herself as if watching it for the first time. This was how Vivian had died and been reborn.

"Okay well I shouldn't be too long. I just have to finish walking Brady and then I'll be home," I said to Aiden through the phone as I looked down at the overweight boxer. Big stuff Brady weighed more than me and then some yet he was gentle by nature... maybe too much.

"Alright, well don't be too long. It's getting dark and its taco night. Love you," Aiden said.

"Love you, too," I smiled and hung up on him. I put my phone in the pocket of my gym pants. I was circling my usual route that I walked most of my clientele's dogs within this area. It shocked even me that I could make a living out of how many people just didn't walk their dogs. Some cities used robotic walkers and services but Shabeah was known for its 'old school' personal 'human' touches.

I looked over the small business that struggled to stay afloat because of its positioning outside the city. I have never lived anywhere but Shabeah. By comparison, visitors had said it was beautiful and glorious but wouldn't stay for long. This was the demon's city and any smart human who dwelled here knew to be in before dark. That was just common sense. I nodded and smiled at the older woman who walked past me and turned left in between two of the stores. On my right was the flower shop that I enjoyed viewing the different arrangements and on my left was a bike shop which suspiciously caught my eye every time.

I had no idea how the small shop still survived but the motorbikes in the window sometimes seemed to call to me. As if I would ever ride a bike. Especially considering the price tag that went along with it. Aiden and I were saving to leave Shabeah. We had to if we wanted a serious future and to raise children together. This city had too many incidences to call it safe, even if with the treaty.

I walked around the back alleyway that stood opposite to the train tracks. I looked up at the giant glowing billboard that advertised current beauty trends. No shock that it was one of Haymen's Guardians, the demon lord who owned this city. She was beautiful and her skin was silk. Her golden locks trailed over her naked body as she advertised a new handbag. A nice signature scribbled 'Destiny'.

"Is this what we live for Brady?" I asked with a shake of my head and placed my earphone pods back into my ears to listen to music. I followed the back street and passed a rowdy bar. It looked a bit rough and so I always made sure to stay clear of it by walking on the other side of the road.

That little mark of paranoia got the best of me and I found myself for the next mile looking back behind me, swearing that I was being followed. The moment Brady began to growl was when I knew that I was more than likely being tailed. Or maybe I was being paranoid. Still keeping in the open space where others might see me. I tried to call Aiden. It went straight to voicemail.

There's a point when you know the difference between paranoia and legitimate fear. I was now hitting that mark. Fear rolled over me as I thought about the increase of my dreams I had been having. I never knew what they meant but they terrified me and I always feared that one day, that demon or whatever it was that followed me when I slept would come to get me as always promised. I began to casually jog. Looking behind me now and then to see if they followed. I couldn't see anyone.

I took a right and jogged up the stairs near the aquatic center. I walked past a younger male who gave me a very charismatic smile. It turned my stomach. I reached the top of the stairs and looked back down but he was no longer there. The hair on my skin rose as I looked around. I could see from this hill the train tracks in front of me and the houses past that. In the distance, the city lights flashed bright. It wasn't yet dusk but the temperature was dropping. I turned around where I could see cars lined up in the carpark to use the aquatic center. Surely no one would attack me in an open space but my body instinctually said otherwise.

I took one of my earphones out as Brady began barking. There was nothing but terrace in front of me, opposing the greenery that I was surrounded by. I couldn't see anyone walking out from the Aquarium to give me a sense of security. I tried to shake the chills that ran up my spine but knew something felt wrong. I looked over the terrace again as I began to walk forward. The setting sun was an array of oranges and pinks in the sky. I had that stupid thought that didn't help my current panic... what if it were the last one I ever saw?

My hurried step stopped as soon as that one changing movement narrowed my focus. I felt as if I had stepped into a square that was ridden with evil and darkness. I was so terrified that I couldn't step out of it even if I wanted to. Brady barked, his usual calm nature in hysterics and with hackles up.

The laughter surrounded me and vibrated up my spine. Surely someone would come out and help. Surely someone would see. But suddenly all that became irrelevant. I had entered somewhere different, cold and a new place to the world. I was living in the Demon city. That was all I could think of. Was I being attacked by a demon mid-day? Would I be one of those murdered and splattered as another casualty on newspapers?

"We've been looking for you?" the voice said to me and I wanted to drop in terror and cover my ears, hoping that it would go away. I still couldn't see anything, only hear the voice, the feeling was all too familiar. They have finally found me. My nightmares, they have become real and they've found me. I was so terrified that I couldn't speak.

My eyes widened as an all-black and muscular demon with rows of teeth appeared out of nowhere. I couldn't look away from it. I stopped *breathing and all fighting spirit left me. This was it, I was going to die. My legs trembled as I sobbed. The demon had cornered me. Run. Just run! But I couldn't move. All I could do was slowly loosen my trembling yet firm grip on Brady's lead. Run. It's not here for you. Brady ran for it, and a tear dropped as I was grateful to watch him try and escape. I watched after him making sure he got away safely. Another one of the demons appeared.*

"Brady!" I screamed before he was able to leave the square that we were trapped in. I stepped forward to run to him but the demon grabbed him from the side and ripped out his insides. The screeching that came from him forced me to reach a hand to my mouth as I sobbed. Would they rip my insides out? The demon began eating at him, enjoying the splayed guts.

"Stop it!" I screamed and grabbed my phone and pegged it at the demon. I was going to die anyway. I had no weapon to defend myself and not a chance against whatever these things were. But somewhere I mustered up some trembling strength. I had been running away from these demons who followed me in my dreams all my life. I wouldn't let them so easily take me down, no matter how pathetic that sentiment. One of them lunged for me and I dodged him, tripping over an uneven part in the pavement. How pathetic and predictable. I scurried up to jump out of the way but not in time as it bit into my shoulder and flung me across the pavement.

I screamed in pain clutching at my shoulder. Suddenly all my strength vanished and I was pinned against an invisible wall that barricaded me into this square. One continued to devour Brady as I curled my legs beneath me, trying to get further away from the one that walked towards me.

"We will drag you away and take you to Master." The voice said again. I couldn't see the person that spoke but I knew they were close. I could almost feel him standing behind the demon that was about to pounce on me. I wanted to look away but I couldn't. I stared into the black piercing eyes of the demon that was about to rip out my intestines as the other one had done to Brady. Tears spilt down my cheeks. Brady. My life. My everything. Everything was gone. I was soon to be gone.

The demon lunged for me and I covered my face with my arm. It latched on and I screamed as I punched it with my other hand to no avail trying to keep it away. It flung me across the wall again. This time I couldn't get up. I was in too much pain. My body was shaking and bleeding out. I sobbed as I tried to push myself up. The smell of blood hit my nose, the copper in the air would be the last of my memories. Blood. My death was to be covered in blood.

The demon lunged again and I tried to roll away. A loud crash interfered and I could almost feel the walls that kept me barricaded in being broken down. A darkness swept around me and lashed out at the demon before it could lunge at me again. It yelped and was flung into oblivion. It had literally vanished into nothing. The darkness that swept around me snaked in a blanket and I was more terrified of it then I was the demons who had been attacking me.

A beautiful man appeared in front of me. Porcelain skin, with contrasted black hair and well dressed. I recognized him straight away, had seen images and articles on him. Haymen Davolch, the demon lord of Shabeah. Waves of darkness pooled from him as he turned and those icy blue eyes that screamed terror turned to me.

He leaned down and ignored my bleeding arms. His intensity made me uncomfortable but I was going to die anyway so I didn't look away.

"Why do they want you?" he asked me in a voice that vibrated through me and enticed me to a place I could never understand. When he spoke, it was almost like he was coaxing me into a world filled with evil and lust. I couldn't speak and felt his waves of darkness rub up against me as if trying to pry open the answer himself.

The second demon lunged for his back and in mid-air the darkness wrapped around him and the demon exploded. Blood splattered everywhere and I shook, the scream unable to leave me as its blood coated my face. I could feel my life draining from me. I looked down at my shredded arms and realized that my injuries were a lot worse than I had realized. I was shaking and cold, too scared and pumping with adrenalin to have noticed.

Even if it felt like Haymen and I had stolen a moment, it took me away from the reality of my death. I choked and spluttered red. I looked down at my blood coated front. This was it. I was going to die. I looked back at the predator who gazed at me through blue eyes.

With no consideration of fear anymore because I knew I was already dying, I looked at the most powerful man in front of me and thought of the only way I would want to go out facing such a demon. With a smartass comment. "The scowl is a bit too much wouldn't you say?" I coughed out another patch of blood that didn't reach him and keeled over. Instead of falling to my side the darkness that oozed out of him seemed to support me.

"I could give you another life," he said, in that voice that was coaxing. "There is something about you that draws them to you. You will be of service to me," he said.

"I don't want it," I panted through a coarse breath. My body slowly became irrelevant to me as the surroundings began to swirl in colors of orange and pink. "I'm done with being hunted," and that was the truth I had never been able to admit that to anyone else out loud. No one knew what I have suffered or what I see when I sleep. No one could protect me from it and all my life it scared me. Finally, they have come for me and a part of me was relieved to know that I could die instead of the graphic unknown that they tried to show me so many times before. At least this way, I could die as me. "I finally get to be free."

He smirked at my dying words and pressed his lips against mine. It was fiery and demanding and my body could only react. He stared into my eyes as I did his. He pulled away and licked my blood from his lips. What a sinister man to force himself on a dying woman. Not man— demon.

"So, you've returned," is all he said before dark needles, no his darkness pierced into me and raped me of the person I had once been. I screamed as everything I knew, loved, and felt, was taken from me and darkness filled the void that would remain. The last thing I saw was his blue eyes before languages and demons crept from the dark. There was no battering. No denial. They instantly filled me and created my being. I screamed as they merged into my skin making me feel unbearably hot. I couldn't even see their faces but felt the evil fill me. If I could've *attempted to claw them out, I would have. But they seeped into my skin as quickly as they had come.*

And then there was one... one woman... not woman, but demon that came forth. The odd feeling was that she didn't enter my body but had only awaken. She was beautiful as she was deadly. And yet I couldn't see what she looked like. But a part of me knew and felt that she had been the one to react to Haymen's kiss. That somehow both of them felt... familiar. As soon as she took her place inside of me, my body felt as if it went up in flames and the life I once knew had vanished.

Evil. Lust. Blood. It was all I was and craved. I was a creature of darkness and the only way to creep out of my newborn egg was to tug on the string that was attached to Haymen. It took me the longest of times to creep from that darkness. But slowly I came and was reborn, into the hands of the Master that would never let me go.

I gasped as Vivian pushed me out. As if the doorway that had just been opened was as a shock to her as it was to me. I looked down and noticed that through the ritual I had already resealed her arm. The trace of my light pink lining marred it. The completion of the Angel Kiss ritual. Vivian had returned to her human form. Exhausted I leaned back against the hollowness to the inside of the tree. It was dark outside now. I must've been doing the ritual for hours.

She was still unconscious. I don't know what came over me but I pushed back the hair that clung to her sweaty skin. She had spoken the truth, she had never chosen this life for herself. Haymen had forced her into it. And to so intimately feel that violation and life taken from her, I wanted to hug her and so I did. I gave her the hug that she had wanted when she was scared and alone. When everything was being taken from her and she so very much wanted to die.

But she chose now to live, for a second time, accepting my aid in her survival. I could sense the difference of the person she once was and what she had become now. I continued pushing back her hair, almost feeling protective of the girl she had once been. I knew that wasn't her anymore but something was taken from her and I knew with all my unanswered questions about the interest that I had taken in her, that there were others who still wanted to take more from her. And there was only one person who could answer that. Haymen had a lot to answer for. Vivian might have not realized it at the time but it was the Volv that spoke to her in her dreams when she was human. What was more alarming was the demons that listened and attacked her. Who had been after her and why?

As if on queue, I felt Haymen's presence teleport in. The shuddering coldness he oppressed every time swept around the tree that we rested on. I pressed my own light against it, not letting it touch Vivian any more than it already had. People died every day and I didn't care much for humans. But what he did to her was against the treaty and my own personal morals. I was almost disgusted that someone like me, if not any angel was there to protect her against such wrong doing. More pointedly I wish that I had been the one to protect her. And I pushed that uncertain thought into a place I would never touch again. I walked out of the hollowed tree and confronted the demon lord who for years I've wanted to kill. And now I felt like any control of doing things 'correctly' was a thing of the past.

Chapter Twenty-Eight- Gabe

I walked out of the hollowed entrance and into the dark. My wings naturally glowed bright against Haymen's darkness. I insured that the same safety and protection surrounded Vivian despite her natural defense and aura of darkness that tried to protect her from my own.

I stood in front of the entrance making sure my shoulders blocked his view of her. He snarled at the gesture. Reason wasn't exactly reaching me, even in my weaker state after the ritual. I focused on my bedroom within my own city and teleported one of my spears into my hand, swiveling it and slammed the bottom of it into the ground next to me. I would guard her from him. He began to laugh, the echo cringe worthy as it seeped throughout the trees.

"You seem rather attached to my Vi," he seethed with a cruel smile. I ignored his statement. This ran deeper than her. But suddenly I realized that a lot of Haymen's focus was on her. She was something special, she was a weakness of his that I could exploit. When he forced her into the contract he considered her to be familiar and someone he already knew. I wondered who it could be for him to allow her time to nurture and grow. I don't even think Vivian knew what hold she might have over him. I wondered what she would think of it all now that she had relived those memories that were so tightly tucked away.

"Your assassination attempt failed. How pathetic you've become if you fear confronting me yourself," I said to him. Graphic memories of years of our fighting consumed me. The war which we both desired a serious outcome. Those many years were challenging on my people. To be the head of war and lead my angels was an honor but the truth was, I barely made it out intact. With that much shedding of blood and carnage it was hard for any man to stay sane let alone stay 'pure'. I was close to the edge of darkness and I wanted it to consume me. Killing would be so much easier if I was a fallen angel. It is harder to be mighty and great opposed to becoming a dark angel and allowing that which came natural to me to be my entirety. But then I would be no better than him.

Haymen brushed his hand through his black hair, the silk fitting for the charming evil that he was. His black tendrils misted from him as throwing knives and blades began to hover around him as he teleported them in. He offered me the vicious smile that I had too often confronted. Our fight had been prolonged to just under five hundred years now. Not because of species and power, but it was personal. Has been since the last war.

"I despise those who take interest in my property. I've allowed this ridiculous following for too long now. It's beyond entertaining. Have you fucked her?" The weapons began to increase and the way he spoke of her only grated on me more. "Do you know what happens to those who touch my property?"

"But she's more to you than just that, isn't she? It's not Vivian you're actually referring to," I said coolly. His black eyes mixed with gold, as the mass of his power pillowed out. It was a reaction I'm sure not even he realized that he had let escape. For all his power, there was one thing he always lacked and that was restraint. I didn't know what laid dormant in Vivian that he wanted or even who he wanted, but it was important to him. He defiled the woman I protected now for his own means. I gritted my teeth. I didn't know if it was because of the ritual or a protectiveness I carried for generations but I didn't want him touching her anymore. Especially when she couldn't defend herself like those two years ago.

Haymen sniffed the air and his head crooked to one side. His eyes fixated on me as they turned to that gold and then black again. His eyes were pulsating as his wrath surrounded me and thickened. "You defiled her?" His voice was only a whisper. "Angel Kiss."

This had nothing to do with the treaty, the council or even Vivian. I cocked a smile. "Looks like you're not the only one she is bound to."

He vanished as the knives propelled forward towards me. I grabbed my spear circling it in a motion so fast that it knocked the blades away from me. In that second, I vanished from the claws of darkness that would dare try to penetrate the light that countered it. I teleported to meet him in the shadows. Teleporting was for only the old and those who could master it. If not done properly some would be lost forever. It was rapid speed and movement as we fought in that motion. For most, to fight while teleporting would be a death sentence. That was most regular warriors. Particles spread around us as we brush past one another time and time again trying to collide and find each other unguarded for a fatal blow.

There were lots of countering as our darkness and light fought against one another trying to counter our physical hits. He was the demon king and I was the war angel. This dance had been playing for far too long. I teleported with my spear aiming to stab him in the chest. He deflected it with his own weapon. I changed my own, teleporting my twin blades and countered his.

Minor demon crows swept in aiming for me as he teleported them in and out. Vile creatures that swooped and ate away at their enemies. I teleported through flocks of them, slicing through them as they came near and countered his next attack. Flames crept towards me and I surrounded myself with water, teleporting in part of the ocean and cocooning it around me.

In every way we were opposites. We would only agree and come to terms on the surface of death. My one irritation was that I knew I was weaker right now after the ritual and I could only keep this up for so long. The ritual had taken a lot of energy from me, taking part of my life to complete Vivian's.

We fought close to the hollowed tree. I purposefully kept it close, so I knew that he wouldn't venture any closer to her. It irked me so much to think of him touching her, of commanding her like he did. But within reason, she was his Guardian, contracted to work for him and never had she led on that she opposed that.

I growled and snapped my wings tight in infuriation. Why did I even save her? Was it to get back at Haymen? Because I knew it would end in a fight I had been waiting for, for so long like now?

On the outside of our continuous teleporting there was a presence that crept up. Three to be precise.

"We will end this soon enough. Away from the treaty and commandments," Haymen said before disappearing completely. I teleported to the front of the hollowed-out tree and swept my wings out allowing my light to destroy the remnants of Haymen's darkness. We were both technically governed and had to keep the charade up. But one day one of us would end up dead at the others hand. And I would make sure that it was him.

There was a minor cut along my rib that I healed instantly. I waited for the three to arrive who carried light instead of darkness. Angels. But at this sensitive time of just completing the ritual no one would be considered a friend. I tried to rule my head with logic. Why had I performed that on Vivian? A Guardian, a woman contracted to demons and Haymen most of all.

I tried to reel in my protectiveness of her. The ritual was a profound thing. Binding your life to someone else's... the days following that until we were both completely healed often led to over possessiveness and protectiveness. I had seen a very old friend once save his lover but be executed for the lack of his control after the ritual. He wouldn't let anyone close to either of them... even his own kind.

I stayed guard out front as the three approached. They were familiar and three faces I didn't want to see right now.

"Why are you here?" I asked the woman that led them. Tahlia and the two men behind her were in fighting form as usual and security to my father. Tahlia was beautiful in her own right but lethal. Her short bobbed brown hair allowed her tattoos to be seen even up the back of her neck. Her arms were covered in stories of wars she had fought and gruesome stories that she had seen. The interesting thing about Tahlia and the reason my father kept her close was because speckles of her feathers were black. Whether still close to rolling into becoming a fallen and dark angel, she was not all pure. As soon as an angel was compromised they were shunned and discarded but my father made sure to protect Tahlia until that day.

"Your Father requested that we find you after hearing that you were within Shabeah instead of your own post ruling your own city. A bit old to be playing detective don't you think?" She said. The other two men looked around. Although I swept away the remnants of Haymen's presence, we could still feel the evil around us and I tried my hardest to cover the smell of Vivian. I hoped that they couldn't sense her on me after the ritual.

Tahlia was only short in size but her wings compensated for the size difference. She shut them in tight as she walked closer and the twisted greens of her tips glowed to suppress the darkness from touching her.

"Lyra sent word and concern for how you've reacted to Luke's death. Trailing a Guardian doesn't seem all that dignified."

Every part of me wanted to wrap my hand around her throat to protect Vivian and prevent her from stepping closer. I didn't look towards the hallowed tree but I couldn't stand the thought of them imposing on her. The other two swept the area and the notion wasn't unnoticed. They were surrounding me. No one was friend or foe. Even my father at times I had doubts. I was his son, but only by blood. The moment I took to the field he had me only revered as a glorified warrior as he gave pretty military speeches in the background. My father's power and age surpassed even that of the Council. And very few times would he waste his time checking up on me.

"Then I will make sure to punish her for her disobedience and interference when I return. I was granted access and suspicious rights by the Council."

One of the men scoffed to my left and this time I snapped. I lunged for him and pinned him to the tree with my hand around his throat. I snapped the blade shut back in its sheath at his waist as he tried to take it out. I snarled at him and stared at him long enough for him to realize his mistake of hierarchy. He might follow my father but I could definitely kill him. My father might've eaten well, given pretty speeches as the last war almost destroyed us against the demons; but I was the one leading and gaining that respect of fellow warriors. This young one here, although strong, had no understanding of that. And when I looked him dead in the eye he looked away to Tahlia unsure of what he should do.

I noticed the other angel's interest heading towards the hollow tree and so I let go of the current one I held and paced back. My maneuver was a tactical one. I was making sure I was in the middle of all three in a defensive position. I opened my wings fully and widened my stance. It was a display of muscle and size. I allowed my power to leak and radiate in a show of hierarchy. But the true purpose of it was to block out the view of the tree.

"Your Father requests you leave here at once. You are creating small talk that raises questions and possible embarrassment for your father," Tahlia said matter of fact.

"Tell my Father to speak to his son himself instead of sending his dogs. After fifty years of not speaking to his only son, this is what he calls my attention for?" I hissed. "Get out of my sight. Now." I reiterated to the man standing behind me who seemed to be taking subtle steps closer. "I have another three weeks that I am sure will go by before he knows it. If you do not leave within five seconds I will acknowledge it as a challenge."

I could feel the wind reacting to my temper as it whirled around us. The storm had reached my eyes and I would not tolerate disobedience. Perhaps I had to send Father a message to stay out of my affairs.

"Gabe, we didn't come here to fight. All we ask-"

"One," I began counting to Tahlia. I watched the two men as they slowly circled me. "Two." I watched them closely. If I wanted to, I could kill all three within minutes no matter how powerful they might be.

"Gabe-" Tahlia hissed. To her I was being a fool. Her patronizing reminded me that of my Father.

"Three." I clenched my knuckles and the first flash of lightning flickered in the distance as the clouds came over.

Tahlia hissed. "Disengage," she said to the others. And with that they followed her as she whipped her wings out wide and boosted into the treetops. I waited until the rain began to pour. Minutes went by and I was certain they had completely retreated. I was certain that they didn't notice Vivian or the residue of the Angel Kiss ritual. If anything, Haymen's interference had cleared up the remnants. I stepped back into the warmth of the tree and sat across from Vivian watching her as her eyes moved and her eyelids fluttered.

They would report back to my father that I was investigating the forestry outside Shabeah. Let him scoff at the childish detective work he thought I was doing. As I stared at Vivian I wondered to what extent and role she would play to the storm I felt brewing. I looked down on my right forearm and noticed the curl and burn mark of the new tattoo engraved in my skin. It was an array of swirls that had three distinctive lines through it. I looked over at the light pink tattoo that had marred Vivian's skin matching the exact same imprint. I dragged my hands through my hair and shook my head. Why did I save her? Why would I offer her something so sacred as my Angel Kiss? Angels and demons were not companions. We were two sides of a separate coin, separated by worlds of darkness and light.

I stayed far back from her avoiding the intimate touches that I craved. The few days after the angel kiss would be the worst. Fighting against the urge to protect, claim, and be within the same room as her at all times would be something that would test even me. I wondered if she, the host of demons would feel the same? I looked out at the hammering rain and sighed heavily. No, I couldn't let it happen. A debt had to be paid after she saved my life. That was all that this was and all it could be.

I had to focus and keep in mind that I was in search of Luke's killer and the source of the Volv that has taken particular interest in Vivian. My gaze crossed between Vivian and the storm. Where has my logical mind gone and what have I done?

CHAPTER TWENTY-NINE- VIVIAN

The flicker of heat and flames warmed my skin. I winced lethargically and pushed myself up from the hard, rocky ground. In front of me was a small fire pit, not that weather or temperature change affected me. I looked past the flames and into the intense forest green eyes of Gabe. We stared at one another for the longest time. I'd never cared much for other's thoughts or opinions but so much intensity coursed through his eyes and pinned me. It didn't unsettle me but I wanted to know what he was thinking, why such a storm was raging in those eyes and the outside of the hollowed tree we were staying in. Rain pelted down and wafted in a fresh smell from the forest.

There was a part of me I realized with great confusion that wanted to touch him. To see if he was real and moving. His face was stone cold and restrained. It led nothing on. Just raw power of light emanated from him, even if he didn't realize it, my own darkness cocooned me uncomfortable by its sensitivity to it. No words emitted as I tried to rally my own memory of events.

"I was certain I was going to die," I said and finally broke our eye contact to look down at my left arm that was intact. My gaze hit the soft pink markings of a new tattoo that marred where my arm had been reattached. I moved it back and forth with full motion. The pink tattoo, but... I looked back up at Gabe and knew that he had done something. The marking felt light, angelic and good. It was uncomfortable on my skin, like the remains of a burn mark to my usual acquainted and familiarity of darkness. "What did you do to me?"

He still stared at me and didn't move. His knuckles were white and I realized that for whatever reason it was, he was holding himself back from me. I didn't understand the compulsion to reach out for him either. The darkness that guided me told me to stay on the other side of the fire. But the reality of the situation was, the one man who knew what had happened to me while I was out cold and near dead wouldn't speak to me. Irritation began to boil. I stood up and headed for the opening. His gaze followed me.

I could smell and feel the rain but as soon as my foot reached the entrance I was blocked in by the light that surrounded the tree. A protective barrier of sorts. It felt and smelled like Gabe. It wasn't as powerful as Haymen who emitted the same raw power of darkness but I did attempt to press whatever I had against it. Nothing, not even a budge. I blew out a sigh of frustration.

"So now you're going to trap me in here?" Again, he didn't speak but he took a harsh swallow. The singular motion had me fixating on his neck and the subtle change turned my rage into lust. His arms were defined nicely through his shirt, one that I very much wanted to take off. The room suddenly felt a lot hotter than I wanted it to be and I licked my lips to distract me. But I couldn't look away and his gaze didn't leave mine.

There was a pull that didn't make sense. It was beyond my usual desire of lust and sex. I needed him in me. I needed to... *claim* him. That key word, claim. Still with the feeling of the light burning the tattoo on my arm, I walked over to him. The tattoo felt like him, was a part of him, and I couldn't describe in words what I felt against my usual lack of emotion. His knuckles seemed whiter as he clamped his fist in his hand. I knelt in front of him, my eyes tracing over his every muscle and line as if it were the first time I had seen him. No resentment, hatred, or games like we had before. This was a marring I couldn't understand. I couldn't love but this felt like the intensity closest to how I imagined it to be.

"What did you do to me?" I asked coolly. Every part of me wanted to pull him in. I thought he was a fine specimen prior and could admit I wanted to have my way with him but something had changed. I have changed and from his firm grip and cock which I noticed had hardened against his jeans as he sat cross legged, something has changed for him too. Before I could lean closer into him and touch him, he pressed his hand towards me to stop. He swallowed hard before he spoke. As if talking to me might be the unleashing of what he tried to hold back. I wasn't sure of how much restraint could be put on me as he pressed his light against me, which demanded my inner darkness to repress.

"You were going to die. You bled out and lost your arm. There was a ritual I performed to keep you alive. Don't look into it. It was in exchange for you aiding me and protecting me when that witch had cast her spell."

I didn't care much for the cheesy stuff. "What ritual?" I asked. His forest green eyes flashed with a harsh color as the thunder around us responded and somewhere close, a bolt hit and shook the ground. It vibrated through me only turning me on more from the display and release of his power. I swallowed as I looked down at his size that pressed harshly against his jeans. He noticed and tightened his jaw. He wouldn't so much as move. His positioning seemed to be his only power of restraint. "What have you done?" I asked. For us to have both changed so much it must have been some serious ritual. From this small tattoo I felt connected to him somehow and the brightness of that irritated me. What had he done to me?

"It's called Angel Kiss. It enables me to transmit some of my life force into yours and to heal a fatal wound. There are side effects, however." He took a gulp. "I ask of you Vivian, please stay close to me over the next few days. If you don't it will turn me into a madman."

"What are the side effects?" I asked and surprisingly my voice was quiet. I pressed my hand to my throat surprised by the soft tone that came out. Now what was that? A feminine response to his masculine and clipped one. His eyes followed the movement of my hand.

His jaw clenched tighter as his rough voice responded. "Don't you already feel it?" My eyes flickered to his gaze and the raw lust that was there snapped me. I pushed away any rational thought and let my body act, as I had always done, even if it were under some weird ass angel spell right now. I pushed through the light he emanated against me to keep me at bay and paused in front of his face to search his eyes. His breath hitched as did mine. I sat in front of him on my knees. I felt weak and powerful all at once. Human and demon all the same. I felt...

woman in front of him, a sensation and complexity I haven't wanted or known for a very long time.

I had only a second of hesitation. What if this feeling was irreversible? I wasn't one to doubt my actions but I genuinely feared if this was how I would feel all the time. Because looking into those stormy green eyes that looked like a vicious storm on the sea, I would not be able to restrain. I hitched another breath, not having realized I haven't breathed since the moment I moved on him. The flames flickered on my back. There was no going back but I couldn't move.

"Vi," his voice came out as a husky growl. "These are side effects that require our restraint." The restraint in his tone was choking him. Vi, that was the first time he had called me that. I took my first breath in what felt like a lifetime and the coolness of my own mingled with the warmth of his. Already I could feel him inside of me, filling me from my insides and lungs. I wanted that in more ways than one.

He took another gulp as I poised slightly over him. His eyes didn't move from mine but if possible, his body went more rigid. "Please have restraint," he said clipped.

"I can't do restraint. But I can do you," I breathed into his ear. His hand grabbed the back of my hair, the first movement he had done since I awoke. I felt his light pulsing around me, which made me only thrum annoyingly with desire between my legs. He arched my head back, trying to push me away. He fixated on my exposed neck and I lowered myself back to the ground in front of him.

"Sometimes we don't need to think about right or wrong. There is the instinctual habit of an indescribable need that requires to be filled," I said closing my eyes and sinking into the niggling feeling of his light against my darkness as if it alone were rubbing against me and stimulating me. I let a small moan escape my lips anticipating how Gabe could make me feel and it was nothing short of savage. A low grunt escaped him reacting to my own imagination and noise. I flashed my eyes open and looked at him. Hungry. Predator. And no angel. That restraint snapped.

He pressed his lips against mine, claiming me. He continued to tug my hair back as if controlling the motion as I kissed him back. He pressed his other hand to my back, pressing me into him, almost crushing me as he did so. I molded into him perfectly raking my nails down his chest and stomach.

His wings curled around us as if every part of him had to be swept up and touching me. I lowered my hand to his hard shaft that pressed painfully against his jeans. I went to undo them but he spun me in seconds and pressed my back against the bark of the tree. His hand slid under my shirt scrunching still in attempt to restrain himself. His larger frame pinned me as his other hand slid up my inner thigh leaving me to tremble in anticipation.

I twisted my neck so I could kiss him behind me. I bit down on his lower lip, growling at the hotness that devoured my body. I was already on my way to climaxing from our darkness and light that opposed one another. And he hasn't even touched me. He shuddered, his every action a response to my own. He pulled back staring into my eyes once again.

"This is the ritual. The claiming part of it. We don't want this," he said heavily breathing. He was trying to convince himself out loud. I slid my hand over his bulge and he buckled into me. As he did, his light pressed harsher against me. There was no malice tainting it. Only lust and passion. Every hair on my body rose as it continued rubbing against me. I did the same to him as a natural response.

"I don't care what it is. I want it," I breathed out pressing into him. I rubbed my ass against his cock and he rubbed against me his cock rubbing against both of our jeans. He inhaled my breath as I continued to motion into him, in desperation to come undone. My tattoos began to glow bright blue and that was the wash over of water for Gabe. I haven't turned into any of my demons but I was losing control. He stepped back shaking his head. And suddenly that seductive and hungry light that wanted to devour me pushed up again in resistance.

"No." Is all he said before pressing one final kiss to my lips which put me in a drowsy state. He walked out. His light which held as a barrier still kept me in but I could sense him not far from the tree gathering his breath. Rage fluxed through me as I considered the rejection as well as my drifting body that fought the sleep he had placed on me. He had done this to me before, unsuspecting of the kiss that would put me to sleep. My body was still hot for him, needing him to fill me which only pissed me off more! What has he done to me?! I resisted the urge but fell to the side as I fell into an uncomfortable slumber.

CHAPTER THIRTY- GABE

I teleported Vivian into her sleeping quarters. Every touch was like a flame wrapping itself around me. It both burned and was pleasurable. I knew the claiming would be hard to resist but I didn't realize I would lack control to the extent of almost having sex with her. The claiming was often described as the person who did the ritual was trying to claim part of their self that they put into the other. For most it ended in sex, but in years for the elders who could do it, often it was only designed for long term lovers.

I didn't want to resort to putting her to sleep. One of the many useful skills I learned over the years but it was the only way I could put a halt on our lack of control. That was an action that couldn't happen no matter how much I desired it myself. It was dark in the room and no one had woken to our intrusion. I tucked her in the blankets and pushed part of the hair that had slid to her eyes. She was beautiful. That much I would admit. I teleported out knowing that she would be asleep until the early hours or the morning. That gave me plenty of time to start my own investigations once again.

I swiped over my watch and made the call. It had already been two weeks since I wasn't present to govern my own city. I phoned my second in command, Torrin, who was my current fill in. I waited for him to answer with the small implanted ear piece as I walked the dark alleyways of Shabeah. My light was constantly pushing away the pollution of darkness and evil that lingered in every space of the city. Heavy population of demons often created it and it was disgusting to know that humans not only lived in it but revered it.

I walked to the end of the bricked apartments and looked towards the city and glow of the night. Bright lights shone like a beacon and a hot air balloon drifted overhead slowly advertising the reverence of the Guardians. One each side for all five members–one of which I hadn't yet seen–stood there like idols advertising some kind of weaponry seller's store. I focused on Vivian in her succubus form as Torrin finally picked up.

"It's midnight," he breathed through the phone with little agitation. He would never dare speak to me how he did some of the others.

"Don't tell me you were sleeping already?" I teased him.

"No. But I was enjoying the company of a certain brunette until my boss called," he said and I could hear him shuffling through sheets and the mumbles of a woman by his side.

I laughed at him. The sound of a familiar voice was rather refreshing after the hellish two weeks I'd already had. "Obviously I'm doing them a favor. Should you pass over the comms device so I can show them what a good time really is?"

"I don't know why you don't just teleport here and see me yourself. A bit old school of you to call me," he said seriously. He was one of the few who knew I could 'officially' teleport.

"I have to stay close to my marker on this one," I said thinking of Vivian. I had to stay within the city and close so I could feel if anything happened. And with the remnants of our ritual she was all I could sense and feel. Even the fresh air wasn't blurring that burning focus. But I had to get out, remove myself from her before I did truly drive myself mad.

"Have you pinned that Demon Summoner yet for Luke's murder?" He snarled through the phone. I walked down another alleyway where a rowdy pub housed a bunch of drunks. Across from it was the bike shop that was in Vivian's memory. I continued walking towards to find the staircase to the aquarium like I had been vividly shown in her memories.

"I think we might have more serious issues here than we thought. I need you to do some searching yourself for me. I've picked up the presence of the Volv within Shabeah."

"The Volv?!" He hissed through the phone. Torrin was one of the few who fought along my side in the last war and survived. He knew too well of the carnage the Volv left behind. "I thought they were killed."

"That would be our mistake for presuming so," I said as I walked up the cemented stairs recalling her own heartbeat and fright for being followed. "Have you had any issues while I've been gone?"

"We've had a few issues. A couple of demon break-ins and attacks but nothing fatal. We have noticed a slight increase but nothing that hasn't been manageable."

"From what I'm seeing here and whether it's demon central or not, there seem to be a lot demon attacks and activity here." The aquarium was across from me and I walked into the section where Vivian breathed her last goodbyes as human. It has been two years but scorch marks still remained on the cement. Her scream and pain vibrated through me at the memory of her life being ended and filled with demons instead.

"Surely you don't have to investigate this yourself. I can follow the Demon Summoner-"

"No!" I snapped possessively. There was a surprised silence on the other end of the phone and I tried to breath out my frustration. I rattled my brain back and forth chastising myself for having reacted to the bond. Why did I do this to myself? I could have just let her to die instead. But looking at the ground where she had died already once and remembering her crawl to throw herself off the cliff, I was sad for her. She never had time to value or mourn her first death.

"I'm sorry Gabe. I didn't mean to insult you," he said on the other end of the phone. A shadow caught my eye close to the aquarium entrance. I could hear the laughter from a woman as a cloaked figure pushed off the door of the building to catch my attention. I could sense from here that she wreaked of vileness but beneath the robe was a light blue glow. One that reminded me of the Guardians.

"I've got to go," I said hanging up on him. The concealed person began to walk away, leading me. I could've confronted them but for whatever reason they were leading me somewhere and unlike the witch sneak attack last time, I wouldn't leave myself unguarded. My light was bright around me, protecting me against any hidden attacks or ambush.

I kept to their pace which sped up and ended on the edge of the block in an old run-down shrine. It looked like an old one where people once prayed for religion and a God before the introduction of Angels. I hadn't seen a church for years and it was almost in bad taste that they still had one standing in Shabeah of all places.

The dusty and worn-down building looked as if it had almost once been burned down. The wooden front door was left open slightly for me to enter behind them. Inside, candles were lit lining the room. I stepped inside the room that was dusty and uninhibited. The cloaked figure was standing beside the podium.

The room was drenched in darkness and vile that meant this wasn't the first meeting place for the guardian in front of me. But there was something twisted and dark that wrapped around the room.

"Who are you?" I asked the figure stretching out my wings in dominance. A woman's laugh echoed the room and then the woman took off her hood. I instantly recognized her as the woman who was on the hot air balloon. So, she was the fifth member of this generation of Guardians. But her beauty was no longer there. All that remained of what was once her was the blonde of her hair. Now her face had strained blue veins popping out especially around her mouth and eyes. Her eyes lit with a darkness that pinned in and out to focus on me. It only confirmed what I have been thinking.

"You're a part of the Volv." Her laugh echoed the room and I honestly thought that maybe it was her real voice box. The Volv that had mingled with her had so forcefully claimed her.

"They used to call me Doreen," she said looking over her face in the reflection of a puddle that had leaked from the roof.

"What is your kind doing here?" I demanded from her. The shift in the darkness stirred and her tattoos glowed bright blue. Her face began to twist into that of one of her demons.

"I'm just here to distract you and play," she began to laugh. "Next time you shouldn't leave your princess alone."

The light from the candles blew out and a wave of darkness swept before me. *Vivian.*

CHAPTER THIRTY-ONE- VIVIAN

It was snowing and I was freezing! Even with my thick layered jacket, hand mittens, and beanie, the chill cut through to the bone. I clung to my books at the university I was walking through. It was old and gothic styled. The ground and cobbled ground hid under the pillows of white. This wasn't a memory. This was new world created by the puppeteer of this dream. I have never studied in a university. Skilled fighting, controlling demons and assassination–Yes. University–No.

I proceeded to restroom. A few people greeted me on my way. The lingering eyes of a guy in a jersey jacket didn't go astray. He looked like such a stereotypical cocky jock. Muscular, beautiful and blonde hair. I have to admit my pace slowed as I considered talking to him. Instead I smiled and kept walking past. What could I say, I was a sucker for an attractive arrogant boy.

I admired the gothic style of the two-story buildings on either side of me. Irrelevant people spoke to one another hidden behind the pillars of the second story before some proceeded to go into their classes.

"Vi!" A hand reached out for me and pulled me into the warmth of a private room.

"Aiden?" I said confused. Even in this dream I knew that we had been broken up for a long time but with a human heart he stirred unsettled emotions within me.

"Look. I know it's been some time but I can't not say anything. You know I miss you," he began. The rest of his words became a blur as I studied his face to etch into my memory even if it was a dream and I wasn't entirely sure where it was leading me or if I was in control of the events that would come. I couldn't help but feel with this human heart that was projected in my dream. If this were real, I might've cried.

Before I realized it, he had crushed his lips onto mine taking me by surprise. The kiss was comfortable and committed. We had been together for five years. We had history, love and passion. His hand trailed under my jacket and pressed into my lower back. I twisted my tongue with his as he pushed me against one of the desks that appeared at the edge of the room. Everything else was irrelevant. Before I knew it, I was laying on the ground with him as we intertwined with passionate kisses. I knew where this was leading and I wanted it but I pushed him back. This was not my dream nor was it a figment of my imagination. I was certain I was trapped in a shadow dream but nothing has yet revealed itself. Was this a normal dream?

But I could never risk it. The consequence of leaving myself vulnerable would be my life. And I had already fallen for sexual content as a form of bait before. That was the thing with these Shadow Dreams. My attacker appeared as anything, could even make me feel enticed to touch and kiss them. Once I was enticed to follow a small girl down a well. When I realized it felt wrong I awoke myself instantly as soon as it started rearing its ugly head. Another time was having idle chat with an aunt who tried to coax me into having a bath. I didn't have an aunt.

Being with Aiden felt so good but I couldn't risk it. "I can't," I said with as much force to push away the temptation and pushed him away. I stood up and left the room having one more glance at the man I was to reject and leave behind, again.

I made my way outside into the freezing cold where people still went about their daily business. I continued to the restrooms taking a right and admiring the monolithic pillars and whitened room. Mirrors circled the powder room. Admiring the clothing that the women wore I realized that this happened a long time ago before the treaty between angels and demons. This must've been in the late 1900's easily. One woman in particular grabbed my attention. She seemed to stick out opposed to the proper young women who had just left. Only the two of us now remained. She had numerous colors throughout her short hair that spiked out and black clothing that might've seemed a little bit too chilly in the current weather but she seemed comfortable.

I walked over to wash my hands and took note of her. Despite her extroverted exterior she seemed shy as she smiled at me. "I'm Louana Smith. It's my first year here studying journalism. It's nice to meet you," she charmed in an awkward manner. She was small and fragile looking *and I furrowed my eyebrows as to why I was taking so much notice of her. She held out her hand as if to shake mine and then saw the time on her wristwatch. "Oh, I have to go. I let the time get the better of me. Nice to meet you," she said before dashing out of the room. The moment she left I felt the presence sweep in.*

When I took a step to follow her escape everything froze including my body. An echoing and entertained laugh encircled the room as the flash of a figure darted past the mirrors.

Wake up! I tried to tell my body. This was bad. Very bad. This was something worse than what I usually dealt with. Every hair on my body rose and I feared for my life. I restlessly tried to run and oppose my frozen body.

Sweat began to drip down my neck as it instantly got hot and I knew that whatever this creature was in my dreams, it had the power to control fire. I had never dealt with that in my shadow minds before. It was like a real demon in the one place I was most vulnerable and couldn't call upon my own.

I was flung and suspended into the air by a gust of wind. Fire and wind! Get out! Wake up! If I didn't make it out now I knew that I would be scorched by flames. The heat began to rise as jarring and rhythmic clubbing kind of music began. Above all of that was his laughing, he enjoyed my suffering and inability to escape. He was theatrical and I couldn't look down to see his face despite trying. I could feel the flames creep up and tried my hardest to wake myself. Somehow, I needed to. He began to speak to me but I focused on trying to make my escape.

Wake up! Wake up! Wake up! Heat wrapped around to envelope me and I began to cry as the tips of those flames licked at me.

My room enveloped my focus as I woke in the state of in-between. I was neither fully awake nor was I still asleep. I had been pulled from the shadow dream. Instead of being confronted by the red spider like creature; red numbers and lines were written all over my roof and walls. The wet spill of tears was what remained of the attack. I was so scared with a human heart in my dream that I cried. My body was frozen from paralysis. The red writing didn't disappear until I drifted into being fully awake. Suddenly in my vision was Gabe who was rocking my shoulders back and forth.

"Vivian, talk to me," he commanded. I couldn't yet talk as my body hasn't recovered from its paralysis. The remainder of my tears spilled over and I had no choice but to stare at the storm in his eyes that were the usual forest green. "Are you okay, what was in this room?"

Slowly I raised my hand to touch the side of his stomach. Real. He was real. And I was real. Which meant I was back to normal. I allowed the remains of the fear and dream wash away from me. I couldn't act like this in front of anyone. No one could know that I had been compromised and feared something so greatly.

"Nothing," I said in a voice that felt raw and had been choking for the longest of times.

"Nothing?!" He said antagonizing. "By the time I got here you were screaming and crying in your sleep and something dark in this room was pinning you down. As soon as I came in, my light forced it out."

I stared at him while the tingling sensation of being paralyzed subsided. I grabbed onto his shirt tighter trying to distract him with my touch. No one could know that he saw something. If Haymen knew I would surely be facing consequences. I grew angry. The reason why I was asleep in the first place was because he had put me in that state with his ridiculous sleepy kiss. His eyes looked back and forth aware I was about to unleash my fury.

He pressed his lips to mine to silence me. His mouth was demanding and exploring. It was erratic and uncertain. But we were both okay. My body could only react to the claim and I allowed him to press me back into the bed as he rested both of his arms above me on the head board. I roamed my hands over his arms noticing the deep gashes and cuts. I opened my eyes to look at the wounds which still haven't completely healed. His shirt and arms had been shredded. He had just been a fight. Before I could demand answers, he bit my lips and slipped his hand beneath the light sheet that was still over me. I sucked in a breath as his hand very quickly slipped under my pants and began to circle. My legs rose as I sucked in another breath. One that he caught into another kiss.

All rationality had left as I roamed my hands down his stomach to feel the size of him. A darkness enveloped the room but the spell we were under was too demanding despite the new threat in the room. The darkness spread between us. In a split second, Gabe was flung across the room and smashed into my bookshelf. He hit it hard but not enough to hurt an immortal war angel.

I jumped out of bed but instantly disengaged from the flowering disgust in Haymen's eyes.

"I told you not to touch her!" He unleashed his hatred stabbing those dark talons of his towards Gabe. Gabe's light pressed against them and his wings swept in front of him pushing a sweep of light. Haymen seemed to have protected me from the blow as his talons spread around the room like an angry vine. "I told you not to enter her room!" His vines contracted and rushed to attack Gabe again.

My door opened as Tahmeed and Destiny ran in shambles still half naked from sleep. They looked from Haymen to Gabe then to me. Darkness enveloped me and I was dumped on a cold and dark floor. I looked around at the cave walls that dripped with water. Only Haymen's eyes glowed with a piercing blue that was entitled and focused on only me.

"You are mine!" He snarled and a flash of those fangs he often hid were apparent. His dark tendrils smashed me against the wall, the rocks digging into my back. I hissed out a breath from the forceful impact. I didn't know what had come over me when it came to Gabe but that was no longer the issue. I watched as the Demon King in front of me paced very slowly toward me. A predator deciding if he were to play or kill. "You've been defiled!" He spat at the ground in front of me. "You've let him see things!"

He slapped me across the face. The ringing in my left ear left me disoriented. "He touched you where no other but me should touch!" He said gripping my breasts tightly. Painfully tight. That raw power was my undoing because it only called forth my succubus who wanted nothing more than to reciprocate the same painful pleasure to

Haymen. My heart beat as loudly as the thrumming between my legs that very much needed to be quenched. I was high on fear, near death, my lust not having been met for almost a week and nothing but teasing for days.

He bit into my neck, the bite instantly stiffening me. I could feel blood draw over my shoulder as I hissed in pleasure. This was the sex my succubus desired the most. My tail flicked back and forth as it was the only thing I could move while he marked me. He clenched down harder the pain starting to crush down on my muscles and shoulder. Despite it, I couldn't control the dampness that came to my core.

He retracted his mouth and kissed me. His fangs unforgiving as it stripped and cut my lips. My own blood being the taste of our kiss.

His claws began to rake up my leg, cutting deep through the pants and shocking me with a painful and intoxicating pain. The darkness of his black talons swept from his body and began to rub against my clit as he overpowered me and his darkness swelled into my pores. Every part of him was intoxicating and filling me. His talons rubbed more vigorously as my body reacted to him.

For one moment, I thought of how different Haymen's darkness consumed me against the feeling of Gabe's fingers and light instead. The friction between my darkness and his light.

The room iced over those talons that were carefully exercising on my clit, stopped. Haymen's hand was around my throat with claws digging in. "You dare think of him while I touch you?!" Any harder and the tips of his claws were sure to make permanent damage. The pain became too much for my succubus as she retracted despite the thrumming of the still expectant pleasure. I hissed at him and for the first time instead of being limp in front of him, of being obedient, I dared defy him.

My body might react to him; I might be excited by the closeness of his power. But what I couldn't stand for in this moment was being overpowered and my lack of control got the better of me. I threw my head back and head butted him. It wasn't enough force to actually hurt him. It was Haymen of all people but he took a few steps back as if to entertain me.

225

Instead of hatred for my defiance there was a flash of something else in his eyes. My tattoos glowed bright blue as I allowed my Hellhound to come forth and growled at him. Fangs that were larger than his, well in this form. I looked at him at eye level on all four legs.

His smile widened. "Ahhh," he said and held out his hands in the way someone might appreciate art. His mood so quickly changed. From sexual, to kill me, to something I couldn't recognize and now appreciation.

"You are nothing but my creature," he said and that truly did resonate with my Hellhound demon more than the others who felt loyal to him. "Did he tell you that the Angel Kiss ritual is made for lovers? Angel lovers and it connects them more personally than any other ritual yet known. For the next few days is the period known as the 'claiming'. He's defiled you and that calling for you to fuck him is nothing but you falling for his little spell. He only wishes to enslave you to his own means."

Haymen seemed smug as he said it, his anger receding as he took pleasure in watching me stiffen in the dark. I didn't change my stance or facial expression. I did however pull back my lips further and growl with my ears pointed back. I wouldn't return to my original form to speak with him. I had nothing to say. He wanted me to be shocked by that information; to hate Gabe which I already did. We were natural enemies and I might've already known that something of that effect was already happening. And yes, I had fallen into the moment of it. But I was a creature of darkness, blood, and lust. I would be fulfilled either way.

"Lick your wounds and think on your actions. I am imprisoning you in here until I see fit to release you. And if you ever try to pull a stunt like disrespecting me like that again I will slit your throat." I growled lightly again and he charmed a smile. Although he said it, it seemed as if he almost enjoyed someone daring to defy him for once.

His darkness emitted through the room and he vanished. I changed back to my original form and sat against the wall. I took pleasure looking into the darkness of the cave that led to nowhere in particular. I was certain this was one of Haymen's personal prisons.

There was nothing but four walls entirely enclosed. There was no escape until he says so.

I wanted to make sense of any one thing that happened in the last fifteen minutes starting with the shadow dream. That was the priority. It gave me chills still thinking about it. But somehow Louana Smith was relevant. I couldn't put any of it into a factual presentation for Doc but it was more so a feeling. I never asked people for their names in my dreams. She was important and I had the sickening feeling that the demon in my dream was the same one who attacked her in which she had suffered and died by. When I am set free, depending on the amount of days or years Haymen saw fit, I would research and see who Louana Smith was.

Locked in my prison, I just hoped that Haymen would release me in two days so I could make it to the black market and find out where the witch had taken the possessed children. I rolled my eyes in annoyance. There were so many things to focus on right now. What I knew and had to avoid was a certain Angel who seemed to complicate everything.

CHAPTER THIRTY-TWO- HAYMEN

"Sir, it's been posted," my assistant's voice echoed through my room. I charmed a smile. Good. As soon as the photos hit the media of Vivian and Gabe it will strip him of his credibility. Despite my desire to kill him for daring to touch her and what was mine; consequently, it worked out in my favor. This would destroy all faith from those who followed him. Their infamous War Angel to have such an affair with a Guardian of all things, it was almost worse than a pure demon itself because it was connected to *me*.

Vivian could deal with the backlash, if any at all. Shabeah celebrated anything fanatical and they adored the Guardians of this city. Other Guardians weren't so renowned or desired in other cities. This would allow me to strip credibility from Gabe and slowly break into his city in the coming months from the rollover of mistrust and broken treaty in his own accord.

There were other ways to distract and win a war. I thanked the human entertainment of media for making it far easier and spreading such distrust publicly and quickly. Everything else that would happen between the two would only destroy his leadership. I had to ensure I weakened every player in this game before future events unfold. It seemed my dear Vi was more helpful than she would ever know. Her beauty is bewitching to even that of one of my greatest enemies.

Her defiance had surprisingly made me hard for her. Where most would've been killed, I wanted to play with my little Vi for a little more. I smiled and summoned Destiny. She was there within seconds. She went to speak but my effective gaze told her to otherwise keep her mouth shut. I might allow slight questioning and defiance from Vi but no one else. I fisted her hair as she silently dropped to her knees and began undoing my belt. She only had one purpose to serve right now.

CHAPTER THIRTY-THREE- GABE

I could no longer sense Vivian. I was certain that Haymen had taken her to the Underworld. Tahmeed and Destiny stared at me, shifting into their preferred demons and ready to attack. I jumped out over the lake and propelled to the sky before any fight could break out. They deemed me as their enemy and I was by default. But this had nothing to do with them. This only involved Haymen, Vivian, and me.

The wind was a reassuring cold slap to my face as I raced between the clouds trying to strip away the heat and hard on that had come over me. I wanted Vivian. Every inch of me screamed to claim her as my lover and I knew the logic in that was ridiculous. I complicated this mission by using the Angel Kiss ritual but even now I still had no coherent reason as to why I did it other than a life for a life as she had protected me. Trying to find Vivian and aid her in escaping would be a direct challenge to Haymen and that was something I had to do strategically and leave for another day. I was certain that he wouldn't kill her.

I snapped my wings shut and dropped through the air towards the city. The lights glistened in rapid speed as I dove closer enjoying the inevitable rush that swept over me in the cool air. My heart pounded as I dropped between the tops of skyscrapers looking down at the traffic below on the main street. I snapped my wings open and glided over them zipping between the bright lights enjoying the distraction. I let my light spread out and push against the darkness that constantly encased the city. I etched through the hub of the city searching for the old ancient darkness of the Volv. I made sure that I was too quick for anyone to take credible photos or close ups of my current state. I could imagine the phone calls I would receive if anyone noticed that I looked like I had been in a fight in a fellow treaty city. But I needed to exhaust some of this pent up sexual energy.

One of the big screens caught my attention and I swooped up to the highest building. I rested on the tip and wrapped my wings around me concealing half my face. I looked down on the screen in the city center in the early hours of the night. Photos of Vivian and I tangled within one another's embrace has been captioned and gone viral. I could feel the rollover of storm, wind and clouds follow my mood. This was in Vivian's bed. Only Haymen could have authorized photos to be taken so closely and leak them. What was worse was I didn't even sense someone spying on us because I was so focused on Vivian.

The image of her arching into me as I took her lips flashed onto the screen. My body thrummed with that same intense desire. Another image flickered over. People pointed and spoke amongst themselves. This was bad.

A call began to ring through. I touched my wrist watch and answered my audio piece. "Torrin."

"I don't know if you've seen it-"

"I've seen it," I said. I wondered how much he would seethe my involvement with one of Haymen's Guardians.

"Graphically manipulated?" He asked with a stern voice that noted he would kill the person who would try to defile my name.

"No." I would never lie to my people. Especially the man who I would trust my life with. Our conversations never went further. There was utter loyalty. "I performed the Angel Kiss ritual on Haymen's guardian. I'm trying to refrain from the aftermath with evidently lack of control."

There was a pause on the other side. "You what? Why? With her? Why?"

"A debt. She saved my life but traded it with her own."

"Yea but she's one of Haymen's Guardians. Who cares? The one who killed Luke at that!"

"She didn't kill Luke," I said adamant as I watched the images continue to flicker with crazed reports and wording. It was the first time that I had admitted it. And I hope I was right. I hadn't found any proof that she had. When did my opinion of her change so much? "I don't know. She has something to do with the Volv. They're following her. I couldn't let my main lead die."

"Her? It. She is an 'it'. A creature filled with demons. A creature of darkness. I understand some of our younger ones might have been tempted but you of all people, Gabe?"

"You've followed me for over five hundred years. Don't tell me you're doubting my instincts and agenda now," I said harshly. Haymen would have released these to create doubt and friction amongst those who followed me. What Haymen forgot was that loyalty was not built on media, images or words. It was gathered through blood, personal sacrifices and the loyalty that led me here to find Luke's killer. He doubted my city and army of angels far too much.

"You know I would never doubt you. I am just worried. You've never involved yourself in such an affair. When your father sees this it will be bad," he said as much as he did as a soldier as well as one of my closest friends.

"It's not an affair. It's just an aftereffect of the ritual that no one is to know of. If you could I would appreciate if you could realign everyone and dispel such rumors within my city. I'll deal with my father when the information crosses his desk."

"With your reputation it won't take long to dispel the rumors. But Gabe, you need to come home soon. Your time is almost up." He couldn't see me but I nodded my head in agreement. I hung up. I had to end this quickly. I came here to find Luke's killer and couldn't even find any trace of his killer that had dumped his already dead body in the middle of the sea. His death wasn't in vein, it has led me to the resurfacing of the Volv. And that meant war was certain to be on the horizon. Drops of rain began to sprinkle as the dark clouds rolled over and lightning spread in the distance. I dove towards the ground once again, powering through the city to pick up on the slightest scent of mishap and where the Volv I had fought previously might've vanished too. We still had unsettled business. I might have injured her greatly but it was still able to escape.

Chapter Thirty-Four- Vivian

Trapped. Darkness. Silence. To most that would strike fear in their hearts with the inability to escape. For me it acted as a comfortable silence. All I had to do was wait in silence until I was allowed to re-enter the real world. Although I was parched and starving I knew that Haymen wouldn't let me die. Perhaps be uncomfortable and near death, but not truly die. Of that much I was always sure of.

What I was painfully reminded of was the memory that Gabe had followed me into when I was nearing my death. It was my first true death and the start of the contract between Haymen and me and the demons that now filled me and were entitled to my body. I don't know who Haymen thought I resembled but it was added value to keeping me alive. So far I couldn't think of anyone who might've had that kind of hold over Haymen. It might have some connection with the very reason why I had been fighting darkness in my dreams for as long as I could remember.

As a human it was easier and none of it felt like the Volv itself. Perhaps those dreams had attracted only smaller demons that couldn't actually possess my body. I wish whatever protection I had against them as a human until that fateful day still remained. Now greater demons were attracted to me and I had no idea whether they were in alliance with the Volv or a new range to enjoy the pleasure of accompanying me and trying to kill me. Volv, why had I only learned of their real name up until now? Why didn't Haymen call them by that name with us?

The air chilled and I knew that Haymen was present within the room. In silence he teleported me back to my bedroom. He vanished as quickly as he had disappeared. My bookshelf that had been destroyed had been repaired and realigned. Always so quick to clean up after any incident. I quickly had a shower and changed. I had the scent of two of the most powerful men on me and I was still waiting to be ravished.

That was something I would soon have to quench or I would go savage soon if my needs weren't met. Because of my succubus demon that dwelled within me I was certain that my sex drive was sketchier than the others. At most we could last a few weeks without having our needs met. I however went feral if I left it for too long.

I walked over and beeped my request for Doc. I would have to report my dream and I wondered if she had any insight or had seen a similar thing happen to any of the previous Guardians. I wasn't sure for how long Doc had been working for Haymen but I had the impression it has been for a long time now. Age for witches is irrelevant much like Angels and Demons. If they were powerful they could obtain immortality.

Before going to meet with her in the Shadow Minds room I quickly raced to the kitchen to grab something to eat. It has been two days since I was locked in that prison and I was utterly starving. I grabbed two raspberry muffins from the counter and looked up with a mouthful of muffin. Looking over the lake was Alexa. She almost had no presence about her since her return. I gulped it down and walked over to her. She almost looked like a statue and didn't look to the side where I stood starring at her. I casually placed my arms over the railings and continued munching on my muffins. It didn't take me long to devour them. When I didn't think that she would talk, I turned to visit Doc. She would already be waiting after my request.

"I wanted to become a Guardian," she said grabbing my attention before I had gone back inside. "I was a human king's daughter and the thought of adrenalin pumping fighting, action, and fame drew me in." She paused again. "I met Haymen only once and was drawn in to the existence of demons. I wanted to become one and so my wish was granted."

I rested back up against the railing looking into the house. It was the most I had heard her speak in the past few months. And she wasn't one to speak unnecessarily. Like all the Guardians I had met and some were visiting from other cities, all of them had been volunteers to be reborn. And all of them were some sort of impressionable human prior. Haymen was picky as to which Guardians he chose for his 'elite

233

team' within Shabeah and close to him. If he could not eat the humans then he would take their leaders and have them do his bidding against their own kind. And that was at times what the Guardians enforced on his behalf. Guardians in different parts of the world had varying purposes.

"The shadows in our dreams..." she continued and that caught my attention more than anything else she said. It wasn't something we spoke about. We only reported it. It was our greatest weakness so we never dared exploit it even to one another. We could all end up as enemies one of these days. "I know I don't have much longer. I've been in this position for twelve years and I've only gathered information as to where their outdated camps and dwellings were. These demons, whatever they are, are smart. And Haymen fears that. I fear that."

"We don't fear," is all I said. Though I knew that sometimes we did. But we weren't meant to. That wasn't who or what we were created for.

"Do you think that they are trying to take Haymen's throne and that's why he's scared?" she asked me and looked directly into my eyes.

"You seem to not know fear if you are asking that question out loud," I said looking around to make sure we were alone. If this conversation was being recorded we would be in big trouble. Then I realized Alexa had the ability to mangle anything technology. That was a gift I could use to my advantage.

"Alexa, can I ask a favor of you?" She diverted her eyes again but nodded her head. She was scattered and I too had the feeling her time was close. All life had been drained from her. It was evident both physically and mentally. I wondered if there was any coming back from that but previous Guardians opposed that notion. All of which were dead. "Can you gather as much information both public and off record on both Gabe and Haymen for me? I want to date it back as far as the last war, if not more. I want to have knowledge of their origin and birth year. I want everything from the start."

She furrowed her eyebrows and focused her eyes on me. What I was asking could lead me into further punishment from Haymen if she were to report it. She turned her back to me and nodded her head.

"There's one more thing, Vi," she said looking over her shoulder. "The shadow creatures are drawn to you. Often your image appears in my dreams or they will pretend to be you. I'm certain that you are often their focus. They might not reveal it purposefully but I've had that opinion for a long time."

Despite our madness for talking so openly we didn't stay put any longer. She walked through the kitchen and out the front door as I ventured down the hallway to meet with the Doc.

I opened the door just as she was about to open it herself. "I've been waiting five minutes since you requested me," she said irritated.

"Now, now, Doc. It looks like you might have to practice some patience," I said with a charming smile. "I got caught up deciding what shirt I should wear. It's always something special, our visits." I offered her an antagonizing smile. I had gone with the long sleeved black shirt despite it being a summer day and the temperature not having much pull over me. I didn't want other people seeing the new light pink tattoo that was identical to Gabe's. It wouldn't take long for others to figure it out even though I myself had never heard of such a ritual.

She didn't seem to enjoy my mood and took a sample of my blood. "Is there any other way we can identify my other contracted demons besides taking blood samples?" I asked her rubbing the skin of where the needle had been. She rolled my sleeve back down and prepared the probes to attach to the back of my neck.

"Unfortunately, no. You know the few spells I had cast and trialed has failed to reveal those who were still dormant in you. Whatever species you might have obviously has a strong repellent to block even my magic," she said matter of fact and attached the four prongs into the back of my neck without warning. I hissed at the rudeness.

"You seem to be in a rush as of late Doc. Aren't you enjoying the time together like I do?" I said and began watching the screening of my dream and attack. Her usual witch scribble splashed across the page. I caught inconspicuous glances, reading her notes. When Aiden appeared, she wrote vigorously. *Subject tends to have relapse of emotional connection to previous lover. Possible relapse or fault in conditioning.*

I could've growled at her. I wasn't sure how I could read witch scribble writing but for whatever reason I was realizing that this wasn't the safest place for me to be because I wasn't sure when actions were taken against those she deemed compromised. I wondered if she has done anything to Alexa who never appeared to be the same after being with Doc for those few days.

We watched on the projector as the fire wind demon guy crept up on me and she gasped with recognition. Before I was pulled out of the dream she casted a spell. It summoned Haymen immediately into the room. He was wearing long pants with no shirt. I blocked him out of my sight ignoring him.

"Rewind by one minute," Doc requested of the Shadow Minds Journal. It did exactly that stopping at the end of the conversation between Louana Smith and I. So, it wasn't her they were focusing on but the demon.

I could feel Haymen watching intensely. "Determee'," he said in a foreign tongue. "I haven't seen him for some time. He's been in hiding since the end of the last war. Track him," he said to Doc. "I want you to find him. Good job," he said placing his hand on my shoulder before vanishing.

"Who is Determee'?" I asked Doc. It didn't sound as ravishing as it had coming from Haymen's mouth. Finally, we have found something.

"An old fire demon. He's renowned for feasting on beautiful women and scorching them alive. He's rather theatrical and usually seduces his victims from clubs and parties. He was known as the Fire Feeder to those who didn't yet know of the demon's existence and haunted his continent. He helped in the war periodically but fled shortly after. He was a coward with no desire to stand against the Angels despite his strength. His commitment to the war could've made a difference. So instead of partaking, Haymen purposefully hunted out his kind killing majority of them. Only few remain to this day. He's a fool for showing himself in your dreams and attacking you."

She pinched the four prongs from my neck and pulled the Shadow Minds out. I rubbed the back of my neck from the remains of its irritation.

"When you find him, I want to be the first to know. I owe him a debt," I said jumping off the seat.

"I imagine that Haymen might want to deal with this himself," she said from behind me. "Haymen can be rather protective of his property." I held in my scoff. He wasn't doing anything to help Alexa or any of the other Guardians who had fallen. I had almost died numerous times on the field of battle and yet he held the impression I was invaluable and not expendable. Yet death had come knocking for me more than once.

Perhaps somehow I could manage to find this Determee' before Doc did. I did have a visit to pay at the black market tonight. Perhaps I could purchase a locator spell on not only my green haired witch friend who took the children from the orphanage but also Determee' by name and description. I tried to have one more glance at Doc's board but she had covered it up. I smiled at her and walked out. I didn't know the consequence to being compromised but I had the chill that it wasn't good. Was it outright death or something worse? And perhaps she had turned Alexa into a mental potato to keep her hushed from the brink of displaying crazy. The cracks before she was taken had been covered. *She* hadn't been recovered. More than half of her seemed to have been wiped.

I walked out and Alexa was standing there. Not that I truly looked at her, besides expression and face nothing there remained of Alexa.

"Which demon am I talking to?" I asked wondering if one of her demons had taken over completely in a last effort to keep her body and fellow contracted demons safe. That had to be the chill I felt whenever I thought of the consequences. If a Guardian became compromised then they would be erased. Not their body or their demons, just them. So how did that make us different from the Volv's intent?!

"I am one of the few that are your ally," she said. It was Alexa's voice and face. But it was by far the remains of her. From the smile that crept, it was one of her demons who had been talking to us all along. She didn't try to stop me and I wondered if I was the last to speak with Alexa overlooking the lake, or if I had been tricked by this demon in her stead. What I did know for certain was that Alexa was now gone.

I continued walking past her. I had to fill the day quickly and act upon the night.

CHAPTER THIRTY-FIVE- VIVIAN

I had never begrudged anyone's presence more than I did Gabe's that day. His absence had me walking around the house more times than I would like to count almost pining for him to be close. I decided to sit on the couch and read the last of the romance novel that the old woman in the diner gave me.

Satisfied by the ending that if happened in reality, I would vomit. I snapped the book shut and poured my first whiskey straight. I ventured back to my room and took out the Trinity necklace from my safe. I was certain that Gabe wasn't coming back today. Although seeming like a dog in heat for him, I was satisfied to know I would have time and luxury to explore my private dimension again. I slipped it on and was instantly transported to the barren world I so fondly felt comfortable in. Crows squawked around me as if my arrival had disturbed them. I looked into the direction that I had last explored which led me to nothing and headed into the opposite one.

I walked for a while. My dress drifted behind me in a never ending cloth vapor. The sky was grey and dull with very little light. I continued for another ten minutes on an incline before standing at the top of the hill. Beyond the hill was great walls to a city. I wasn't foolish to think that I might be the only one on this planet but from where I stood it seemed abandoned. I cautiously walked over the hill making sure not to walk into any obvious traps.

The bricked walls were tall and I could imagine the days when warriors of what every species of demon lived here, might've monitored and guarded atop the wall. I walked through the abolished wooden gates that splintered over the ground. As soon as I stepped through to have a closer look, a red laser type scan buzzed over my body. I prepared myself to fight an impostor, but there was no one. Only a little small levitating dome that had scanned me. It flashed the color green and then vanished into the distance. Odd little fellow.

The dust swelled around me from a low breeze as I looked behind me and noticed that the tall cemented wall was the second threshold. The city glowed with a light blue lighting. A second layer of wall surrounded me as a defense force. I imagined if it considered me an enemy that it would push me out. An interesting layer of defense. Whatever species of demon they are, they're clever and advanced in their technology. Whoever had defeated them must've found their weakness. I continued to walk through as noises swept around me. Lights and voices whispered from screens of music and commercials which now stayed on the same scene, looping because of the damage it had taken. I looked down admiring the singular blue glow that would advance under my foot as I stepped. I came to a fork in what I considered to be the city.

The architecture was sleek and beautiful. Metal and white. Even the dusty ground I had once walked on is now polished flooring through the entire estate. The dress I wore seemed to sparkle against the flooring as if enjoying the life brought back to it. The entire city felt alive. From what I could see or sense no one lived within it but the entire city seemed to have a life force of its own which rubbed against that of my own skin.

I looked down the two paths unsure of which way I should go.

"Hello Lady Trie'," a hologram of a sleek blue woman spoke before sparkles of her form came from the ground and manifested before me. She looked as solid as any real person might be. She wore slimming silver wear and cusped her hands delicately in front of her. Her black hair was slicked back tightly as she smiled with expectation.

"What are you?" I asked her.

"I am one of your many assistants designed to support and do as you bid. What would you like to do today?" her voice was milky and placid.

"Are you a real demon?" I asked.

"No, I was created by your people. Would you like location to be saved to your Trinity Necklace as last checkpoint?" she asked.

"And what demon is that?" I asked ignoring the last question. What homeland was this and to what demon? Who had destroyed them?

"With your best interest Lady Trie' I have saved this as your check point. Your next appearance will allow you to instantly come back here." She charmed a smile. Before I could ask her another question, instinct hit my stomach and I pulled my necklace off. The world around me collapsed as I was thrown back into the visual of my reality and walk in robe.

"Vi, let's start getting ready!" Destiny was banging on the door. "Glorious sex won't just come find us. We have to go out and catch it!"

I quickly shoved the necklace back into my safe and opened the door.

She already had a flask in hand. "I could use that," I said grabbing it. "I'm over this week already."

"That's why I brought this," she said pulling out a bottle with her own empty glass. She pushed me aside and walked into my room. It was daring for her but expected with what has been happening lately. I knew that Haymen had her watching me carefully.

"No stalker angel in here if that's what you're after. I think he might've finally gotten the message," I said walking her into my walk in wardrobe anticipating the clothes I would wear for tonight.

"Well he is a fine specimen. Hard not to want to tap a war angel and then leave him in the dirt," she said fishing and indiscreetly as well.

"I had my fill with the last angel I fucked. I don't need a trend. I need a demon to fulfil me tonight," I said searching through the racks. She went to speak again but I gave her an effective look. If she continued to pry it would end in only one way. And that would be bloodshed. Enough of these games and tracking.

She charmed a smile and filled her own glass. "Well then, let's get you fucked by a demon," she said smiling as she took a sip.

After the first two bottles went down swimmingly, Tahmeed joined us. I enjoyed the nulling companionship. I needed to distance myself as much as possible from the current pull I had on Gabe and his disappearance was blissful by my logic just as much as it was spited by my ruling connection to him.

I zipped a tight leather skirt that didn't leave much to the imagination, with leather boots that went past my knees. A one-sided sleeved silk grey shirt assured my new tattoo was covered but allowed the others to scandalously show. I straightened my usual curly crimson hair and opted for a night dye instead. I swept the little gadget through my hair that changed the illusion of my hair color from red to blonde. I put it up in a high ponytail and anticipated what the night might be like. This was a night for both pleasure and business.

I would distract everyone with my public party habits clubbing at Ravish and slip later on to the black market where I could find the answers I have been waiting for all week. Much to our surprise Alexa decided to tag along and chose not to drink. Which in previous years was rare for the renowned alcoholic Guardian. But the thing was, it wasn't really Alexa anymore and I wondered if the other Guardians have noticed yet.

Hours later we found ourselves on the doorstep of Ravish, walking past the line-up of those who waited and hoped they would be allowed in tonight. A group of girls screamed as we walked past them and reached out for us. I walked further away so they wouldn't touch me. We ignored them and continued walking through to the security who greeted us promptly and scanned us in the dome one by one to make sure we didn't conceal any weapons.

It didn't take us long to take to the bar. Tahmeed was in her usual 'party' demon form seeking out her preferred type. No one was here yet and she seemed disappointed. Instead she grabbed one of the fish out of the small holes in the bar. She swallowed it and hissed as it cut its way down her throat. She was definitely in for a party night. I quickly made my way to the dance floor before they could offer me one. I needed to make sure that they were too drunk to consider tracking me. I needed to keep somewhat sober for the end of the night. I looked at the clock. I had about two hours to kill and could fit something or should I say someone in that time.

I looked around the bar and found a few interested patrons. I began to dance, my hips swaying in an inviting manner. It wasn't long until Tahmeed and Alexa joined me. Destiny chose to enjoy her time with her favored human bar tender, Brady.

It wasn't long until we found ourselves circled by a few humans and demons. Admittedly it has been a very long time since I had fucked a human and it piqued my interest. Instead of hot hard sex I felt like something innocent and pure. They were unknowing to the aphrodisiac I could create. There was a tall blonde man with blue eyes. As far as humans went he was attractive and very fit. I don't think you could drain much of a conversation out of him, but I wasn't after chit chat. When I got closer I realized my mistake–he was a hybrid. A weak demon that must've had one human parent. His skin heated with a complex tan that wasn't of human origin. His thin thread like pointed ears were what gave away the human appearance.

I was impressed by the inferior demon who despite being weak knew his beauty and approached me with a cocky smile.

"I wanted to call you over to the bar but I imagined you weren't one to come when told, so instead I thought I might come and collect you instead," he said offering his hand.

"You certainly have some balls considering your inferior disposition," I said. He shrugged his shoulders not at all discouraged.

"Where I lack in power I make up for in other departments. I can only distort demon's presences, make them near invisible to others. An ability that is limited but both handy," he said with a suave smile. Everyone else in the room began to vanish one by one as he smiled. "I could make you cum anywhere you want to in the world, inconspicuously." The charade dropped and everyone crowded around us once again. Or should I say they had been the entire time. My demons fed me knowledge of his kind. Rather common and weak but that little trick of his could give me a few hours to kill in a back alleyway and then furthermore into a black market while hiding from a certain angel.

"Tell you what," I said curling my fingers around his neck with a smile. "You know who I am, yes?" And he nodded. This was certainly going to be one of those treats that he would talk about for years. "Say we have fun for the next few hours in an alleyway. And by fun, I mean you better be balls deep in me making me scream as rubble scratches against my back."

He chuckled and furled his arms around me. He was an attractive creature. For a demon who could conceal the presence of someone he certainly had a presence himself. I looked around the room and noticed the fellow gawkers. It appeared the human women and men had a keen eye trained on him. "But afterwards I need you to conceal my presence for a few hours. Can you do that for me?"

He smiled and his grip firmed on my hip. The single gesture spread warmth across my body as it began to yearn for the one thing it had been denied for days. The tattoo that connected me to Gabe seemed to burn at the betrayal which only infuriated me more. I had to do this. I had to rid of this spell no matter how illogical or how much it actually made my stomach flip. All I could visualize was this to be Gabe instead and every part of me tried to push away that attachment.

"I don't even have to be present to conceal your presence. Tell me for how long and you'll vanish from the world," he said breathing lightly before pressing his lips onto mine. The room seemed to spin and everything else became irrelevant. We had vanished from the world and surprisingly that vile feeling that began to rise up my throat with thoughts of Gabe fled too.

My entire body and focus was on this stunning demon who I didn't even need to know his name. He was my tool that would finally unleash this build-up of sexual frustration that had been gaining for far too long.

It wasn't long before he had my back up against the outside walls in the alleyway as promised. I moaned and groaned as people at the end of the alleyway still waited in line. No one could see us or even hear us but the rustle of trash cans being thrown about might've creeped a few of them out.

Despite his rather feathery touch, my beautiful demon was rough in all the right places and I would've thought he was more prone to be a sex demon than anything else. I moaned as he pumped me for those hours which filled the time and had me climaxing more than once. His hands and lips that pressed against throat was exactly what I needed. Just a casual fuck. Not an intense claiming of an angel or domineering of a propaganda demon boss.

I moaned into the beautiful demon's mouth as he continued to pump into me. The distraction and absence from the world was just what I needed to kill time.

Chapter Thirty-Six- Vivian

Being invisible, I didn't have to consider being inconspicuous as I walked into the local bookstore that was the entrance to the black market. Usually I would pretend to show interest in books and purchase some. Well, to be more precise, I would end up walking out afterwards with about ten new romance novels to read. I loved reading romance novels both in my human life and in this life. I imagined it had something to do with trying to resonate and understand an emotion that I was no longer capable of.

I walked through the few patrons of the store sweeping past two old-school wooden bookshelves. Most books were electronic and memory transferred these days it was a true delicacy to be able to smell and feel the old material which I had an interest for. Sure, upload one to my mind in seconds. Cool. I was all for efficiency but the old tailored books reminded me of what we came from and the old days we used to live. Not that I had ever lived close to those generations.

I walked to the back of the store shoving someone and laughing as the human male looked back over his shoulder unsure as to what sent his shoulder and books flying. I could get used to this little disappearing act. In the small door on the left was a restroom for customers. I entered and closed the small door behind me. I looked up at the blank white wall focusing to find the panel. The light green glow of one grabbed my attention and I entered the passcode by memory pressing on the panel. Within seconds all nineteen of the tiles lit up and began crumbling away the wall. Rather dramatic considering a slide door would've been easier. A guard looked over the entrance, unable to see me like everyone else. Tusks came out of his mouth as he straightened himself and weapons in alarm.

As soon as I stepped into the black haze of the underground market which was in another dimension, I became visible. The black market was always hosted in this dimension. It was a small fraction designated on the land built for illegal deals and trading. My facade dropped and the guard tsked at me speaking in a language that I understood and could translate. He wasn't one for visual games.

"I knew the haze would burn it away, don't get yourself all huffed and puffed," I said slapping him on the shoulder as I walked past. Weak demons couldn't survive on this planet nor could their magic. The façade was simply to get me here without a trace in case a particular angel tried to follow. Now being here, there was no way Gabe could find me. This was the place and world for demons only. Sometimes I saw a few dark angels but they weren't exactly welcomed and often found themselves mysteriously not finding the item they were after or being hunted themselves for their wings and feathers which did catch a high price.

Rows of tables on filthy grounds were displayed around me. Most have a tent or shop with their merchandise hidden inside. On my left was the illegal trading of demons and auctions. Most of the time it were women and children that are being sold. I turned a blind eye to it. I wasn't anyone's hero. This trading existed far before my own parents were even born and I relied on the resources and items I could obtain here. This was where I had purchased my Trinity necklace. In the world of demons, you were either powerful, weak, or defenseless. The latter two would ultimately cost you your life in either death or eventually slavery of some kind.

I kept a watchful eye on the weapons and jewelry I walked past. Most of the shop fronts were tools, items, and jewelry. What I wanted was further down the rows where the witches manned their stores. They weren't technically demons and they could either be light or dark. But those who practiced dark arts were definitely welcomed here. A demon was limited at times within their own capability. Depending on how powerful the witch is, she could even control that of a strong demon and become a puppeteer. Most known demon lords have clans of witches serving their houses for as long as time went back. Witches were the initial connection to something 'other worldly' for humans. They didn't take well to the announcement of witches so one could have only imagined what came about when demons started making their activity known. And that's when the darling Angels swept in. Everything after that led to the human world. Either celebrated or hated. Everyone had claim to the human dimension as well.

The human's world and people were resourceful. Overpopulated and with rich and equal living atmosphere. The only reason they haven't been entirely killed was because the Angels prevented it and demons quickly learned of the entertainment and food they supplied. It didn't take long for the cat to pretend that it let the mouse escape.

Few shady demons approached me and I made sure that my look was so effective that no one would dare speak to me unless invited. I didn't too often change to demon form at the Black Markets. If anyone were to attack me I'd rather take them by surprise. That and most of the demons I was contracted to were rare. That rarity might be seen as gold coins to some. Not that they would survive if they ever tried to kidnap me but I made sure not to draw too much attention.

The two suns set in the background igniting a purple tone over the horizon. There was nothing but desert and surrounding hills. The thick miasma often had newcomers choking as their body tried to adjust to the pressure.

I looked at the long black lavish coat on my left which was certain to be some kind of pelt of another demon. The slithering shop keeper crept over with a smile. "It's very nice," he hissed.

"And it want to be very cheap," I added. He mocked me with a laugh and my eyebrow rose. For how long would I have to tolerate him? His venom was strong, one of the strongest amongst demons but nothing ever trumped my succubus venom. That alone could kill him or make him awfully sick depending on how powerful he actually was. His tongue poked out at me and he smiled showing me his fangs. I leaned in closer making sure that part of his tent concealed me from others.

"Five gold," I offered and he scoffed laughing at me. He spat at me and I grabbed his throat pinning him against the table. He slithered out of my grasp in seconds and latched onto my arm. His poison secreted into me as quickly as it took me to turn into my succubus form. It was a tickle. The shift startled him and he slipped back behind his wooden desk.

My tail flicked back and forth as I gave him a seductive smile. I picked up the coat with one claw holding it over my shoulder so passersby's couldn't see me in this form.

"I meant four gold and I won't kill you now for being so disrespectful," I snarled at him but my voice was honey and seduction. His slimy body wavered with the lustful tone and atmosphere I emitted. I had yet to find someone who could deny my succubus. I have met many demons but her kind was by far the best at seduction and manipulation.

"I'm so sorry to have upset such a beautiful customer," he began as he coiled in front of me to come closer. There was the mixture of fear and pleasure in his eyes.

I pulled four gold coins out of the small pocket on my breasts and flicked it at him. I wrapped the beast like coat over me and changed back to my usual form. I liked and enjoyed the barter at the markets. He all but gasped from behind me as I walked away and he realized that he had been trumped from both fear and deception.

There were many forms of currency but gold and silver were often accepted in currency conversion no matter what dimension you were from.

Besides my anticipated visit to a certain witch I also made sure to visit one other. I turned into the gross smelling alleyway and to the shabby looking building that was as disgusting as it was daring to participate at any drinking and gambling. One demon was weakly bleeding out in front of the entrance having been robbed and beaten. As well as drunk.

I stepped over him and creaked open the wooden door which did little to hold back the rowdiness inside. It smelled of all disgusting things. I pointed my finger in the air so the bartender behind knew to follow me with one pint. I scanned the room checking if there was any immediate threat. Eyes wandered over me but nothing I couldn't handle. I located my guy and walked over to take the seat across him in the corner of the already dark lit room.

Heads of different demons were stapled to the wall and smoke misted throughout the room. If you stayed here for too long you would often lose your mind. Most newcomers were victims to the cause. The waitress, a scrappy looking wench who wore no clothes and purposely offers herself and services, brought over my pint. I threw her a silver coin not even daring to touch her in case some disease jumped from her skin and onto my own.

I offered the pint to the hooded demon in front of me. "How goes my favorite customer?" He purred with a beautiful smile. I have never seen his face because his hood has always concealed it. But from the power that radiated from him and the way he spoke, my body definitely would want to mix business and pleasure with him. He waved his hand and the beer soared towards his mouth as he opened it and took a sip. I raised an eyebrow.

"You don't seriously expect me to touch the glass?" He said with a mocking smile. He did this every time. Always aimlessly flirtatious and I hadn't yet a guess at what kind of demon he was but he served a purpose. I slid over three gold and like the beer he waved his hands and then the gold was off the table and he accepted his payment.

"A lot of demonic activity is happening everywhere, internationally," he added before I could protest that I already noticed the increase in Shabeah. I suspected he would've done his research and knew who I was. The Guardian tattoos gave away our ruse but if anyone with half a brain used their resources they would see me on various magazines, campaigns, and fashion articles, of all things. I was renowned but isolated to Shabeah. Other guardians might have the luxury to dip into assignments elsewhere but being Haymen's head guard and enforcer of his city, I wasn't so lucky.

"I found a few leads to armies building in the demon worlds. Nothing has yet happened but different dimensions and their kings are preparing for something. I tortured a few various species who haven't yet been advised as to what their mission is and can only tell me the same thing–heightened security and some offerings to the mighty Demon Lord himself." We both knew he meant Haymen but it wasn't a name one would say so lightly in a place like this.

"The Angel Council is aware of it and are also preparing their arms in case an attack is made. Again, it's all precautionary but it makes you question whether it will be like the old war with demons and angels again or if something greater is coming. So, me and a pretty little angel friend talked," he said shrugging his shoulders with a smile that said they did much more than talk. "Turns out the infamous War Angel, Gabe, who has been following you was asked by his father to focus on Shabeah. Seems like it came in handy in the time that one of his subordinates was murdered and had a connection to you, who is one of the most connected to Haymen." I wasn't at all surprised by that; he was here for far more than just investigating his friend's death personally. He was *the* War Angel and had strategy written all over him.

He took another vacuumed sip and continued. "So, it adds a further plot twist as to why he Angel Kissed you, who might become his enemy and be on the forefront to the soon to be war unless he has a motive to use that connection between you two for something else."

I wanted to lunge at him and swipe the smile off his face. I didn't know how he found out that information. But that was the reason why I relied on his resources so much. I knew better than to question how and why he took interest in it.

He continued. "So then I took particular interest in you, Darling, and did some background research on your heritage," he paused to see if I wanted him to continue.

"I didn't ask you to do background checks on me, Sweetheart. I specified your attention to be on the Shadow people," I gritted between teeth.

"But doesn't your angel boyfriend prefer to call them the Volv? Look, Darling, you either want my information or not," he said shrugging his shoulders. A fight broke out behind us and we watched with little interest until the victor was quick to claim his gold pieces by shoving a blade through the others demon's skull.

The Black Crow was as great an asset as he was a liability, sometimes he was too good at what he did and if he got too close to home then I would have to discard him.

"Turns out your turning despite being a simple dog walker was intentional. The Volv's interested in you was targeted. You see when I looked back into your birth parents and way, way back into your great, great, great, Aunt, Louana Smith." My eyes shot up at him. Louana Smith was the woman I had met in my last dream. He charmed a smile and continued. "Turns out she was also targeted by the Volv. They seem to be rather sloppy when they hunt. All bang and guts left behind. Turns out they didn't get what they wanted out of her. She had a sister who surprisingly wasn't victim to the Volv and so she continued the bloodline. It changed a few times in name by marriage but then on your birth, the Volv suddenly held interest again. So I continued tracing back from there and let me tell you how difficult that is when you have mixtures of humans and demon children."

"My heritage is human," I interrupted ordering another drink.

"Your knowledge is a lie. But it propels so far back that I doubt anyone would've noticed. Have you ever heard of the Disdaint demon or clan?" I shook my head. Something about the name rang familiar. All of my demons have knowledge on that name and yet none of them spoke up or offered me that knowledge as if all of a sudden they were shamed into speaking. "An old clan, a very powerful demon race. Well known for their technological advances and control of blue fire but above that they could see and feed off demons without form. In essence, when the war came they were highly valued against the Volv." The rowdiness continued behind us as demons continued to lose stakes and make large wins. "And guess what, Darling, you have a tinkle of that demon heritage. The Volv made sure to extinguish the race. Including Haymen's Queen." The room went silent at the mention of Haymen's name. I looked over my shoulder with an effective look. They all continued their business but I could feel ears were now on our table.

"I want you to become more accessible to me," I said sliding over another two pieces of gold. In exchange, one black feather landed on the table in front of me.

"I imagine we will be doing plenty business together Miss Vivian," he said offering the feather to me. "If you require my services simply call upon me through that. "Despite your shackles that chain you, I advise that you should find allies very quickly."

"And is that what you are?" I mocked as I took hold of the black feather. It felt heavy and menacing. As if blood had poured over it far too many times and attempted to be washed. I tucked it away in my coat.

"For the right price I can be," he smiled and then vanished leaving the half empty beer on the table. I stood up and walked out. Our business was now done. On to my next purpose of being here. I couldn't help but recall the path that Gabe and I walked together when I neared my death. The memory of my contract to Haymen and death began piling a few questions that I could never ask. Did I have a connection to his last Queen, was that why I was protected from even his own wrath? Was he hoping to restore that heritage so he could eliminate the Volv once again?

CHAPTER THIRTY-SEVEN- VIVIAN

I made haste down the loud and sneering merchants making sure not to tread on the vermin that had three heads and hissed at me from the broken ground that glowed a light green every step I now took in the dark.

I walked down a few more corridors before I found myself in an open space. Shi-Shi, the witch I used frequently for locator spells, wasn't one to be found easily and appreciated privacy. What she loved more was the gold that matched the services of her power and skill. I stood there chanting the incantation that would summon her. A small black cat crept out of the invisible wall that concealed her business. The human child looking cat was far from innocent and its golden eyes stared with expectation.

I changed into my cat demon and used my own claw to draw blood across my hand. I hovered my fisted hand which dripped with my own blood into the cat's mouth. Insurance if I weren't able to pay what Shi-Shi demanded for her services. The cat licked its lips and meowed. It usually hissed at most; I wondered if it had favoritism for my cat form. I changed back to my usual self and followed the cat as it opened the invisible door between the black market's and Shi-Shi's stall. I followed the cat and felt the layer of invisibility sweep over me. It felt of electricity along my skin as I uncomfortably stepped through.

"My, my, look what the cat dragged in," Shi-Shi said as she preoccupied herself over a kettle that burned over a lumber of wood. Her beauty was that of fairy tales. Olive skin that had never known the damage of sun, age, or stress. Her black hair trailed down to her ankles with a fleeting golden dress. Her golden eyes were against red ruby lips that tricked most men into her lair. Which I imagined was exactly what she had been doing only hours before as she poured the hot mixture of herbs and water into a large mug. At the bottom of it was ruby red blood and a clean finger bone that she stirred the concoction with. She devoured men and only men regularly to keep her immortality. Who knew how old she actually was and I never cared to ask.

Colored and rare materials messily straddled the room as birds inside shrieked at my intrusion. She purred at them enjoying their struggle as they were caged and hanging from the roof. Her cat perched itself upon the black leather sofa in the corner, the only modern ornament to the entire room. I took my seat at the table that was built of bones. The bones were melted by a small magic that actively knitted them together in a small stemmed black swirl of living magic. She took her seat across from me with a smile as she placed the mug in the air and it floated beside her.

"And what does the talk of the town Guardian want from me?" she asked with a ruby red smile. Even I was entranced by her beauty but I knew that it wasn't her true form, it more than likely was rotting flesh. Because despite everything else about her was beautiful, the smell remained. That was what constituted that she should've long been dead.

"Two locator spells," I said offering her the green threaded hair I had from the witch that had intervened at the orphanage. She looked at the hair collecting it with her elongated nails and sniffed it with disgust.

"How did you manage to mingle with a Tolar Witch?" She asked detaching one of her pristine and pointed teeth from her mouth. She cut open her own hand and let the droplets splatter on the bones that were hoisted at a table. She threw the tooth in with it.

"I don't know what kind of witch that is," I said. Again, I had the sensation that my demons were familiar with the race but refrained from telling me. Irritation flickered through me. Why so quiet now?

She toyed with the tooth rolling it into the bones as her golden eyes glowed like a cat's. There you could see the wickedness at work. The emptiness behind that held no such beauty.

"Well considering most of the powerful witch clans are far and few, I don't blame you. I myself don't hold high regard for them." Despite her honey voice you could hear the venom and croak in every word if you looked for it hard enough. "They deem themselves royal to our kind but nothing that I would respect. There are three high bloods of witchery. Tolar are the more political, prim and proper. Often inclined to be white witches, healers blah blah," she said snooty like. "Golem Witches, my own kind, well," she said charming a nasty smile. "We enjoy our taste of men and dark rituals. The very presence of darkness charms us from birth. And the Antic Witches, more solemn but unpredictable. They follow the muse to their own magic opposed to rituals and tradition. Their power depends on the witch itself. To have crossed paths with a Tolar witch must mean you've done something to piss them off to grab their eye. They are usually the executioners. We do it for fun. They do it for purpose. Whatever reason you've drawn its eye. I would suggest you try to stay clear of them."

"They took something of mine," I said thinking of the children and the Volv that were possessed within. They were my lead and I couldn't let it die because of a warning.

"The price has increased. I don't think you understand how much effort I have to put into this. It's much harder to find a witch who is heavily guarded by their own magic," she said looking at me to see if there was issue with the payment.

I nodded. I was fine with whatever the payment but was very clear when I said, "As long payment is restricted to *only* gold." She smiled at me.

"Always the clever one," she replied pulling out a knife and asking for my hand. I knew better than to agree offering her whatever she wanted. Deals were not made lightly, especially when she held part of my blood already as leverage. She cut my hand deep making me hiss. She pressed it to the bones that were smoothed over. The black magic that conjoined the table together rolled over my fingers.

A vision came to me as I looked around and was lost in woodland. Across from me was a small hut. The dew and mist attempted to conceal its location. The hooded witch with green hair stepped outside. The jingle of her golden bangles stopped as the hooded figure looked up at me.

"I've been waiting for you," the feminine voice said. "But you are not here physically. As soon as you step out of that witches lair I will call you forth. We have much to discuss." I was back in the room with Shi-Shi. She snarled at the bones that began to sizzle under a taxing acid. She swiped it with her hand the tooth and long strand of green hair flew across the room and the bones seemed to absorb both our bloods.

"Spiteful Tolar witch," she hissed retracting her hand that already began to heal. She took a mouthful of her blood mixed drink. "There. I'm sure you saw what you came for," she said. I looked down at my own hand that also began to slowly heal. The skin was mending from the scorch marks and blisters that began to immediately form.

"I did. I have another request. Are you able to locate a demon for me if I have nothing physical of theirs?"

She looked at me for a long time. "Do you have a name that I might be able to associate with this demon?"

"Determee'." Her eyes locked on mine and the veins in her neck sucked in horrendously.

"I deny your request. You shouldn't be daring to locate such demons. You might be a Guardian but learn your place girl," she snarled at me. "Three hundred gold for the singular locator spell," she said brushing her hair away.

I wanted to mock her and call her a coward but I held little patience to prevent me from doing so. Shi-Shi was resourceful, I wasn't going to push something when I knew the witch was already determined to stand by her decision. I didn't press the matter any further obviously those who knew him by name had witnessed or heard stories of the wrath that he had used against me. I threw a large sized ruby that she instantly fell in love with. She collected it from her table with admiration of all things beautiful.

"Payment in full plus more so you remember who your silence and continued business will come from," I said as I stood up and went to step out.

"You know young Guardian, I'm quite fond of you," she said not looking at me but stroking her dainty fingers over the ruby. "You and I shall interweave often in the future I feel."

I stepped out of the hut feeling the bites of her electricity nicker at me. As soon as I stepped out into the night of the black market, a symbol traced beneath my feet and a circle overlapped it. I was sucked into darkness before I reappeared in the woods I had witnessed only moments ago. There, the Tolar witch waited.

"It's nice that we can finally meet properly," she said dipping her head and crossing her hands gently in front of her.

"Well, you kind of ran off taking my leads before we cold properly speak last time," I sneered.

"I apologize. I'm not fond of angels that trace our movement," she said and removed her hood. She was a very beautiful *he*. "My name is Loclan. It is my greatest pleasure to finally meet with you, Lady Vivian." His cheekbones were sharp and pointed. His lips a soft pink with eyes that held no color; only white with no pupil. Despite his gender everything else about him was soft and delicate.

"Don't give me that Lady bullshit. You don't like the angels but you're happy to help a fulfilled demon conjuror?" I laughed at him.

"Please don't confuse my actions with preference of company. I only helped you at the request of one of my own. That very witch that lays dormant within you now was the one who requested me to help you at that orphanage on that fated day. My loyalty is to her not to you."

"I'm sorry to point out your mistake but I don't possess any witch. And besides, a witch isn't a demon. I can only contract with that of demon blood."

Loclan pressed a beautiful smile that showed sharp teeth. A wave of wind fluttered through and I could smell the flower-scented skin he held. Not like that of Shi-Shi who smelled of rotting flesh. He smelled clean and almost... pure. Raw refined power. "Haymen's Guardians have always had inconsistencies in their contracts with the demons. They can only contract to those of the dead. Not necessarily that of demonic energy but of great power. The Tolar witch that resides within you is just that. The contract is based on mutual agreement obviously you benefit one another in some way. Considering the way that particular witch died and who she is I can definitely admit that she would have much unfinished business."

"No witch has presented themselves through my contractual agreement. Again, I believe that you're mistaken," I hissed. I had recently been able to start reading the Doc's witch writing, if any amount of what he spoke was the truth that might be the reason as to why.

"Well she was very shy even when she lived. She would often only reach out to me, which surprises me so much that she agreed to bind a contract with a Guardian, whether you recall it or not."

"You speak as if you know her," I said assessing this dainty looking witch.

"She was my twin sister, which is why we still speak. Both after her death and now while she is hidden within you," he said with little remorse as he spoke of his sister's death. If he was in fact speaking the truth.

"Prove your claim," I said to him. We began slowly circling one another in small steps. The wind around us swirled unsettled.

"And how would you have me do that, young Guardian? There is nothing I can do until she presents. That's the only way you will believe me. If I wanted to kill or manipulate you, I would've done so already," he said unflinching. I growled at him, part of my hell hound coming through my lips.

"Then let's see if you're capable of that too," I said pissed at his accusation that he was more powerful than me. I shifted into my demon cat. The jingle of the bell on my tail swished back and forth.

"I have no interest in fighting with you. You came for these did you not?" He clicked his fingers and the hut vanished. The three children were suspended in the air, their hair adrift in an unseen wind. "I kept them like this because I knew you would follow. I've also frozen the Volv within them. I tell you now though, they have rooted in strong. Most demons can be exorcized from their hosts but these ones possess and rid of the souls as soon as they sink in. You cannot save these children."

I watched the three children who drifted in the air as if only asleep. My ears pulled back as I hissed at Loclan.

"Vivian, I would like to add that your master can't know of our intimacy," he continued. I tried not to choke on a laugh as he said 'intimacy'. This was far from intimacy but then again, the man looked like he hadn't spoken to another person in years. "I don't wish to abandon you at dire times but our association cannot be found out. Someone is tracking you as we speak. Also, the weak demon that cloaked your presence has abandoned his agreement with you. It's now losing its strength. You will be visible soon. You are currently being hunted. You should run."

I cocked my head to the left aware of the intense power that came from the trees at a rapid pace towards me.

"I will teach you the ways of our people because of the request my sister has asked of me. But do stay alive until then," Loclan said. A symbol appeared beneath him as he started a chant. He paused it to say his goodbyes. "I think that your Golem witch might've betrayed your trust. It is Determee' that comes. I will keep wards up that will keep him at bay for a few moments. I warn you: run." And with that he vanished. I hissed at him. Was this entire thing a set up? A burst of flames powered through the trees burning everything alight. I changed into my hellhound who could absorb fire. But the flames never reached because a barrier stood between the oncoming force and the suspended children and me.

I growled at the laugh that began to circle and cackle at the trees. To his word Loclan had built a barrier. But for how long would it last? I dared a smile. Well at least I got my two birds with one stone, now I just had to figure out how I would kill a demon this powerful.

CHAPTER THIRTY-EIGHT- GABE

I felt it as soon as Vivian dropped off the grid. I paused myself for minutes in the rain. I had been exploring old buildings that held the remains of demonic energy. I stood there willing myself to think logically. I couldn't allow myself and my thoughts to revolve around her no matter how great the pull of the ritual. I was almost starting to believe that it was something more. She was not *my* woman and never would be. I growled as I took one small step after another trying to push myself further into the building.

Minutes after, I realized there was no way I could possibly focus on my task. Acknowledging her disappearance was driving me insane. *She* was driving me insane. I purposely did my best to put distance between us and she either pulls a stunt like this or she was in serious trouble. I knew that she could handle herself and that Haymen wouldn't hurt her because he returned her back to her estate earlier today. I confirmed it myself trying to rein in this possessiveness that swept over my usually collected self.

I let an hour go by as I tried my hardest to focus on my search. Nothing. So far it appeared that I would only find remains of the Volv when they wanted to reach out to me. And since my last encounter no one stepped forward. The orphanage hasn't had further attacks after confronting Vivian. Which very well might've meant they had been baiting her.

I growled as I swept up the high building no longer patient for her reappearance. Surely she should've returned by now depending on whatever situation she was involved with. But the tugging sensation of something happening at her gnawed at me. I felt that she was alive and safe in my gut but worry still sickened me. And that revolted me as much as it panicked me.

I followed the last location I had sensed her at. A club I had heard much about and was a hotspot in the city of Shabeah. Despite the rain that continued to pour over the city, the distinct smell of Vivian and another demon's scent mingled with intimacy. Every fiber of me wanted to rip that demons throat apart for daring to touch her. It was the worst thing that could've happened while I was under the intensity of the ritual. Another man claiming what was mine.

I swept into the alleyway where I could smell her. She had left a while ago but the demon remained. As soon as I dipped into the alleyway women squealed behind me and gave chase. I spread my wings wide so they could only see my back. I pressed my light to the entrance of the alleyway so no one could step out.

There, standing over the remains of the demon who had touched Vivian, was Haymen. He didn't seem surprised as I walked towards him. He charmed a smile at me as I approached him, wiping over his hands with a cloth that evidently didn't even touch the demon that was gasping for life with wounds that would not heal in time. Silver blood drenched the cemented ground and splattered the walls.

Mixed emotions pumped through me. I was pleased to see another demon dying, more specifically one who dared touch Vivian. Discretely I would've tried to kill him myself. Vermin. I tried to push away that second thought that reared its ugly head. A demon's death was always nothing but joyful to me. I was sharp on the reality of the situation despite battling the barbaric inner monologue.

"You killed him because he had sex with her," I said in a low enough voice that only he could hear. A crowd began to gather behind me as a few photos were taken. No one would be able to see past my wings. The dead body on the ground in front of me should've been blocked from their sight. The darkness around Haymen advised me that he was concealing his physical form from everyone but me. Which meant I walked into a trap and the subject of murder. I let the storm unfurl like my emotion. The heavy downpour and lightning that flashed would force everyone into cover. The rain would assure no one would be able to see past their own hand.

"Weren't you coming to do the same?" He asked me with a knowing smirk. Information of our kind and ritual wasn't meant to escape past our own knowledge but somehow during the years, certain rituals such as the angel kiss had. It wasn't general knowledge but Haymen made sure to be informed as much as possible against those who were his arch enemies. Likewise.

"I wouldn't do an unauthorized kill. Especially in your city," I said, formally. He laughed at that. A deep chuckle that drew out his true menacing nature.

"You're right. This is my city and I don't allow those who touch my property to live," he said pointedly. It was both a threat and an admittance. I clenched my knuckles, aware of those who still tried to take photos behind us.

"You killed Luke, didn't you?" I said as it all made sense. It wasn't Vivian who killed the men that she had slept with but Haymen who spited anyone who dared touch her. She was something to him or whatever remained dormant in Vivian was what was most precious to him. And it had cost my friend his life.

"You'll have to be more specific," he said with an antagonizing smile. "I don't make it common practice to ask the name of those I kill." The final gasp of the demon who bled out on the floor was the only thing that came between us. The downpour soaked us both. He was smug because he knew I couldn't go to the council and openly claim him to be the murderer without proof. My restraint held me in my position. I wanted to kill him more than anything but I had to be smart about the way I would execute him. This was politics and any irrational action I made would affect even those who followed me. The time I had been given to mourn Luke made me more logical and restrained.

At the moment of the demon's death the veil was revoked from Vivian. Obviously, it was this demon that withheld her presence. If I had taken a better look at him I might've realized what demon he was.

I almost wanted to drop to my knees as soon as I felt her again. I almost choked as if the life that her and I shared was being extinguished. Haymen seemed to feel the same effect through whatever connection they had and within seconds had vanished. I teleported myself screaming out to that thread that connected us, to where she might be. I didn't focus on any location or image because I didn't know where she was. I only focused on her. The one thing that felt insufferably freezing to my usual warmth and light. The darkness drew me in and the pull was so great that it felt like a form of home. A place that would be my yearning for years to come.

I would make it there before someone truly hurt her.

CHAPTER THIRTY-NINE- VIVIAN

Determee's laughter continued to swirl around me. Flames shot from different angles on the barrier making it hard for me to focus on his location. I growled with my ears pinned back tiring of this game. The hackles on my back had risen as I anticipated the barrier to break at any time. I was pacing back and forth unable to attack him myself until the barrier between us was shattered.

"You were a fool to seek me out personally but I do thank you for making it easier to locate you. Perhaps before you use a Golem witch's service you should research and know that their kind has worshipped my own for hundreds of years," he continued to laugh. "Catch you and bring back the others, looks like this will be rather easy for me."

I had millions of questions for him but I could ask them when I had him chained and gasping for his life. He'd made the mistake to attack me and try to end my life in my dreams. I wasn't able to conjure any of my demons and lacked the strength to match him evenly there. Now, it was game on.

The three children were still suspended in the air, a wind drifting through them that I couldn't feel myself. I crept closer to them waiting as every bashful force of fire hit the barrier close to its rupture. If he was after the children then it was likely he would kill them to release the Volv inside. Like the one who had possessed Alice and now the girl with plaited hair. It would only continue jumping from host to host. But only death would allow it to do so. If that was part of their goal then I had to prevent that from happening.

I couldn't see the barrier but I could feel it chipping away weakly. The vibrations left from the force told me the time was close. It was about to break. I still tried to track where Determee' physically was himself. I would give chase and kill him when I found him instead of fighting through his circle of flames. The fire my hellhound form could handle. The power of his wind however might be a problem.

The sound of glass breaking shattered after another flame busted against it, this time pushing through the barrier and reaching out for me. I lunged for the flames drifting between them with little hesitation. If anything, my hellhound loved rolling around in fire and would never fear it. I tunneled through the flames using them to hide in.

Suddenly the air was sucked out of my lungs and I couldn't breathe. I choked and my feet dragged against the ground and fire that was no longer beneath them. I was being levitated in the air. I still couldn't see him but his laughter circled me. I was unable to gasp for breath as I continued to choke. I changed into my water demon. She wasn't equipped for being outside of the water but one thing that left ears bleeding on land was her siren. Being breathless on land wasn't as sufferable as I shifted and gills split underneath my ears, ribs, and legs. She could never breathe on land prior to that. I opened my mouth and released my siren that was like a high pitched canon straight to the ears. I dropped to the ground and changed instantly back into my hellhound sniffing out the blood I could now smell trickling from his ears.

His disorientation would last only for so long. I ran through the trees with the speed of a high-class demon. The hellhound was fast. I smelled him in the treetops, his whimper coming to an end as the bleeding began to stop. I changed back to my water demon and as I looked up and released my siren, flames shot at me. I took the blow to my left arm, moving slightly so I could still isolate the scream into his direction. I didn't dare look down at my arm. He held steady in the tree, began bleeding and becoming disorientated.

I shifted into my cat demon making sure not to let her tail jingle. I dove my claws deep into the tree, climbing up on it in two jumps. As I rolled around it, I shifted into my succubus form smiling as I stood over him. The force of his wind and fire came towards me at once. I pierced him with my tail ejecting my poison into him as I grabbed him and shielded myself from the flames and wind. I dropped towards the ground taking him with me. I shifted into my hellhound grabbing him by the throat and using him as a shield against his own artful flames and wind. The fire I was protected by but the wind sliced around me, no matter how tightly I curled into him.

I was captured in a vortex of wind. I had to release him and escape before it sliced me apart. I let go of him and jumped through the wind. Deep cuts tore across my body as I rolled out. I scraped back on the back of my heels and shifted into my cat demon. I watched him with interest as he scampered on the ground.

"Turns out not even the great Determee' can survive my succubus's poison," I purred watching the black shadowed figure gasp on the ground. His body took the shape of a man but was charcoaled, cracks of flowing flames licked outside of him. He began choking out blood into the ground as I kept my distance. I wanted to be smug and walk over but watching him die alone was more satisfying.

"St-" He began to stutter. "Stu-"

"What? I can't hear you." I said raising a paw to my ear.

"Stupid is what he is trying to say," a voice came from behind me. I whipped around not having even felt their presence. The three children stood in front of me. The smiles were as corrupt as what they themselves were now. Black veins threaded their face and their eyes spoke lengths of evil.

Determee' began bellowing out in laughter behind me. I angled myself so I could be at the point of our positioning like a triangle. Determee' stood up dusting himself off. The coaled smile smoldered out flames.

"Poison, really? My body does not grow the same flesh as most demons. Tricks like that won't work on me," he said with an irritated laugh.

"Vivian, we will take you to our Master now," the girl with plaited hair said. It was the same Volv that had possessed Alice's body in Aztec prison. I could feel darkness circle me, as if a few more Volv were surrounding me but those who were not yet attached to hosts. Fuck. Fuck. Fuck. My cat demon's sixth sense enabled me to feel them but I knew I was outnumbered and before Loclan had trapped them and teleported them, I myself had been pinned with their attack once before.

I hissed as they circled me. "I can take her back, I don't need your help," Determee' said to the others.

"She is for our Master, not you," the girl seethed in a different language but one I could translate.

"Neither will be necessary," Haymen's voice startled us all as his darkness swirled around me as a barrier and he stood beside me. He looked down at me proudly and directed his gaze to Determee' with a smile. Behind the three children Gabe swooped down with wide wings, standing tall behind him.

"Haymen," Determee' seemed to entertain. "Old friend, it's been a while." Determee' didn't fear Haymen as he should but I could sense he was looking at plausible places of escape despite his eyes never leaving Haymen's.

"I see that you're besotted by my Guardian," Haymen said to both Determee' and the children. "Your Master is a fool for trying to steal what is mine." Haymens darkness pushed back the other Volv who had no physical form. I felt Haymen's darkness swirl around me and kiss my skin swimmingly so that they couldn't break through his barricade. I knew it would protect me from their imposing possession.

I looked over at Gabe who watched between me and the children, his wings glowing bright as darkness swirled around him trying to break in. A spear was in his hand, one that hadn't been there before. Perhaps Angel Boy had the gift of teleportation. Despite flying in I didn't think of it as coincidence that he came here with the exact timing as Haymen.

"Change into your hellhound for me Vi, I wish to see your beauty again," Haymen said to me as if the others were no longer present. I nodded and shifted as he asked. He smiled and began rubbing his hand through my fur. The ruffle and touch electrified against my skin. And there it was I realized the adamant loyalty and expectation for me to only be his pet. He smiled as I looked up at him, as if knowing it all clicked into place. I was exactly that. His. Master and pet. He was here to protect his hound.

"Our King will end you once and for all, Haymen," the girl seethed through bleeding gums as she spat. "Kill them!"

All four of them lunged. Haymen gravitated towards Determee'. Flames swept against his tendrils of darkness.

"You will be placed under arrest and questioning," Gabe announced as his wings glowed. The shadows became restless as his light ate away at their darkness. The girl was focused and lunged for me. I met her mid-air to counter her attack. Before we could make eye contact her eyes went wide and she dropped floppily to the ground. As soon as her feet made contact with the ground her head slid off her shoulders and blood splattered. I growled at the disgust as it sprayed over me. The two behind them that Gabe had been trying to capture also died, their heads sliding off their shoulders as well.

I looked over to Haymen who had killed them so quickly and already had Determee' pinned against a tree. His swirls of darkness appetizing on him as he screamed. I couldn't see what was being done to him but the darkness that ate him alive could only be that from Haymen who would wipe out kingdoms in days.

"I said alive!" Gabe shouted. Haymen was only amused as he stepped towards Determee' focused. "You know that they will just keep capturing new hosts!"

"You are going to tell me everything before I kill you Determee'," Haymen said ignoring both Gabe and me. "Good job my darling, Vi," he clicked his fingers and the swirl concealed both him and Determee' as they vanished. Gabe seemed to vanish after them. One second later I was teleported with a nauseous black swirl into my room.

I looked around catching my bearings. I was back in my room. My tattoos glowed blue as I looked around in the dark room. Blood was splattered all over my clothes and face. I began tearing them off as I headed for the shower. What just happened? Everything happened so quickly and I wasn't happy about not killing any of them myself. I needed to shower. Haymen wouldn't tell me anything about his capture or torture of Determee' which only pissed me off more. I wanted to be able to interrogate him myself. Especially considering a lot more seemed to be a part of the picture then what others were leading on. Especially Haymen.

We were his race, his Guardians that were not meant to question and yet the irritation of always being the hunted when I was created as the hunter overwhelmed me. I lathered my hair with shampoo thinking as to why Gabe and Haymen were there almost at the same time. Haymen had no difficulty with beheading them. Within seconds I hadn't even felt the presence of his darkness. An image came back to me and clearly seemed to come into the forefront of my mind. Alice from the Atzec prison has been killed in a similar manner. Directly behind me before that demon that was being guarded entered me. I still couldn't feel it stir within me but I definitely felt it merge with me that night. But Alice had died in the exact same manner.

Slowly things began to click together. Haymen was eager for me to go to that prison. I didn't gather any helpful information from Alice but I did obtain something that day, that much I was certain. I wasn't sure what but I was certain that something else resided in me now. I pressed my hand to my stomach as if I could feel the swell of the demon within me. But it stayed silent not even the faint bickering of something that shouldn't reside within me.

Despite the ordeal with Gabe following me around and using Angel Kiss on me–Haymen hasn't yet killed him. Law, treaty, moral, a higher war angel–none of that meant anything to Haymen if he wanted someone dead he would assure that they were dead.

Even my memory of my death and contracts–there was something I had that Haymen wanted and protected and for some reason he was involving outsiders to play. He was watching my steps and playing me as a puppet that much I always knew since our contractual agreement. But I couldn't help but realize he was brewing and leading this all into something.

I felt someone creep into my room. I fell silent as I listened to them come closer. I washed the last of the shampoo out my hair. The presence was being sneaky and so instead of turning my shower off and offering that person a very painful lesson as to not enter my room, I crept along the white tiles and pushed my back to the wall, waiting beside the door.

The figure seemed to mimic me on the other side. It felt familiar, but I could recognize that something about it had changed. Something seemed off.

"Shit," I said before jumping out of the way but not in time as a steel blade smashed through the tiles and sliced my arm. I skidded back towards the shower in the middle as Alexa walked in. Her eyes had no pupils and were now black. Veins were protruding from her face and arms as she smiled at me with a doll like presence. Both her arms had shifted to blades. Alexa had been compromised.

"Those who decide to host in a child's body were always going to die quickly," the echo of a woman's cracked voice said pushing through Alexa's voice box. This Volv was different to those I had met.

"Who are you?" I asked with irritation changing into my succubus form.

"You may call me Gardanor and I am the bringer of your death," she said with a smile and lunged for me.

I dodged as she swept her arms back and forth, one cut from her steel like blades would scatter my guts to the floor. Water poured over me from the showerhead as I dodged her second blade. I changed into my water demon. The water glittering like specks of air over my gills. I speared my retractable titan nails at her. The escalation of their length split my own fingernails and my hands went bloody and wet.

She dodged my attack coming down on me with her own blades again. I let them graze close to me, grabbing her shoulder with my retracted claws and running against the tiled wall, twisting her behind her back and flinging her across the room. She busted through the tiling and was plunged into the river outside. I lunged outside diving after her in the water.

Her tattoos glowed bright under the surface of the water but this was my domain and I knew that she had no demon that could counter mine in water. I splintered my nails towards her again harpooning her through the stomach. Like a fish on my hook she thrashed around as a pillow of black blood surrounded her.

A disorientation stirred in my mind as I thrashed back and forth. An electrical current streamed up my nails and coursed through my veins. I was shaking and unable to get closer as the current only grew harsher. I could hardly think as my body thrashed back and forth in the water. I released her waiting for a few seconds for the conductor to stop. Damn technology demon.

She darted for the surface of the water. When my limbs could move of my own accord again, I began slowly following her, disoriented but focused. My body just couldn't keep up. Blood trailed her as she broke through the surface and pulled herself up onto the docks.

Like the hunter I was it didn't take me long to give chase. The sky was clouded and left us in the dark. Although some passersby pointed at us in aww and celebration. She still held her stomach that was spilling through her hands and smiled. Before I could jump to stop her, she had already begun her killing spree on the humans. Screams echoed throughout the wharf as people quickly realized the fun of our presence was misrepresented.

I shifted into my hellhound and gave chase as she shifted into the only demon that could outrun my hellhound. I ran through the city with my heart pounding through my body. Despite her wound she was outrunning me. Bodies were left in her wake as the green small demon with speed flashed across them, shoving people and splattering them against the buildings. Humans were so weak and she only left a trail behind her.

She was no longer attempting to challenge me, that wound obviously having been just as severe as I had aimed for. She was running for security. And shortly after she received it. I trailed back and forth after losing her scent in the underground sewer. Oddly enough unlike the others who surrounded me in numbers she had confronted me on her own.

I continued walking through the sewerage discovering more bodies than what should be down here. It smelled of demon blood and vomit. The city of Shabeah was definitely increasing in demon acts against the treaty and killing of humans. After an hour of trying to find her again I relinquished my keen nose and climbed back onto the outskirts. I shifted into my cat demon choosing to stick to the rooftops as I ventured back home. Already the bodies that were massacred had numerous scenes on them.

Human police. Media. Haymen's cleaners. I looked into the distance at one of the wide screens that had recorded footage of myself in hellhound form running after the green demon that killed numerous passersby in her way. Children, men, women—no victim was excluded.

I had only been talking to Alexa, well what remained of Alexa hours before. The Volv that possessed her must have only recently taken over her body and it was rather bold that she decided to attack me prior to even understanding the demons she was contracted to or their abilities.

I hissed in agitation of the footage that had been taken but was charmed by the beauty of my hellhound which begrudged with red eyes. My coat was beautifully black and decorated with scarring and on top of my head, which was something I hadn't noticed before seemed to be a crown which grew from the skull.

I furrowed my eyebrows in confusion. I had seen paintings of such a magnificent hellhound before. And she was not just any; that hellhound had been mother and alpha to an elite pack. Now that was something I had to look into. There was no denial nor was there confirmation from the hellhound within me. And I wondered who else might recognize the beast for who it truly was and what I had contracted with. I continued my walk on home disregarding the human bodies and squad teams that layered the streets. Someone else would clean it up. They always did. What interested me more, was learning that the heritage of my demons seemed to be either rare or queens in their own right.

Chapter Forty- Gabe

Footage streamed live of the massacre throughout Shabeah and I knew that it would be political hell from here. Included was Vivian's involvement. She might've been giving chase or she might've been aiding in the kills but all anyone could see live and being reported was two Guardians slaughtering humans throughout Shabeah. I was perched on the highest building in Shabeah looking over the carnage. I spread my wings out wide letting the rain wash over them.

As soon as Haymen escaped with Determee' I couldn't track him. They had teleported somewhere into the Underworld where I couldn't follow. I considered how I should kill Haymen after he admitted murdering Luke. Haymen would play dirty but I had already gone through my vengeance and lack of control when I came for Vivian the first time. Now, I had to execute things cleverly to actually have his death announced and approved.

Now that the Volv were present I had to consider that as well. If Haymen were to disappear there would be a shift and perhaps breakdown of the treaty when it came to the new Underworld ruler. No matter what happened I had to make sure it wasn't the Volv that claimed the throne.

My earpiece began to buzz and I swiped my watch to answer. "Torrin?" I asked, watching the repetitive footage of the big screen in front of me.

"You have to come back. There's been a situation. One of the soldiers turned on civilians only moments ago. So far the kill count is at thirteen… We think he might be possessed by a Volv," he said. I watched the monitor of the screen that now focused on the Guardian who was once Alexa. Even in her green slick demon form you could see the deformities of her face already.

"So, they're making a move on all accounts," I said, pissed that I had allowed such demons into my own city. "Keep him detained. I'll be there in ten."

I swiped my watch to end the call. So, the Volv truly had come back. At least now I had one I could interrogate myself. It seems that Haymen was making sure that there would be no loose ends. Somehow this had his involvement and I was still to discover what Vivian had to do with it. Until I found that out, I had to make sure my own kind was safe and ready to fight. It wouldn't be too long now until we would go to war.

Chapter Forty-One- Vivian

I stepped out of my second shower and towel dried my hair. I made sure not to wear one around my body as I stepped out and greeted Gabe who is leaning against my bookshelf. The light glow of his wings surrounded him as he stood in the dark.

"Big night?" he asked. I shrugged and looked at him lustfully.

"I wish something 'bigger' would find its way to me in the dark instead," I said with a coy smile.

"You know the kill rate so far up to twenty-three," he said with a distant tone. But I knew he was pulling away, trying to guard against me. Whatever we had between us was distracting for the both of us. But when I had him so close to me and my bed… well I didn't want idle chit chat or talk about massacres.

"I don't deal with the aftermath or politics. I was chasing after the Volv," I said rubbing over my hair one more time before flinging it onto my bed. "What happened to Determee'?"

"Ask your Master," he all but gritted. "I came to say goodbye."

"How courteous of you," I purred. "But I prefer saying goodbye through action and not words." I prowled over to him. His eyes were distant as he stared at me and ground his teeth. The white of his knuckles grew tense as he physically held himself back from me.

"Just make sure you stay alive. If not, remember it will hurt me too," he said tapping on his matching tattoo that linked our angel kiss. I considered him for some time still taking my not so cautious steps towards him. I looked up into the green of his eyes appreciating their majestic sharpness. His holiness crawled along my skin but it was no longer the bile that made me want to vomit. There was something alluring about him, perhaps the raw power that my own enjoyed to feed off. We would never see each other again. A part of me that I wanted to deny so fiercely, reacted poorly to that.

I studied the tattoos that were inked into his skin and saw the small one that linked him and me together. I was so curious as to hear the stories about the other ones.

"Why did you do it?" I asked. I didn't care for sentiment. We were natural enemies. I felt as I asked him the question, I was asking myself why I jumped in front of him and took the fatal injury myself.

"I was indebted to you. A life for a life. My favor was returned," he gritted out quickly which made it sound all too rehearsed. There was silence between us as I snaked my hand to trail against his forearm. He didn't pull back from my touch and the push of his light and my darkness rubbing against one another was electrifying friction.

"But why did you really do it?" I asked locking my eyes with his again.

"I don't know," he admitted with hesitation. Suddenly the façade between us seemed very broken. The angel kiss ritual had pulled some shit stunt on us. It would constantly draw us in like this and I was glad to see it go. I wanted him to vanish so I wasn't undermined by this uncomfortable pull.

"I'll never be able to turn good," I said to him without shame. We were on opposite sides of the spectrum. Our eyes might meet, and our bodies might react to one another but we could never fulfill one another. We were opposed in everything we did and stood for.

"It's what I hate about you the most," he admitted as he intertwined his fingers with my own. I looked down at our hands that shifted slightly within one another. Every movement was like tiny flecks of lightening on my skin.

"I hate how self-righteous you are," I said with venom behind my words. He charmed a smile and a chuckle came out.

"Just don't destroy the world. I hope that we don't meet again, Vivian, but if we do, I dare say I'll meet you in war," he said seriously as he let go of my hand.

"Hopefully between each day we can sneak into one another's camp and fuck. Slaughter and sex, you've just described my greatest fantasy."

"But that would involve me taking you to bed. Which will never happen," he said leaning in and kissing me on the forehead. The heat of his kiss seemed to sting and I twisted my face disgusted by the sweet moment.

He chuckled at my expression before stepping back.

"If you ever decide to, you know, hit the dark side and become badass, call me." I said with a coy smile that only my succubus could produce. His eyes continued to linger on my own and dart over my body with an appraised smile as he turned and flew out of my room.

Hot and flustered once again. Fuck all of these men who wanted to have a bite but nothing more.

*

I walked into my wardrobe surprised to see an electronic box which needed to scan my finger to open. I sighed over the old text and leather-bound books. Although now gone and having tried to kill me, Alexa had left me one parting gift and in the form of text that I liked to read best from. She could've simply given me a chip to open in my computer but somehow this felt safer. I closed it again, assuring myself that I would soon read the information she had obtained for me after my request. This would help me piece together some information of the past for both Angel Boy and my master who I haven't seen since he took his play toy to torture.

I walked over to my own safe slipping on my Trinity necklace. I transported to the place where I had been last standing in the sleek metallic and quiet city. This time I was not greeted by anyone but was given the luxury of walking in silence throughout the streets. It was obvious that housing began outwards and upwards. The buildings were impeccably tall, larger than those in Shabeah.

I made point to walk to the center. Behind it was a castle I was yet to explore. What grabbed my attention in the center that was empty and large was the slick egg like looking throne that was perched on stilts in front of me. I walked towards it assessing it. The open space in front of the throne might've been used for leisurely things.

Dances, festivals, fights, offerings. Looking around I realized that there was not one speck of dust, no splatter of blood or remains of any life prints. The city was too clean. Curious to see if I might be able to dirty it, I walked over to one of the side shops and entered.

The door opened as a slick white screen for me. There were jars of liquid I have never seen before. Some were bright, others had creatures swimming in them. I took the one that looked closest to some kind of demon blood tapping it and watching gold flakes stir.

I walked back out to the center and looked at the clean floors. I held out the jar of blood and let it slip through my fingertips watching it smash on the ground. Blood splattered everywhere. As soon as the red began to dye the white, the floor beneath it liquefied and enveloped the blood, glass and remains of anything that tarnished the ground. In the blink of an eye nothing remained.

I looked around the city again, so that's why it looked so clean. Despite it looking like war had found itself here. Somehow it automatically cleaned itself. As if the city had a mind of its own. I looked back to the throne that seemed to call out to me. Behind it was clear water that circulated in the air ornamentally with no vase. It simply rolled around, glittering a pale blue.

I walked up to the water tapping it. The water ruptured only for a moment before continuing its course. I looked back to my left to the throne that was stilted high. As soon as I got closer, one small platform rose in front of me. As I stepped on it, another appeared. White steps appeared in front of me as I reached the throne. I looked behind it at the castle.

I could explore that soon. But I was interested to see what the previous ruler might have watched from this very throne. There were only whispers of ghosts here and a barren land outside the wall. I was curious as to what demons had lived here. I twisted and sat on the throne surprised by its comfort. A shudder came over me as I grabbed both edges and rested my hands on the side.

I looked over the center square and further past the sleek buildings and a sun that glistened in the distance. There was nothing but barren land. And yet here, I could sense the power and life roll over me. Like something was whispering to me and something responded from inside.

I charmed a smile as I crossed one leg over the other. Somehow–this city felt like home.

Writing this made me not so scared.

THE SHADOW MINDS JOURNAL

SERIES WILL CONTINUE.

READ ON FOR A SNEAK PEEK OF THE NEXT BOOK.

Chapter One- Haymen

Y ou are cordially invited to the Annual Trevis Games. Please have nominations of five fighters within the week. Accordance to the treaty and entertainment agreement, placement will continue to be held in the city of Celtia governed and overlooked by War Angel, Gabe Christain, within the Coliseum. There will be a total of fifty fighters from ten different ruling regions. Assure that your nomination meets the deadline or you will forfeit your position.

Let the games begin.

Sincerely,

The High Council

So, the games begin. I released a small tendril of my darkness to envelope the invitation in flames. I sat swirling the blood in my wine glass in contemplation. My room engulfed in darkness like always. The crackling flames of the fire pit was the only source of light within the room. Shadows leaked from me and danced over the walls in swirls as if trying to fight off the light from the soulless shades arrayed from the flames. My shadows were always living and breathing. They were after all an extension of myself. I could never fully contain the power within me. To do so would near suffocate me. My darkness always swirled around me, if only to give me breathing space.

It had been a long time since I was able to release that pent up frustration and I built up for only one reason, and that was the war to come. I looked down at the dead woman who bled out at my feet. She had displeased me greatly. My hunger and need for Vivian was only thirsting more, now not even an outsource harem could quench any appetite. I looked at her now crusty face that was covered by her yellow hair. Her mouth and eyes were wide open in horror. The most beautiful of her court, they said. What rubbish. She was nothing but a sincere whore trying to steal my power. Thus the ability of her kind to drain and eat away at another's strength and power. But to so carelessly attempt to prey on me, especially while I was on edge was ludacris and something I wouldn't stand for.

I swatted my hand in the air so a small amount of invisible force would push her hand off my chess board in front of me. I gazed at it longingly and took another sip. My hackles were rising and I wanted this game to come to a close. I didn't anticipate the Volv to make a move so quickly. The massacre on the city weeks ago was only a side result of them not being able to take Vi. Because of that though it put her under scrutiny and so I couldn't send her out for many jobs until the media simmered down. My poor kitten was getting frisky just from staying in the house for so long. That attack had slowed my plans and now I have to deal with them alternatively. The interlacing and timing of the Trevis Games might be very convenient. A smile pressed on my lips. I knew exactly how I could place Vi in this pile because no matter what, almost all of it centred around her whether she realized it or not. I just had to keep her alive long enough to reap those rewards.

All I could see was Vi on the board. Her face, her lips, her body– sprawled in front of me for my delicacy. I needed to take her. Had to claim her as mine. But I knew the moment wasn't right. I rubbed at my clean shaven jaw that hasn't grown hair for lifetimes now. I required control for how I would next play this out.

Another player had recently introduced himself in my game and I found many ways for him to partake. I took another gulp of the heated blood that never cooled trying to bite back my hatred for Gabe. He had imprinted on what was mine with that stupid fucking Angel Kiss ritual. I tapped on my glass in impatience. It could however work in my favour. But I would me contending with my own self-control. I could destroy him from the inside–through that bond I could force Vi to drive him mad. He now knew it was me who killed his friend, Luke, and yet he hasn't said anything to the Angel Council. Because he couldn't, he didn't have enough proof.

I smiled again at the chess board moving my prized piece and admiring its positioning. That plan might work very nicely, I thought to myself as I scanned the board and saw all the pieces I could wipe out from that position. Yes, I liked that plan a lot. From the Queen Chess piece to the images of my Guardian Vi, all I wanted was to lap in the silky milk of my kitten. My cock thickened in size just thinking about it and again I growled in frustration. My claws edged further out from the tips of my fingers and clawed at my leather seat. This blood flow would only pound for her and I needed her to truly suck that out of me, if only to relieve me for a few minutes.

"Destiny," I summoned. Within seconds she had used the bracelet I had given her to teleport into my room directly. Her hair was in upheaval and her eyes were still dazed. She must've just been sleeping. She looked over my naked form that sat on the leather couch and glorified at my hard cock.

A shade of jealousy crossed her face as she looked over the woman who had tried to please me only an hour before her body now going cold. That temper of Destiny's flared in her eyes like her fire demon might burst through. I gave her an effective look. I didn't desire her nor appreciate her jealousy. She swallowed hard and walked over to me sassily. She dropped to her knees obediently and suctioned her lips around my cock. I arched into her, threading my fingers through her hair.

This is why I summoned Destiny so much. Because her hair was similar in length and curls to my beautiful Vi's. Although her hair, scent, and everything else was different, I could still envision this to be the very thing I had been meaning to claim for thousands of years.

My Vi, before you know it, you will be mine. I pressed her head down further and sighed at the noise of her choking and unpreparedness to take more of me.

CHAPTER TWO- VIVIAN

"And remind me why the fuck I have to do this again?" I snapped at the pompous photographer. I was balancing on a light see-through floor floating on the lake just behind our Lakehouse. Little digital balls hovered in the air to create projections and reflect the sun so it wouldn't interfere with the lighting of the shot.

Since the massacre within Shabeah and the attack made by the Volv I was under heavy scrutiny as to whether I was a part of the attack. I was basically housebound for two weeks now and instead of kicking ass I was requested to promote a new bikini line, to make my fame look once again a little more humane.

"Because we need to erase images of you covered in blood as a Hellhound rampaging through the city with stunning human-like images to glorify you in a different light," the blonde bimbo with a high pointed ponytail said from behind the plump photographer.

"Who the fuck are you again?" I asked her. She had cosmetic planted pointed ears, cheekbones and eyebrows. I could've grafted her face myself for free if she really wanted. Small pink pointed lumps textured her skin. I don't know what fashion craze or demon she was trying to be but I certainly didn't see the allure. She huffed at me, those fake slitted cat eyes trying to pin me.

"We've gone over this. I'm your publicist," she growled calling over the hair stylist. I slapped his slow-moving hand away as he attempted to 'fix' me.

"The fuck do I need a publicist for? I'm a Guardian not a model," I hissed at the photographer who tried to sneak in a few photos.

"I've been to all of your photoshoots already," the human publicist snarled. "I've been working with all of you Guardians since day one. You remember me so quit pretending like you don't!" I bruised her ego more than frustrating her over the photo shoot itself.

"It's going into Winter and you have me out here in Bikinis!" I spat crossing my legs and sitting with my hands strapped over my chest snarling.

"Oh for god's sake you don't even feel the cold!" The publicist snapped. I ignored her and looked down on my silky floral pink one piece that was vibrant against my too pale skin. The edges of the swimsuit were crisp and flicked out like metal sheeting. Large slick shoulder pads rounded near my face. Parts of my glowing tattoos were visible on the edges of my collar bone. The pink tattoo that marred my shoulder thanks to Gabe himself was completely covered. I covered it every day with a concealer so no one would ever see the marking of the Angel Kiss that connected us. That would be dangerous for the both of us if anyone else found out. Besides the two of us, only Haymen knew and that was one person too many. I began playing with my numerous earrings in boredom.

"I am over this! It's infuriating I just can't work with you!" She threw her hands up in the air and turned to take a breather. I charmed a wicked smile. It was true, I didn't feel the cold but I couldn't help but want to piss her off.

Click. I looked at the photographer in shock as she smiled over the photo she had just taken. "Perfect," she said. Her short curly black hair bobbed as she nodded vigorously in approval. The publicist swung around and smiled at the result. I breathed out heavily in the grumps. I was done with this glamor thing. I was penting up with far too much sexual frustration and hunger to hunt. Surely, Haymen knew what he was doing to me. I was riding stir crazy up the walls. I looked over to the back of my Lakehouse noticing the orange alleyway cat that hung around more often during these two weeks. Even from this distance it looked as if it were almost smug. I growled under my breath. A swirl of wind swept through and everyone gasped in a cold shudder, tightening their thick coats. I didn't feel the chill they felt but breathed out the piece of my crimson hair that had blown into my face.

"Why the fuck are we even promoting a bikini line in Winter?" I asked tapping an extended claw onto the glass flooring. Part of my succubus was now crumbling and revealing herself.

"Just do as you are told. I am here–" The publicist began until her eyes widened in horror. I smirked down at the small crack that began on the see-through flooring. I only eyed her but noticed the six others, including the photographer squirm. "Now Vivian," she began. I clicked my extended claw that was my succubus's against the flooring again to shut her up. The crack spread wider.

The vicious smile spread on my face. "Dear chatty publicist," I said sweetly, my menacing smile unable to be contained. "I am a rather good swimmer," I said having in mind my water demon. "Are you?"

"Haymen will be angry! The amount of money it would cost to replace this equipment and–"

My cheeks rose further into a devilish smile making my eyes almost squint. My smile was far too big. I tapped one more time into the hub of the crack with triumph. It began cracking all the way through and made a defiant split. I jumped back into the water turning into my water demon and splashing into its depths. Gills split open along my ribs, under my arms and legs. My ears elongated into thin tips as I reached for the surface again and broke the surface so I could watch.

The entire flooring cracked in half. The six of them began to awkwardly squirm and scream as they yelled out to others on the docks. I watched in triumph as they sank and screamed into the icy cold water that I personally found rather refreshing. The screams of mortification and swearing from their embarrassment was music to my ears.

i lapped them as they swam back, making sure they made it. I swam briskly throughout on my back luxuriously enjoying the swim. Miss publicist would often spit acid like words of having Haymen reprimand me. Pfft. Like she had the power to convince him to do so.

I made sure they got there safely. It was a prank after all not a death sentence. When a small boat came out to collect them I knew that they were safe and continued towards my lakehouse. I jumped out of the water and onto my personal veranda to my room. I shifted in the air, my light blue tattoos glowing as I returned to my usual form.

As soon as my feet lightly padded the ground I ripped off the tragic one piece that was iconic to fashion these days.

I stood there naked with a smile on my face as I watched the humans be rescued.

Meow. I looked up onto the rooftop to the orange alley cat that didn't fear me, surprisingly. It jumped off and onto the back of my neck. Its claws digging in as it almost slipped off. It was a welcomed pain. The cat only began visiting three weeks ago and I couldn't sense anything demonic about it. It seemed to enjoy me most when I shifted into my cat demon form and she didn't seem to mind the curious alleyway cat. Now it loitered around from time to time. I haven't begun feeding it yet but it was often on my mind. The stupidity of a Guardian having and feeding a house cat was what had stopped me.

I scratched it behind its ear as I walked over to the open box on my office table. I padded around the bottom and collected the first romance book on top of the pile. I had ordered twenty just to try and get through the few quiet weeks I was housebound. I walked over to my bed, still dripping from my luxurious swim and sat upright against the headboard in my bed and began to read. The alleyway cat jumped off my shoulder and began to rub against my leg in appreciation of idly being patted as I began on the first chapter.

I didn't dare use the Trinity necklace while I was housebound because Haymen had been sporadically checking up on me more often than usual. He already knew that I had the necklace but I didn't want him to see the compulsion I had towards it. There was something very special in that world and broken city, something that I felt connected to and instinctually I knew that I had to keep Haymen away from that. I had to keep him away from anything that sparked my interest or was deemed special to me.

I waited out my opportunity. Since the city and personal attack on myself the Shadow Mind dreams and attacks had lessened. For now, everything seemed to be at a stand still. The calm before the storm, I thought. I flicked over to the next page accidently slicing my finger. A small nick but I allowed the dark black substance to make one fine droplet on my book. I breathed out a frustrated sigh as my thoughts unknowingly rested on Gabe and when I saw him last those two weeks ago. I heated in my core instantly, sexually frustrated and derived from the one creature my body wanted to claim. I curse this Angel Kiss. I growled and pushed the alleyway cat off me, walking over to have an icy cold shower. I hated how my body reacted only to the thought of him.

CHAPTER THREE- GABE

I gazed out the window as a lightning bolt struck outside the city. I was sitting in my office chair, stretching out my wings along the span of my slick wooden desk. They stretched powerfully, igniting a small burn along their frame and muscle. I tenderly lowered them again. I rubbed the knots in the back of my neck, rolling my shoulders. I was only now coming near the end of piles of paperwork that was left while I was in Shabeah, the renowned city of demons. It had been two weeks since then and I was caught up with the concerns and attacks within my own city. Sixteen humans and one fellow angel had been killed. One of my soldiers had been compromised by the Volv and gone rampant during the same hour as the attack within Shabeah. It took only a few minutes for him to be taken down but the loss was a heavy blow.

Torrin, my second in charge, had ruled over my city in my absence. He maintained it as expected except for the paperwork he conveniently forgot about. Only he could ever get away with it. Sly bastard, I smirked to myself. Torrin was the only person I had told in depth about my discoveries while in Shabeah. About the Volv, that Haymen was Luke's rightful killer... and about Vivian. Torrin, my old friend and one of the few warriors that survived alongside me during the last Great War didn't say much about the Angel Kiss that now intertwined Vivian and me. The damage had already been done.

Another bolt struck the ground in the distance. The rain poured against the glass in buckets. I stood up and pressed my hand to the glass, looking over my city, Celtia. My breath fogged it before me. The bright lights of the night and city glowed. Restaurants hovered in the air reacting to the magnetic force beneath the city. The waterfall within the center of the city flowed up instead of down. A central park for only angels to play on top of. It was bare now because of the late hour.

I myself was standing in the highest building. At the very top of my own enterprise where I overlooked the city. Forty levels up, my office was on the thirty-ninth level. My second apartment was at the very top. It was to accommodate for those times and days I couldn't leave the office. It seemed a constant these days. I couldn't remember the last day I had actually spent in my own mansion which overlooked the city opposing me. I imagined it in the distance, hovering like most of the CBD singular mansions.

I have a revolving office so as I waited patiently, I was able to see all parts of the city. Hundreds of cars still functioned at high speeds despite the hour. Colorful garments and furs caught my attention on the big screen central over the stadium as a game played. It was a traditional sport played by Angels involving one singular ball amongst a brut of two angel teams. To say the least it was rather brutal. We had an outside team come in tonight, I could hear the stadium roaring from here.

Across the stadium was the Coliseum. I sighed in angst. It couldn't have come at a worse time yet I couldn't delay it either. The lights were bright as cleaners and painters varnished the seating and walls. Only a few weeks now until the Trevis Games begin. It was built on the old city, parts of it still surrounded by ruins and cobbled stone. Opposed to the rest of the high-tech city, it momentarily looked like a part of Shabeah had been placed there. It disgusted me to see. I never wanted a reminder of that demonic, disgusting city again.

Even with that said... I teleported out into an alleyway within Shabeah. It was the same spot that I had first met the orange alleyway cat and she ventured to the same spot every night. She meowed when I appeared and jogged over to me. I scoped to make sure that no one was watching. I had met this alleyway cat when I was first investigating Vivian. This was where Vivian had killed the monster who abused and murdered children within the orphanage that he looked after. That was the evil that would've drawn the Volv in there to kill and cripple so many of those tiny minds.

This alleyway was when I first heard the jingle of Vivian's cat demon and from there we ran to the pier and fought. It seemed like a lifetime ago and yet it was so close to my heart that it hurt. I could sense her within the city and I knew more than likely when I teleported into this city for only those few seconds she probably sensed me. As tempted as I was to see her, I had to make sure that never happened. Ever.

I picked the cat up and teleported back to my office. The alleyway cat was very open to me and had played to be my spy master ever since our first encounter. Much to my surprise it quite enjoyed Vivian's company so it didn't mind sharing its encounters and impressions of her. It began visiting her when I first stayed in her Lakehouse. We were divided by rooms but what she was up to I was later informed by this furball.

The bright lights of my circular room hurt my eyes in comparison to the darkness of the stinky streets of Shabeah. I sat down in my chair scratching the back of the cat's ear. She dared to play with me, fearless she was. She struck at my fingers; rather savvy. I smiled at her as she opened her mind to me and showed me her memories and impressions of Vivian.

The furball had been watching her from a distance when she was posing in bikinis. Some absurd fitting one piece. Although I couldn't deny that she certainly made it look fantastic. It had nothing to do with bikinis. It was just her. All curves and pouting lips. I smiled when she looked directly at the cat almost pissed off as she watched on. I even sensed that the little furball found humor in it herself. I was surprised when Vivian played a prank on them and shattered the sleek, invisible flooring they stood on. I shook my head almost laughing with her.

She was as menacing as always. And despite being filled with demons and destined for evil, she hovered close until safety was close by. That was something I imagined no one noticed about her and she would never admit herself. The same happened with the children at the orphanage. She mightn't speak or intend to do good deeds. She wasn't good. But against her own beliefs she had a conscience.

Either that or I was hoping she did. The pull was far too great to deny after the Angel Kiss and I wondered if I were simply seeing things that I wanted to. To justify that the person I chose to perform such a ritual on was deserving. I hoped that over time, being separated by space, I would be able to move on and not find this heavy weight in my chest that yearned for her. I performed the ritual so that my debt was repaid and her life was saved. Now, I wasn't so sure if that was the only reason I had decided to keep her alive. I growled in frustration unsure as to what my own feelings were anymore. Was it all from the ritual or was this truth from my heart?

The ginger alleyway cat clawed at my hand to shake me from my daze. Snarky little thing. She drew me back into her own memories of Vivian. She was very fond of her and was almost gloating that she could share that comfort with her instead of me. Vivian manifested out of the water, dripping and *very* naked. I pushed away from the memory for a moment. The way the alleyway cat and I saw her was very different.

My body coated almost in a cold sweat with desire. My cock was aching rock hard from the vision alone. What has that woman done to me? I ached to touch her, to thread my hands through her soft hair, to kiss her and fully complete the ritual–to entirely claim her as my own. Small patches and memories of her grabbing a romance novel and reading it began shifting through my mind. I internally laughed that she was still reading them but my body caved in heats of fluctuating desire distracting me from all sense of humor.

The cat showered me with images of itself rubbing against her naked and still dripping body on the bed. I shot right up eyeing the evil creature who sauntered off fully aware of the strings she was playing. I stood up again and shuffled uncomfortably. I was rock hard and envisioning the beads of water that slowly dripped from her thighs. I looked down on my right forearm at the three distinctive lines and tattoo that matched the one on Vivian's shoulder. Our imprint.

"You're a little shit," I said to the cat before placing my finger on the corner of the circular glass at the bay of the window. The cat meowed in response walking over to its food and water bowl. From my touch the glass slowly opened and removed the protection between myself and the pelting rain. I freefell from the window enjoying the cold beating snap of the thundering rain. I dropped close to the ground, liberated by the fall until I snapped my wings wide and beat them back to the top. I swept through the pounding rain, coating my body entirely with freezing cold water.

Images of her naked frame continued to creep in. Her delicate swirls of tattoos, her curves, silken skin, the long-curled hair. I scanned over the city within the pelting rain trying to take my mind off the images.

The Volv had been after her. Of that much I was certain. For unknown reasons, Haymen kept her as a prized mare and after seeing how he had been a part of her death and rebirth, I knew that he had history or knowledge of who she truly was. There was something special about her which is why I kept a watchful eye on her through the alleyway cat. No one else loitered around her for the time being which meant for now she was safe. I had no doubt that she could look after herself but what she was up against was more than her typical demons. If Haymen and I hadn't intervened that time the Volv ganged up on her… who knows what might've happened to her. I ground my teeth at the thought. And it had been Haymen who absolutely obliterated them. His power when unchecked was a lethal rage. It was my only assurance that he wouldn't let anything happen to her but it didn't devoid the question as to whether he would put her in harm's way for his own gain.

My head began to ache and my wings were freezing and numb from the wind and cold. I snapped my wings shut and freefell again.

I just had to make sure that I never saw her again because if I did… I wasn't sure what I would do or if I would let Haymen walk away with her again.

ACKNOWLEDGMENTS

Thank you to everyone who has been a part of and supported my author career so far. My journey has been trialing but every step of the way I've been encouraged by all of you.

A special mention to my younger sister, Jasmin who for the longest of times has been my biggest cheerleader. No doubt in mind of my endless possibilities and many coffees and late night chats. You don't know how much you inspire me and I am grateful to have you backing me up in my corner.

I love you all and honestly find the courage and strength to continue writing because of how much support and kind words you offer. I hope you enjoyed this read x

ABOUT THE AUTHOR

Kia grew up in the Darling Downs Region in Queensland, Australia. Graduating High School, she pursued a career in freelance journalism. In 2014, having always had a passion for writing fiction, she decided to follow her dream of becoming an accomplished author.

Now living in Edinburgh, Scotland Kia has a can do attitude, a strong will and the touch of kindness that makes it hard not to fall in love with her. Announced 'The Best New Author of 2015' by AusRomToday, and being awarded numerous awards, she has no intentions of stopping. Kia Carrington-Russell is definitely the new author to be looking out for.

Learn more about Kia at www.kiacarrington-russell.com and follow @kia_crystal on Instagram.

ALSO AVAILABLE

The Three Immortal Blades
Possession Of My Soul
Possession Of My Heart
Possession Of My Fate

Phantom Wolf Series
Phantom Wolf
Sia
Phantom Eye
Phantom King

Token Huntress Series
Token Huntress
Token Vampire
Token Wolf

The Shadow Minds Journal Series

My Escort Series
My Escort
My Exception
My Expectation

Taming Himself Series
Aroused
Taste

www.ingramcontent.com/pod-product-compliance
Lightning Source LLC
Chambersburg PA
CBHW030629110726
47901CB00002B/377